THE ETERNA SOLUTION

THE
ETERNA
SOLUTION

LEANNA RENEE HIEBER

A Tom Doherty Associates Book
NEW YORK

THE ETERNA SOLUTION

Copyright © 2017 by Leanna Renee Hieber

A Tor Book
Published by Tom Doherty Associates
175 Fifth Avenue
New York, NY 10010

www.tor-forge.com

Tor® is a registered trademark of Macmillan Publishing Group, LLC.

The Library of Congress Cataloging-in-Publication Data
is available upon request.

ISBN 978-0-7653-3676-7 (hardcover)
ISBN 978-1-4668-2927-5 (ebook)

Our books may be purchased in bulk for promotional, educational, or business use. Please contact your local bookseller or the Macmillan Corporate and Premium Sales Department at 1-800-221-7945, extension 5442, or by email at MacmillanSpecialMarkets@macmillan.com.

First Edition: November 2017

Printed in the United States of America

0 9 8 7 6 5 4 3 2 1

THE ETERNA SOLUTION

CHAPTER
ONE

Clara woke to whispers and dread. The shadows of her small cabin on a cross-Atlantic steamer bound for New York were too close, and the cramped space seemed even more claustrophobic than when she'd fallen into uneasy sleep.

The first days aboard the packet, a vessel chosen for top-of-the-line speed rather than luxury, were filled with victorious, albeit harrowing, tales as the American Eterna and English Omega teams recounted their climactic, supernatural encounters outside Parliament. Those who had battled the horrors of the Vieuxhelles estate and saw to its destruction shared their victory.

The warmth of reconnecting, marveling at the strength of their colorful compatriots' varied gifts and bravery in the face of madness, was so powerful that Clara had not yet fully registered the concern for what they'd find upon their return.

Clara had been a gifted Sensitive from an early age, and her gifts had been sharpening at an exponential rate since her lover's death. Upon waking to unease, her first instinct was to call, to bid him come to her in luminous, spectral visitation and talk with her about the state of the spirit world and what she might expect, but she stopped herself.

When Louis Dupris died and in doing so discovered that he had made the protective Ward of localized magic that was the Eterna Commission's great legacy, the knowledge he brought from the beyond helped Clara mend the torn, bleeding tissues of grief, giving her something to fight for and with instead, making his sacrifice meaningful. But their souls had said their good-byes. Their story was at an end and she was, now, finally at peace with his spirit moving on to help guard his native New Orleans. For all that she might feel lonely, she was not alone.

Not because her dear soul sister, Rose, lay sleeping in the bunk below, a woman recently awakened to the paranormal but less attuned to it. Not because her former guardian, Senator Bishop, a man she had loved all her life though she had shuttered the sentiments deep belowdecks, was across the corridor, perhaps lying awake and thinking of her . . .

No, because some other *thing* was awake and aware of her. The shadows across the room were not only too close, but unnaturally dark.

Not one to be afraid of a resident spirit or haunt, she felt the hairs rise on her neck and arms, the familiar, unsettled twist in her stomach. Her body did not yet call for her to be on a countdown to collapse, but she had to be wary, as the epileptic seizures that accosted her whenever the spectral world crossed a line from a pleasant encounter to an onslaught of something altogether malevolent was often a quick and dizzying shift.

There was no remaining still any longer, so she clambered down from the upper bunk as soundlessly as she could so that Rose would not be awakened by whatever next occurred. Water was a charging and shielding element for Clara and she felt safer in the open than in close quarters when something was sniffing her out, so she resolved to seek solace and safety on the uppermost deck.

Throwing the skirt of her burgundy riding habit over her head and buttoning the matching jacket somewhat messily, she palmed her cabin key and quietly slipped out the wooden door, locking it behind her. Clara trod quietly up a stair and stepped out from a narrow archway to the deck where she found herself alone with the sea. All on the deck was still save for two great steam stacks exhaling vapor.

The tang of the salt spray on her tongue and the sea air's moist kiss against the open collar of her bodice were an immediate tonic. The lace panel lined with glass buttons that was meant to cover her neck flapped in the breeze, the buttons thrumming against the hollow of her throat in a rhythm that matched the cracking of the Union Jack flying above her head as she stepped farther out onto the aft deck. Nothing made Clara feel so alive as the sea.

Closing her eyes, she communed with at least three past lives lived most vibrantly upon the water. In doing so, she felt exhilarated and replenished. Gathering herself, renewing her psychic and spiritual shields, she breathed in the vitality of the ocean and snapped energy out from her body like a whip, breaking off the tendrils of any negative spirit or demonic murmur that had managed to cling to her after the battle in London.

She spun slowly, surveying the ship and the waves around it, lifting a hand to sweep aside stray, dark blond strands of hair that wanted to experience the same freedom as her skin. In their number were a few fresh gray strands, her connection to the spirit world hastening the silvery growth. She was twenty-nine, and the graying was premature, but Senator Bishop, had gone silver in his twenties and had always blamed it on the ghosts. She would, too. She looked around for them, or for the worse company: demons.

The shadows retained their normal angles, depth of light, and expected shapes; nothing was lurking. Not anymore. But something still was not right. The salt-infused air held a slight tinge of copper. Sulfur even.

The foul air was one thing, the sounds were another. There was a howling off the water, something not human, but not altogether industrial, something that Clara had never heard before. She could not imagine what creation, entity, or machine could make such a noise.

Clara's mentor, the clairvoyant and ever-elegant Evelyn Northe-Stewart, exited the cabin corridor onto the aft deck, her gaze immediately pinning Clara, to whom she nodded in acknowledgment. The medium wore a thick saffron dress robe and cloak over her nightclothes.

Not far behind her, the Omega department's Miss Knight, London's lavishly theatrical psychic asset, approached, her raven hair in a long braid. She wore an elaborate crimson kimono. The layers that were not bound to her person whipped behind her like a scarlet flag in the wind.

The moon shone blindingly down on them and bathed them all in silver, an incredible, almost staged effect. Clara could not help but recall lines from Macbeth's witches, chanting in otherworldly meter in her mind's ear.

The three Sensitives looked at one another with a mixture of confusion and fear. Clara pressed her hand to her bosom, where the protective Ward created from her late lover's research still lay—she'd created a sort of poultice of the contents and had been loath to remove it from her person—and felt a little surge of power for the press. Perhaps it was just a trick of the mind, but it did seem to offer a bit of shield against the difficult sounds.

Movement drew their attention, and all three turned to see that Rose Everhart had joined them, rubbing her eyes and seeking out Clara first, as if she were an anchor. The two, born a sea apart, had found in one another the soul-sisterhood of lost lives, and the bond kept growing.

Clara responded by placing a firm hand on Rose's trembling shoulder once she stood at her side, in a plain workingwoman's skirt and shirtwaist with buttons not quite aligned. If Rose was indeed first discovering otherworldly communication and instincts that Clara had fielded all her life, it would be a confusing time for her. They needed to be mutual ports in supernatural storms.

"I don't suppose any of you have any idea what woke us," Rose asked, her voice shaking.

Evelyn indicated an area at a distance from the ship but about a meter up from the rail, just above their eye-line. "I assume it happened because we are not alone. Those dark shapes are *not* clouds."

Clara's blood chilled when she finally noticed the contrast. A sequence of ink-black humanoid forms, bodies in silhouette floated off the port side like an artificial horizon. It wasn't the first time they'd seen such lightless things; Beauregard Moriel had a whole army of Summoned, vile presences that had slipped through a fissure he'd created between the natural and unnatural worlds. These shadows were no more welcome here than they had been marching up the Embankment with the aim of tearing down the stones of Parliament.

"The two walks," Evelyn continued, her voice trembling. "Two paths between the living and the dead. The Society opens these corridors and hell slips through to float along the water."

"They appear to be inactive. Summoned and awaiting orders?" Miss Knight queried, studying the predators.

"Waiting, or ready, either way we have to try to banish them," Clara stated. "They are a danger to us, to everyone on this ship. What if our trajectory passes right through them?"

Evelyn began to softly murmur scripture used in exorcisms, simple renunciations of devils and evil.

Clara imagined that Evelyn's words lessened the opaque density of this pitch-black armada, but she couldn't be sure. The bright night sky seemed to be playing surreal tricks on her; Clara didn't feel her regular faculties of sight could be trusted.

"Clara, you brought more of the protective Wards we created, yes?" Rose asked quietly. "I . . ."

"Yes. I've a doctor's bag full of them in our cabin," Clara replied. "I made sure Senator Bishop traveled with a case, and Andre and Effie with their own. Lord Black supplied his own cabin with them and made a small fort of them around our beleaguered Lord Denbury." She chuckled mordantly. "I think your proud nonbeliever Mr. Spire remains the only unarmed person among us."

Rose looked at the silhouettes. "I feel we'll need many, to keep them from noticing us. To give us room . . ." She shuddered. "By God, I feel like I did in front of Parliament, with all of the damnable silhouettes parading . . . It's stifling."

Clara placed her hand on Rose's shoulder and she could feel her tension ease. They had that ability to balance one another; their souls always had.

"That's likely what the wretched forms are there for," Evelyn said grimly. "A certain show of strength from whatever of the Master's Society is holding on after Moriel's death. We should mount as many Wards as possible on this ship at once."

A strange tearing sound to Clara's right sent her whirling, nearly knocking into the woman who appeared suddenly as if propelled by an engine.

"What the bloody hell?" the woman exclaimed. The voice was familiar, as was her small stature and great presence.

"You . . ." Clara said to the woman known as the visitor, who had appeared in heraldic capacities throughout her life like some combination of philosopher, guardian angel, and prophet of doom.

Known to some as Lizzie Marlowe, she was inexplicable. A woman of sharp angles, a petite redhead with a braid down her side, she was dressed as a proper Victorian explorer, in a thick white blouse, a split skirt, boots, and a seaman's cap.

A peculiar belt of instruments wrapped her waist. Clara peered at the devices—was that an astrolabe?

"Why am I here? What have you done, Templeton? This is 1882, yes?" Marlowe barked. She looked the women up and down studiously, her gaze softening only once she seemed to recognize them.

Clara raised her eyebrows. "What have *I* done?"

"I was minding my own business," the visitor continued, "hardly eavesdropping on you and your lot, and now I've been dragged here by my spiritual hair."

"Well now," Clara said incredulously, "isn't *that* turning the tables?"

Marlowe thought a moment. "Yes, I suppose it is. You *are* powerful, Clara. Center of the storm indeed. A magnet, even, pulling the likes of me here? I'll have to do more research on you!" She paused for breath and seemed to assess her surroundings for the first time. "Good God, what is that racket?"

"I was hoping you could tell me," Clara replied. "And for once explain how you come and go like a ghost."

"I'm human, a mortal woman named Elizabeth Marlowe."

"What do you want with me?" Clara asked.

"You know, you're a bit demanding, my dear," Marlowe admonished.

"I think I learned that from you," Clara countered.

The visitor loosed a deep chortle. "I'm so proud. But you must have brought me here for a reason, so let's discern it, shall we?" She gave Clara and her companions a curt smile and angled her head toward the sea, narrowing her eyes at the eerie pall of the horizon line. She slowly turned completely around.

"Hmm. No. That's not right," Marlowe muttered, and began tapping along the brass-trimmed rail of the ship with a small wrench plucked from her leather belt. She listened to the way the metallic clinks changed in pitch as if she were striking a tuning fork and scowled. "Very, very wrong . . ."

The howl changed, as if incorporating the *ting* of the brass, as if it were two notes in a reverberating chorus, and the visitor made a face of supreme distaste.

"Before we take on those dreadful forms out there, where exactly *are* we?" she asked.

"In the middle of the Atlantic Ocean in the middle of the night during a full moon in Jupiter," Miss Knight said, then pursed her lips and strode toward Marlowe and Clara.

After offering Knight a prim, unamused smile, Marlowe stormed off toward the wheelhouse, calling over her shoulder, "I need details! Latitude and longitude, direction and route."

The three ladies were left to stare at one another.

"She's not a ghost, yet I cannot get a sense of her," Knight muttered. "It's maddening. She burst into our Omega offices once, then vanished without leaving a trace. I thought if I just had another chance, I could see what I'd missed. It seems that she is beyond my gifts," she finished, unhappy at being bested by this mystery.

"I'm relieved someone else has finally seen her," Clara confessed. "I used to think I'd gone mad whenever she came around. She's been . . . an infuriating mirage my whole life, flitting in and out at the most critical and dire moments. Not at all how I imagined a guardian angel, but then again, I've not led a normal life, I doubt I'd be assigned a normal angel. . . ." She finished with a weary little laugh.

"She's human," Evelyn stated firmly. "But *more*. I've never seen anything like her. This is astral projection at its most sophisticated."

"Ah," Miss Knight murmured. "Astral projection. Yes. If that's the case, well. Incredible." Her tone was now a bit jealous.

Rose was silent, staring, baffled, in the direction Marlowe had gone. A sharp and logical woman, Rose would find no solace in gifts that offered a range of vagaries.

Marlowe soon strode back toward them, brandishing a chart that flapped in the wind. Clara wondered if she'd snatched it right out of the captain's or first mate's protesting hands. Marlowe spread the wide paper atop a small table that sat between two deck chairs. As the others gathered around, Marlowe seated herself and began pointing.

"We're *here*," she said, placing an ungloved finger at the center of the ocean between North America and Europe. Dotted lines arced across the chart, denoting sea-lanes and major currents.

"This is the transatlantic cable," she said, indicating a relatively straight line across the Atlantic. She pointed at the line of black forms. "Those shadows are directly above it. On our current course, we shall pass right over the cable and therefore right under *them*." She looked at the women. "But there is an alternative. There's a sea-lane to starboard, above a *protective* line that is not on this map."

"Can we convince the captain to change course?" Evelyn asked.

"Leave that to me," Marlowe stated. "But as I've not much time, I need you to understand something. The harmony of the earth is off. Someone is transmitting something unnatural along that cable. But that's not the only thing you're hearing."

"Yes, there's an echo," Clara confirmed.

"It's not the only line across the waters. There's all these." She danced her fingertips over the cartography. "They denote currents and routes, intangible yet forces of nature, beholden to wind, water, and tides. But life, since ancient times, pulses along the greatest of all lines. And that is, I believe, how you summoned me, Clara Templeton. And if so, I am beholden to you, because I am *of* the great lines," Marlowe stated. Clara blinked at her. Did she mean lineage? She pressed on, "What's important is these lines above all else."

"What lines?" Clara asked, finally exasperated.

"Ley lines," Evelyn finished.

Everyone stared.

"Oh, come now, don't be surprised," Marlowe scoffed. "You're all clairvoyants, aren't you? Aren't ley lines a given in your world?"

Rose opened her mouth, and as a small sound of protest issued forth, Marlowe batted her hand.

"The weight of all of you brought me here," Marlowe continued, attempting a patient tone, "Clara being my most potent tether along such a key ley line as the transatlantic. Here *between* the lines of natural ley force and the man-made wires, something is trying to interfere.

"Maybe someday you can do what I do, Clara. If you were able to access your past lives differently, on a different trajectory . . . It grows a bit tedious, being the only one stretched this far across time. I could use a companion."

Marlowe smiled. When she smiled it was alternately endearing and terrifying, as there was something nearly ancient about the expression. Marlowe was too human, too much of one all at once. She was overwhelming.

"Is that what this is about?" Clara asked softly. "Companionship?"

"Ah, no," Marlowe said definitively. "I could never take you away from your most important time line. You began to understand, by wielding localized magic, and deploying a soul compass, the lines along which life runs."

"Ley lines are the . . . latitude and longitude of magic?" Rose asked, grasping for purchase on the topic.

Marlowe grimaced at the word "magic." "Do you have to call it that?"

"Life-force, energy lines so powerful they are nearly super-natural," Clara offered.

"Yes. Can you *feel* those lines?" Marlowe asked.

Clara thought a moment. "No."

Marlowe leaned in. "Try."

"How? What do I look for?"

Marlowe clucked her tongue. "You're clairvoyant, you don't *look*. Not in the normal way."

Clara reflexively thought to ask what sense she should sharpen but remained silent when she knew the answer would be her sixth; the maddening sixth, *knowing* without being able to prove *how* in common terms. But if there was one thing the Eterna Commission had demanded of her, it was that she stop second-guessing that knowledge and begin treating it with proud certainty.

There was a long pause. All Clara could hear was the water, see was the endless horizon, smell and taste was a salt wind, and feel was that moist wind on flushed cheeks and the sensation of a speeding vessel beneath her steady feet that had no trouble with the pitch and yaw of the boat.

As for her sixth sense, Clara wasn't sure what indicators to consider. She could feel Elizabeth staring at her, through her, perhaps seeing more of her than even she could. It was terribly disconcerting, everything about the visitor always was; she made no sense to any of her senses, especially not her sixth.

Very often her sixth sense was a hybrid of other senses, a slight tweak to her hearing or a flicker to her vision.

The visitor suddenly smacked her in the abdomen. Clara yelped. Had she been wearing her corset, it would have been like hitting a cage, considering the steel bones; instead, with her being in only soft layers and with her body being on high alert, it had a higher impact.

"Your gut will tell you where the lines are," Marlowe

stated. "Don't think, just feel the flow of energy and tell me which direction it is from where you stand right now."

Clara stared at this unprecedented, unpredictable woman and then faced the prow. The hairs on her head rose a bit and there was a visceral stirring sensation within her. She felt her left hand lifting, pointing forward as they headed west, every movement coming from that visceral place. Her body flooded with a warm, luminous power. She smiled, unable to help herself. She could, in fact, feel this line.

There was an audible component, too. Something soft lifted from this peaceful thrall, a thrumming, vibrant hum that was not the steam engines, not the water, a faint violin string in vibrato across the waves.

"That's the ley line," Marlowe murmured, pleased. "Toward where you're pointing, ahead, behind, we're nearly on top of it in this sea-lane. But the direction you turned? That thing that made you perk your ears up port side and come out here to see what was wrong? The rest is—"

"The transatlantic cable ringing with a sour note, comparatively," Clara finished.

"Dissonance. Yes." The visitor sighed. "The cable was put in unfortunately close to our line. Doubt the planners had any sense of it, but who can blame their instinct? Something drew them, literally along this line. Humans gravitate to these old lines constantly, but sometimes I feel like what happens upon them are at cross-purposes."

Evelyn, Miss Knight, and Rose had all been listening at a polite few paces off, but Evelyn took a step forward, Marlowe's nearest rival in terms of sheer force of presence.

"The force of the world doesn't like to run on man-made wires, but goodness if mankind doesn't like to run along the force of the world," Evelyn offered.

"If that's not the truth, I don't know what is," Marlowe murmured, and looked up at the stars. If Clara wasn't mistaken, the one toward which the visitor stared winked out. At this, the strange woman frowned, as if personally wounded. She turned fierce eyes upon Clara.

"So. Remember this lesson, Templeton. *Never* forget it. These lines are life or death. For you, and for me. . . ."

It was Miss Knight's turn to step forward, her long crimson robes billowing dramatically in a gust of wind. "Do you know, then, what will happen next?"

"No, not exactly," Marlowe replied. "Beyond the fact that the amassed, negative energies are a distinct threat no matter where they appear. I mean, I could try to see your future if I concentrated very hard, but there are too many variables to say for certainty and my consciousness can only focus in on you for so long before I become a danger."

"Are you, then," Clara asked, "in more places than one?"

At this, Marlowe smiled. "Aren't you?"

Clara thought of her lives, lives she could see at any point if she concentrated hard enough, lives that each chewed upon an important crux. She had a sense that the lines were her crux, the one that this life hinged upon. There was a truth to the visitor's idea of a broader consciousness. At that moment came a gust of wind so strong and sudden that Clara had to close her eyes against the salt spray. When she opened them again, the visitor was gone.

While she'd been focused on Marlowe, Rose had gone to their cabin to retrieve the doctor's bag filled with protective Wards and was now returning to her.

At Rose's side walked Senator Bishop, an additional bundle of Wards in his hands. He was tall, striking, and distinguished, dressed in a black satin robe; his silver hair positively glowing in the moonlight, giving his face a preternatural halo.

The moment he caught sight of Clara, his eyes sought out hers and spoke volumes of his care. She moved to meet him nearer the door he'd come through; the magnetism that had grown between them was dizzying, and she put her hand on the rail.

"Warding the ship," he stated with a smile. "Leave it to a group of brilliant women to be working through the night for the benefit of all."

He turned to nod out at the water and the still-floating shadows. "They woke me, too, a thrumming racket in my ears and a dread press on my heart. I have to imagine anyone with even rudimentary sensitivities either won't be able to sleep or will have a miserable set of nightmares to show for it," he said grimly.

He shook off the pall and turned to Clara, beaming. "What may I do to help, my dear? I am ever at your service."

His deference and respect, his radiant smile, as if her rising to leadership was the source of his greatest pride, moved and inspired her. Her fingers ached to touch him but she had to recall herself to the moment and task at hand.

"Thank you, Rupert," she murmured. She turned to the rest of her company and spoke with calm authority. "We should Ward each flank of the ship, and at different levels, but in inconspicuous places. It will be done quickly if we divide up the vials."

"All the more quickly for extra hands," came another voice, from the deck door directly behind them.

Harold Spire, the leader of London's Omega department— "a policeman turned circus manager," as he termed himself bitterly—strode toward their number, dressed in shirtsleeves that accented broad shoulders and an open waistcoat that mirrored the company's haphazard dress, his brown hair mussed.

The default scowl of the dour man was affixed until he saw Rose step out from behind Clara and his expression softened.

"Have you worked around us Sensitives long enough that

the presence of the paranormal affects you as it does us? Drawing you to the front lines?" Clara asked with a hopeful smile.

"No, that honor goes to Lord Denbury," Spire replied with a sigh. "Poor boy had one bloody hell of a nightmare, woke moaning about his mother, his razed home, the demons. . . . He wasn't quite to a screaming fit but I heard enough on the other side of the cabin wall. Lord Black thankfully was able to quiet him, he's like a mother hen, that one."

"Cluck, cluck," Black said with a small laugh, his turn to speak from the doorway, his own box of Wards in hand. "He'll be all right. He just needs time to heal, grieve, and to frankly be away from all this. Warding will help, I'm sure."

An immaculate, handsome, fashionable man who usually dressed in light colors, patterns and pastels, a stark contrast to the darker and bolder shades of most of the rest of the teams, Lord Black was currently arrayed in an emerald silk smoking jacket with a loose cream ascot, looking far more put together than the rest of them.

Wards were distributed among the group.

"We'll affix them inconspicuously *how*?" Spire asked. Rose lifted up a small box of twine, cloth, and scissors. "Miss Everhart again wins the day with usefulness," he stated. She beamed, and Clara could feel the little ripple of light and warmth that resulted. Energies and moods were atmospheric conditions, and despite Spire's thick clouds of skepticism, his deepening bond with his second-in-command made for clearer skies.

The small glass tubes were mostly filled with London's protective recipe, and a precious few still held New York's ingredients; Clara hoped they would work here, in the middle of the ocean, for both shores.

Without a word between them, Miss Knight and Evelyn began lashing Wards to various out-of-the-way places along the prow. Lord Black, Rose, and Spire went further aft and port.

Clara instinctively went starboard, toward the ley-line side, and Bishop followed. They were silent, knowing that prayerful contemplation was the best way to attend to their work and to charge the Wards with their own personal fire. She felt the Wards vibrate in her hand as if invigorated as she neared the ship's rail.

Once she'd tucked two of the glass tubes into a notch in the wood, striking a match to light their contents, satisfied by the ethereal light that burned in the glass, she reached out to feel the ley line again. It was like it was singing within her.

As she felt it, she turned to the port side. In the distance, one of the wavering, inky human forms hovering above the transatlantic cable faded into the bluer night sky. Clara smiled. Magnifying the lines within her, an amplifying resonance, there was an effect. The full line of shadows was gone, and she heaved a sigh of relief.

The rest of the team had vanished, leaving her alone with the senator in what likely was a message of encouragement. No one could doubt what an indomitable partnership Clara and he had become. "Do you believe in ley lines?" Clara asked finally.

"Yes. I could feel what you did. You seemed to be tapping directly into them, a refreshing jolt all around you."

"Better than a cup of coffee," Clara chuckled before she looked out again at where the inky silhouettes had floated. "We have to fight to keep the ley lines clean, wherever they run, and try to keep industrial lines clear. Wards can cleanse any ley lines that industry sullies and they can in turn bolster the Wards. A symbiotic protection."

Bishop placed his hand on her shoulder. "So we shall. Fight the deadly shadows with the potency of our life. I'm so proud of you and your widening power."

"Thank you for being so very good to me," she said, turning to him, intuiting that his touch invited closer contact.

"You have kept me good all my life," he said earnestly, keeping the hand on her shoulder but sliding his other around her waist, as if he were about to dance with her.

"My powers of mesmerism could have taken me down a very dark path," he continued. "The 'two walks' as Evelyn always called them. Life and death, war and peace, illumination or obscurity, generosity or greed. Because of you, the great responsibility that was providing for inimitable you, there was no choice but to walk the upright walk. Being good to you has always meant what is good for me."

"And . . . now?" she asked, tilting her head to him. Just what kind of power could she wield indeed? His fingertips inched down her back and further around her side, beginning to envelop her in a covetous embrace.

"I want to be very good to you indeed," he murmured.

She let herself fall against him with a soft sigh as his arms fully enclosed her, having longed for a kiss since the last night at Lord Black's estate. There, something definitively changed between them; an agreement that she would carefully open herself to feelings buried deep in her heart. In that compression it had become far more precious, a diamond waiting to be mined.

A laugh sounded around the side of one of the great steam stacks. At the sound, Bishop turned his face, taking a step back and letting his arms fall away, breaking what had been the promise of a kiss, ever the gentleman of public propriety, offering Clara an apologetic look.

She turned to the noise to see Louis's twin, Andre Dupris, and Eterna's best spy, Ephigenia Bixby, deeply engrossed in conversation, dressed as though they'd not yet gone to sleep, Andre in the navy evening suit coat he'd worn to dinner and Effie in a white linen dress with ribbon trim, her tight brown spiral curls tucked up under a felt and feather hat.

The two had partnered together in England, sliding between classes and cultures, saving as many lives of the struggling as they could, striving to keep them from the Master's Society's vile clutches. The moment they made out the figures at the side of the ship as their compatriots, Effie gasped.

"Oh, I'm sorry," she said, looking from Bishop to Clara, "I hope we didn't . . . interrupt anything."

"Indeed," Andre intoned with a slight, knowing smile that made Clara blush.

"Ever since the nights trying to convince the dockworkers not to work for Apex, trying to warn as many of London's underclass of the dangers as possible, we've not been able to keep regular hours and find ourselves pacing the night," Effie confessed.

"I was awoken by the sense of Summoned forces and we've just been Warding the ship," Clara offered.

"Ah!" Andre exclaimed. "I'm no Sensitive but I was there when those shadows snuffed out Eterna's researchers and not a day goes by that I don't yearn for the Summoned to be banished from the face of the earth forever. I'm sure they're the reasons I couldn't sleep tonight."

"But perhaps we should all try again," Bishop declared. "I think our Warding has made the night sing more sweetly." He bowed his head. "Until morning, friends, for soon we are home," he said, and walked off with a lingering look at Clara before disappearing beyond the door to the cabin halls.

"Good night," Clara said, casting one more glance over her shoulder at the water before striding ahead to the deck door, hoping to catch Bishop in the hall beyond. But he was gone, down to his room, and she didn't dare pursue him there. Not yet.

Lying in her bunk, Clara drifted to sleep with an unresolved question on her mind, wondering if her new skills of ley-line sensitivity would increase the likelihood of epileptic attacks. If fully attuned to the great dynamos of the earth's life force, would she be paralyzed in the face of danger? With every gift there came physical consequences, and she prayed she wouldn't suffer unduly in the process.

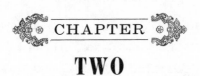

CHAPTER

TWO

Lady Tantagenet, lounging in her boudoir, reached out her hands, raising them in the moonlight like large, climbing spiders over her head.

She stretched to feel the ebb and flow of her magic along all the lines she had begun to co-opt: rail, telegraph, and electrical. She liked to think the pulse of energy whispered her name, *Celeste,* with every chug of a steam engine and every whir of a dynamo turbine.

It was time for maintenance and renewal of the leeching boxes. Her stations on both sides of the Atlantic, pulling on Master's Society channels cut deep between the two countries, had lost their potency. Commissioning renewals would be tomorrow's task.

Tonight, however, her whirring thoughts turned to consider what had brought her here, closer and closer to her ultimate goal of transcending her limited flesh.

The day she had first arrived in Manhattan, the train ride was as smooth as she hoped it would be, which gave her the assurance she needed: that the tokens she'd been laying anytime their train stopped were having an immediate, amplifying effect.

The arsenic-laced tea and alcohol she'd fed to her ailing, dazed husband, a boring man whose title she'd needed to further her aims, helped keep the ride enjoyable, and she was blessedly able to focus on nothing but how her latest ventures had changed the breadth and scope of her gifts.

She felt younger, more energized, and moved with far more ease. O, how this petty age worshipped youth and beauty. People bent to her will like willow branches, responded to her with eager haste, as if the requests she had made were ordered by royalty. She could sway the world, mesmerize it, and finally be at peace within it. . . .

Nothing is worth doing if it can't be felt, she maintained, and remembered opening herself to the train as if she were inviting in a lover. The hum, the vibration, the turning wheels chugging from one industrial station to another, speeding and screeching, sooty and steamy, a shrieking metal monster across the vast tracts of wilderness. She felt it all.

Like many other burgeoning empires before it, the United States was founded on slaughter and blindness. On genocide and slavery. On fear, feast, and famine. Arrogant and often without principle, it was perfectly suited to her purpose. The country had belonged to the shadows since its beginnings in seizure and violence.

Celeste was much like the society of her birth. A usurper. Soon she would collect her due, the country seeing her as one of its very own. Grateful to men like Cornelius Vanderbilt, who sought to monopolize certain industries, she considered consolidation far easier to leech onto and undermine than individual businesses. It was easy to hide within conglomerates.

She'd dipped her toes into an assortment of the various blood pools of Chicago industry, the slaughterhouses beautiful visions of hell on earth, but when she began worming her way into the railroad industry, she knew it was her best fit. As New York was the hub and the heart of the rails, relocation was inevitable. The rails and the electrical grids would best fulfill her widening needs.

The last station before a ferry after which another train would screech its way into the heart of Manhattan and bring its mass to steaming rest at the great depot had been a quaint little platform in eastern New Jersey. Celeste took advantage of the pause in her journey to briefly disembark, wandering out along the platform with a small black box in hand. She eventually found a place for it; stepping down onto the tracks, where a screen of smoke and steam obscured her, she left the seemingly harmless token at a track change.

Her soul-binding tokens, placed beneath arches, at intersections, at track changes, at booster stations, at turbines and dynamos, held the divinatory quality of forks in a road. If each side of an intersection represents a decision, movement of any kind—turning, continuing in the same direction, or even reversing course—makes the choice. She would collect those decisions and allow the mass to power her future, part by dead part.

That was how she'd gotten here. Shifting in bed, arms still upraised to feel the prickling jolts of the industries that were offering her every other beat of their unnatural hearts, she rejoiced that eventually she wouldn't even need this female assemblage of carbon the world considered a second-class body; she would float above it all, a spirit supreme.

* * * * *

Sleeplessness was now the new rule of law.

Perhaps, Clara thought, it was a consequence of feeling and hearing the lines, perhaps because what they'd fought in England still wafted over the earth, in one form or another, when she'd hoped every last Summoned had been banished on the bloodied stones of the Embankment. Of this she was as sure as instinct and portent could be; it was not mere imagination.

What, then, would be the point of what they hoped to do in New York? Would there ever be a final nail driven in this particular coffin? Could there be? Might a systemic evil gain enough momentum from the magnitude of its own near-impossible virulence, springing up from the grave in cycles like a penny-dreadful *vampyr*, to become immune to all of folklore's remedies?

She had to trust in the city, the power of the local magic, to strike back, as it had done in London. Yet she feared that her work ultimately made little difference. Did she make any ghost's afterlife any better with her work? Was the spirit world as a whole moving toward peace?

The practical and localized magic Clara and her companions wrought—did it do right by the living and the dead? She could no longer ask her late, beloved Louis this question, certain as she was that his call to the world was trained now upon his beloved New Orleans, so she would have to ask Evelyn Northe-Stewart. Perhaps Evelyn would be willing to hold a séance to ask Lady Denbury, and others in the spirit world that had helped them, what more the living could do to help those who had crossed over, who had so many times come to the aid of humanity.

If she was feeling ill at ease, did that mean the Summoned had returned to float again over the cable? Marlowe had made sure their path wouldn't cross over it directly, but she was up on her feet and half-dressed again, because if they had come back and no one else was awake to fight them . . .

Trying to be as quiet as she could, as there was no sense in sounding an alarm until the threat was assessed, she rushed up and out to the rail and looked out in the direction of the line.

There was a floating lightless body again, as unnatural as it was unnerving. One. Perhaps two; it was hard to tell in the dark night and the movement of the water.

Closing her eyes, Clara felt for the ley line behind her, as if she were reaching back and drawing out a sword of light. . . .

The hum filled her, a sense of peace soothed her, and when she opened her eyes again the demon, or whatever trick of the water and night that had made the demons appear, was gone. The Wards tucked into inconspicuous places glowed from their nooks and crannies, her surge recharging them a moment. Clouds fled from the moon and suddenly the water danced with diamonds. She smiled and clenched her fists in pride.

It wouldn't always be this easy, and she had only sensed and seen one Summoned, but having a new spiritual weapon at her disposal, one that had yet to put her into epileptic danger, was the most exciting development ever.

Out of the corner of her eye she could see Miss Knight approach, her elaborate crimson kimono replaced with a far more somber aubergine taffeta that swished as she walked.

"Trouble sleeping; a psychic bane," Knight murmured, turning her focus far out into the deep, toward the fading glow of the horizon line. Neither broke silence for the sake of nicety.

In Clara's experience, when two clairvoyants spoke after a long quiet, one tended to pick up on what the other one was thinking; this did not disprove it.

"Thank goodness the water and the horizon line are clear," Knight said. "We've done good work, thanks to you."

"Thanks to us all."

"I wish I could simply take comfort in our talents as enough. But I fear we may not be enough, strong and unique as we are," Knight murmured. "What if there is no end to the plague of demons, Miss Templeton?" Miss Knight placed her long fingers on the rail and gripped it. "I've been having visions. Terrible things. A war in the ground. I cannot tell if I am awake or asleep, but I see the future, decades from now. The whole *world* is at arms. Is destruction mankind's foremost instinct and nature? There are beautiful women on this boat and normally that would be enough to assuage my romantic heart; that there are at the very least lovely creatures walking this earth that I may daydream about. But beauty is not enough for nights such as these."

Clara did not turn to her newfound colleague, as she couldn't bear to see what Knight saw if she were to look into her eyes. The empathy from one Sensitive to another would have to be enough. The gifted were often as alienated from another soul as they were drawn to one another, beings magnetized trying to wrest apart for safety.

"If the Master's Society's demonic, soul-splitting, and resurrectionist terrors can't be thoroughly squelched and driven out from under every rock under which those practices have lain hidden, we won't *have* a next century," Clara replied after some consideration. "I'm worried about protecting the here and now. That's why I'm awake right now, I wanted to pray to the Wards and keep them vibrant."

"Will what we fight not always regroup?" Knight asked. "Is this not the most exhausting of prospects?"

"Humans will always have the capacity for evil and terror. All I hope is to keep the demons out of the mix. Humans, I can't answer for. I won't."

"I may have to borrow some of your fortitude. I'd once prided myself on it." The medium sighed dramatically. "I'm getting vulnerable in my old age!"

At that, Clara snorted, as the woman couldn't be much older than her, and while by society's standards the both of them should have been married off by thirty, they were hardly elderly, and certainly didn't live by society's rules. Clara didn't find "spinster" an insult. It was, for so many, a freedom to live for oneself.

"You know, Miss Templeton," Knight began, still staring out at the water. The breeze buoyed loose strands of her black hair, creating a wispy Medusa. "You have become the cornerstone of this entire foundation. You hold us all up."

"Clara, please," she replied earnestly. "As for my conviction, it waxes and wanes. Tonight I felt myself waning, but I can't afford to be a crescent right now, I must be full, and so I pull on forces far greater than myself. I have a feeling New York will not be so simple an equation." Clara sighed. "So much about my land defies redemption. How can we effectively Ward the inherently flawed and harmful?"

"England is much the same, with its flag piercing any patch of land it seizes, thinking it knows better than the places and people it destabilizes," Knight replied. "I'm sure our grieving Mrs. Wilson could regale us with complicated feelings about what and who she considers home and country, as could Zhavia about his escape from pogroms to English safety, and our compatriots of blended race who have to navigate their circles carefully at home and abroad.

"As for me, I've fought hard to be solvent, to have certain freedoms. And yet I have to hide who I am, hide behind Mr. Blakely as a beard. And Lord Black; more privileged than us all and yet he cannot be open about the man he adores. I resent the heavy hand of imperial interests, I feel too keenly, see too much, as do you with concerns of westward expansion and stolen native lands. But the Society's vision is no *alternative* to the horrors citizens have wrought on both our shores, foreign and domestic."

"It is not, and we are its antitheses. Now and no matter the future to come," Clara declared, looking out at the moon, choosing to remain at full.

Miss Knight took to reclining in a deck chair while Clara couldn't seem to tear herself away from the railing. It was the old sea captain in her.

After a long while had passed, she turned back to find Miss Knight gone, the moon lower, and an entire loss of sense of time. Despite the moon's rounds, where it was in the sky seemed like another place and hemisphere; even the constellations seemed askew, and the sound of the sea lapping against steel sounded far away. There was a *zap* from the shadows behind her. Something very specific, that sound.

Clara turned away from the railing when something caught her eye to the side of one of the great white stacks periodically venting great gouts of steam: the figure of a man peeking around the impressive cylinder. She remembered when she'd first seen those eyes, sparking in the shadows, unnerving and unnatural. It had been on Pearl Street in Manhattan, shortly after the street had been electrified. The streetlamps and the interior lights of the homes along the street flickered whenever this particular small, unassuming, yet terrifying young man stood below the orbs.

Mr. "Jack" Mosley, who had taken the name of his dead brother and the name of England's first lit street as his own. Wielder of electricity, grand leveler of Moriel's Vieuxhelles estate, and the greatest aid in cutting the Society to the quick. Mosley was the one among their number who was the most unpredictable. *How* he worked, Clara could not fathom.

Dressed in a brown frock coat and matching waistcoat too large for his thin frame, he stared at Clara. His mousy brown hair was wind-tossed and his thin mustache traced an uneven line over a pressed mouth that frowned in concentration. The sight of him filled her with as much fear as fascination; he could harness electricity the way a rancher might a lasso or a driver a whip.

Mosley was, so far as she could tell from his work against Moriel, an ally, though driven by a desire for vengeance rather than justice. He was also the reason for one of the Omega department's casualties: Voltage from Mosley's hands had leaped through a wire and electrocuted Reginald Wilson from across a park. It had not been intentional murder but the man had still died, leaving his wife grief-stricken and his friends heartsick.

Yes, this was a man to be feared and kept at a distance.

What was he doing on board? He was an Englishman. . . . Perhaps New York City had become his home and he was simply returning after being removed to London by Moriel's people. Perhaps he knew something none of Eterna nor Omega were aware of—something about what lay ahead.

She couldn't just stand there and stare at him as much as he could her. She had to speak or move; she couldn't pretend she didn't notice him any more than she had when he'd raised the hairs on her arms by his very presence on the street where she lived.

A nod. That was all she could manage.

He returned the gesture, then spoke. Though they were many feet apart and she should not have been able to hear him at that distance, over the noise of the sea, his voice came to her clearly.

"I've been waiting for a moment alone with you," he stated in a way that Clara wasn't sure how to take. "I can't bear to be around all the people in the daytime," he continued, rubbing his temple. "It's very noisy—all the power lines, the cable lines, the passengers and their chatter, so much *humming*. But you're at the center of your merged departments, all orbits around you so it's been impossible to reach you."

"Well, you have my ear now, Mr. Mosley," she said carefully.

"It's good you're learning how to differentiate between the feel of natural lines and man-made. I'm glad your guardian angel came to help. I was watching."

Clara stared at him, horrified by the idea of someone noting her every move. Perhaps her sentiment was made manifest in her expression, as the small, awkward man blushed in shame and stammered an explanation. "She makes a distinct sound, that woman, a specific note I never heard before. I had to see the source. I hear energy signatures like music, you see."

"That's . . . very unique," Clara replied, and forced a smile.

"With so many devils we need a few angels," Mosley continued, "to help us take care of unfinished business. So many frayed wires . . . A live, frayed wire is very dangerous, Miss Templeton," he said ominously. "Be an angel and keep listening for beautiful notes. Not sour, rotten ones. You are a natural. That's the key to turning the tide for good; picking the signal out of the noise." A moment later he vanished behind the stack as it belched a fresh channel of steam into the air, obscuring the view. When the white cloud dissolved, she was alone again on the deck.

Why make himself known solely to her? While he made her uneasy, she didn't get the impression that he thought of her as prey; she felt as though he sensed something of a kindred spirit in her.

That was, in a way, more terrifying than the ability to carry and disseminate a charge. She couldn't do what Mosley did, but what did he think her capable of?

"Be worthy of the squall," she murmured to herself, a line directly from the visitor's mouth. It was one bad forecast after another and she hoped she could get a bit of rest to weather the next downpour.

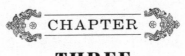

CHAPTER

THREE

The bulk of the voyage was spent bolstering one another's spirits, telling stories, toasting each other with pints or cordials, and Clara tried to enjoy every minute of it, relishing the bonds of chosen family as sacred food for the soul.

Andre Dupris and Effie Bixby, encouraging others to join them on their deck laps, shared their love of French poetry, and the importance of Frederick Douglass, and took the time to explain to their compatriots the infuriating complications of existing in two separate cultures as people who could "pass."

Knight and Evelyn played clairvoyant guessing games with the company, nothing that revealed anything too personal, but Clara assisted when she felt so inclined. Lord Black gossiped about members of Parliament and Bishop about Congress, and the senator indulged his mesmerism only in so much as to procure them an occasional extra bottle of wine for their table.

Even Harold Spire told a few unexpected jokes and regaled his compatriots with sordid and outrageous tales of his London beat. While his distaste for the supernatural remained, he did seem to care for his fellows, and no one could doubt his devotion to seeing justice served.

Only Lord Denbury kept himself apart, for the sake of his fragile health, carefully tended by Lord Black and his mother-in-law by way of marriage, Evelyn.

The ongoing ache between Clara and Rupert was as

distinctive to her tongue as the sea spray and as deep in her body as an old wound. Countless times they would open their mouths to say something to one another, yet didn't speak, unsure. For all their mature talents, they were timid children in this new realm of intimacy.

When the time came for everyone to see to their bags and packing out, Miss Knight whispered in Clara's ear, "Good heavens, dear girl, just kiss him already, I can no longer *bear* your pining minds!"

The striking psychic walked away, teal taffeta swishing in her wake, leaving Clara's cheeks to turn scarlet in private. Perhaps she was correct. Bishop has always given Clara time, space, and autonomy. It was wonderful, all this freedom, but might it mean that she needed to be forward, to act, to grant him explicit permission . . .

She sought out Rupert's cabin once she'd seen to her things. Perhaps he sensed her nearness, for he opened the door just as she was about to knock. Sensitives; taking the surprise out of everything.

Taking her arm, Senator Bishop led her into the cozy space. His eyes were full of heat. The wall between them, constructed from decorum and shy awkwardness, was coming down brick by brick, revealing an ever-burning hearth. Clara longed to warm her hands in the gently growing fire of their more intimate companionship.

He stared at her for a long time before reaching toward her face. Two fingertips edged around a braided tress of her hair, then traced down the side of her ear, causing her a shiver of delight, before grazing her cheek. His mesmeric gaze was fastened on her, those powerful eyes that shifted between shades of blue, green, and hazel depending on the surroundings and emotions.

"I'm simply . . . so glad of you, my Clara," he murmured. "So glad."

He seemed to take a delight in "my." She tried out the concept. "As am I, my Rupert. . . ."

He beamed, sculpted lips curving into the most inviting of expressions.

As they balanced, transfixed, in an endless pause, there came the loud blast of the ship's horn and the echoing call to disembark. At the reverberate sound, Bishop seemed to remember himself, turning away to grab a leather case. She seized his shoulder to turn him back, wishing to relish the moment full of aching promise and seal it with a physical gesture.

"There will be time for us, for everything we want," he promised in a delectable whisper, and bent to deposit a kiss upon the hollow of her throat, then her cheek, then her eyebrow, each evoking a little hitch of breath from her. His lips landed last on her ear, where he murmured, "We've been patient this long and I will not rush anything . . ."

The horn blasted again.

Stepping out onto the walkway, he offered his arm to Clara. She took a deep breath, calmed her racing heart, cooled her burning cheeks and slid her arm onto his.

They found the rest of their cadre assembled on the main deck, looking as groomed as ship travel might allow. Clara studied them for a moment, taking their measure. They all shared the look of wartime soldiers.

The ship approached the busy harbor, where the brown stone spires of the still-unfinished Brooklyn Bridge impressively defied the sky. The teeming harbor and bustling city were an intricate, moving tapestry of countless colors and shapes. New York was, in and of itself, magical, inimitable.

But she could not forget her worries about the scars, the bloodied land still reeling from slavery's shame, and what kind of toll was taken on the magic itself? No matter the bent of her own heart, if the society itself was flawed, unjust, unbalanced from the start, what hope did this island have to Ward out more oppressive evil? They were heading into unknown territory, into a nation that took possession of land day in and day out, in ways ruthless and unforgivable.

Perhaps that was why the Society chose New York, or any part of the U.S. territories; so much blood on the soil, for many centuries, spreading ever westward. That humankind took and retook territory across every culture did not console her; it was the kind of excuse one made to keep stealing from others.

As open psychically as she ever was upon water, she saw, in her mind, the wafting sorrow of the Lenape tribe's ghosts still lingering on the edges of the island just ahead of her; the atrocities of Willem Kieft and his bloody war, when men and women were chased down, babies ripped from them, heads dashed on rocks, and the severed heads of tribal leaders he placed on pikes along the Bowling Green. . . . A psychic scar remaining upon the tip of the island. She wished she could rewrite their suffering and exchange it for a retrospective coexistence.

Or perhaps it wasn't their ghosts she sensed at all, as Native beliefs of the spirit world and the afterlife were different than hers, each tribe with their own tradition. She couldn't presume. Her guilt was the haunt here; that she was of a people who benefited from stolen land now beholden to localized magic. This was a depth of worry to address.

Her devotedly Quaker parents, and Bishop, too, had raised her to always be aware of injury, to seek to repair it, and to live in peace. Increasingly attentive to the slightest change in her these days, the senator noticed a pall come over her and he touched her elbow as the boat made its final approach into the clanging, whistling, roaring, teeming harbor.

"Taking in the sight of New York, all I can think is how can we protect what is so deathly flawed?" she murmured.

"What is sacred or Warded ground when so much unholy slaughter came to pass here?" She felt tears rise to her eyes.

"Advocacy is far more useful than tears, Clara," Bishop said gently. "And I promise you I will attend to the issues as best I can. We mustn't excuse the human need to conquer and its deadly momentum, a runaway train that left from its station the moment European powers touched this shore. It is ironic, perhaps then, that we are here with English allies, but then they, too, must join in the righting of wrongs, affixing better brakes to that insatiable engine."

Their entire crew, the American Eterna colleagues that had gone to fight for England and those of Omega who had boarded to return the favor, stood near to the disembarking platform, the smaller of their luggage in hand.

Bishop turned to the company with all his powers of persuasion and magnetism radiant in a palpable aura. He gestured toward the ever-climbing skyline and teeming cityscape.

"Welcome back to New York," Bishop said, turning specifically to Rose and Knight, who offered polite smiles, Rose trying to stand so that Knight's elaborate peacock feather fascinator wouldn't tickle her face, there in the powerful crossbreeze of the rivers' confluence at the tip of Manhattan Island.

Bishop then turned his magnetism to his elegant peer Evelyn Northe-Stewart, who seemed to take his mesmerism as if it were a passed plate at a communal meal, and she instinctively, protectively placed her gloved hand on Lord Denbury's back.

The young man stood silently, expressionlessly beside her, always dressed in some simple but magnificently tailored dark-colored suit. His beautiful face, now far too drawn, seemed antithetical in the bright sun. Clara's heart swelled with empathy for the man; torn from his family to fight old demons he thought long dead, subjected to a constant and familiar torture. The young man's health had steadily declined and he needed to recover far away from demons' clutches and reminders of their evil.

"To those joining us here for the first time, the senator, Clara, and I, and the whole city, thank you," Evelyn added, turning to Spire, whose expression was more a grimace. Everyone knew this was no tourist trip.

"But of course and we are happy to be here!" Lord Black exclaimed with a bob of his top hat. His cream-colored suit with a golden ascot and light blue waistcoat made him appear like clouds, sun, and sky, a perfect visual companion to his warm tone and ever-cheery disposition.

Andre Dupris, in his usual vibrant style of russets and bright accents, a light green cravat magnifying the piercing quality of his hazel eyes, glanced around at the bustle of the nearby docks as if getting his bearings. Taking in nearly everyone in the company, he avoided looking at Effie, who stood adjacent. His expression took on an air of finality, and Clara understood what was about to happen.

"My friends, before we disembark and go on our ways, I must confess: This is where I leave you. Not because I do not wish to fight fires here in New York, but there are similar conflagrations in New Orleans, as I have seen reported in what papers I could find. The Crescent City is another port town, another bulwark where the Master's Society and their corporation sought to sully industry. You have, in yourselves, an impressive company; New York has the best and brightest.

"New Orleans can claim only its beleaguered but passionate communities, the economic struggles of Reconstruction and the ghost of my brother, in his final rounds, struggling to make sure whatever has been upturned is righted once more." He spoke quietly, and Clara assumed that, as she did, he still battled with the strange grief that was losing Louis over and over again; having parted with his mortal coil first, they were hit by secondary waves of loss whenever Louis's ghost came and went.

Clara was sure Andre, like her, did not begrudge his twin brother peace, but goodness how he was missed, in death as in life; his spectral presence as much a balm and help as his mortal flesh.

Andre continued. "Of course my city will always have its art, heart, and indomitable soul. No demon can come for what is inherent."

No demon can come for what is inherent. That phrase echoed in Clara's ears as if spoken in a cavernous cathedral. It echoed with the resonance of lives past, which always meant it would be important, now and in the future.

"I can't bear to see the reverend, or Mr. Stevens," Andre added. "Please. If I see those dear friends, I'll want to stay and help them. But New Orleans, she needs . . ."

"Go on to the Mississippi, Mr. Dupris," Bishop said. "I agree that it is best if we spread our knowledge and experience. We know that Apex had holdings in New Orleans, and we cannot abandon that charming city."

Ephigenia Bixby's face was unreadable as she adjusted the calico shawl over her layered eyelet dress. Clara was ever impressed by her coworker's impeccable mettle. But the way she stepped toward Andre, hands clenching the sides of her shawl, made Clara think she was not ready to part.

"Now. My inimitable Miss Bixby," he said solemnly, looking straight into her eyes, "I wish to say in front of our friends and colleagues that you are the *finest* woman I have ever known. Should you wish to come to New Orleans, I would be honored, and the city would gain a beloved sister in you. There are . . . kindnesses for people like us. Allowances for our heritage, a pride in our Creole class, to which you would be welcomed. Please consider it."

"I shall, most heartily, Mr. Dupris. I make that visit a promise," she replied earnestly as color mounted in her cheeks.

"I'll hold you to that," he said, a fond sparkle in his eyes. The work had bonded them indeed, and if Clara wasn't mistaken, they'd calmed something within one another. She could see anchors in storms, ships in ports, when she took a closer look at what their bodies seemed to say; at the unspoken words of their entwined auras.

"To the rest of my fine folk," Andre said, turning to the rest of them, "I will wire you when settled. I remain tethered to you in heart and soul. Louis . . . taught me that such a bond is an indelible, unbreakable cord. I tie my soul to you and may all of you be bound to me."

"If there is a finer sentiment, I cannot dream of one," Lord Black said, stepping forward to clasp the man's hands in his in a fond gesture. "Thank you, friend, you've been a great asset."

"I've been a coward," Andre countered sharply. "I appreciate your giving me a chance at redemption. All of you have taken part in my transformation. I am less bitter a man, for all the horrors I've seen. Perhaps it takes monsters to cure a man from becoming one through a hardening of the heart."

This notion seemed to hit the assembled company like a small push toward a mystery solved. From what Clara knew of this man, he had grown indeed. Louis's influence was obvious, a bit of the mad chemist and poet-philosopher bequeathed unto his twin.

The ship horn blasted and the plank lowered.

Andre tipped his hat, a brown bowler with an orange feather, picked up his bag, and walked away. Like Lord Black's, his style made him notable against a sea of somber tones. They watched him go on ahead until his flair was lost in the shifting sea of Manhattan's constant coming and going. Clara assumed he would seek out the nearest ship heading for the Mississippi.

"So, let me ask my good New Yorkers," Lord Black began, clapping his hands and returning their attention to one another. "Once you've gathered your things, as we Brits have the lighter loads coming here on emergency, where should we meet? Which of your ghastly anomalies shall we attend to first?" He smiled gamesomely, platinum hair and bright blue cravat tousled in a harbor gust. The dear man was undaunted. Clara's heart warmed.

"Lady Liberty first," Clara, Evelyn, and Bishop chorused at once, Clara continuing, "If you please. Her poor hand. We've a hellfire to put out."

CHAPTER
FOUR

Once the team reassembled outside Eterna's Pearl Street offices—where none of their staff was in—after returning luggage and freshening up in actual washrooms rather than cramped quarters and insufficient basins, three hired cabs managed to take their company up the angle of Broadway to Madison Square Park.

Rose, Clara, Spire, and Bishop took one cab; Black, Miss Knight, and Effie followed in another. Evelyn Northe-Stewart would join them later, after seeing that Lord Denbury was safely reunited with his wife and child.

While hardly matching the Arcadian splendor that was Central Park, Madison Square was a welcome swath of green among the bustle of theaters and retail palaces. Throngs of well-dressed ladies met there to walk the only avenue where society allowed them to stroll unaccompanied by a chaperone. The Sixth Avenue stretch known as Ladies' Mile featured palatial stores showcasing the latest in international fashion.

It had always offended Clara that the only place that society's judgmental hand allowed her to be seen without a designated shepherd was focused solely on dressing prettily and spending money. Clara could have been that kind of woman, trapped on a pedestal. Instead, with the full support of her hardworking guardian, she had refused the beautifully gilded cage.

For a moment she watched the birds of those cages strut about, hold their hats against the wind, pick up the folds of their skirts and dart laughingly out of the way of trolley car and carriage with their fellow flock of extravagant plumage. While she admired some of their fashion, she didn't want their lot. Her work was unlike that of most women but it was her own, and in happier times had given her much satisfaction.

Nearing the park, the carriages slowed; the horses stamped and whinnied, sensing something off in the atmosphere around them. Animals had a pure, untainted clairvoyance Clara found at once both unnerving and inspiring.

On the southern side of the square stood an elaborate pedestal constructed to showcase the hand of Bartholdi's Statue of Liberty. This gift, which hopefully would one day rise on Bedloe's Island, represented Edouard de Laboulaye's hope to cement France's identity as a democracy and to honor the United States' own revolution. Her sister sculpture already stood proud beside the Seine in Paris, but fund-raising efforts for Lady Liberty had stalled and the arm and torch had been left standing in Madison Square Park.

It really was a sight to behold. Uncanny and entirely out of scale. A hand. A hand bigger than the struggling park trees.

Just a hand with a torch, as city leaders remained ill at ease about the "signal" she would send in the harbor. *Rabble rousing,* thought the elite of the city, disquieted about the thousands of unwashed masses who arrived on Manhattan's shores year after year, pouring in from around the world.

It wasn't the copper hand or torch itself that was the present trouble. It was the fire leaping from the sculpted flame. Green fire. Not because of copper patina, but something foul that smelled of sulfur. Fire and brimstone, if someone were to think too long on it.

The great arm emerged from a stone pedestal; a stairway at

the rear gave access the arm. To the side of the structure stood Franklin Fordham and the reformed chemist Mr. Stevens.

Bishop had wired the office when they'd be arriving and attending to the matters of request, this being the first. Their team was clearly awaited by these two weary men who had remained behind to guard the city. Clara could see worry, fear of failure, and shame on their faces.

"Thank you for returning as soon as you could," Franklin said to the group.

A stocky, auburn-haired man who wasn't half as imposing as his stature, Franklin was nearly Clara's age and had been sought out by her in visions and premonitions, a reconnection from a past life. He had been brought into the Eterna Commission to help expand the department's reach, a man with a melancholic heart and a shocking gift of psychometry. He seemed surprised by the British contingent.

His usually neatly trimmed beard was unkempt, his eyes were deep-shadowed, and the tilt in his posture due to his bad leg was more pronounced than usual. His smile was genuine and his relief palpable at the sight of his colleagues. The poor, dear heart, Clara thought. He was not made of stern stuff.

"Of course, Mr. Fordham," Bishop replied. "We never intended to abandon you. There is much to discuss, and actually much to celebrate despite so many aftereffects still lingering."

Clara turned to Mr. Stevens, who looked just as tired as Franklin but not nearly as harrowed. Upon their arrival, he had accepted a hug from her with a small sound of joy and appreciation, as if he had been offered treasure. His work with Eterna had given the former criminal—who had once been in league with the Society—a resurrected spirit.

Just then, out of the corner of her eye, Clara saw a familiar presence strolling up the street, gaze focused intently on her. She did not bother to hold back her audible groan at the sight of the lanky, thin man in a plaid suit that did him no justice. He wore a brown bowler low across his forehead; light brown hair poked out in tufts from beneath the brim.

Instinctively, Bishop stepped toward Clara as the man reached the group. He glanced up at the torch, then cocked his head with an infuriating expression of playful curiosity, focusing his attention once again on Clara.

She sighed. "Mr. Green. I should have known you'd miss me and search the city over to find me out."

"I'm sorry, he's been dogging me about you this morning and in my exhaustion I let slip I might see you," Franklin muttered. "He read English papers and assumes it's all related."

"Green. The prize thorn in my side," Bishop declared. "Come to make yourself useful?"

"That has only and ever been my aim," the man replied as if offended.

"Paying too close attention to Miss Templeton along the way," Bishop reprimanded him. "It is ungentlemanly, Green."

"You've been gone awhile," the reporter replied, "and therefore free of my attentions. Where were you?" When he received no answer, he gestured to Bishop and Clara's companions and asked, "And who are these fine fellows?"

"Tourists," Harold Spire declared. "The senator and Miss Templeton are expert guides." His London accent made all his consonants more pronounced. Rose said nothing, simply smiling primly at Spire and then turning wary eyes to Green.

"Listen," Green said. "Allow me to be of use. I saw a strange man around this torch, in workman's clothes, carrying something that he did not have with him when he descended. I assumed he was with the commission responsible for the statue, but it was not long after that I noticed the odd fire, so I thought perhaps there was a connection. When I went to your offices to see what you might make of this, I found the place quite understaffed." Franklin opened his mouth to retort when Green continued.

"I have watched the arm for the past several days. This park is my haunt, and before you ask, I have not seen that man again."

"Was there anything odd about him, physically?" Spire asked, his policeman's habits immediately taking hold. "Anything about the eyes?"

"Yes, actually, I was profoundly unnerved by him," Green said, for the first time in the conversation looking visibly shaken. "He caught my eye as he took to the pedestal, looking around before darting up the stairwell. His eyes were dark, and shined oddly, like those of an animal at night when they catch the light from a lantern."

Her team and their allies shared a look. Possessed, then, Clara thought, her stomach sinking. There were still tainted properties and active possessions. Shouldn't this all have died with Moriel?

Clara sighed. Over the years, Green had tracked her to too many different sites; dissuading him would be impossible, redirecting him was the only hope. Perhaps she could appeal to pity. This was a risk, but she thought if she appeared to him vulnerable, it might keep him from thinking her powerful. Women sometimes had to use this trick and she hated it every time.

"Mr. Green," she began wearily, "as you know, inexplicable things are my pastime, and, frankly, my obsession. As I am an epileptic, paranormal interests can trigger seizures, and so I have a host of guardians and friends, all you see here, who help me. Some share my interests, others follow along, humoring me.

"I cannot make this public," Clara continued, "as all of New York would come to me with pleas for intercession and requests for advice. You seem fond of me, despite our constant demands that you stop pestering us. If you value me or my health in the slightest, you will take this under advisement and stop trying to expand our hobby into some sort of government initiative, am I clear?"

"Hobbyists," Green repeated slowly, looking skeptical.

Clara said nothing more and everyone else held their tongues and stared at him. As the silence lengthened, the intensity of their glares grew, conveying unmistakable dislike. Finally he lifted his hands in surrender. "Hobby it is, then. Would you please, however, render an opinion, to another follower of the unexplained, about this sulfuric hellfire? I can see it, others have remarked upon it, but it seems not everyone sees the same thing. Some see nothing at all but the metal itself. What do you see?"

"I don't dare speak to it," Clara replied carefully. "Even an opinion can set me up for danger, if printed. Those desperate for answers will still seek me out and all will escalate. Write what you must of the unknown mystery but leave me out of it."

Bishop stepped closer. "Or city officials will finally close you down," Bishop said, the quietness of his voice somehow strengthening the threat. "I've a note ready at City Hall, just waiting for me to ask my friends in offices to act."

Clara's body reacted to Bishop's forceful energy as he utilized his power of mesmerism against Green. Bishop was subtle in the use of his abilities; people listened and assented to his wishes of their own free will. All the more reason for him to remain supremely careful with his intoxicating and appealing gift.

With a sigh and a shrug, Green walked away, glancing back up at the torch in consternation.

Clara immediately began ascending the stairs at the rear of the monument. Stevens and Franklin were quick at her side.

"My dear fellows," Clara said to them, "tell me what you've been dealing with."

"I admit I am late to addressing this site," Franklin began mournfully. "I ought to have had this in hand before you returned. But both Mr. Stevens and I kept hoping the flames were a bit of staging, trying to inspire the populace to pressure city officials to raise Lady Liberty in the harbor. I assumed this was one of the many campaigns."

"I'd likely have thought the same," Clara assured, trying to relieve Franklin of the guilt he was always so quick to pile upon himself.

"Miss Bixby and Lord Black have agreed to keep watch below and discourage onlookers," Bishop interjected from behind them. "Mr. Spire and Miss Everhart are taking an investigative look about the park grounds and Miss Knight ran after Mr. Green, probably to use her own psychic powers on him."

Franklin led the party up to a small landing where there was an entryway into the arm itself. The door into the statue's framework, which presumably would disappear once she had an actual body, was locked.

"I don't suppose, in the time you waited for us, you troubled the Trust for a key?" Clara asked Franklin.

"I tried, but there was neither answer nor aid," Franklin replied. "But no matter."

With a flourish, he flipped up the long collar of his brown frock coat, one he'd had specially made by Miss Carter, a talented seamstress in the theater district. Franklin would have caused casual onlookers a good deal of unease had they seen his array of hidden implements. On the underside of his collar gleamed several lock picks, each nestled in a small holster and visible only if the collar was raised. Whipping one from its place, he wasted no time in picking the lock.

"Is there room atop the arm for all of us? Will it hold?" Clara asked.

"I've seen up to six permitted up there at a time when they've opened the observation deck," Mr. Stevens replied as Franklin gained entry and bolted up the interior stair, his boots setting a clanging echo bouncing off the copper. Clara ducked her head as she passed through the temporary doorway.

The interior of the arm was dark, but they could see well enough to make their way thanks to light coming from the grate of the torch above. Indeed, the supernatural fire cast an eerie green glow down through the space. A narrow stair at a difficult angle allowed only for small steps and required a firm grip on the iron rail. It was not a good sport for the ladies' skirts but Clara kept her complaint to herself.

At the top, a short, narrow notch gave access to the platform surrounding the torch. About two feet wide, with a circular railing about at waist level, it afforded a lovely view of the park along the outer edge. Franklin offered Clara his arm as she stepped out, but she shook her head and moved smoothly past him, gathering her skirts close as she saw the flames up close for the first time.

The bulk of the fire roiled within the beautifully wrought brazier of the torch. The copper sculpture's dynamic, left-leaning flame reached gracefully up into the sky, staid and stoic above the chaos below.

Taking a careful walk around the narrow circle demonstrated that the fire entirely filled the brazier and confirmed for Clara that heights were not her favorite places, especially when one rail of relatively small circumference was all that kept her from tumbling two stories to the ground.

Uncertain whether she would be burned by the strange illumination, Clara reached out a palm, testing whether the infernal blaze emanated heat. Though she felt no warmth, the core of her palm suddenly stung as if it were attacked by a horde of wasps, the pain rapidly escalating in intensity. With a hiss she drew her hand away.

"Clara—" Bishop made to admonish her.

"It does not burn but stings," Clara stated, interrupting him without hesitation.

"Like an acid," Stevens surmised, inspecting her hand and the already-swelling tip of her first finger. With a gentle eagerness, he offered, "I've a salve for that, I'll be sure to provide some for you."

"Thank you, Mr. Stevens," she replied, all too aware that he thought of her and Bishop as saviors and had to be dealt with delicately.

"Mr. Stevens, what do we have in terms of chemical properties at work here?" Bishop asked.

Stevens began peering, sniffing, and poking at the flames; he even stuck his tongue out near them, as if trying to taste their eldritch surface. He did this for some while as the others watched, regularly flinching back from the sting of the fire and flicking the edges of his jacket out of the way.

"Well, the sour sulfur should be obvious to everyone—it's the source of the green and yellow coloration. I detect barium chloride, as well as a lime and limestone residue. Phosphorus creates the brightness, and a sodium nitrate or carbonate enhances the yellow. Plus there is something else I cannot quite put my finger—or tongue—on."

"This is elemental then," Bishop prompted, "rather than . . ."

"Supernatural?" Evelyn finished. She had climbed the steps behind Bishop and joined the others on the observation deck.

"Mostly elemental. With a shade of mystery," Stevens said, almost excitedly, invigorated by the puzzle. "Brilliant stagecraft, really."

"How is Lord Denbury?" Clara asked.

"Safe. I daresay his wife won't let him out of the house again and I'm sure that'll be just fine with him," she replied, then gestured that they continue. "But do go on."

"How, then, do we render all this inert?" Bishop asked.

"It's been burning for days, without end," Franklin said wearily. "Like I said, when it was first reported, I thought it was part of its show."

"To neutralize the sulfur, which herein has become sulfuric acid, we require a base of at least seven or eight on the pH scale. Water will dilute, however, from personal experience, I can attest that it won't entirely extinguish. And the mystery element here, well . . ."

"For that, we'll need a bit of magic," Clara said softly, "to tip the scales, pH or otherwise, in our favor."

Evelyn made a face at the sight of the chains wrapped around the statue's hand and wrist.

"What's this?" she said with concern. "These chains are not a part of the statue's design."

"To be fair, we don't really know what she'll look like when completed, Evelyn," Bishop countered.

"I do," Evelyn stated firmly. "I've been one of the few of my station campaigning to get her erected! Lady *Liberty* doesn't wear chains, that's rather the point . . ."

"Surely to keep all the pieces together—" Franklin suggested.

"But they aren't *attached* to anything," Evelyn retorted. "Look, they're just fastened about the arm." She bent closer to one of the padlocks, where something white fluttered behind it. "There's something written here," she continued, thumbing a tag affixed to the lock then read it aloud: "'Provide more piercing statutes daily, to chain up and restrain the poor. . . .'"

There was a long silence.

"Shakespeare," Clara blurted finally. The company turned to her. "That's Shakespeare. From . . . *Coriolanus*. The beginning. Text from the starving citizens."

"A keen memory," Bishop said with a smile.

"Do recall that ill-intentioned, dramatic period of time in my youth when I wished to become an actress, dear senator," Clara said, returning his smile. "I daresay I committed several plays entirely to memory in those days. All aching tragedies, of course."

"Of course," Bishop chuckled.

"It's part of the magic, then," Evelyn stated. "Part of the spell. This makes me think of the Baudelaire poem, written out but missing a name; that was a part of the magic surrounding Lord Denbury's soul prison.

"Perverting great literature seems to entertain the Society as much as fouling religion, though I've not seen this sort of riddle repeated since Denbury's case. I think it was too time-consuming, since they've gotten more efficient and ruthless, in their parsing of soul and body. Where once it was a sport, it's become a business."

"Could this be the same operator, or someone copying those previous tactics?" Franklin asked. "Someone who admires those early days?"

"I'm not sure it matters just now; our priority is to counteract this spell," Evelyn replied.

"Perhaps we need another verse?" Clara posited. "Something in contrast?"

"Perhaps," Evelyn nodded. "Moriel at heart believed in English superiority above all else."

The mention of Moriel seemed to darken the mood, as if his very name was a poison. Clara focused her thoughts, seeking a rallying cry from the greatest of lasting literature.

"Something of freedom, perhaps, something of an opposing sentiment to break the will of this fire, to meet its magic word for word . . ." Perhaps Hamlet: *We who have free souls, it touches us not . . .* No, that text wasn't quite right. She needed a counterpoint to the visceral cruelty of the Society; opposing it with a demand of restive peace.

She closed her eyes, and as she did so, the vibrant, energizing hum she'd first noted on the ship when truly feeling the ley lines for the first time was again present. They must be close to one here; a resonant thread Manhattan usually drowned out. She recalled some esoteric text once positing that Fifth Avenue was thought to be Manhattan's ley line. Perhaps the eldest of forces could help her here. Just then, a suitable text came to mind.

A statement of longing and rejection from Clara's favorite tale of the woeful capability of human horror came to the fore instead. Opening her eyes, she spoke in a clarion tone.

"'We may again give to our tables meat, sleep to our nights, Free from our feasts and banquets bloody knives, Do faithful homage and receive free honours: All which we pine for now.'"

As she recited, the fire flickered a bit, as if losing some of its oxygen. The tallest of the flames grew lower.

"Well done," Bishop murmured. "*Macbeth*?" Clara nodded.

"Indeed, but as the secondary flames persist, I imagine we'll get nothing done without a bit of chemistry," Evelyn stated.

"Let me see to that," Stevens said with certainty in his voice.

"Thank you for what you've done and will do, Mr. Stevens," Bishop said. "Whatever resources you need, we'll attend to." The two men shook hands on it.

"We must break her hand free," Clara insisted. "She stands for everything the Society is against—people raising themselves up from nothing. She is female, triumphant, free, not enslaved, she . . . offers light and shelter for all. . . . She is not an aristocrat and that's threatening to them, hence the chains—and our mandate to release her."

Moved by this speech, her companions stared at the padlocks with renewed determination.

"She's just a hand now, just a light, a lamp, and yet, she inspires as if she already stands tall in the harbor . . ." Bishop mused.

"Just think what she'll be like when fully finished, welcoming and impressive," Evelyn said, reaching up to run a gloved hand gently over a graceful sculpted tongue of metal flame, the low-licking preternatural fire not reaching that height, held by an awe-inspiring hand that was larger than Evelyn's whole body.

After studying the locks, Franklin again whipped up his collar, selected an implement, and set to work liberating the emblem of the free.

The first was opened in quick time; the chains clanged down along her forearm once the lock was removed. As Franklin reached for the second, an arc of green flame shot toward him like a thread of lightning and he yelped, dropping the lock pick on the grate-like floor of the landing, where it thankfully didn't fall through.

"Careful!" Clara said. "Are you all right?"

Franklin nodded, rubbing his arm.

"We may need to fully banish the fire first," Clara said, trying to assure him that he had not failed. Franklin nodded and walked back toward the chains, where he fiddled for a moment with the tag bearing the quote from the Bard. Releasing it from its place, he pressed it between his palms. She watched as he engaged his psychometric touch, trying to glean information from the scrap of card.

"A house, a relatively fine one, but not a place I know.

And a pen, likely the one that wrote this. That's all," he said, pocketing the tag. "I'll keep an eye out for the property, but there's nothing to commend it," he finished, his disappointment and disenchantment palpable.

"Thank you for trying," she said, reaching out to squeeze his hand. He tried to smile but it wouldn't hold.

Clara returned her attention to the ornate, grated cup of the brazier, examining the black pitch that lined the torch deck. The low, clinging flame that rose from this bore a deeper color than the rest of the sulfuric glow. She peered closer, holding her nose against the acidic, rotten smell.

It looked a lot like the mixture of blood and tar that had caked some of the floorboards in the disastrous house where Louis had met his end.

"Mr. Stevens?" she called, waving him over.

"Yes?"

"This pitch, it is used in Society rituals."

"Indeed, Miss Templeton."

"Mightn't it be directly counteracted by our Wards?"

"Why, yes, Miss Templeton, that's a wise suggestion. Alas, I have no more Wards, having set many out in any place I could think of and given others to anyone who was amenable. The reverend promised to have a small box ready by the time you returned."

"Indeed, and we used the last of our New York Wards on the return voyage, to protect the boat as we moved through troubled waters." She looked down at her team below to find that trusty Josiah, their best and brightest young hire, was returned from an errand at the behest of Franklin.

When she descended with Stevens, the boy was at her side the moment he saw her, offering a wide smile, his brown skin flushed from movement. The boy had an uncanny read on her, and anticipated her in ways that were good instinct to the point where she believed he must be a burgeoning psychic.

He was only about ten years old; by the time he became an adult he would be one of the best assets their ragtag company had managed to develop.

"What is it, what do you need, Miss Clara, you have that look," he said with a grin; his spirit was as restless and eager to take on the world as hers.

"That look that always finds great comfort when it falls upon you, my trusty right hand," she said approvingly. The boy glowed with pride. She decided it was time to share more of their work with him, both as a sign of her deep care for him and to continue his training. "There's a pitchy substance up above, around the torch. I think it's some of the same stuff I've seen in buildings tainted for the Society's purpose. What do you think about placing one of the city's own Wards directly onto that foul muck? Not just lighting it like a candle in prayer, but directly mixing substances. Do you think it would have the desired effect of countering the offal?"

"You're asking my opinion, Miss Clara?" he asked, wide-eyed, recognizing the unusual nature of this revelation.

"Yes, Joe, I am. You've watched this latest madness crop up and you're sharp as a tack, so what do you think?"

"I've seen the city Wards do a lot of good, Miss Clara, especially if they're personalized by those who set them. And when some Wards were spilled, they still seemed to have an effect, like standing on blessed ground. I'd say it can't hurt. I could go procure you some from the reverend."

"Hire a cab to take you up; it will be too exhausting and take too much time otherwise."

"I . . ." He looked away, ashamed. "I don't have the best of luck hiring a hansom. Maybe if you . . ."

"This damned city," Clara muttered, her ungloved hand entwining with his darker one as they walked toward Broadway. "If we can save this rock, I will demand it treat *all* its children better. . . ."

When she obtained a hansom, she handed over more than the journey was worth and said, staring at the driver hard, "Please take my precious charge, Mr. Josiah Garvey, uptown to the Right Reverend Blessing, as they are both employed on the business of Senator Rupert Bishop and the Secret Service of the United States. You will then wait and return him to this spot, doing your part in the most important business of protecting this city. Am I understood?"

"Yes, ma'am," the Irishman said in a thick accent, staring at Josiah with a bit of awe. The child was unable to contain a smile as he bowed his head in acknowledgment, as if he were already the statesman the senator and Clara hoped he might be someday.

After closing the carriage door, Clara saluted Josiah through the window and he did the same in return. Even the driver saluted before he cracked the whip, taking off uptown at a canter.

* * * * *

Sitting in the parlor in a fine mansion that was situated a little farther up Broadway than was precisely fashionable, drinking a concoction she'd taken to at an earlier age than one should, Celeste felt a ripple course through her.

Someone was disturbing her art.

It was inevitable that someone would; it could not go unnoticed forever, nor did she want it to. She wasn't the only gifted creature on the island, and more had arrived earlier that very day. She would deal with them where Moriel had failed.

Moriel. She could still feel him. She resolved to use this to her advantage. She would summon and contain—that would serve him right.

Painful memories flooded her mind and her body.

Celeste had been in the public gallery for Moriel's New York trial and that was when she'd first realized someone else like her existed, when she'd experienced the life-altering yearning to cast off her solitary misery for a true partnership. Here was a man who saw the world much as she did and wanted to take innovative, unprecedented powers into his hands.

Humanity would never cease to be stratified. Simplifying the layers and leaving the control of it to only those who were willing to get their hands bloody and dirty was only just—and efficient.

Like Moriel, Celeste knew she was born for grandeur. He was an aristocrat and she, the poor daughter of an unmarried actress, but she'd learned very early to endear herself to the landed class and how to pass herself off as one. She'd done it so well she'd nearly convinced *herself* she'd always been an heiress. She paused her search for a rich, easily manipulated husband and devoted herself to getting closer to Moriel.

During his extradition to England, Celeste posed as a nurse aboard his ship. She introduced herself in careful whispers as someone interested in learning his great work.

They met in secret, her wiles and psychic talents ensuring that no one knew of her comings and goings. While he had been slated for execution, the queen herself was too fascinated by the possibilities of his work to kill him, her interest in immortality her fatal flaw. Celeste kept the nurse role going throughout his internment in the secret cell in the Royal Courts of Justice.

She recalled their love letters. Her gifts. She was beautiful and he liked that. He was not but it wasn't about him.

His betrayal was the worst of the memories; a blade, slipped neatly through the bones of her corset. The greedy man even took one of his gifts back from her as she stumbled away to die in a London gutter.

While he had never said so, her mental gifts told her the

reason. She was too powerful for him and he resented her gifts, as well as her inability to be the bland, subservient queen he required. Still, Celeste had thought she'd have time to gain the upper hand and, like her inspiration and idol Lady Macbeth, seize opportunity and demand it in equal measure. But sadly, he was a petty, little man, and his inability to share glory and narcissistic greed would become his downfall.

The night he tried to kill her she anticipated it, intuition and clairvoyant clues saving her life. Leaning in a certain angle when he lunged with the knife to make it appear it had gone deeper, she stumbled away in a great, dramatic fashion. Once she cleaned and patched herself up, she swiftly removed herself from England and headed directly to hectic, industry-filled Chicago before he could send any of his Summoned to come looking for her corpse.

His violence toward her hardened what little heart she'd been granted. It was for the best, as working for herself sharpened her every gift. When she found out he'd died, in a spectacular blaze of demonic glory outside Parliament, she smiled.

Wiring a bribable English policeman instructions and money to procure a souvenir for her from the wreckage of his estate meant she had an incredibly useful tool at her disposal, and she planned to use it.

Oh, his spirit should fear her now. . . .

Someone let loose the doorbell, recalling her to the present. Betrayal and hate were acrid upon her tongue and she spat into the smoldering fireplace.

The bell rang once more. No staff hurried to answer it, as this was forbidden. Celeste oversaw who came and went and none did either without her permission. Especially her husband.

She went to the front hall, where a small square box wrapped in thick brown paper and tied with twine waited on a table. She opened the door to her courier, a ragged-looking man in a shabby but nicely kept brown coat. He stared at Celeste eagerly from under his dusty bowler, his expression painfully readable; he was desperately glad for whatever work he could gain, the kind of man who would build a robber baron's empire without gaining a shred of credit or capital. Such men she used, pitied, and sometimes killed.

"Please deliver this to Mr. Volpe at Edison's plant." She handed over the package, which smelled distinctly, if one was familiar with the scent, of embalming fluid. From the look on the courier's face, the smell meant nothing to him. "Volpe will pay you upon delivery."

"Yes, ma'am, thank you," the man said.

As he turned away, she added, "Please return at the same time next week." He nodded and, satisfied, Celeste closed the door.

As she took a step toward the parlor, she spotted her husband standing half in shadow, half in the light of the stained-glass window behind him, peeking out from the narrow gap he'd left between the parlor's pocket doors. He froze under her stare like a rabbit before a dog.

"What is it, my dear?" she asked sweetly. "Finished with your meal already? Don't you like my trying to fatten you up?"

"I . . . heard the bell," he said, as quietly and simply as a child.

"It wasn't for you," she replied, using the gentle tone she reserved for him.

"No . . . I suppose not . . ." he said sadly. "Never is."

The poor thing wanted to be important. But he was not.

She, on the other hand . . . her power would expand this week, encompassing another few blocks. While her tricks of stagecraft and chemistry and her offering to the demons would keep those who might peer into her affairs distracted, she would grow ever closer to her unstoppable tipping point, when all of the city's energy and momentum could be wielded by her body as easily as turning on an electric light.

* * * * *

It wasn't long before Clara had a Manhattan-specific Ward in hand, the driver having returned Josiah in as quick an order as Manhattan's midday bustle would allow, a mere hour and a half. She'd celebrate the little victories. During this time, Bishop provided their company with a welcome picnic of beverages and tasty, roasted morsels from street vendors along Broadway and they enjoyed the park as it was intended.

Josiah gave the Wards to her in a small box where as many as could fit were wrapped in tissue paper.

"This is what he can spare, and he hopes you'll come relieve him soon," Josiah said. "Just when he thinks he has the area settled down, another body surfaces," he said worriedly. "It has gone in fits and starts for over a week."

"Of course," Clara promised. "Right after this, if my colleagues can endure it. If not, I'll go myself, I can't have that dear man stretched too thin."

Bishop came close, patted Josiah on the back, and then followed Clara as she darted back up the stairs.

"While fighting fire with fire might have an effect," Clara explained her plan, "I'd like to experiment and see if the earth, mixed with the other Ward elements and made powerful by our respective prayers, once poured onto the offending substance, has an effect. If so, should we, heaven forfend, have to Ward large plots of land, this might be a substance to bury, till, and add to any protective bulwark. Let's see."

On the torch's rim, Clara swept her skirts clear of the oddly licking flames once more and shook the contents of the vial before tilting it to evenly sprinkle the mixed ingredients of the Ward about the rim of tar, pitch, and blood. As she moved around the torch, she murmured several benedictions that she hoped would be useful, if only to strengthen her own energy, prayers she'd learned from Evelyn. Bishop bolstered her prayers with his own, keeping silence as was their Quaker tradition. The fire flickered.

A few more prayers, a renouncement of evil, some Shakespeare, anything about freedom and free thought, about love and kindness, about democracy and the ideals that she felt her city and country strove for, what Liberty herself could symbolize . . .

That this beautiful hand had been defiled struck Clara to the core. The anger that roiled within her gave every utterance from her lips the weight of righteous conviction.

The battle of freedoms, of wills, seemed at a tipping point and at last the flames lowered. A sulfuric stench still hung about the rim of the torch, but the ungodly fire of it seemed mostly doused. A few burning tongues refused to die. That would be for Stevens to manage with science. Whether this damnation flame would prove an eternal one was yet to be seen.

Bishop squeezed Clara's shoulder.

"There is an effect for the better here. You remain the heart of the matter," he said softly.

In Louis's recipe for Wards, that exact phrase was boldly scribed at the top of each local iteration he had managed to concoct. Clara smiled, hearing Bishop speak what had become sacred text.

They descended again to street level.

"I've done as much as I can do and the hellfire is mostly subdued," Clara reported to the company.

"Now what?" Rose asked.

"We have to knock down these abominations one by one,"

Bishop replied. "Next, Columbia University, north of us some thirty blocks, an ongoing site of grave concern."

"*I've* a concern," Spire began, adjusting and smoothing his dark brown waistcoat. Everyone turned to regard his natural authority. "That these are mere distractions while some larger plan is being put into place."

"Likely so," Bishop agreed. "Is there something you think we should be paying attention to?"

"Industry," Spire replied. "The Edison plant. Places that have exponential capacity to cause a disaster, like that warehouse of toxins back in London. We need to assess if we're here to play cleanup or if we've another active enemy at work."

"Would you like to undertake an examination of electrical companies and outposts while we assess the reanimate, Mr. Spire?" Bishop asked.

At the word "reanimate" Rose stepped forward, folding her arms so that her gloved hands each rested on the opposite elbow of her white shirtwaist blouse.

"I'd like to be with Clara when encountering those creatures," Rose said. "We've . . . particular experience. Not to disregard your instincts, Mr. Spire."

"No offense taken," Spire replied. "And you're wise to suggest we stick together to create the widest net against any of those horrific, shambling creatures."

"With all due respect, I'd like to wait this one out," Franklin said quietly, his face pale against his unshaven whiskers. "The nature of the reanimate . . . all the patchwork bodies, I just . . . It's a bit too much. My brother, may he rest in eternal peace, his body was all in pieces after Gettysburg and I can't help but see *his* . . . parts . . . in those bodies . . ." Franklin faltered and Clara put a hand on his shoulder.

"Go home and rest, my dear," she said gently. "You're not on your own anymore. It will do our tasks no good if we're all not at our best."

Franklin nodded and walked away without further word, his limp exaggerated by his evident exhaustion.

"And the cavalcade of horrors continues, like the old days of our circuses, only all the acts are made of nightmares," Miss Knight said quietly.

FIVE

En route to Columbia, the noise and bustle of New York folded in around Rose in layers of sound and color. It wasn't that this city was noisier than London, it was simply *more*. Everything she'd seen of America so far bore similarities to England but it was bigger, bolder, louder, faster, more urgent; desperate. It was exhausting.

Squeezed into a hansom next to Mr. Spire, Rose was powerfully aware of his closeness despite her doubled skirts. Glancing at the dear partner she increasingly admired, she saw that he was steeled and focused, ready for the tasks that gave his life purpose. She determined to prove the same.

"Any idea what we're expecting to see when we reach the place?" Spire asked of Bishop, who sat across from them, between Clara and Evelyn. Rose smiled at his tone; his skepticism was unchanged despite all the improbable things he'd both seen and taken part in.

Clara leaned forward, addressing Rose. "A repeat of the City Hall display, I would imagine, using any number of medical students' cadavers as fair game." A shudder of revulsion visibly swept over her.

Rose recoiled, too, at the memory of those patchwork, Frankensteinesque bodies rising up, tethered to wires and current, black swollen mouths hanging open like something out of one of Poe's worst nightmares. She wasn't looking forward to confronting them again either.

"Reverend Blessing may have the situation mostly in hand—he's put to rest something like this before," Evelyn said sadly.

Columbia's stately grounds lay north of Longacre Square but south of Central Park, in the Fiftieth Street range, not far from the line of elaborate mansions and accumulated, ostentatious wealth; set behind ornate, wrought-iron gates, all of which were locked.

In the courtyard beyond, a spindly, brown-haired man paced nervously back and forth, frequently looking toward the street.

Police officers stationed at each corner dissuaded any passersby from the premises, citing disease; a rotating cast of curious onlookers asked if what the papers reported was true.

"I'm frankly surprised there isn't more of a crowd," Rose said.

"A good number of citizens must have considered the news to be fake," Clara stated.

"I'll take that as unexpected providence then, lest we have a frothing doctor's riot on our hands like a century ago," Evelyn muttered.

When the two carriages discharged their passengers, the man within swiftly darted toward them, opening the gates from the inside. He left the gate ajar to greet his fellows.

One of the nearest patrolmen came over to make sure Bixby wasn't being harassed, and Senator Bishop showed the officer a card marking him as a statesman and Spire flashed his Metropolitan badge for good measure. The officer bowed his head.

"Let me know if you need anything," the officer said. "But if you're going to be there working on the scene, you all need to do so from inside the gate."

Fred Bixby ushered them in with wild gesticulations and

slammed the gate. The officer eyed all of them, and looked into the courtyard beyond worriedly, before returning to his post.

Fred, whose center of gravity seemed to hover in his elbows, had not inherited the grace displayed by his sister, though his pale brown skin tone matched hers, as did the dusting of freckles across his prominent cheekbones. Bright brown eyes wide, he directed a heated declamation at Bishop before the senator said more than hello.

"For the record, Senator, sir, I do not like this. For the record, *sir,* I am a man for records. Papers. By the grace of the ever-loving Lord, please get me the hell away from any kind of organic detail. I find the human body a deeply flawed machine and I've seen far too much of its complications these past few days!"

Amused, Effie stepped forward and wound her arms around her lanky sibling, calming him. Spire turned to Rose and commented that this man was their kind of person, at which she smiled.

"I've missed you, Brother," she said with a chuckle. "Now don't be rude, you must meet our new friends and colleagues."

Fred ran a hand over his closely shorn head and murmured, "Yes, of course, do forgive me."

Effie performed the introductions quickly, ending by explaining that her brother maintained the files and account books for the Eterna Commission.

"How's Gran?" Effie asked her brother quietly.

His unnerved rant was forgotten for love of family. "Not doing well. Effie, we should—"

"Take time with her," his sister declared. "Yes. We will."

"Take what time you need," Bishop said softly. "Your family needs you as much as we do, and if anyone needs to be moved somewhere safe—"

"We'll be fine," Effie said, an edge to her tone.

Both siblings shifted back to the task at hand, though Effie didn't remove her hand from her brother's shoulder.

"I happened to be at the chemistry department when this all began," Stevens explained, "seeking supplies for Wards and antidotes, when I saw the first corpse shamble onto the green." He shuddered. "From that point we've tried to keep the situation as contained as we could. I knew it was important to immediately quarantine the campus. Fred here contacted the right city and college officials to ensure it. But, as you can hear . . ."

The wails were like sirens at a distance, a distressing blanket of audible horror over one of the most opulent parts of town.

"Come see," Fred said before turning to Clara. "I know you've your limits, Miss Clara, due to your condition, but Reverend Blessing sure could use some help. The poor man hasn't had a good night's sleep since this began."

"He and I worked hard to settle the dead," Stevens explained, "then just when we would think it over, one of the patrolmen says another one is shambling across the green again. We don't know who's been winding them up and setting them loose."

Lord Black steadied Miss Knight, who seemed overwhelmed by what she was sensing from the green. On her other side, Evelyn offered grim guidance.

"I wish I could say it gets easier to hear them. It doesn't. All you can do is try to get used to it." Knight nodded, her lovely face blanched.

Resolute, the team moved through the campus, turning a corner around a stately neoclassical building to confront a field of four patchwork corpses standing and swaying, draped in ragged, blood- and tar-stained medical gowns.

Spire let out a quiet curse. Rose put a perfumed handkerchief to her nose to block the overpowering stench of moldering decay, soot, steam, formaldehyde, and other embalming fluids. Clara drew a sharp breath and Bishop placed a steadying hand at her elbow, energizing her with the anchor of his presence.

The patchwork nature of the bodies was evident in the large, inelegant stitches binding sections of yellowed skin together. The air around them shimmered with bright auras, the spirits of the dead tethered to the parts of their bodies melded in each terrible golem. Their ghostly sparks, the last gasps of their life force, served as the igniting strike of the dread match that powered these beings into shambling momentum.

But what a champion stood before them.

* * * * *

Clara's sensitivities were in awe of the sheer power radiating from Reverand Blessing's body. At the center of the courtyard surrounded by grand buildings surmounted by statues of philosophical greats and quotes of enlightenment stood a brown-skinned man whose tight brown curls were peppered with gray, his black suit coat dusted with ash and smeared with God knows what. His arms were held wide and his voice boomed scripture.

A dash of dark crimson marred the reverend's white cleric's collar but he did not appear to be injured otherwise. Clara took note of the mark to make sure it did not spread.

Two shambling corpses in bedraggled medical gowns, jaws hanging open in an unnatural scream, shambled toward him. Their banshee wails were horrid death knells seeking to disassemble the mind and to sow the seeds of hopelessness. The Master's Society had created them for the purposes of supernatural terrorism. They carried ghosts attached to their patchwork parts; the specters' siren wails a harrowing effect of the system that made the bodies animate.

The reverend swayed almost in the exact rhythm of the corpses, moving either with the power of the spirit or from sheer exhaustion. His strong arms lifted again into the air as he recited another verse from the Book of Common Prayer in a compelling voice.

Blessing was a man with a heart as vast as the pain and torture of his ancestors was wide, ever choosing love over bitterness, a man who bore his duties as an exorcist as calmly and efficiently as he supplied his congregations with what suited their diverse needs. For all Eterna's respective powers, he was as equally armed with faith and fearless conviction.

A few new shocks of those telling gray hairs were invading around the reverend's hairline and temples, more than when they'd left for England.

Evelyn strode up beside him to bolster his work and began admonishing the bodies with renouncements of evil pulled from the Christian scriptures and those of other faiths. As New York was as diverse a city as any in the world, so were its ghosts. Evelyn's appearance prompted an intense, bright smile from the reverend; his relief was immediately palpable in both face and body. Clara could almost feel his tension ease.

Clara made for Blessing's other side but Rose held her back a moment. "Are you breathing?" she asked gently. "Do you have your balance?"

It was so important she take stock before a supernatural or spiritual battle; Clara lost track of her seizure protocols and countdowns if she didn't take the moment to center, ground, and shield as Rose was encouraging her to do. The soul energy that connected them as reunited twins was such a vital tether for Clara. She nodded and offered Rose a smile, which she then turned on Bishop, who watched their exchange. With these loved ones near, Clara felt doubly protected.

"If I were to *shoot* the bodies—" Spire said, striding forward and withdrawing his pistol.

"No," the reverend and Evelyn said together.

Evelyn explained. "They're already dead, it won't affect them. We have to untether the spirits. When we do so, the bodies slow, still, and become inert."

"Very well. But them mauling us in the meantime also isn't an option," he said, looking around. Spotting an area where some maintenance was being done, he stormed over and returned with a rope in hand. He tied a quick, noose-like knot and slung the loop around the neck of a burly, vacant-eyed man whose arms came from another corpse.

Moving quickly and avoiding the grasping hands of the shambling dead, he circled the nearest corpses with the rope, gathering them in like a shepherd until they were bound together. Even as the reanimate strained against the rope, Spire tied it off with impressive nautical knots.

"That does make our task much easier," Blessing said. "We can direct our energies against them in groups and worry less about being attacked. Thank you, Mr. Spire. Any scrap of attention I can spare is enough to keep me going that much longer. . . ."

Pleased, Spire looked around for other useful things; the paranormal nature of this task clearly made him uncomfortable.

As Clara feared, their presence attracted the specters' attention. While the banshee wails could unravel any person's sanity, the ghosts attached to each body also served as a siren call. Another body came around a corner and onto the green.

"How many are there?" Spire said incredulously, gritting his teeth.

Clara's mind swam. With at least five ghosts attendant to each assembled body, the spiritual "noise" was overwhelming. Rose's and Bishop's white-knuckled clamp on her arms would only keep her from seizing if she could access their aid.

She closed her eyes to stay focused. *You're at the center of the storm. Be worthy of the squall.* . . . The voice of the visitor, the ineffable Marlowe, cut through the banshee wail. Thinking of herself as a column of fire, she tried to expand a barrier ring around herself, creating a psychic shield that flew out in all directions, a habit she used to break away from cloying, negative energies.

As she did, everything went suddenly still and quiet; she could feel time, space, sound, and energy take on a different weight, tone, and density. There was a familiar hum she'd come to know as the sound of the ley lines. Fifth Avenue was just beyond. In that hum was so much *life* . . .

Her past selves began to peel away as if she were shedding layers of clothing, stretching out from her in concentric circles. One by one, pasts floated out like petals escaping the tight bud of a rose.

If she hadn't had these dear souls of Rose and Bishop to keep hold of her as anchors for her soul, perhaps she'd have peeled off into time, wafted away into her pasts like a feather taken by a gust and buffeted into another life.

She stared at her selves. There was a woman in a robe, perhaps druidic, who held her hands up to the sky and seemed to be deep in a prayer or rite. There was an Elizabethan man who pored over maps and charts. An eighteenth-century ship captain was peering through a long telescope. An early nineteenth-century young girl in a white Regency gown had a pen in hand and was feverishly writing as if her very life depended on it.

All these lives searching, searching, creating, willing this current self into existence. This extension of her soul captured the interest of the ghosts themselves.

Caught where sound was slow and underwater, Clara heard scripture and holy text from all backgrounds, peppered in with what names Evelyn could glean as the gifted medium she was, assisted by Miss Knight, the flamboyant psychic having found her sea legs, the two of them holding hands to magnify their connection as they tried to get as much out of the specters as they possibly could. They encouraged each spirit to uncouple itself from the vile desecration it had been cleaved to.

The ghosts spoke back, in whispers, in aching pleas. Clara had to block them out, pretend she didn't hear them as she could feel her body go into its three-minute countdown until a seizure.

While those in touch with the paranormal were focused on the reanimate, Harold Spire focused on the surroundings. One of the college hall doors a few paces away was open, and he strode toward it. Turning back to Rose, he called out.

"I'm going in for anything useful," Spire declared before disappearing under the eaves. Effie and Fred went inside with him.

The chemist Stevens, undaunted and steadfast in his re-formed spirit, had gone to retrieve a box from the chemistry department. He then returned to light a sequence of Wards that he and Blessing had managed to corral for this ongoing task and getting them as close as he could to the bodies, putting some directly in the grass to burn and smoke their power, though the corpses all tried to knock them over or snuff them, clearly averse to the protective nature of the Wards.

Clara's lengthening of time allowed for this interchange to go forward with more success.

Lord Black, interestingly enough, was going around to various flower beds around the grounds and laying bouquets directly on the laps of those bodies that had sunk to the ground, or tucking little makeshift bundles into their ragged clothes. In some cases he placed certain leaves found on the grounds along with the stems.

This was a curious development, and made Clara wonder, in this mental space where expansive thought was at its most inspired, about the many pots of ivy back in Black's mansion. His own personal magic of flora and fauna was coming into its own. She would have to ask him about this when they had a quiet moment together.

Spire returned with Effie and Fred, carrying more material to bind bodies, and they saw to securing those that remained and helping Stevens with Wards. Everything was now within the center of the green and more manageable. Evelyn, Blessing, and Knight stood as a powerful trio around the growing knot of faltering dead, some on their knees, some lying down, others pawing at one another.

Swiveling her head, trying to catch something in her peripheral vision, she noticed something new.

To her left and right, there was a gray area, a long rectangular swath where it looked like the world was blotted out in those monolithic sections. She wondered if it was an intrusion of the spirit world, for it had the same kind of colorless quality that ghosts had when they appeared to her eye. There was nothing she could discern *within* those rectangular swaths, but they stood sentry on the horizon line of her many selves. Perhaps they had been there all along, and as she was becoming accustomed to this ability of hers, she might be noticing details that had always been present but that she'd been too focused on her lives to see. Was she opening herself directly to the spirit world?

Regardless, she could feel that there were more ghosts on this campus green than she should entertain an audience of, filling up the whole space around them. Her body was well aware of the danger.

A second wave of seizure symptoms accosted Clara, and

she swayed on her feet as her vision went dim and the sounds, muted and faraway as they were in these elongated moments, were cut into abrupt silence. The extension of her lives snapped back into her as if she were slapped, an echoing slamming of a cosmic door that stung all over.

She could hear Rose cry out and in moments she and Bishop had led Clara to a park bench at the edge of the green, near enough but out of the direct pressure and thrall of the reanimate.

"Breathe," Bishop commanded, pressing a hand directly onto her sternum and channeling power through her in a laying on of hands.

A wrenching gasp tore from Clara's lungs and she breathed deeply, involuntarily, sucking in the scent of death and preservation. The sharp, disgusting nature of it acted like sick smelling salts and her eyes fluttered open.

"We've turned the tide, Clara," Bishop insisted. "Thank you for your spell. The very breadth and gravity of you makes all realms open up to us, to our advantage. I don't know how you do it."

"I'm not sure I do either," Clara murmured, "but I am glad it is useful. I want to hone it."

"For the moment, take pride in the powers themselves," he bid. She nodded. Rose squeezed her shoulder in agreement.

The reanimated bodies all lay slumped, finally, as if they were asleep. Spire wasted not a moment in making methodical rounds, undaunted by the idea of touching death, straightening each into a peaceful, respectful position, closing their swollen, blackened eyes. Fred and Lord Black followed his lead. Effie hung back, eyes closed, either in prayer or to shut out the horror that had grown too intense.

Reverend Blessing followed to pray over each body, his patience and energy as boundless as the scope of his heart.

While most of his invocations were Christian, he offered Hebraic and Islamic blessings as well, learned from his friends and colleagues of other Abrahamic faiths. Listening to him calmed Clara and made her clenching heart relax. Somehow Miss Knight had managed to scare up candles, which she lit near the bodies in an additional bid for spiritual peace; a spot of gold against a gray day.

"Reverend, Mr. Spire, everyone, step back," Evelyn said urgently, grabbing Miss Knight and pushing her toward Clara. "You know what the spirits, collectively, will wish to do. . . ."

"Ah, yes," the reverend said sadly. "Unfortunately I do recall this finale. Everyone, be aware, there's about to be quite a fire."

A vibration crested in the air, culminating in the assembly of bodies bursting into flames. They burned quickly, the embalming fluids acting as accelerant. The stench was overwhelming and everyone had to breathe through kerchiefs for the minutes it took the bodies to become ash. They did not dare leave the scene until all was finished, no matter how gruesome.

Fred and Effie had retreated to the gate, arm in arm, hands to their mouths and noses. Spire approached Clara, thankfully downwind of the spontaneous pyre of bodies.

"I assume that at least parts of these bodies were pulled from the Trinity churchyard disruption mentioned in that first telegram for help?" Spire asked

"I assume so," Senator Bishop replied. "But not every grave was unearthed; the unsettling there was piecemeal. Here, there are too many disparate parts for Trinity to have been the sole source, I hate to say."

"The rest likely came from here," Spire declared, brandishing a yellow paper marked with a corporate, pyramid logo. "I found this inside on a board." The billet read:

ANATOMY AND SURGERY ENTHUSIASTS:
The Apex Corporation can provide you with a reliable
supply of human body parts managed ethically and
responsibly. See the wonders of electricity on human
tissue when Columbia showcases its first electrical
turbine, its power solely for your use. Harness life and
death in your hands today. Write to Postbox 99 in this
area to request further details. The top of the future's
pyramid begins with you.

"I'll investigate that postal box as soon as possible," Spire
stated. Rose caught his eye and nodded her agreement. "But
we're losing light now and those offices will be closed."

"To whom do we trust the interring of these ashes?" Lord
Black asked.

"I'll . . . I will deal with it," the reverend replied. "The pas-
tor at Trinity, a fellow Episcopalian, has aided me before and
is open-minded about such matters as these."

Spire said, "For now, lock the gates again and cover the
remains with burlap; it will appear to the casual observer to
be renovations until the premises can be fully cleaned."

"Considering that posting," Black began, "where, and
who are, the 'doctors' that did this?"

"I'll make inquiries," Stevens offered. "Academics prefer
speaking to their own, as this is the chemistry department.
Just as soon as I've gathered the final ingredients to put out
any last troublesome flickers of Lady Liberty's foul fire." He
smiled at Clara. "Somewhere between magic and science
we'll best these moral offenses once and for all."

She tried to return the smile and share in his hope, but her
memory was jogged by the chemistry department. Barnard
Smith, Louis's partner in the Eterna Commission, might they
both rest in peace. He had once had an office in this building; Clara had visited it, seeking more documentation on the

Wards. Was Barnard's spirit somehow wrapped up in all this? Or was there an instinct for these haunted creatures to remain near already haunted spaces?

Clara put her hand on Evelyn's and suggested the medium reach out to his spirit.

"I will try, when the effects of all this have passed," Evelyn said, staring at the ghastly assemblage of death. "I understand the Society tempting isolated doctors to this Frankenstein witchcraft, but a whole *class* of them? This couldn't have been the work of just one or two lost souls."

"It is the greatest lure of all, is it not?" Clara murmured, shifting on the bench, pressing against the stays of her corset so the muscles of her back wouldn't spasm when she undressed. "To find the cure for death, to resurrect the dead. It was the very start of Eterna, after all, and remains one of mankind's perpetual desires."

No one argued her point.

* * * * *

Evelyn insisted, as they were not far from her home, that she host as many as wished, for an evening refreshment as night was falling. Blessing and Stevens recused themselves to hours of overdue sleep.

Clara felt like she was walking with leaden feet, but she kept a cheerful face for her compatriots, as every action and battle they faced together made her care all the more for each and every one. Bishop didn't seem to mind that she leaned on him a bit more than ever before, and in fact he quite encouraged it.

If the maids were daunted by an unexpected crowd, they did not show it; likely daunted by little, considering the lady of the house and her compatriots underwent rather ungodly circumstances time and time again. When Evelyn inquired about the status of her husband, she was told he would be held late by a Metropolitan Museum function and she chuckled, saying that was for the best. She turned to Spire.

"Like you, my good man, my husband isn't one for ghost stories. Thankfully he cares for me enough to overlook the constant one I keep living." She smiled and this actually got a bit of a laugh out of Spire.

Once the company had all settled into Evelyn Northe-Stewart's fine parlor, all were soon armed with delicate, gilt-trimmed cups of fine bone china, filled with a rich, hot tea to banish the chill of death. There was blessed silence for a while.

However, Spire, ever the consummate policeman, could not stray from duty.

"I again can't help but wonder if the displays we have seen to today are merely distractions from other dealings going on in the city," Spire began carefully. "Will matters come to a head in your capital as they did in ours? While I'm hardly clairvoyant, I'm rarely wrong when it comes to such things.

"Considering these spectacles we dealt with today—well," Spire continued, "I cannot, for the life of me, see how anyone might profit from them, but they might gain time from keeping us busy while infiltrating hearts of commerce and your capital, just as Moriel wished to take down Parliament. Your mesmerism of Congress was a start, but I am certain there is more to do there to maintain protections."

"Likely so," Senator Bishop replied. "I'll wire each of my most trusted Washington contacts in the morning. In the meantime we must keep fighting these battles when they arise and rest when we can, but let us not think the resurrectionist terrors are all that is in play."

"For my part," Spire began, "Miss Everhart and I will investigate the postbox from the Columbia billet and Edison's plant. Of course, we must consider the docks. Apex is still in operation; a business in body parts. The Master's Society heir, if there is one, is whoever is running Apex."

Effie took her brother's hand and volunteered. "We'll be active at the docks," she said wearily. "I know what to say and what to look for. I'll make sure Franklin knows, too."

"Thank you," Bishop and Spire chorused.

"From what we understand of the reanimate," Bishop said, "there would have been a great deal of energy created and expended to make those dead rise in the first place, presumably electricity from the display dynamo Columbia received. Is one Edison dynamo that powerful?"

"The war of the currents rages between Edison and Westinghouse," Evelyn said. "It is a war Mr. Edison is shrewd and ruthless enough to most certainly win. Whole blocks downtown have become a playground for his Pearl Street plant. He's likely to court every college or other institution where he might expand."

"Then I'll make inquiries in this war," Spire said, setting down his cup on the silver tea tray and standing, smoothing his brown waistcoat. "Thank you for the tea, it was bolstering. But while I might not have much light left, these things thrive in darkness. Progress can yet be made. I've been cooped up on a ship for too many days, I'm far too glad to have my feet back under me again to stop now."

"No, Mr. Spire, if you please, did you not advocate rest?" Evelyn stood in protest.

"You were tireless on our soil, we'll be the same on yours," Spire declared. There was no arguing with the man.

Clara watched Rose glide to his side as he rose to his feet. Those two were connected in partnership in the way she and Bishop were, an effortless pair. Their connected movement was like an equation, a chain reaction creating the next step. The corners of Spire's characteristic frown curled upward as she joined him, reflecting his quiet pleasure.

"As we'll already be downtown, we'll return to our safe house," he added. "Thank goodness for government embassies and their amenities. We've all a bit of settling back in to attend to. Shall we rendezvous here in due time?"

Evelyn nodded. "I'm always happy to host."

"Thank you for everything," Spire stated.

Rose offered the same, turning to Clara. "We'll not be far from you if you need anything."

"The very same, my dear," Clara said with a wave as the two strode out the door in tandem.

Once they had exited, Lord Black, who had been watching Spire with a mixture of pride and exhaustion, commented:

"Good man. Hiring him was the best decision I ever made," he exclaimed. The nobleman rose to his feet and took a few paces about the room.

Black was struck by something, looking out the window. "Is that your great, famed Central Park there, across the street?" he asked excitedly.

"Yes," Clara replied, sharing the beaming smile he turned upon her.

At this, his entrancing eyes danced. "Miss Templeton, if we've a spare moment, would you mind showing me your magnificent park?" He turned to Bishop. "With, of course, your permission, Senator. Though you know I am devoted to my Francis and am of no concern."

Clara turned to Bishop with a smile, daring to draw back the curtain of her emotions. "My dear senator is not a jealous man. He knows, now, where my heart lies."

At this, Bishop actually blushed.

Clara swiftly took the pressure off Rupert from having to respond, turning back to Black. "I'd be honored to escort you, milord," she added. "But may I ask why you're curious? You've the air of someone hoping for more than a tourist experience."

Something about what Clara had seen him do in Columbia strummed the telling, internal lyre of her instincts and she knew, with a knowledge that was very old indeed, that a trip to the park wasn't merely about a nice stroll. Entering the park would be about power and she wanted him to say so.

"As we talk about protections," Black replied, "I want you to understand mine."

"Wonderful," Clara replied. "Let's do so in the morning. May we meet here, Evelyn?"

The medium nodded. "I remain your home away from home."

The assembled company, exhaustion setting in all around, rose to be on their way with pleasantries and embraces all around.

Bishop turned to Clara with an inviting smile, holding out his arm for her. On the carriage ride downtown, Clara allowed her facade to fall and leaned against him fully, no longer hiding her aching exhaustion. Folding an arm around her, he kissed the crown of her head in a benediction. It was as if this were a spell, and she fell into a deep sleep.

She did not remember being carried inside, or up to her room, until she stirred there in the middle of the night, realizing she remained fully dressed but was tucked gently under her covers. There, she smiled and thanked heavens for heart and home.

CHAPTER

SIX

Rose and Spire took an East Side trolley car downtown with the aim of at least taking stock of Edison's plant, to see what it was doing after hours, conveniently near their safe house for their well-earned collapse afterward. After they'd ridden in comfortable quiet for some time, Rose couldn't hold back a thought.

"May I speak boldly about a difficult subject, Mr. Spire?"

"Of course."

"Lord Black once told me that he'd chosen us for Omega because our having each lost a parent to murder made for a better-prepared, dauntless team. Do you think he was right? Are we better able to face the strange unknown because we have survived formative horror? And did that steel us enough or should we be armored even more?"

Spire set his jaw. "He said something similar to me, early on. At the time I thought he was being flippant, but now, I think he was speaking honestly. Were I some innocent lamb pitted against such lightless forces as those we face, for I do feel the evil Moriel has wrought, even if I don't see the demons, I doubt I'd have the strength to face the work."

"I empathize and agree," Rose replied.

"Perhaps," Spire continued thoughtfully, "the righteous fury of our youth might be as much a protective Ward for us as any of Miss Templeton's vials. To each their own magic, I suppose." He smiled as the trolley came to its downtown stop.

They alighted near their Whitehall Street safe house and strolled east along Pearl Street, the riverfront busy at all hours, toward the large brick building with cast-iron pillars that was the home of Thomas Edison's infamous dynamos, lit brightly, garishly, with electric lights along its facade, a buzzing advertisement against the darkening sky.

"Jumbos" one through nine had only recently begun generating their massive amounts of voltage at the tip of the island. These new engines powered and fueled restless, sleepless Manhattan Island and its endless hunger for commerce and capital. Even from the opposite end of the block one could hear the great, whirring hum of turbines, the intense hissing of boilers. Rose could feel vibrations over her skin and below the soles of her boots. Stopping before the four-story structure had her feeling like she stood on a hornets' nest.

Several stacks thrusting into the sky poured steam and smoke into industrially ashen clouds. Though they stood near the confluence of the Hudson and East Rivers, with the sea just beyond, there was nothing refreshing in the air. Instead, the scent of oil was thick in Rose's nose, nearly prompting her to gag and cough.

The edifice had several front doors, all of which proved to be locked. This was no surprise, as this was not an office, exactly, nor were they within traditional business hours, but there were silhouettes within; an occasional workman moved around the dynamos, like a bee around monstrous flowers. Edison was known to keep certain things hidden or off limits to the general public. Locating what seemed to be a doorbell, Spire pressed the button; he and Rose heard a ringing sound within.

There was no answer.

"No one will answer the door at night, you've got to have a key," came a voice from behind them. "I used to have one, but they changed the locks."

They turned to find a small man staring at them with sparking eyes. Mosley.

"Hello, Mr. Mosley," Rose said, trying not to appear as nervous as he made her. "What brings you here tonight?"

He narrowed his eyes at Rose. "You already know I live on this block. I keep an eye on the plant."

"On behalf of Edison's Company?" Spire asked.

Mosley snorted. "No, our association ended some time ago."

"Better to understand the war of the currents, then?" Spire posited.

Mosley laughed hollowly. "If only they'd all destroy one another in the process." Rose opened her mouth to query further but then thought better of it; she didn't want to stoke the man's bitterness. "No," Mosley continued, "I'm here to listen. Things are even more discordant. The grid is expanding, but it's taking on a terrible noise."

"I'll have to take your word for it," Spire replied.

"Come back in the morning. There's something I want to show you. Meet here and then we'll walk. You'll want to see what's happening," Mosley stated before disappearing around the corner of the building. A streetlamp across the street guttered and the glass of its globe cracked along the side in the shape of a lightning bolt.

"I think we're done for the day," Rose murmured. "Let's not press our luck. We've earned that rest you spoke of," she said, and Spire did not fight her.

Knight and Black had arrived ahead of them; their doors were closed but low light spilled out from underneath. Rose and Spire moved so as not to be disturbing presences. It was important for all members of their team to have their moments alone. Especially, Rose was learning, if they were prone to sensitivities, as everything was simply *louder*. . . .

A letter lay on the console table addressed to Mr. Blakeley

in Knight's hand. Seeing it, Rose felt a pang for their missing compatriots, the late Mr. Wilson and those who had remained in England, Blakeley and Adira Wilson. It was for the best that they stayed; someone needed to keep tabs on what had been only so recently settled, and it wouldn't be fair to bring Adira back here in her grief.

"Good night, Miss Everhart," Spire called softly as he moved to close his own door.

"Good night, Mr. Spire," she murmured, turning away to take stock of this plain, drab place and try to rally hope and strength.

* * * * *

They tried the Edison plant again in the morning, and Spire kept ringing the buzzer until someone answered. A bespectacled, ginger-haired man, perspiring and harried, answered the door.

"Hello there," Spire said jovially the moment the door was open, the greeting uttered in a far more robust manner than was his custom.

"How may I help you, sir?" the man said, adding, "My apologies, but we're not open for tours."

"I'm just in from Mother England, my boy"—Rose nearly broke into laughter at a phrase she hadn't heard Spire ever utter—"and I'm looking to snap up some valuable Manhattan property, but only near places that have access to your incredible current!" He chortled and Rose had to keep from raising an eyebrow. "Do you have a map I can peruse, noting the present reach of your electrical grid? I'm eager to become a customer. And if I like what I see, perhaps a true patron of your endeavors."

The man's expression shifted, becoming more welcoming. "By all means, sir. Mr. Volpe, at your service," he said, bowing slightly and admitting them to the premises. He turned deferentially to Rose, who offered a snooty upper-class expression, deliberately offsetting Spire's forced cheer. "Madame," he said with a nod.

"Tom Hamilton," Spire said, "and my sister."

Rose bristled a bit at "sister," which made her realize she liked it better when they played a couple—this shifted uncomfortably within her. But Spire wore no ring today, as he usually did when they posed as married. He must not have brought one along for the ruse, or thought to have put on the detail outside. She hoped her blush at thinking too closely about the matter didn't distract. Spire seemed not to notice, instead focusing on the entrance, and two of the great generators beyond.

Volpe bid them climb a few steps and enter into an open foyer with high ceilings befitting an industrial space, the interior painted with a neutral beige tinged with soot from the coal fires below that powered the turbines above.

The focal point of the wide-open space was the dynamos, the building's main feature and star. Wooden stairs and landings on either side of the main floor led to the upper floors, where there were still more dynamos whirring away, Volpe explained proudly.

The behemoth things, well over the height and many times the width of a single human, were like nothing Rose had ever seen; large, circular machines with great coils and thick metal casings. The sound and vibration were so intense and all-consuming, Rose didn't see how any of the men could handle it for hours on end.

Volpe escorted them to the side and into a wood-paneled office near the front doors. Here, he drew their attention to a large map spread out on a wooden desk. He dragged his finger along various downtown streets, tracing the pale yellow lines already drawn there.

"You are here, in the heart of it all, in district one, the

square defined by Pearl, Nassau, Spruce, and Wall Streets," he explained, running his finger along the electrified districts and where expansion was planned.

The way Volpe passed his finger along the grid was as if the man were examining and explaining anatomy. Rose thought of their eccentric Dr. Zhavia murmuring the contraction of each muscle as it led to movement. Here current was shown as winding, forking, and thrumming lines just like veins below New York's street skin. To disrupt this burgeoning grid would be to disrupt the industrial pulse of this increasingly mechanized city.

"Your wires run underground, yes?" Spire queried.

"Yes, here in the city they have to. In other areas, such as Menlo Park, there are aboveground wires."

"Ah, yes, the Wizard of Menlo Park," Rose declared. Edison's familiar nickname was taken from the location of his studio in New Jersey.

"You don't have trouble . . ." Spire began carefully, "keeping track of things, do you? Is there any errant or aberrant usage of these new dynamos? I have heard Edison will win this war of the currents with his innovative, efficient mind. Not a drop or volt of waste. At least I would hope."

"That is most certainly true, sir!" Volpe blinked at them from behind his glasses, his eyes a bit watery. "There is no aberrant usage. All is accounted for."

Rose could tell by the flick of his eyes to the side that this was a lie. She wondered what else he was hiding.

"Say I was to invest less in property and more in . . . your company," Spire asked, "who would my fellow investors be? I'd like to see a list as I'll want their glowing recommendations of you before I commit a pound—ah, a *penny*—" He chortled before continuing. "—to the cause."

Volpe forced a smile. "While I don't have such a list to offer you at present, I can assure you that only the *best* people are with us. The Morgan residence, as I'm sure you know, was our first triumph, and we're expanding daily."

Rose leaned in to press him, speaking as if conferring a secret, putting a hand to her pearl-buttoned collar. "Now, Mr. Volpe, I have heard concerns about singed carpets and furnishings, sometimes perhaps *explosions,* what do you have to say—"

"Stuff and rumors," Volpe scoffed. "Unsubstantiated."

"Are you *sure* about direct current?" Spire said, leaning in, too, so that their trio appeared almost conspiratorial. "Have you not heard alternating current might be more sustainable, safer, and better for use at a distance?"

Spire's knowledge of this new technology surprised Rose, but she recalled him saying that he liked to learn everything he could about things he did not trust—and he had spent a good deal of the sea voyage reading.

"No," Volpe replied simply. "I have heard no such thing nor would I entertain it." Another lie, Rose was sure. All the ticks and nerves were there; body language its own code she enjoyed cracking. The employee continued indignantly, "Don't listen to a word of what those raving Tesla sycophants have to say."

Eager to take the focus off himself, the nervous man gestured to the great turbine machines past the window. "Now. As I mentioned, there are several jumbos on each floor," Volpe explained. "Number nine alone could power the square I showed you, but of course we have backups, in case of unanticipated outages. And to supply our planned expansions, of course."

Darting to a desk, the clerk produced, from a drawer, a handsome little pamphlet positing the company as a sure bet and inviting patrons to invest in the future and illuminate the world. Spire pocketed it with a smile.

"I'll be in touch," he assured.

Rose glanced at the few workers in shirtsleeves and suspenders, tinkering and reading valves, before turning back to watch Volpe's face. She couldn't shake the feeling that this plant was, somehow, doomed.

They were soon on their way, sent out the door with friendly waves. Once they were several paces away and Rose could speak without shouting, she shook herself, realizing how taxing the roar and vibrations had been.

"He was lying about efficiency and safety, as well as their control of the market," Rose stated.

"Glad you noticed, too," Spire replied. "Of course, it would be his business to lie."

"Something there is spinning slowly out of control, charge by charge," Rose murmured as they strode up Pearl Street, away from the shadow of the great Brooklyn Bridge behind them, a bridge whose brown, stone feet stood mind-bendingly grand above them, the rough-hewn legs of giants.

Across the street, as he had demanded, stood Mosley, staring. The man jerked his head to the side, gesturing up the street. He turned and began to walk toward the East River, away from the downtown confluence and toward the great bridge. He looked back over his shoulder, clearly waiting for them to follow.

Spire remained expressionless and began walking after him. Rose kept pace. They wove up through Manhattan's busiest, most dense district, full of people and businesses. Between the brick buildings and industrial stacks, Rose glimpsed the masts of ships, moored in their narrow slips. They were close enough to the waterway to hear the noise of seafaring: bells, whistles, and deeper, resonant horns of ships, the calls of stevedores loading and unloading cargo. Trolleys and ferries plied the rivers, adding to the bustle. As they broke out toward the heart of the seaport, beyond lay busy Brooklyn, its own vibrant city, rival and sister to Manhattan.

Nearly complete, the Brooklyn Bridge was a masterwork of German engineering, a great testament to the Roeblings' vision and sacrifices. When Washington Roebling suffered caisson disease, an ailment that took many who worked on the bridge when the casks below water were brought up too quickly, it was Emily Roebling who stepped in to manage the situation and ensure the near completion of the project. Bridge and woman were awe-inspiring and fascinating, making Rose feel that it put London's bridges to shame.

Mosley sped toward its vast stone feet, two Gothic arches lifting unto heaven, bearing a webwork of coiled wire rope—enough wire to wrap around the earth, it had been boasted. Ships passing beneath were dwarfed by its leviathan scope; their passengers and crews looked up as if at something divine. A cathedral of traffic and a monument to engineering, when completed it would bear the crown of the tallest man-made structure on the North American continent.

Mosley darted up a side street at a sharp incline, leading them up several streets, toward City Hall Park, and turned to where the pedestrian and vehicular level was to meet with the park and allow for flow of persons, carriages, and trolleys.

The opening was presently slated for the next spring, interestingly enough, on Queen Victoria's birthday. At the moment, layers of great steel reinforcements were being laid on the roadway. The grand structure, with its wire rope web streaming from those Gothic towers in an attractive lattice, teemed with workers.

Spire and Rose had kept as fast a pace as they could but they were both out of breath by the time they reached the higher ground. Mosley was awaiting them before a chained metal gate that barred anyone from walking out onto the still-unfinished bridge.

The thin wisp of a young man studied them. Rose found him to be a terribly unnerving presence but she tried not to let that show, tried not to stare at how his eyes were not just piercing, but *sparking*.

"What do you know about electricity?" Mosley asked quietly. A sudden gust of wind off the harbor blew his thin brown hair over his moist forehead. Rose put a hand to her sensible little hat, worrying that its pins might not withstand the winds.

"I know enough. What about it?" Spire asked, playing the safe tack.

"Do you understand what direct current requires every mile or so?"

"An outpost? A tower? I don't know the technical term," Spire replied.

"A booster station to continue the flow of current. They are being built all around the city. Something's off about them," Mosley replied. "And about the plant, too." The man screwed up his face in disgust. "Gone off like soured milk."

"Is there meant to be a booster station here? At the bridge?" Rose asked.

A gust of smoke and steam rose from the Edison plant like a dark cloud and passed through the skeleton of the bridge.

"Not at present," Mosley said. "Though there are electrical plans for the future."

Again gesturing for them to follow, Mosley kicked open the gate without a second thought, a spark springing off the chain as it clattered to the ground.

The wind picked up grandly the moment they stepped onto the walk. They'd walked a good distance across the span when a ruddy-faced worker approached, waving them off with worn, brown gloves. In deference to the wind, his dusty bowler hat was pulled down close to his brow.

"You there, no, stop," he said in a thick Irish accent. "The bridge isn't open yet. 'Tisn't safe, ye can't continue forward."

Spire reached into his breast pocket and with a fluid motion pulled out his silver Metropolitan Police badge. Though he was technically off the force, he was an officer to his core, and always carried this token, wielding it with sense and purpose, and Rose expected he would ask to be buried with it.

Without looking closely at the badge, the Irishman lifted his hands in a show of deference. "Is there anything we should be worried about and looking out for, Officer?" the fair-headed man asked. "Save, of course, for the danger that is this bridge itself," he muttered.

Rose tried not to think about that aspect as she noticed the patches of open slats that had yet to be filled in. Watching her step and her skirts against the construction supplies and debris, she stared in wonder as the city fell away from them; they were gods above it.

Mosley quickly explained their presence, gesturing down at the Pearl Street dynamos. "We've concerns regarding the electrical plant."

"That makes four of us," the Irishman muttered. "I don't mind the soot and the smoke coming up, that's what all factories do, but I've heard places can just blow up with that direct current. Dangerous, if you ask me. And with all this wire? Could kill every man on this bridge, not that anyone cares."

"I care," Spire said quietly. "Very much."

The man pressed his lips together, registering Spire's plain honesty while his expression spoke of centuries of strife. "With an accent like yours, I'm surprised, if you'll forgive me saying so. And you, miss." He bowed his head to Rose. She simply smiled at him, allowing an empathetic warmth to cross her face. The man seemed satisfied that he had not offended.

Tensions between the British and Irish were high across the Atlantic, and evidently here, so many driven to immigrate to New York due to political strife and famine. Rose considered this grimly. She owed her job in the Omega department to the very fact that Special Branches were being created in London as intelligence-gathering offices particularly to deal with the "Irish threat." It troubled her that there was so much fear, division, and mounting friction in the world, when new innovations should be bringing everyone together.

Mosley turned his attention to the brick outpost that formed part of one of the two main turrets of the bridge. There was a narrow metal door level with the walkway, and the young man toyed with the knob and lock.

"That's what might be part of the electricals when we're done," the workman said. "None of us goes in there but Edison's men."

Mosley surprised them by brandishing a key. "I work for the company," he said confidently, even though he'd confessed that was no longer true. "You may leave us now, sir, thank you," the young man said stiltedly, his awkwardness with social conventions suddenly apparent, as if he'd exhausted his ability to communicate. Rose thought to soften the command but the workman simply bobbed his head.

"Let me know if you need anything else, Officer, folks, I'm Bill."

"Thank you, Bill." Spire extended a hand. "Harry."

Rose didn't allow the surprise of that word to register. Harold Spire hated to be called Harry, but he offered a fellow workingman's gesture and a less formal name. While stories were told of the privileged and history was written in their image, the world was moved and maintained by its workers. Bill shook "Harry's" hand heartily before returning to his work.

Rose considered this compartment within the body of the bridge and its implications. Edison did like to be seen, and here he could integrate himself directly into the most iconic man-made structure on the North American continent thus far.

That was what disconcerted Rose about electricity: It was lying on, grafting onto streets and avenues, ferreting below the earth or darting along in zinging wires like an unending aerialist's wire, all for the purposes of turning night into day with manufactured light. To become a world that did not stop. It was the definition of unnatural.

For the first time, for all her interest in a more informed and educated world, a less hateful and limited world especially for women, Rose wondered if she was indeed more of a traditionalist. If there was a limit to how much of the "modern" world she would truly embrace.

Mosley rejoined the issue at hand.

"Since I returned to shore I've done nothing but walk as many lines of the grid as I could," he said against the wind. "The moment I arrived, I heard the difference."

"Heard?" Rose hoped for clarification.

"The lines sing to me, mum," Mosley explained. "You've heard the buzz or whine of a current." Roe and Spire nodded.

"I hear the most subtle variances in their pitch; crest and fall, it's symphonic to me. The delicate song of the current is beautiful." He looked away, his youthful face suddenly tortured. "Violent sometimes. Murderous, even." At this, Rose held back a shudder. Spire remained impassive.

"What has changed?" Spire queried.

"There is an addition, something that was not here before." He tilted his head to the side as if listening, thin hair blowing in front of his thoughtful face. "It's a particular hum that's changed. Downtown Manhattan whines at a certain specific pitch, in varying notes depending on the proximity to the turbines, dynamos, and boosters. All currents have a song; different voltage changes its tune. I don't expect anyone to hear it, but I wouldn't understand the world without the singing of the lines . . ."

"When did your ability first manifest?" Rose dared to question.

Mosley blinked his dark, sparking eyes at her and spoke matter-of-factly. "I was struck by lightning as a child. I lived. It changed me."

Rose felt her mouth fall open in surprise and snapped it shut again. The man shrugged then turned to walk further, toward the nearest of the great Gothic arches. When Rose and Spire caught up to him, he left the matter of his unique adaptation and returned to the present.

"Yesterday I followed the lines out of the city to see where the interference was strongest," Mosley explained. "The problem crests at the booster stations, which exist as one might expect; to boost. Sometimes these stations are elaborate edifices. Sometimes tucked within grander fare as this. Some have called them entirely inefficient. I admit I'm far less the Edison devotee than when I arrived on these shores but I remain impressed by his mark on the world. He wants everyone, everywhere, to know what he's about and what he's doing."

They stopped in front of a door that was built into the stone structure of the bridge. Mosley held out his hand and there was an odd snapping sound, a small spark leaped into the air. The key had just been a prop to convince Bill.

The door swung open to reveal an unadorned inner chamber that held a huge, round turbine—a squat, vast sentry within the bridge. The dynamo was a silent behemoth, rooted to the floor by metal bolts the circumference of a wide hand. On top of one of these bolts sat a black box. The three investigators entered the room, their eyes adjusting to its dim interior.

Mosley walked quickly to the box, then turned back to face Rose and Spire. In the dimness the alien nature of his eyes was fully apparent—they sparked like tiny Tesla coils, fascinating and terrifying.

"Mr. Spire, Miss Everhart," he began quietly. A gust of wind made the bridge sing behind him. "I know you have seen terrible things. This is no different. I beg you, brace yourselves."

He opened the box. Rose covered her mouth both to block the smell and stifle a cry. Spire turned his head away with a cough, then steeled himself and brought his gaze back to the horror.

The container held a large, severed hand with an eyeball implanted crudely into its palm. Runes and numbers had been carved into each digit. Somehow this isolated body part was more disgusting than the patchwork corpses they had helped put to rest just hours ago.

Rose forced herself to inspect the awful offering. Though on first look it was as terrible as anything she'd seen in Tourney's cellar of torture, this seemed a more dreadful innovation, bearing a horrid symbology.

The *hamsa* had been utilized by many cultures and traditions for centuries, merging a symbolic eye at the center of a hand as an icon of protection against curses, warding against the "evil eye."

As usual, when it came to Master's Society work, what could be considered of faith and tradition was made disgustingly opposite, *creating* the evil eye, not protecting against it; feeding on sacrilege by direct perversion.

"There is no way this contributes in any way to the electrical route," Mosley said, staring into the dead eye as if trying to glean some meaning from it. "What a terrible thing to mix with such beautiful, clean current," he continued mournfully, then closed the lid.

"Do you have any idea as to why? Why this?" Rose asked, gesturing to the box.

Mosley shrugged, setting the box down, not wanting to hold the thing any longer. "Someone may be trying to lay their own energy on top of the network Edison is creating."

"Building a conduit for evil?" Rose posited.

"I have no other explanation," Mosley replied. Taking in Spire's skeptical expression, he shrugged again. "You don't have to believe it, but if this has a result, you'll feel it."

"Since you once worked for the Edison Company, can you help us find who is doing this? Can you help us look into the company further, see who in its employ might be turned or outright possessed by demons?"

He stared at the hand. "If this unholy box, like that dormant dynamo, is a booster for some dark energy, then there must be a greater source somewhere. Perhaps below the Pearl Street plant. I will try to root out that source, and to assist you. Provided you don't find *me* suspect in all this," Mosley clarified.

"We do not," Spire reassured. "And I'll be honest with you if that changes."

An expression that might pass for a smile appeared on the young man's face. It was unnerving. "So, then, will I."

"I look forward to your insights, Mr. Mosley," Spire said. "You have been a great help since the moment you joined our team."

"I'm not on your team—" he snapped.

"Since you became an ally," Rose countered. The poor man wasn't making the case of trusting him any easier. But Rose was accustomed to unique, if not difficult, personalities. She was surrounded by quite a collection.

"I'll do what I can," he said, before looking away. "But don't expect too much. I . . . I'm doing this to atone for terrible things I've done." He steeled himself and again stared both Rose and Spire down with that uncanny gaze. "But I don't want you thinking of me as an *operative*. This is not how I want to live. I want to be left alone. I am not a part of your commission."

"Of course, Mr. Mosley," Spire assured. "Whatever you can help us with we will be grateful for."

"You see and feel things we simply cannot," Rose added. "I know it may seem like a curse but truly, it is a gift."

Mosley tried to smile at this, a pained, drawn, pinched expression.

"I'm going to go track the song awhile," he said. "See how muddied it is. See if there's more interference." Grabbing the box with the severed hand, he carried it out onto the bridge, followed by Rose and Spire.

Walking a few paces, suddenly he cursed at the abomination and hurled it away, off the unfinished structure and down toward the river. As it fell, the lid opened and the hand tumbled forth before it and the container finally hit the water.

Spire opened his mouth, probably to say something chastising Mosley for destroying evidence, then stopped.

"Good day," Mosley said over his shoulder. He walked quickly back toward Manhattan, moving more in a scurry than a stride. They watched him go a moment before Rose spoke, brushing the hairs the wind freed from the loose bun atop her head behind her ear.

"He is a nervous creature at heart, but I do believe he was telling the truth as he knows it," she said. "Who, then, is this amplifier of death?"

"Who indeed," Spire said. "I want a list of all Edison employees to cross-reference whatever Mosley might think. We're going to have to tell our poor, beleaguered friends about this latest ugliness."

"There are only so many body parts anyone should have to consider in so many days, but if we delay, they'll worry for us."

"You're very brave, Miss Everhart," Spire said quietly. Rose turned to him and raised an eyebrow.

"You say that because I should have a lady's 'delicate sensibilities'?"

"No," Spire said matter-of-factly, "I say that because in Tourney's cellar I turned my head and vomited. You did not. And here, again, you managed to keep an impressive calm. My stomach simply nearly couldn't abide it."

At this, Rose couldn't help but laugh. A truth deepened within her, the delicate opening of a hardy flower; when Harold Spire was at her side, she felt she could endure anything. She was not melancholic by nature, but next to him, she was fearless and content. Until this point in her life, she had been a solitary soul, so this revelation was profound.

"You delight me, Mr. Spire," Rose said as they left the bridge and turned onto Broadway.

Spire seemed surprised by this, his scowl softening in pleasure. "Do I?"

"You do. I find you to be . . . my favorite company."

"That is . . . high praise."

Neither was prone to giving or receiving compliments, making their exchanges stilted, but their sentiments were no less genuine for being awkward.

"This work, it taxes the spirit," Rose added, "but I find it to be less so, with you beside me. I hope I—"

"You are the only thing that has made life bearable in quite some time," Spire replied hastily, as if that bold declaration had been bubbling up behind a dam, aching to burst forth.

Rose's cheeks colored. Glancing at him, she found his cheeks were as bright as hers. The small gestures and hints she had perceived in the past month were not wishful thinking, then. He cared for her. Their affection was mutual and growing.

She could feel his gaze upon her and wondered what he would say next. But this was not the time for sentiment. Or was it? She spoke.

"As we have agreed to wait a bit to share the latest dreadful turn with our American colleagues, unsettled stomach or no, would this be a bad time to ask if you'd care to have a drink at Delmonico's?"

"You're full of good ideas, Miss Everhart," Spire replied. She smiled.

They picked up their pace a bit, or perhaps they merely accounted for the spring in their steps.

"You should call me Rose, Mr. Spire," she said quietly.

"Harold then, Rose. It's time . . ." He offered his arm. She took it.

As they walked past newspaper buildings and fine municipal halls, Rose felt that the gas lamps burned brighter and the sky turned a richer shade of purple twilight. . . . New York was now magical.

CHAPTER

SEVEN

When Clara woke, after what her mantel clock told her was twelve hours, her first thought was of Rupert. She listened for him but the town house was silent.

Once she changed out of the clothes she'd been deposited in for a fresh day dress in a dusky rose hue with an embroidered shawl, she went to check on him, but he was nowhere to be found in the house.

She suspected the senator was already at a legislative office near City Hall, determining what lawmakers in the city were doing about the strange goings-on. Knocking on his door, she found it open and the bed made, confirming that she'd missed him, and reminding her how much she liked seeing him in the morning and before she went to bed. A twinge of desire shot through her as she envisioned a future of such greetings and partings, of waking up and going to sleep together . . .

She peered into the open door of his study, and a note on his desk confirmed her suspicions.

My dear,

Out with government associates to get a read on the needs of the city and Washington. You know dealing with politicians is worse than herding cats, it will take a good part of the day, but Lord Black will entertain you. Enjoy the park.

XO, Rupert

She ran her hand over the smooth surface of his desk fondly, smiling at the daguerreotype of her he kept in a silver frame facing his chair, her heart full to bursting.

She stood on the floor they shared, their set of rooms a hallway apart, she looked around at all the fine wood, the plush carpeting and pleasant furnishings, she wandered back into her room of gauzy lace curtains and beautiful porcelain things and yes, it was good to be home, but none of it meant anything if her anchor wasn't there to share it, to bring her surroundings to life.

Rupert was home. Everything else was a shell. She had never felt that so clearly or deeply. It was freeing in its own way, terrifying in another; to need someone so much. A vulnerable port for an independent soul to have docked in. She descended to the dining room in hopes of a large breakfast.

While their housekeeper, Harper, was out at the market procuring fresh food, she'd left a note, too, lest Clara feel abandoned, and set out a spread of bread, butter and jam, and, most importantly, a pot of still-warm coffee. Clara ravenously partook of two cups of the expensive stuff Bishop kept on hand just for her, and most of the loaf of bread.

While intelligent, Clara simply wasn't as swift in the morning as she'd like, especially if having seized or narrowly avoided it. Coffee allowed the wide net of her paranormal mind to narrow into sharper measure, and she simply didn't know what civilization had done without it.

Looking out the window, she saw that the sky was slightly gray but that the October day was pleasant enough, built for strolling. "Now, Lord Black, talk to me of your magic . . ." she murmured, and was off.

* * * * *

Lord Black awaited her in Evelyn's parlor, having donned a waistcoat and ascot in shades of bright blue that matched the layered blue piping on the tailored lines of his gray suit.

"Why, don't you look dapper as ever!" she exclaimed. What, on others, would look ostentatious, on Lord Black appeared simply celebratory, as if his every day was a holiday.

"I had a feeling you'd sleep in, and good, you needed it. This allowed me time to go *shopping* and it was divine," he exclaimed, smoothing his new satin waistcoat. "Our Evelyn and Knight are off on their own adventure. Knight insisted on meeting Madame Blavatsky, and Evelyn felt passionately about obliging."

Clara chuckled. "Ah! Won't those two be a sight to see?" Clara had a feeling that the preeminent psychic, founder of the Theosophical Society and fascinating eccentric, would absolutely adore Miss Knight and fold her immediately into her circle. Evelyn and Clara had always kept a polite distance; it was safest that way.

"I didn't think you'd mind if we declined the invitation," Black said.

"Ah, no, Blavatsky is an engaging, wonderful character in her own right, but I confess I find her somewhat exhausting," Clara confessed. "The park is exactly what we need."

Lord Black held out his arm for Clara and she took it happily. Lord Black, a perfect gentleman, treated Clara as a person of great worth, his opinion unaffected by her gifts, her epilepsy, her remaining unmarried at her age, or her devotion to her work.

In turn, she felt nothing but warmth for him and the man he loved, and she dearly appreciated how the nobleman used his position to help those around him live their best lives. He was one of those people who seemed like a higher being bid walk among mortals.

They had to wait for a break in the steady stream of fine, two-horse carriages that were clopping up Fifth Avenue before they could cross into the park.

The eight hundred and thirty-two acres of Central Park

belonged, as its visionary designers had hoped, to all the people of New York City, and countless numbers were out enjoying it.

Clara led Lord Black through winding paths to Bethesda Terrace, the crown jewel of the park, ruled by the Angel of the Waters and her fountain, and further into the interior of its carefully planned wildness. The "park of a thousand parks," as it had been called, evoked a gasp from Black the moment they turned a corner and saw a new, sweeping vista unfold, one picturesque setting after another.

A staggering amount of flora had been planted in this place during the park's long construction, over a million trees of over six hundred different varieties, placed in soil that had once been quite swampy and unremarkable, the water table now rerouted into gorgeous ponds and reflective surfaces.

At Clara's side, Lord Black looked at the innumerable plant life. The last of the fall colors cast the whole vast, layered array in shades of yellow, orange, red, deepening brown, and the stalwart evergreen.

After only two decades, the park was already a haven. Inside, there was a distinct difference of temperature, a palpable change in the scent and quality of the air. The effect was energizing.

"You know, Miss Templeton," Lord Black began.

"Clara please, milord, after all we've been through," she said, interrupting him with a gentle smile.

"Edward, then, if you will. I'm very glad to have you all to myself for a bit."

There was a wide, nearly childlike grin on his face and Clara felt the keen force of this kindred spirit. He had been part of her family in a former life, and that sense memory underlay their current friendship. Clara was flooded with an overwhelming feeling of comfort that was difficult to put into words.

"Are you getting the sense we've done this before, you and I?" he asked with a delightful youthfulness that might have been positively intoxicating if not for her love for Bishop— and Edward's for his dear Francis, whom they'd left behind in London.

"I am, quite strongly." She stared at the aristocrat. "I don't have the specific sense of a sibling like I do with Rose, but you were very close to me, at least once."

"I am glad you feel the same," Black said. "Bodies get sorted into one of what society sees as only two categories, building distinct prisons for them both. The soul is not so codified. Especially not an old soul, one that's been every-thing the human experience can offer. For old souls, identity remains far more fluid."

"Absolutely," Clara agreed, relieved that someone could understand the many different versions of her soul she saw stretched out before her, understanding life as containing multitudes.

They turned a winding corner into a stretch where trees arched branches over them like a clerestory walk. Black took a deep breath.

"This, Clara. This is heaven."

"You're such a metropolitan soul, Edward. Who unmis-takably brightens beneath leaves, and leaves grow green when near you. There's a bit of fae to you," Clara stated.

"In more ways than one," he said, arching one eyebrow, and Clara laughed. "I've a way with plants," he declared.

"I know, I watched you gathering leaves and flowers at Co-lumbia, placing them with careful deliberation on the bodies. I then understood why you keep all those small pots of ivy in your Knightsbridge home; why your garden is so lush and filled with such diversity of species. You speak their language."

"I'm what one might call a green witch, though the term

takes on pejorative qualities depending on who wields or answers to it."

"Botany is one of the world's most important sciences," Clara continued eagerly. "As a child, I spent hours poring over books on the natural world. My parents, may they rest in peace, demanded that any child of an unnatural man-made city be mindful of the natural cities, every tree and every different clime having its own metropolis of organisms."

"Couldn't have said it better myself."

Lord Black strayed off the winding path to bend over a peach-colored rosebush in raucous fall bloom. A branch near the bottom of the shrub had been nearly severed by some passing creature or person. Breaking it free, he offered Clara the stem, bursting with a delicate blossom. Clara was moved by his desire to gather only that which would have withered if left alone.

"To counter the hysteria of Victorian secrecy, our century has created something wonderfully resourceful," Black began. "The language of flowers. I speak in this language as often as I can. What am I saying to you now?" he asked. She took the sprig and studied it for a moment before tucking it behind her ear.

"Seeing as how you have presented me with a peach rose in full bloom, with a leaf attached," Clara replied, "this color of rose symbolizes immortality and modesty. The first speaks of our commission's original aim, the latter speaks of the humility we must maintain in moving forward with new information, tending to the sanctity of our souls. With the addition of the leaf, perhaps you remind me to remain hopeful in dark times?"

"Indeed, Clara. Precisely so. You speak my language fluently . . ."

"Why then, as a practitioner of green craft, did I see no flowers inside your home?"

Here Lord Black pouted. "On account of my poor Francis. He happens to be terribly allergic to pollen and he's far less handsome with a red nose."

Clara chuckled. "That is a most unfortunate ailment, the poor dear. But why were you not more open about this particular discipline during the Warding process in England? You would have been vital to the recipe in those vials!"

"Oh, I was *quite* involved," Black assured her. "It was simply a secret between Dr. Zhavia and me. There was dried *Hedera helix* in each of those vials, Knight's Cross ivy, lovingly raised in my home. It represented the beauty of green, faithful England, a verdant knight fighting for her in the darkest hours."

"Wonderful," Clara exclaimed. "What a blessing indeed. But I wish you hadn't hidden your talents from me. It's a relief to know. Now you make more sense."

"Please understand," the lord said, an earnestness offsetting his joie de vivre, "I have to hide so much about my life, about who I am, who I dare to love. And if I were decried as a kind of *witch* on top of it all?" She heard the pain in his voice and responded reassuringly.

"I do understand, most certainly," she said, reaching out a comforting hand. "We keep our armors, and for good reason."

"Please don't tell Mr. Spire. He's so leery of everything about our departments—I think this revelation about me would tax our burgeoning friendship."

Clara couldn't help but chuckle. "I promise. And I think you're right. However, I do think your gentle guidance on some bouquets for Miss Everhart might be a welcome service to him."

Lord Black gasped. "Really? Those two?"

Clara pursed her lips. "I'd have thought it were obvious."

"Well, I admit, I am too protective and shortsighted when

it comes to my dear Rose. But, now that you mention it, goodness, they are perfect for each other!" He grabbed Clara's arm. "Let's plan a wedding!"

Clara laughed again, realizing it had been a while since she had felt so unburdened and so full of hope. This was Lord Black's greatest power: ebullience.

"But in all seriousness, my dear Clara," he continued, "what I wanted to impress upon you during our stroll is something I've worried about for quite some time, long before these nightmares reared their heads."

"What's that?"

"The balance between the natural and the unnatural world," Black continued. "As your parents said, I live in a very industrial city but surround myself with living things and try to create natural systems within as many spaces as possible. I have been to your country before. To this city. The balance is very off here—the only thing that has rectified the tipping scales is this park.

"I know the planners have been passionate about it but I'm not sure anyone knows how vitally *magical* it is. But *we* might do well to consider that, to protect what is natural. Not at the cost of progress, mind you. I believe in steel and plumbing, in the possibility of electric light and the wonder of the telegraph cable. But if we do not mind our leaves, our branches and roots in equal measure . . ."

"We'll be lost," Clara agreed. "I'm grateful for your perspective, Edward. Because I taste a sourness—a metallic bitterness in the air. If there is a rhythm to this city, it has gained a strange murmur, an off-tempo beat." She thought of the visitor, of the ley lines. "Speaking of balance and forces of nature, Rose told me you met a woman named Lizzie Marlowe."

"You know her?" Black exclaimed. "What the devil is she? Something is either very wrong or too right about her."

"I can't explain her, but she has appeared to me at irregular intervals since I was a child. I used to think I was mad, but, then, don't all of the gifted think that at some point?" Clara gave a short, bitter laugh and continued.

"She appeared to several of us on the ship home, and though her visit was brief, she trained me to feel a certain source. Much like latitude and longitude, there are other markers—"

"Ley lines," he supplied without hesitation.

"With the principles you espouse, I'm sure you feel them far more strongly than I. She encouraged me to be aware and to find ways to amplify them."

"Because the industrial energy is amassing in a way that will shift the balance between man and nature," Black said, clapping his hands together. "*That* is most certainly true."

They strolled now beside one of the park's many beautiful ponds, passing below the hanging tendrils of a weeping willow. Black continued with contagious enthusiasm.

"It is my strong conviction that Warding with flowers, trees, and shrubbery will be very effective in maintaining the balance—and in protecting humanity from the deleterious effects of industry, both spiritual and physical. Given this land's many different climes and populations, it may be the most effective local Warding there is, something cross-cultural and without ties to individual faiths."

"That is brilliant, Lord Black," Clara said, filled with genuine admiration for his quick mind. "I will tell Rupert to bid all his congressional colleagues institute that principle immediately."

"It can be a type of game," Black suggested. "Legislatures can debate which tree or flower best represents a state and its people, put it up for a vote, and all the while it's a statement—giving something natural a greater power, protecting the area from the encroaching unnatural offense."

"A loving point of pride and thus a shield," Clara agreed. Then her stomach clenched and she furrowed her brow. "Congress notwithstanding, those native to this continent have their own customs and beliefs, and considering everything the government has done, it would be a further imposition if the white man were to tell them how to protect themselves. They need a Ward against our people as much as anything."

"Colonial powers become pathological," Black said with a sigh. "I know all too well. I have tried to dissuade Her Majesty from overreach, but she seems rather more enchanted by the brass band symphony of manifest destiny."

Clara nodded. "It keeps me up at night, really, that there seems to be an utter inability to coexist. That violence and seizure is simply what human beings do. That doesn't sit with me. With *any* of me that has ever been."

"We have to do our best within a broken world," Lord Black said quietly, lifting Clara's downcast head with a gentle finger to her chin. "I have to reassure myself of that, every single day. We must be healers in a universe of ills."

This rallied Clara. Lord Black and Rupert Bishop were two sides of a bolstering coin.

"I'll have to remember that phrase, Edward, about being a healer; that will be very helpful when I feel helpless."

"How can we feel helpless when we are surrounded by so many talented people?" he declared.

"How indeed," Clara mused.

"You know, speaking of weddings and talented people, when will you and the senator, finally, make honest lovers of each other?" Lord Black asked.

It was Clara's turn to gasp. She sputtered, "But, we . . . haven't . . ."

"Oh, Clara Templeton, come now. I'm not a prude, now don't you be!" Black exclaimed as they turned a curve in the perimeter of the pond. "I don't care what you have or haven't done together and that is truly none of my business, but my *goodness* does that man love you. He oozes it. It would be sickening if he weren't such a wonderful soul and if you weren't worthy of such adulation."

Clara's blush flared right up to the rose behind her ear.

"I see I've made you speechless," Black said with another of his contagious grins. "I'll make note of that, as nothing else seems to have that effect. Now." He held out his arm again. She took it with a nervous chuckle. "Come, show me more wonders of this vast, beauteous temple!"

* * * * *

Returning to bid adieu to Evelyn after traversing most of the eastern half of the park, Clara was told at the door that there was someone awaiting her in the parlor, and Lord Black was shown to the library to join Evelyn for tea.

In Evelyn's lavish parlor Clara was delighted to find a familiar figure dressed in layers of black lace and crepe, head covered in a tulle veil.

"Lavinia Kent, I've been wondering where you were since our return!" Clara exclaimed, running to embrace her dearest friend, the guardian of the stairs at the Eterna offices.

The young woman's black garb did not signify mourning; it was simply her way, every day. If anyone could be said to be the living embodiment of a Gothic novel, it was Lavinia Kent and her fiancé, Nathaniel Veil, who made his living as a performer of Gothic texts reinterpreted for the stage. Now Lavinia lifted the tulle, revealing a few shocks of red hair pinned beneath her hat.

"I'm sorry, Clara," she began in a bit of a rush, "I had it in my head that you didn't arrive until today. I know you wired the office . . . I've been . . . overwhelmed by what's been happening."

"I'm sure," Clara said gently. "I'm sorry to have left you to it."

"Nothing for you to be sorry about, but I will be frank with you. I'm not comfortable being the only woman around. I love the boys, truly, but I need a respite. The reverend, Fred, Franklin, and Mr. Stevens have done wonderful work with the Wards and in aiding those who were discomfited by what happened at Trinity churchyard and the goings-on around Columbia. However none of them are any good at expressing their own emotions and I just can't do *all* the feeling for them. Or explain what they're feeling *to* them. After a while, it's a positively *vampiric* drain!"

Clara laughed as she embraced her friend, whose keenly empathic nature was one of her greatest strengths. "I know. And I'm sorry," Clara said, kissing her on the temple. "If there had been a way to set another strong woman at your side—"

"At another time, I'd have had Natalie. But seeing as how *Lady Denbury* now has little Eve, how could I in good conscience bring any of these troubles to her doorstep? Not when she's so worried about the pall Jonathon can't seem to shake."

"I hope he's doing better now that he's home."

"I'm sure. I haven't seen him, I plan on giving space. But I do know Natalie and Eve do wonders for him. They reverse all the lines on his beautiful face, take the dark circles from his eyes and replace their hollows with joyful twinkle," she said, enjoying a bit of poetry in regard to friends who had all seen death together and fought the reaper with their brave, bare young hands.

"I am so glad to hear that," Clara replied. "I'm racked with guilt bringing Jonathon back into this."

"It wasn't you! It was finding out Moriel wasn't actually killed," Lavinia spat. "I only wish I could have seen him go up in flames in person, or delivered that blow myself. But I digress. I'm here to . . . ask your counsel."

"Anything, my dear."

"I've been spending every moment I can with Nathaniel. He is in New York for the foreseeable future," Lavinia said excitedly.

"Well I should hope so, he is still your fiancé, isn't he?" Clara said sharply. Lavinia held up her hand to show the black pearl of her engagement ring, set firmly on her finger.

"I know everything going on is, well, devastating, and that we have to fight against any last shred of the Society at all costs, but I was thinking . . ." She bit her lip.

"Go on, love," Clara urged, pouring her friend a cup of tea from the samovar. Lavinia fiddled with it a bit, then took a single sip before setting it aside.

"Her Majesty's Association of Melancholy Bastards, you know, our little fraternity," she said with a smile as Clara nodded, "well, a lot of our members have been deeply upset by what is going on. One would think a group that wears all black and celebrates the supernatural would rejoice, but actually it is quite the opposite. And of course these events are not joyous, not celebrations but desecrations.

"Our group is so sensitive. Not all are Sensitive, mind you, but many have some gifts, latent or awake, that take quite the toll. They're such delicate souls that I fear for some of their lives. You know how hard Nathaniel fights to prevent suicide, it's his personal mission."

"I can imagine, and, of course, I understand."

"So Nathaniel and I were talking about what we could do. He could perform, of course, but he . . . well . . . he's ready to marry me and he thought inviting all our members to a huge, theatrical, elaborate wedding would turn the emotional tide. What do you think?"

"I think that is brilliant!" Clara exclaimed.

"It isn't that I don't think the supernatural terrorism isn't of utmost importance—"

"Darling, no, it's brilliant. May I tell our friends?"

Lavinia nodded eagerly, allowing herself to beam, and bounced a bit on the divan, no longer holding back her excitement.

Clara opened the parlor door and called for Evelyn and Lord Black, who were in the library.

"Lord Black, overseer of England's Omega department; may I introduce Lavinia Kent, our Eterna gatekeeper and the fiancée of one of your famed countrymen, the legendary Nathaniel Veil."

"I loved *Beyond the Veil*!" Black cried. "Genius! His *Castle of Otronto* bit was my favorite, but I loved the Poe set to music. Do give him my regards!" he said, kissing her outstretched hand.

"I shall, Lord Black, thank you and welcome to our city."

"My dear Vin wants to help turn the tide of this city's supreme melancholy. She and Nathaniel would like to make their wedding a lavish public affair. One we could heartily Ward. What do you think?"

"Of course!" Evelyn exclaimed.

Clara turned to Lord Black. "You know the wonderful thing about weddings?"

He raised an eyebrow. She continued, "We can utilize a lot of flowers!"

"Brilliant!" Black exclaimed. He turned to Evelyn. "My dear, would you mind terribly if your home was turned into a bit of a makeshift nursery in the immediate future?"

The grandly elegant woman shrugged. "Be my guest. My gentle husband will much prefer a room full of flowers to one of ghosts."

Lavinia smiled, having gained a team of assistants.

An additional instinct struck Clara. "Have you thought about where you would like to hold the ceremony? Because I've an idea."

"It depends on who will marry us. Not many priests or

reverends take kindly to actors, you know. Many can't even be buried in upstanding lots," Lavinia replied sadly.

"You leave that to us," Clara demanded. "How would Trinity Church sound?"

"*The* Trinity? At Wall Street?"

Clara nodded. "It needs beauty. Love. Magic. Healing from the recent exhumations. It needs help, particularly now, and we'll need a great deal of benedictions and positive blessings." She turned to Evelyn, who was nodding in agreement with Clara's logic.

They could also carefully inter the ashes from the Columbia University bodies, then conduct a lavish Warding ceremony and put everything in better order.

"I'll make sure Blessing knows and I'll talk to the diocese immediately," Evelyn said.

Lavinia's eyes widened. "Thank you. It's perfect."

"Because it's a dark little church in the most Gothic of styles?" Clara posited with a grin.

"Precisely!"

"Now that that's settled," Clara said, frowning as she looked out the lace-curtained window at what had turned into a rainy afternoon. "Good that we took to the park when we did, milord!"

"Indeed," Black said.

"My darlings, while I am loath to leave your comforts, I have not yet checked back in at my office and I must do so."

"Let's go downtown together, then," Black said. "I must see if Everhart and Spire are on the trail of something useful."

"My driver will take you all where you're needed," Evelyn assured. "I'll send for him."

Clara kissed the medium on both cheeks. "Whatever would we do without you?"

* * * * *

Soon enough Clara was walking in the familiar door of her Pearl Street offices, where she found Franklin at Lavinia's desk. During her trip downtown she had held tightly to Lavinia's joy, hoping she might feel something of that luxurious emotion herself when circumstances settled down. Love and care could be her new compass moorings, strengthening her actions. Despite these cheerful thoughts, uneasiness plagued her. Danger was right around the corner; she could feel it.

Clara was glad to see that Franklin had retained the building's two guards, who stood silent sentry just inside the entrance. She gave them a nod of greeting before crossing to the cozy nook beneath the stairs where Lavinia usually spent her daylight hours. Franklin looked a little less tired than when she had last seen him, but lost in thought.

"Lavinia won't be in," Clara explained. "I see you've taken up her post, and wanted you to know she'll be off for the next week, planning her wedding."

"Quite the timing," he said bitterly.

"Oh, no, we encouraged her to," Clara countered. "She'll be doing it at Trinity, and the preparations and the ceremony will provide cover for a whole host of Warding and smoothing out any remaining damage to the plots."

Franklin considered this. "Well, that's useful then."

Clara ducked into the small rear kitchen, where a potbellied stove held several kettles of different sizes. Nearby was a cabinet full of china cups and saucers and canisters of various tea leaves as well as one of ground coffee. That cabinet, to Clara, was life. "Coffee or tea?" she called back to Franklin.

"Neither," he replied, and she could hear his tread on the stairs to their upper-floor offices.

"Never heard you turn down a cup of pekoe in your life, but suit yourself," she murmured, and stoked the stove to heat water for coffee.

Minutes later she headed upstairs, gathered skirts in one

hand and a teacup full of coffee in the other. She went straight to her desk, a haphazard space where files and papers seemed piled entirely out of order—but to Clara's mind, the arrangement was entirely precise; she could tell in an instant if anyone had been rifling through. Indeed, as she looked, she could see that things had been . . . shifted . . . a bit.

"Franklin, did you try to clean my desk again?" she asked grumpily.

"I did," he said, implying his defeat at the hands of almighty clutter.

"Despite my asking you not to?"

"Clara, mess makes me nervous. It's been a nerve-racking time. I couldn't help it, it was like a compulsion, but, you see, I stopped myself." He spoke so earnestly she could only loose a good-natured laugh.

"I've missed you, my friend."

"You have?" he asked, genuinely surprised. "Well, thank you, I've missed you."

He always seemed surprised by any actual show of affection or appreciation, a sign of his low regard for himself, something that frustrated her as much as her disorderly desk did him.

"I expect to hear shortly from Mr. Spire and Miss Everhart. Anything in the papers?"

"Nothing beyond the normal New York madness. Missing persons seem to be the theme."

"Perhaps possessed, perhaps stolen for parts."

"I wonder if this is what the Society wanted, this slow, subtle creep of dread and despair."

"Hopefully what we're witnessing are the final pangs after Moriel's death," Clara assured. "If there is an American head of the Society, or Apex, we'll find them. Or, they might find us. That actually seems to be more probable," Clara said sadly, then rallied. "This grim stuff won't last forever. The Society never thought they'd meet a resistance. While we have underestimated them, we've been underestimated, too."

"You're right, as usual. My sun through dark clouds." Franklin smiled.

In a past life she had literally saved this man from drowning at sea during a storm; his soul seemed to remain in her charge.

"The tag you took from Liberty's hand," Clara prompted. "Anything new? Anything of further psychometric value?"

He fished in his pocket and placed the tag bearing that neatly penned Shakespearean script on his desk.

"No, unfortunately." Franklin shook his head, his voice sounding oddly sad and far away. "I still haven't found it . . . the source," he replied.

"Keep looking, if you would. I'm sure it will prove useful."

He rose, his eyes even more distant than his voice. "Keep looking . . ." he echoed.

"Yes? What about it? I mean, if you'd rather not—"

"I'll keep looking." And with that, he exited promptly.

When he set his mind to something, he wouldn't be deterred, so she let him go his own way just as she always insisted she go hers.

Still there was something off about him, beyond his usual melancholy. Taking steps toward the door, she thought to run after him, to ask him if he was all right, if the past weeks had actually broken his spirit, but she didn't want to seem like she thought him too fragile. Wavering on her feet, she said a little prayer for discernment, but her instincts were an unhelpful neutral.

But maybe her instincts and how to tune them in the city needed readjusting. She'd been away and so much had changed. Facing death and such wild displays of evil invention had aged her, the powers she'd wielded matured her talents and sensibilities. Her heart had broken and renewed itself all over again. Perhaps coming back to New York with a new gravity meant everyone and everything felt all the more changed for her perspective.

She couldn't worry about everyone's moods any more than she'd told Lavinia not to.

Clara considered the empty room a moment, this office her second home, the Tiffany-glass gas lamps with their flames trimmed high, casting a prismatic array of vibrant colors about the walls.

On Bishop's desk sat a wooden rack full of the first Wards, compiled directly from Louis's recipe: a mixture of silt and water from the harbor, chips of bone from forgotten graves—dead whom Clara hoped to honor by incorporating them into the city's protective barriers—and shreds of paper dollars scavenged on Wall Street, as nothing said New York like relentless, merciless money.

The least greed could do was be turned on its axis to shield the denizens it took advantage of.

Lighting a Ward could do her little corner of the world some good. Choosing one of the vials, she struck a match and dropped it in, saying a little prayer for the city and asking forgiveness on the city's behalf.

The Ward began to glow with a strange, gray light, sparked by Clara's life force and intentions. She set it in a brass candleholder on her desk and considered the amalgam of papers and notes she had amassed through years of supernatural inquiry. Despite the battles of recent months, her deep hunger for truths, to know the unknowable, waned. Attempting to find a cure for death had led them down a dark path and destroyed many lives. Only protecting life bore any fruit.

Her reverie was interrupted by the bell downstairs. She went to the top of the landing as the guards admitted the newcomers, whose voices Clara immediately recognized. She called down, asking them to come up.

Moments later, Rose and Spire were seated in Clara's office to tell her what Mosley had shown them on the bridge. Clara shuddered.

"If this is Society business," Clara began, "and what else would it be—one would hope there isn't a *competition* of vile cults these days—they're taking an industrial front rather than a personal one. Moriel wished to build armies of pawns. This, alternately, seems to wish to corral the progress of the machines. Why else put such fetishes onto a working mechanism?"

"I wouldn't know," Spire replied. "I'd like to liaise with your New York police chief. I advise you to be as on the level with them as is wise. The queen withheld things from me, the Metropolitan, Lord Black, and it cost lives."

Clara couldn't withhold a snuff of disdain. "While I understand and agree with you in theory, you'll be confronted with the newly promoted Chief Patt. And for that I wish you good luck. It is my hope he will help and not obstruct. He doesn't believe a whit in the supernatural and he doesn't like working women, so be aware and stand your ground," Clara said, looking pointedly at Rose.

"The Chief Constable and I will get on swimmingly in the former regard; in the latter, I'll take him to task. But I'll get some men out of him to run industrial inspections one way or another," Spire said. "One would hope for brotherhood between precincts but I've been sorely disappointed on that count."

"Mosley spoke of a source abomination," Rose said. "Perhaps akin to what we saw in the London chemical factory or what Spire and I saw in Tourney's basement.

"If what Mosley showed us was a 'booster' of the evil, I can only imagine that the source mimics a dynamo, and while I've no wish to see what horror that might be, I'd hate for the average policeman on beat to find it first."

"That is extremely wise, Miss Everhart," Spire stated. "The average patrolman *ruins* the details of a crime scene. The 'source,' if there is one, should be under our purview. Hopefully Mosley can find it."

The three discussed what other industries might face similar perversions—hopefully Spire could convince the city's police to inspect their factories—not forgetting telegraph companies, considering what Rose and Clara had seen upon the line at sea. Clara advised them about the upcoming Veil wedding and the double duty it would serve, and they agreed to help.

The group agreed to return to Evelyn's the following afternoon for high tea. The medium still felt the need to play hostess, to balance Lord Black's previous generosity. After an exchange of fond pleasantries, Rose and Spire were soon on their way and Clara wanted to return home.

Hopefully Bishop would be there by nightfall and they could reconnect and resume their usual rituals in a space they could Ward together.

A thrill worked up her spine at the thought. What would they do when home, alone, together?

EIGHT

Madame Celeste Chagny, Lady Tantagenet, glanced into the opulent mirror and made a minute adjustment to the position of her feathered hat. Angling her head, she pouted, a practiced expression that had gotten her nearly everything she'd ever wanted, and felt a weight behind her.

Looking over her shoulder, she saw her husband loitering outside her boudoir. "Carlton, why do you lurk there? Come, give us a kiss."

"I . . . never know whether or not to disturb you when you're . . . readying yourself. You've been cross, before."

"You are wise to treat a lady's dressing room as a sacrosanct space. Lucky for you I am ready. Are you interested in escorting me to the lecture?"

"Yes, I am interested in everything you are, dear."

"The very idea of a static picture, *moving*. It's the most interesting thing I've ever heard."

At the Art Institute, a lecturer from France was to discuss new advances in photography and present a moving carousel of images. She had a vested interest in this; if she liked what she saw, she'd hire the man to do a larger display.

Carlton made a small query that was a very big mistake.

"The little boxes you sent out?" he asked quietly. "What is in them?"

"Gifts," she replied honestly. "I'm sending gifts to every

stockholder in the companies I wish to invest in, as if I were sending calling cards."

He narrowed his eyes.

"You don't believe me?" She pouted.

"I want to know if I married a murderer," he replied, sweating visibly.

Celeste's eyes widened. "That is a bold statement."

"There's work you don't want me to see and I think it's . . . something horrid."

"You know what happens when your imagination gets the better of you," she cooed softly. "You and all your fanciful thoughts."

The body parts in the black boxes were retrieved by paid grave robbers and men who pulled bodies from the river when they came to the surface. Columbia students cut up bodies for science and she paid the university for a steady flow of what she needed to create her gifts.

After Moriel's attempt at murdering her, Celeste had given the majority of her instructions via coded letters, which the recipients would burn after reading. Only her few errand runners ever saw her, and they didn't last long—though they never died by her hand.

She wasn't sure what would satisfy her suddenly curious, meddlesome husband, whom she thought she'd made progress on poisoning into submission.

"Not that I am a murderer, dear," Lady Tantagenet began, "but for the sake of entertainment, what would you do if I were?"

He blinked at her, not clever enough for this game. To be fair, he was in failing health. Poor thing.

"I'd . . . turn you in," he murmured.

"No you wouldn't." She scoffed. "You'd inevitably be an accessory. So don't even think about it. Wherever your mind is going, just stop."

She'd have to rework her enchantments and mesmerism and increase the levels of arsenic in his tea. Soon to be a murderer indeed, and no one would know any better. She smiled at the thought.

The black, beaded bombazine mourning dress waiting in her closet was to die for.

"Now, about that moving *picture* . . ."

She thrilled at the thought of seeing her former lover again, and what might happen when she did. Moriel always wanted to be immortal and she'd try to make his dream come true at last.

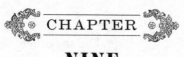
Harper, Clara and Rupert's housekeeper, was working on a meal when Clara arrived, and she felt suitably, a bit maddeningly, fussed over for as long as she could stand and finally ascended the stairs to her room with a weary laugh.

"Has Rupert indicated when he might return this evening?" Clara asked from the top landing.

"No, dear. I'll tell you if I receive any word and I'll fuss *twice* as hard over him!"

At this, Clara laughed more heartily. "Thank you."

She had just lain down for a brief meditation when a sharp rapping sound startled her.

Another strike—a small rock colliding with her window. She rose and moved toward the sill, then looked down into the tiny, sun-choked garden behind the town house.

Jack Mosley stared up at her. With a sudden horror she wondered if he had indeed found the "source" power of that evil extension and had come to give her a private tour. She would have to defer. But how did he get back behind her house? He was looking up at her with a curious expression that chilled her to the bone.

Just staring wasn't going to solve anything. She opened her window.

"Mr. Mosley . . . what are you doing out there?"

"I was trying to help you," he said. His youthful appearance was betrayed by his eyes. The tell of an older soul was always in the eyes. "I've more to say than just about what's going on at the Edison plant. Did the others tell you about it?"

"They did. Nasty business. Did you find the source?"

"The dynamo of the evil? No, not yet. But I will. I think its signal might be hidden by the plant itself. I'll keep looking. But that's not why I'm here."

"Go on."

"There's quite a field about your house. About you." He gestured to the air, not to the ground. He didn't mean a field of grass or flowers.

"A field . . . Our house is not electrified, Mr. Mosley. Nor is next door."

"I know. Yet there *is* a magnetic field about this place. And it's louder, more powerful now, as if something is being routed your way. To you. To this home. I can feel where all the currents are going, Miss Templeton. There's no direct line coming here. But I feel the power."

He smiled partially, a disjointed expression that was deeply unnerving. She wanted to like him but he literally made the smallest of hairs on her body stand straight and it wasn't a comforting sensation. Decorum said she should invite him in for refreshment, but Bishop was not here and her instincts warned against hospitality. He didn't seem to mind or to have any expectation of it.

"Your signature is a note in the air," he continued, and hummed a high, soft note. It rung strangely in Clara's ears, an echo. She cocked her head as if to hear it better. "But this note—" He hummed something low and growling. "—is the signature of a line routing right under your very door. That's where I hear it flow."

Clara shuddered. "What then, if it's not electrical?"

Mosley shrugged. "I'm a director of direct current. You're the expert on all the other stuff. Keep sharp. Listen. You've the ear for it now, you just have to *really* listen amidst the cacophony. Listen before it's too late."

With that, he took two steps toward the lawyers' offices adjacent and retreated down a hole in the ground she hadn't noticed before, replacing a metal circle back over his head. A service shaft for the parts of this block that were electrified— that was how he'd gotten in, coming and going along the ever-expanding grid and the networks underground utilized in Edison's district.

After he left, she considered that patch of faltering green, which seemed dimmer for his absence. Did the green struggle so badly because nothing around it was natural, kindred? Because it could not access sunlight when human towers and constantly climbing stories blackened the sky?

Was electricity in these shadowed spaces created by human interference inevitable? Did they need it? Rumor had it that J. P. Morgan's carpets were browned and his furnishings singed by his own private generator outside his home. It seemed as though electricity lay in wait for disaster. Who wanted unnatural light under false pretenses when it courted such danger?

Lines. Surely he meant ley lines, yes? But that low, growling note, that wasn't what she heard on the ship, or along Fifth Avenue, it was an antithetical note to that of vibrant life. And if it wasn't an electrical line . . .

Were there ley lines that weren't positive? Could there be a ley counterpoint line that was neither positive nor industrially created, and that was what was routing her way? A third kind of line? Heaven forbid, one that devils traveled?

That back "courtyard" saddened her; a feature of her own home—of so many New York town houses—she'd nearly forgotten about. So many buildings had these little ghosts of yards, huddling in rear eaves and standing in for alley shadows, scraps of the old world hiding behind brownstone but away from the cobbles.

She'd always wanted to cultivate a small garden there, mirroring the one she had dim memories of helping her mother tend back when she was a little girl in the wider lands of southern Brooklyn. But the light was insufficient, and the layer of soot, dust, coal, ash, and smoke that coated so much of the spaces of the city had choked out the one rosebush she'd tried valiantly to plant.

This was why she spent so much time after her parents' death in Green-Wood Cemetery; wide open, clean, well tended, sunny in parts, gloriously sacred. So much of the city proper seemed dead and dying, she'd always thought it was the greatest irony to go to such a rejuvenating place that was so alive and vibrant, yet New York's most beautiful city of the dead. . . .

She resolved to bring fresh flowers to her family mausoleum. Roses. Part of Lord Black's Warding idea; she'd love it if all of New York were covered in nothing but. She'd suggest roses as the state flower once that plan was instituted.

And she resolved to find a plant that would survive a coal dusting out back. If nothing else to cleanse the sobering thought of people coming and going around her by tunnels, having access to her in the dark in ways she could not see or predict. Tunnels were for rats, and, it would seem, for warnings.

She thought of the Summoned shadows that had floated along the transatlantic cable, and a terrible thought occurred to her. What if the Summoned didn't need to be placed along industrial lines anymore? What if that was a sort of stepping-stone? What if the kind of dark works that Mosley had shown Rose and Spire were actually freeing up hellish forces to go wherever they liked, unbidden, without rite or direct invitation as had been done before, drawn to snuff out the greatest of life forces with their darknesses? As the electrical grid grew, with dark forces augmenting it, perhaps the Summoned were creating their own grid and drawing their own lines . . .

Darting down the stairs, out onto Pearl Street, she had to ask Mosley this. Gazing about, squinting in the shadows, she walked toward the Edison dynamos, thinking perhaps Mosley would keep close.

There was something compelling about him. Not in a way that made her attracted. Just his field was . . . well, magnetic. Just as hers was, she supposed. He seemed drawn to her similarly. Likely why he'd paused to stare at her before, in those early days before their fates would ever be entwined. Knowing she was something different. Sensing that unique song of her particular wiring.

If she could gain a true understanding of electricity, perhaps it could help her seizures. From what she understood about electrocution, it was not much different-looking than a seizure. Ugly convulsing . . . As she was thinking this, the hairs on the back of her neck rose. There was a slow, building whine in the air. A voice spoke from the shadows of a nearby building.

"Can you hear it, Miss Templeton?" Mosley asked quietly, his voice carrying, despite the busy, noisy, windy city, for no other reason but his preternatural exception. "The sound it makes?"

"The electricity? Yes. Sometimes the whine of it. The hum. I have to separate it from the rest of the noise."

"Yes, it takes a while to sort it out. As I explained to your Omega friends, each voltage is its own song. Each has a note that sings down wires. It has always been beautiful . . ." Mosley closed his eyes for a moment in rapture, as if he were communing with the Holy Spirit in a revival tent. But he frowned suddenly, his God under attack. "But this new energy, trailing along, makes it a dissonant chord."

"What if the dark energies the Society has amassed, especially with this new brand of fetish set along steel and industry, what if the shadows are creating their own grid? What if that's what you're sensing flowing toward me?" She quaked at the thought.

"Perhaps," the man murmured. "I'm not sure. The Summoned still seem to abide by certain laws, and properties. I am of the opinion that you, a wielder of energy yourself, could counter the fouled notes with your own and block the signature out completely; an alternate harmonic to cancel out the note. Think on it. Train your ear, your pulse, your skin. Feel it. And, ultimately, rise above it."

He turned around the side of the building and was gone again as mysteriously as he was ever there. All that was left was the whir, whine, spin, and hum of the dynamos down the street.

Rise above it. . . .

The organic, the inorganic, and the deadly. The delicate and the steel, and she was the one in between fighting off the darkness.

A figure ahead made her heart leap with joy and relief.

She smiled, seeing Bishop emerge from the redbrick carriage house three doors down from their town house. He saw her approaching at a run and waited for her, then offered his arm.

"My dear night owl," he exclaimed to Clara, "what brings you out at dusk?"

The slight admonishment in his tone reflected his dislike of seeing her out alone after dusk. "Mr. Mosley came to visit with a warning about the energies," she explained. "I was trying to get further answers out of him when he vanished. I ran after," Clara said, sliding her arm through his as they ascended their stoop. Bishop raised an eyebrow.

"Mosley. The electrical . . . aberration?"

Clara winced.

"Odd as the man is," she replied, "I don't like that tone or term for him, Rupert. He is a human being."

Clara was sensitive to anyone with a gift being considered a "freak." Anyone.

"Noted," Bishop replied.

They entered, bid Harper good evening, and kept talking.

"What of Mr. Mosley's warning, then?" Bishop prompted, moving with Clara to the parlor, where he took the liberty of sitting next to Clara on the parlor divan, rather than sitting in his usual Queen Anne chair adjacent. A new routine, this closeness, and Clara almost forgot what she was going to say.

"He wanted to warn me of a certain *power* routing here. He can feel and hear it, magnetically. I want to believe it's ley-line energy routing here; that we, as powerful people, Sensitives and forces of nature in our own right, are creating our own sort of spiritual current. But I fear that it's also attracting the darker energies that the Society have so continuously utilized. They know our scent by now, the Summoned, and I fear they're making their own grid, aided by whatever Society holdout is still making hell on earth . . ."

Clara then explained what Mosley had shown Spire and Rose on the bridge.

"Will horrors never cease," he muttered. "How, then, do we fight this?"

"He suggested canceling out any discordant notes. While the buzz of electricity is audible to most, he hears it like a symphony."

"So he suggests fighting energies tonally? Audibly?" Bishop asked, intrigued.

"I believe so, something like a bell, or vibrating at a pitch that might nullify the dissonance and have only the current flowing, not any parasite laid upon it, continuing down the line." Clara spoke quickly as she processed these new ideas. "Perhaps a carillon bell could be stationed various places, disrupting negative currents. The noise could be explained as just a new alert system in testing mode."

"Blessing, Evelyn, and I can talk to church officials about all ringing bells on the hour, rather than just one in a neighborhood. That's bound to shake off some of the trouble, wouldn't it?"

"Yes, of course," Clara said. "Brilliant. Also, if any industrial lines carry negative charge via these death tokens, perhaps the ley lines need a natural and living charge from living tokens. To boost *their* signal. Lord Black and I had an amazing walk in Central Park together. He works in the ways of old, green magic."

"All that ivy in his house . . ." Bishop recalled. "I knew the ancient world whose ways we've forgotten must live in him. The oldest magic; that of flowers and trees."

"Exactly. He and I spoke about Warding with plantings and parks. We mused that what if every state had a flower, tree, an animal, or all, that it chose in a way of Warding, taking localized magic in a new direction in addition to the personal, physical Wards? A state flower, bird, tree . . ."

"That's wonderful. I'll suggest it to Congress immediately. To them it will seem entirely innocuous, and can help broadly strengthen any site-specific plantings."

Bishop was warm and enthusiastic to these developments, but when he reached out and covered her hand with his, it was to address concern.

"But to Mosley's point," he said quietly. "What he brought to your attention. Perhaps we should move. In case what's coming here *isn't* a positive line but a violent one. Seeking to undermine the power we've built together?"

"I . . ." She faltered, unable to put her thoughts into words. The thought of losing this home, a place she loved dearly, cut like a knife. She'd poured so much energy into these bricks. What good was localized magic if one would be deposed anyway?

"I'll do anything to keep you safe," Bishop said quietly. "Just tell me what you feel is wise. In the meantime, we redouble our Wards, agreed?"

"You are so sensible, Rupert," she said with a smile.

She wanted to kiss him. To lead him upstairs. To feel safe in his arms, to be intimate in a way she'd never before let herself dream of. . . . This, too, overwhelmed her.

He must have sensed something of this, for a look crossed his face that was both desirous and pained. He took her hand and kissed her palm, then kissed her again, close to her wrist. Two more delicate kisses followed, moving ever so slightly up her arm. Clara shuddered.

"Perhaps this is the power he meant . . ." Clara murmured.

"You have been my ward. And now you are my Ward . . . Guardian of my heart . . . We must take the greatest of care and caution," Bishop replied in the same quiet tones, his hot breath racing along her forearm like a bold caress. Her shivers made him pause. "I am sorry, forgive me, I am not sure how to proceed with you—"

"Don't be sorry, Rupert. Learn how to interpret when you move me, my dear senator. . . . A shiver can mean delight, and I'd rather you see that and not assume it is the shaking of a seizure."

"I'm learning. . . ."

"We both are. . . ."

Bishop cleared his throat, looking wistfully at her neck, her lips. He straightened up on the divan and smoothed his waistcoat. Clara was torn between leaning back into him and taking his cue to control themselves.

Harper calling that they should attend to some dinner decided decorum for them.

"How was legislative business?" Clara asked as they entered the dining room.

"Necessary. No word on whether Washington is feeling any of the unrest we are here. So I have to believe nothing has erupted there yet. However, while we were away, an Apex holding was found, in old Sleepy Hollow, no less, and the stolen bodies discovered there were returned to their graves. Seems for some doctors, the resurrectionist lure has been just too appealing."

"And with the lore of that town already priming its pump, I can only imagine."

Clara turned to the window, where gas lamps just outside had been lit. The very corner of their offices could be seen from that angle.

"What do we do," Clara mused, "with the Eterna Commission, save for our continuous Warding? Keeping with our Spiritualist patterns? Do we keep searching? For the paranormal? I've received warnings, in various ways, from dreams, to instinct, to a direct order from visitor Marlowe to make sure the Eterna office doesn't become something it isn't. Perhaps this energy tangle has something to do with it."

"It most certainly does," Bishop replied. "The ley lines, now, are the new heart of the matter. Bolstering positive energy as if it were its own industry."

"You know, the fact that our dear Mary Todd," Clara continued, "the whole reason for the commission in the first place, died and neither of us saw her and neither of us went to her funeral pains me. I will forever regret we did not see her before she passed."

"I just couldn't bear it," Bishop added. "I was afraid she'd ask me if we'd made progress. I didn't dare tell her. And so the quest for immortality died with her."

"It died with Louis, really," Clara countered with due reverence, "but the spirit of the commission went with Mary."

"Perhaps her spirit will come in time to give us that closure," Bishop offered gently. "As for what to *do* with Eterna, it will have to change to suit the needs of the city. We evolve like it does, until we're tired of where and what it becomes."

Here, he smiled and stared at her in wonder. "But *you,* my dear. If we were looking to truly bottle immortality, we should have looked to you. All your lives. Your consciousness, your tie to them, the fact that we can see so clearly in you the fact that life is an ongoing cord, an ever-resurrecting link, perhaps that was the key. To *lives.*"

Clara shook her head, thinking of how overwhelming it was when all the lives unfolded. "But better to let that stay, die even, with me, as so few could take on that responsibility, or understanding."

Rupert was discomfited by her words and countered her passionately. "I want nothing to die with you. I want everything of *life* with you. I will awaken to that as slowly as need be. Yes, we must tend to our work. But we must also pay attention to each other."

"Finally," she murmured.

"Yes, finally."

They stared at each other for a long moment, unsure if they should touch, kiss, make vows or plans . . .

"Shall we rest?" Bishop asked awkwardly.

"Indeed," Clara said, rising, deferring to his cue. There would be no discovery of one another this evening.

For all they cared about each other, longed for one another, they seemed equally terrified of taking the next steps, crossing once-so-forbidden boundaries.

"Tea at Evelyn's tomorrow," Clara stated, taking to the stairs. "I have this sinking feeling she has something to tell us."

"Something lovely?" Bishop asked, the hope in his voice an endearment.

"No, I don't believe so," Clara said mordantly.

Bishop sighed. "Damn. Someday the tide of this all will turn. It has to."

"It might just have to be forced, not coaxed. Man-made solutions for man-made complications. There will be a wedding, I can at least say that."

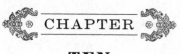

TEN

After the following infuriating morning with Chief Patt—
Clara was right on all counts but Spire hadn't anticipated
just how stubborn the man would be—he wanted to get
something *done* before he joined the others in Evelyn Northe-
Stewart's fine mansion. Thus, he was pleased, upon returning
to the safe house, to find Rose handing him the key to the
postal box associated with the note found at Columbia's little
resurrection club.

"How do you have this?" he asked.

"You can thank Lord Black," Rose explained. "This morning he proved once again that he's the most charming and
persuasive man. It just so happens that the box is associated
with a British bank, and our lord and governor happens to
have rather official-looking documents on his person, indicating that he is not to be trifled with or denied. Shall we?"

"Gladly," Spire said.

They quickly made their way to the bank on Fiftieth Street
and Fifth Avenue, a narrow, multistory, gilded facility with
marble floors and sparkling fixtures. The immaculately dressed
and groomed staff was happy to oblige "operatives of the
Crown." The banker who showed them into the vault was so
delighted to be helpful that Spire sent Rose a piercing glance.
He didn't trust such effusive enthusiasm for the law. It often
concealed equally enthusiastic crime.

The safe-deposit box contained a note with the address

Forty-seventh and Sixth Avenue and a key. *Come calling,* the note said.

"Thank you for the invitation," Spire said to the unknown author of the note. Pocketing paper and key, he returned the box and set out, with Rose, for their new destination.

As they walked downtown and west, the blocks grew considerably less crowded with mansions and their attendant finery, replaced with residential town houses, carriage houses, and businesses.

The address was that of a white stone town house in the Federal style, surprisingly clean considering the soot of the city. A printed sign in the first-floor bay window declared it to be the office of Mr. Ted Swift, Medical Doctor. The white curtains of the window were closed.

Spire climbed the small flight of stairs to the wooden door, which opened to his key. The plain entrance hall bore framed anatomical pictures of the human head and torso on the white-painted walls. An open parlor, which probably served as a waiting room, was on the right; on the left, a blue-carpeted staircase with a simple oak banister led to the upper stories.

The place was silent and there was no one in sight. Exploring the empty waiting area, Spire saw a closed wooden door marked OFFICE. He walked right to it, opened the door, and immediately loosed a vehement curse. Rose hurried over.

Slumped over a desk strewn with occult books, medical texts, and bloodied equipment was a man in shirtsleeves, with a gaping hole in his head. A small black pistol lay in a pool of blood on the floor below a limp, dangling hand.

"Oh, God," Rose said, turning away for a moment. "We need a different hobby than stumbling upon dead bodies."

Spire studied the scene before crossing the room's threshold. Rose followed. They inspected the desk, one on each side.

A broken fountain pen bleeding its own black blood lay atop a letter addressed to a Lady Celeste. What could be read outside the inkblot was, above, an apology, and below, something about the nature of the experiments and not believing in the vision anymore.

Spire went to a huge black metal safe behind them that took up nearly half of the office wall, its door slightly ajar.

A deep metal clank swung the safe wide, and the stench of death accosted them, their nostrils no longer spared.

On one side of the safe were stacked several coils of wire, each with a body part attached—an ear, a finger, a bloody jawbone. Opposite was a pile of metal spikes.

"Railroad spikes?" Rose asked, stepping closer. "Also with attached body parts," she added ruefully.

"Little tokens for the industry. I assume meant to be used as Mosley showed us at that incomplete booster station. To do what, literally haunt the system? Befoul it?"

"I believe so. Attaching the dark magic of the Society to the industrial framework of this city, piece by human piece. Perhaps ghost by ghost, too, if they are connected to these objects as they are to the reanimated bodies. It is rather cold in here, which may be an indication of spectral presence."

Spire ignored Rose's mention of ghosts and bent once again over the desk.

"Lady Celeste," he said. "I don't suppose the poor chap left us an address on an envelope there?"

"You're welcome to move him to check," Rose replied, "but I see no envelope; he seems to be lying on a knot of rubber tubing and a pair of shears. The letter itself—" She peered closer, then cautiously slid the paper out from under the broken pen to examine it. "—has no seal nor any other identifying characteristics."

Spire was looking around the room at texts and certificates on the wall. "The man was indeed involved with a university program. Though it would appear he did not graduate with honors. Perhaps he was trying to gain credibility in other, more insidious ways. . . ."

"He couldn't have sewn up all those bodies on his own," Rose said with a frown

"I'm sure there were medical college volunteers, all of whom knew that what they were doing should be kept off books and records, but wanted access to the raw materials, as it were."

Spire strode back across the room to the safe, picking out a scrap of wire that was free of human flesh and pocketing it as evidence.

"What next?" Rose asked.

"I suppose we'd best alert the authorities and advise them to keep it quiet. I can stop by the chief's office again, loath as I am to see him. Then, back downtown.

"I want to see if this is the kind of wiring that is used by Edison. That, and something about Mr. Volpe continues to irritate me and I cannot put my finger on it. While I'm glad I spared you from grumbling and offensive commentary from Chief Patt earlier in the day, I hope you'll come with me presently."

"Of course," she replied.

* * * * *

At the Edison plant, an effusive worker—not Mr. Volpe—greeted them.

"Hello! Welcome to the most wondrous place on the planet," the man said cheerfully. "I'm Mr. Ansel, and you are?"

"Mr. Hamilton and my sister, we're very interested in all aspects of your company," Spire replied, producing the wire. "A building I have a financial interest in had scraps of this lying about. Are they putting in electricity? Is this a kind of wire your company would use?"

Ansel looked at the sample. "It would appear so. Is the building located nearby?"

"Up by Columbia, actually."

"Oh." The man frowned. "Well, we aren't quite that far uptown yet but hope to be, I know Mr. Edison has been courting folks at the university. Maybe he's had some break-throughs." This seemed to make Ansel doubly nervous. "We'll need more booster stations, though, going that far up. I'd best be prepared! Why am I the last one to know," he muttered.

Rose was looking around the office and noticed that various pamphlets on countless new inventions and devices were set up on a rack near the front windows. She had heard that Edison was interested in getting his hand on every kind of patent by any and all means possible, often being rather an ass or thief about it in the process.

"Perhaps you could be our investment guide," Rose said softly, offering wide, inviting eyes to Ansel, gesturing to the pamphlets. "Mr. Edison is involved in so much, what is the one aspect of his industry you find most fascinating? Most . . . misunderstood?"

The man's eyes lit up. "Mr. Edison, as you know, is at the forefront of audio recording and transmission. I've heard him discuss how *pictures* might be presented in such a manner."

"This would be engaging indeed," Rose said encouragingly.

"In fact, there is a man from France," Ansel continued eagerly, "who has been experimenting with this very idea. After a series of private demonstrations he has agreed to do one at the Park Theatre, Monday at noon. Only the *finest* folk will be there, I am sure. Mr. Edison himself may be in attendance, indicating this will likely be one of his next ventures in the coming years. I would get on board with our company now, if you don't mind my saying so. And you should attend the picture show!"

"Wonderful!" Rose turned to Spire, who nodded in agreement, both playing their roles.

"One last question, Mr. Ansel, what of Mr. Volpe? We met him on our first inquiry here."

"He's not in today," Ansel replied. "He keeps . . . irregular hours." It did not escape Spire's notice that the name Volpe filled the excitable Ansel with either anxiety or concern.

"Curious fellow," Spire said carefully. "Has he, too, always been in the business of illumination, of new industry?"

"No. From what I understand, he used to be a funeral director. Near that big university uptown. But I suppose he wanted something a little more lively!" Ansel chuckled nervously at his own joke. "But I confess, it's he who told me about the picture presentation, and all the possibilities it could offer industry and entertainment. He seems the most interested among us all in the ways the Edison Company can expand."

He didn't mean this to sound ominous, Rose was sure, but it was.

"Ah," Spire began. "Well, do tell him we called, and that we remain serious about our involvement with your projects."

"Will do, sir, thank you." Ansel started to walk away, lost in thought before remembering himself and offering a nicety. "Oh. Thank you for your company, my friends, have a lovely day."

They exited the whirring roar and Rose rubbed her ears a moment before they were far enough from the door to speak candidly.

"Volpe, the former funeral director, and his Columbia connection cannot be unrelated to the recent disaster," Rose said.

"Can't be coincidence," Spire agreed.

"And they kept whatever turbine powered the dead a secret from the rest of the employees. That's something indeed."

They walked a circuitous route back toward Broadway that took them past J. P. Morgan's great mansion. The first electrified house in the country. Even the pretension of great wealth was heeded like royalty here in this country, Rose mused, though Morgan was no pretense; he was likely worth more than most British aristocracy at this point.

Whether or not the rest of the team would have any interest in the show of pictures that Mr. Ansel was so excited by was yet to be determined, but Rose's instinct that they needed to see it was strong. It might be the horror of City Hall Park all over again.

"You're positively whirring, Everhart," Spire stated as they walked up Pearl Street. "I can hear your mind from here."

"Am I truly so loud in my thoughts?" she chuckled. "I'm sorry."

"Never, ever apologize for something so attractive," Spire countered. At this, Rose beamed. "But do share."

"I feel we must attend that show. Ansel may be a zealot for his 'wizard,' but Edison has created a cult of personality, and if there is some new craze the Society could corrupt, I believe that its remaining operatives will try."

"I agree. I hope Edison will attend to inconsistencies in his electricity before long," Spire said. "The distances between necessary boosters, the maintenance, are unsound. Ultimately unsustainable. Whereas the rest of this war of the currents, Westinghouse and whatnot, seem to be about trying to take those inefficiencies and make a sound product to create a, literal, alternating current."

"You're betting Tesla's model will win in the end?" Rose supplied. "Indeed, I wonder about all the problems we've heard about the dangers of direct current; Edison's side has swept them under the rug."

"As any salesman would. While I do not believe him to be forthcoming about the downsides of direct current, I did not get the sense that Ansel was involved in anything insidious. In fact, I managed a fairly neutral read on other staff I saw coming in and around the building. Save for Volpe. He's the problem."

"Agreed," Rose replied. "If something is co-opting the lines, it is being done in private, not as a company directive, and in no way readable from the surface to the average electrician. We need to see if Mosley's found anything. We know where he lives. Dangerous as he is, we'll have to make a house call."

"Should we tell the Eterna team about the upcoming show or just attend ourselves?" Spire asked. Rose thought a moment and frowned.

"I have this sinking feeling that something might be unleashed there. Like that City Hall incident with the scientists . . ." She shuddered, recalling the moment those corpses sat up, enlivened by Mosley's direct current through his own body, one of the aspects of the inexplicable she'd have to leave as such.

"You fear that sort of display?" Spire countered.

"Not that exactly, but something."

"Then everyone should know," he declared. "And we'll tell them tonight. I trust your instincts."

This pleased Rose. That her instincts had sharpened by exposure to the "paranormal" was not a detail Rose felt she should press; that she was understood and heard was vital. She'd not try to convert Mr. Spire to a way of thinking she herself fought at every turn.

* * * * *

They sat in Mrs. Northe-Stewart's grand parlor, sipping the most delectable of teas on the most sunny of days; anyone in their right mind would have treasured such an exquisite home and such fine tastes and such good company, and yet Clara couldn't shake the chill on the air, or ignore how dark gray the clouds were, swallowing up the sun when they crossed over it, the day going from bright to storm-ready in the instant, a chimerical day, one not to trust.

They had started in on tea and refreshments, assuming Rose and Spire would come when they would. Clara was sure Spire was on several hunts, an impressive bloodhound. But Evelyn had been holding back something troubling, and so it was Clara, Bishop, and Lord Black who first heard her concerns as their third cups of tea cooled.

"My dears," Evelyn Northe-Stewart began. "While in London, I received two letters and a telegram I was unable to respond to until my return. But a friend of mine, Rachel Horowitz, a gifted young medium, has dealt with a series of incidents in Chicago lining up with these latter Society initiatives here in New York. She moved there due to our involvement with exposing the Society years prior. There were arrests made then a period of quiet. She thought all was put to rest some two years ago, as we did."

At this moment, the bell of the front door rang, and Spire and Rose were shown in.

"Don't let us interrupt," Rose said quietly. "It would seem we all have news to share."

Evelyn continued as the two leading Omega staff took respective seats on a divan and a wingback chair at the sides of the room:

"Only recently has Miss Horowitz been able to knit together a string of seemingly unrelated Chicago incidents, as the information she has been receiving from the spirit world is sifting into one stream, rather than forking out in opposing directions."

"The spirits are discerning a pattern, or she is?" Clara asked for the sake of clarity.

"Both," Evelyn replied. "There is a central, relative figure skulking in and out of notice on several different aliases, but she has eluded inquiry let alone capture."

"She?" Spire said, sharing a look with Rose.

Evelyn nodded. "Evidently. It seems the absence of my reply to Miss Horowitz's first telegram made her frantic for me and the Denbury clan, involved as they once were. This has prompted her to visit and if the time of her additional telegram is correct, she could arrive any minute now. However, I beg you." Evelyn stared around the room earnestly to make sure she had everyone's focus before continuing.

"Let's take what information she can give us, but not involve her more. Not because she's not gifted and terribly useful. But because she's a young girl, deeply connected to our dear Jonathon and Natalie, and I have made a promise—on multiple graves at this point—to my stepdaughter that I will keep their family out of any further goings-on. We must extend this same shelter to Miss Horowitz. We have between us plenty of Sensitives. With the addition of Miss Knight to our ranks, we are all set for talented psychics," Evelyn stated, and Miss Knight bowed her head, offering a proud smile.

"I wish I could call upon more policemen, if anyone is taking requests for what we're short on," Spire declared. There were pleasant chuckles at this, but the fact that no one seemed to take that seriously made Spire scowl. Rose stared at him, and Clara noticed there was a wordless exchange between them about some other piece of news or statement. Spire seemed to nod to her, as if granting permission.

"The Columbia scientist behind the wandering corpses is dead in his office," Rose reported. "Patrolmen in the area have been informed. He was also employed in the befouling of electrical systems, and there was a supply of railroad spikes with . . . perversities as well. His suicide note mentioned a 'Lady Celeste' . . ."

Before Rose could continue further, the front doorbell rang.

As if on cue for a dramatic turn, the clouds swallowed the sun and the light through Evelyn's lace curtains darkened.

There was a scurrying sound as the maid rushed to the door. Evelyn rose, a mixture of hope and dread upon her face.

Everyone kept quiet and heard the maid's greeting, but nothing from the visitor.

"Miss Rachel!" the maid exclaimed. "Come right in. Madame is in the parlor entertaining quite an entourage . . ."

The maid gestured in a young brunette, compelling but haunted beyond her young years, dark eyes blazing with power and pain. She stood still at the door to the parlor, struck by the sight of so many people assembled. She was dressed in a simple, sharp black riding habit and a white lace-trimmed shirtwaist with a cameo at her throat, a mane of brown hair piled high and pinned beneath a simple black felt hat.

Regardless of what Evelyn had said by way of anticipation, Clara recognized her as a medium immediately. The girl bowed her head to everyone in the room before she fixed Evelyn with a piercing stare, white-gloved hands moving in a series of specific gestures, and it took a moment for Clara to understand that the girl was speaking in American Sign.

When her hands returned to her sides, it was Evelyn's turn, and Clara was shocked that her mentor was fluent in this language, too, as she was fluent in several. Would the wonders of Evelyn Northe-Stewart never cease? No wonder the bond with her stepdaughter Natalie, who had suffered from selective mutism and had learned sign language to counter the condition, had grown so strong.

"My friends, please meet the aforementioned Miss Rachel Horowitz, a truly gifted medium, and a pillar of our efforts to cleanse Master's Society operations from the city of Chicago these past two years."

Evelyn then signed in sequences to Rachel and gestured, an introduction of the assembled company, before continuing:

"Rachel and a companion have traveled halfway across

the continent to give us a report, to shelter her friends, and, it would seem, to grant us all a warning."

At this, Clara steeled herself. So many warnings. Where was the good news?

Clara was impressed by the ferocity in the girl's dark eyes. Eyes that stared down Death and spoke to it by way of a fluid, graceful dance of physical gestures.

Evelyn did not bother to translate her own signing but relayed what Miss Horowitz was here to say, though the girl did seem surprised to have an audience, blushing a bit as she tried to summarize her thoughts.

"While working as a medium in Chicago, Miss Horowitz tracked a woman who supported Society aims in the city. She can't be sure if evil is the lady's doing, or the influence of a foul man in her life, but the spirits contacting Miss Horowitz are rather focused on the lady," Evelyn stated. "The trouble is the aliases. None of the ghosts seem able to agree on exactly who or *what* this woman is; gifted somehow, but that remains unclear. However, there are common factors in what's been under assault. Electrical and rail being the chief sites of trouble and interferences."

Rachel signed in a flurry of words and Evelyn continued the narrative aloud for the group. "The ghosts seem terrified of these industries in particular. More than just a ghost's normal aversion to progress, devices and industry beyond the scope of their lives. She assures us that this is more than the spirits being contrary or reluctant."

As this was being signed and translated aloud, Rachel smiled softly, and Clara read this as a fondness for the ghosts and their old ways. This was heartening to Clara, as she respected mediums who had a deeper connection to the personalities of the spirit world then merely being a receptacle for messages.

"Does Edison or any electrical outpost operate in Chicago

yet? Are lines being desecrated?" Spire asked, directing the query to Evelyn, who gestured to Rachel. Rachel looked between them and signed directly to Spire.

"Miss Horowitz says you may speak to her directly, Mr. Spire," Evelyn said. "Whoever wishes to get her attention and eye, simply gesture so she may be looking at your mouth, to read your lips. I beg you, as the stepmother of a girl who has fought selective mutism all her life, don't act like she's not in the room simply because she cannot speak. A lack of sound does not mean a lack of existence."

"My apologies," Spire replied sincerely, rising to his feet to stand at a better eye line, repeating his question for Rachel. This time Spire referenced the gruesome find in the box on the bridge, but tactfully kept the sentence clear of gore. This prompted a swift sequence of sign in reply.

"Yes, if what was in that box was a body part," Evelyn said ruefully, all of this clearly bringing back dreadful memories for them both. "Rachel is all too familiar with this, and desecration is the certain aim, in Chicago industry and now here." Evelyn turned to the company. "She cites this development as a more efficient perversion, affecting the industry directly at the source rather than taking the time to build full reanimate corpses and terrorize the public. Ghosts are still tied to these disparate parts, and their energy and inherent sparks of electricity affect industry. The full understanding of which we have yet to grasp."

"How can we follow leads on this woman of interest, Miss Horowitz?" Spire asked Rachel. "Would you be so kind as to give us any parts of names you have gleaned?"

Rachel nodded, handing over a small drawstring bag to Evelyn as she signed in reference to it. The silences in communication allowed Clara to fully appreciate just how much information one could share without speaking a word. As an empath and someone who watched body language carefully,

Clara found there was much that could be gleaned from expression and manner without knowing the exact meaning of the signs.

"Rachel says that as much evidence and even postulation as she could manage is included in this bag," Evelyn said.

"You are a great asset, Miss Horowitz, thank you," Spire stated. Rachel smiled and signed toward him, Evelyn seamlessly offering a translation.

"She says she's worked with many policemen, in New York and Chicago, and she realizes she sometimes needs to offer more than a séance or the testimonies of ghosts to aid an investigation."

Here, Spire smiled back.

"I appreciate your understanding of our physical limitations, Miss Horowitz," he said.

At this, Rachel laughed a breathy laugh, appreciating the deprecation. Clara cared for Spire all the more in that moment: a man who didn't believe in the supernatural making a young woman who battled it fiercely feel her full value in a society that discounted her as an "unfortunate," allowing for limitations to be on his plate for a change.

"Rachel and my friends in Chicago," Evelyn continued, "all who worked on Society dealings years ago, were keeping an eye on a particular woman who seemed peripherally involved in spectral disturbances, and then she suddenly disappeared. Soon after, similar things were happening here. She thinks they cannot be unrelated."

"If we can find her," Spire began, "I recommend your police arrest her if she is a person of such interest. Many of the Society ring were being picked off one by one, whether by demons or their own hand, making our ability to pinpoint a wider ring impossible."

"There's nothing to stick until she does something unquestionable, with evidence unshakable. Prosecuting a woman is very tricky," Franklin stated. He'd been so quiet, sunken, and unassuming that Clara had entirely forgotten he was in the room.

"We've hardly any rights, hardly any ability to own property, no right to vote, and yet strangely immune to the law, as we're held to such lofty, pedestal heights," Clara murmured.

"And now we must thank Rachel for her help, but we cannot, we *must* not break these dear souls in the flower of their youth. She and my Natalie have been through one war already, Lord Denbury, now two, we cannot send them back out into another front."

No one argued this.

Across the room, Miss Knight was silent, deep in thought and fastidious with a continuous supply of tea, perhaps searching the spirit world for her own information, conclusions, or ideas. Clara didn't have a very good read on the mysterious woman. She had no idea what was for show, and what was deeper truth. She got the feeling Miss Knight liked to keep it that way.

The young medium then took her gracious leave of their company, with great thanks from Clara, Bishop, Evelyn, and Lord Black.

Spire held back from those who were more effusive, but after leaning in to Evelyn a moment with a question, he then turned to Rachel. He offered the sign for what Clara knew to be "Thank you."

Rachel beamed and signed "You're welcome" and "Be safe, Inspector," Evelyn translating the latter part, which wasn't as obvious as the response. Waving to everyone, she swept back across the threshold and into the hall.

The maid slid the embroidered curtain partitioning the parlor closed, the glass beads at the bottom clicking against one another. The sound of the front door closing behind Rachel made Clara feel suddenly sick.

Overwhelmed by a sudden worry for the girl, in the way Clara worried for any young, gifted woman, especially one with additional obstacles, she reminded herself she didn't wish to be treated any differently as an epileptic; only that those around her understood and respected the condition as a part of her life and tried not to impede or condescend because of it.

She was admittedly glad that Rachel hadn't traveled alone, would soon have the comfort of an old friend, the pleasant distractions of the young Denbury child—that alone could entirely make one forget about the troubles of the world— and that poor, beleaguered Jonathon would have the reunion of dear friends as comfort and return to normalcy. His kind, generous nature was at a distinct precipice, and none wished to make a broken-spirited man of such an angel.

Clara also wished she had any sort of confidence that she would be invited over for dinner, as she liked and cared for these people, and wanted to help protect them, but she suspected that Natalie, the lady of the house, deeply resented Clara having been a part of operations that had so prolonged her husband's absence from home and his involvement in danger. She hadn't yet received an invitation to calling hours and she doubted she ever would. A pang of loneliness for what her work had wrought was fleeting but noticeably sharp.

Spire cleared his throat and, with that simple sound, gathered everyone's attention.

"I hate to add additional intrigue on our already heaping plate of . . . strange," Spire said carefully. "But there is another matter Miss Everhart and I would like to bring up."

"By all means," Bishop said with a sigh. "At this point are we not inured?"

"I'd like to think there is a ceiling for this, however it seems to keep lifting," Spire muttered.

Rose took her turn, mentioning the upcoming light and

picture display in the theater district. Clara glanced around the room to see a mixture of interest and wariness.

Once the matter was explained, Spire put it to the company: "So then . . . who is ready for a show?"

"What a schedule we're keeping," Evelyn said with a laugh. "If you'll excuse me, I've a wedding to prepare! Do come, you're all invited!"

The British company begged leave to spend time at their safe house corresponding in wires with their team back home, those understaffed few who were holding down the paranormal fort. However, Rose promised they'd be on hand to attend the festivities at Trinity Church.

A few days after it had been announced, the event of Lavinia's wedding had given their entire operation the cover needed to fully reconstitute the recently maligned Trinity graveyard and lawn; interring ash and trying to resanctify the grounds that had been so sullied in the recent upheaval used for reanimate parts. It was a blessedly clear late-autumn afternoon, with rolling thick clouds that passed over the sun without markedly darkening the sky.

Clara had taken an indulgent amount of time getting ready. Unfortunate scenes made by her epilepsy meant she rarely went out in society to attend events, so this was a rare and, in her mind, overdue treat.

When she entered her boudoir after a late breakfast, she gasped. The most beautiful bouquet awaited her on her writing desk. The flowers were red roses, signifying the heart, or love; they were surrounded, bolstered, by sprigs of black poplar, standing for courage. Accompanying them was a note from Lord Black.

For the heart of our operation, a dose of courage . . . On the vanity rested a corsage of small white roses, Clara's favorite flower, a message of worth and worthiness. Beside them sat another surprise, a small jewelry box. Opening it, she found peridot earrings set into a small rose pattern with silver stems and leaves. Bishop had been listening the night prior, when she'd mentioned wearing her favorite green silk

gown to the event. His note, written in his neat, careful pen-
manship, read:

> *I could not let Lord Black outdo me. You are*
> *the most important treasure I have. I wish to be*
> *forever worthy of you. Your Bishop.*

A flow of sudden, happy tears as she put these gifts on
with trembling hands and the sentiment they enflamed in her
made the Ward in the small vial sitting against her vanity
frame shimmer with renewed capability.

She stared in the mirror and promised the woman staring
back at her she would not seize like the last time she'd worn
this dress . . . the night she met Louis. The gown had needed
repair and cleaning, which she'd done, then put it in the back
of her closet owing to a complicated tangle of emotions. But
now she could face it again, and once she'd coiled her hair
into a braided crown atop her head, she felt regal.

It had been her favorite dress, peridot green like her new
earrings—and still accented her lines and angles attractively.
The wide, doubled skirts were bustled generously, the lines
of the dress were accented in golden ribbon trim and glass
beads, and a billowing sweep of ruffled satin combined with
the fitted bodice to reveal collarbones and décolletage.
Around her neck she placed a set of small pearls that had
been a gift from Bishop when she had finished her formal
education. Beneath the bodice she kept, as always, the protective carved bird Louis had given her in the early days of
their courtship. It was an effective talisman, and their company needed as much armor as possible.

The last accessory: a Ward. She tucked the contents of a
downtown-based Ward into an embroidered handkerchief,
charging the protection with a small prayer and a frisson of
her own energy, and placed it against Louis's bird pendant

pinned inside the dress. At this connection, the air directly around her seemed to warm.

Placing a matching peridot capelet over her shoulders, she slipped on her cream satin gloves, picked up a beaded bag filled with ritual supplies, and was on her way.

She descended to the ground floor, where Harper clucked and hovered over her for a bit, clipping a few loose threads with embroidery scissors, Clara rolling her eyes in playful exasperation.

"Fred Bixby dropped a note by earlier this morning," the housekeeper stated. "I didn't want to wake you. He and Effie are with their grandmother, who took a decided turn for the worse, so they extend their apologies for missing the ceremony. The senator is already there in preparation."

"Understood, thank you." Clara made for the door but Harper's hand stopped her.

The housekeeper looked her up and down, adjusting the lace bonnet over her head as she couldn't seem to keep busy hands from fussing over things. "Beautiful. May it be your turn next."

Clara sighed, her cheeks coloring. "You, too? Lavinia insinuated the same thing when asking Bishop to be the one to walk her down the aisle. Said he'd be next and then the girl had the cheek to wink at me. A conspiracy, I tell you."

They'd never been pressured before. Perhaps the unmistakable way they now looked at one another gave friends and associates presumptive permission. Still, she didn't like the intrusion of expectations, nosing around intimacy, no matter what society stressed was proper or had a time line.

The Trinity bells tolled four and Clara took her leave.

Entering the wrought-iron gates of the church grounds after a short walk, staring up at the spires of the beautiful brownstone chapel in high Gothic style, its golden stained-glass windows glowing from within, she could feel the spirit of the building itself, as if it were a ghost, trying to rise above the recent horrors on its grounds. This building, this plot, had meant so much to her and to Eterna, she felt it was a character in and of itself; quiet sacred ground surrounded by frenetic Manhattan, it was a precious place and needed renewed protection.

Clara found Reverend Blessing outside, not far from Alexander Hamilton's grave, which was marked by a stately obelisk. Mr. Stevens was at his side in shirtsleeves, suspenders, and trousers with slightly grass-stained knees. Burlap and paper mounds were heaped about—packages containing the ashes and bone fragments that were to be laid to rest in strategic places about the churchyard.

Mr. Stevens greeted Clara warmly and complimented her on how lovely she looked. Though she'd directly helped save him from certain death, the wonder and reverence with which he regarded her remained a bit disconcerting.

He proudly showed her the small, fired clay tags he'd attached to each package. Some bore a person's name, others just a word.

"Whatever Mrs. Northe-Stewart told us of name or quality," Mr. Stevens explained of the demarcations. "I fired these tags in a small makeshift kiln. I think it will help."

"It most certainly will, Mr. Stevens. Lest this plot become a potter's field without any names or religious affiliations, I think this will go great lengths toward peace."

With another wide smile he rushed back to helping the reverend.

Clara noticed that the packages here had small crosses on them, meaning what Evelyn and Knight had been able to glean from the spirits' wishes about where they might wish to rest. She saw no Stars of David, meaning those remains had likely been transferred to Reverend Blessing's rabbi friend Holzman for interring, their allied stand against persecution, discrimination, and slavery running as deep as their blood was red.

"Thank you for your tireless work, gentlemen," Clara said earnestly. "I'm going in to examine the interior."

In the stately sanctuary, Clara overheard Bishop reassuring the deacon that Evelyn Northe-Stewart, a significant patron of the church—and this was no lie—had funded additional grounds restoration before the ceremony. The deacon seemed concerned that he hadn't had the wedding on his calendar; this worry was eased, calmly and quietly, by the senator's mesmeric powers. When Bishop noticed Clara down the long wooden aisle, his eyes widened and he put his hand to his heart.

She smiled, put two fingers to her lips to indicate a kiss, and left him to his work, ducking into the shadows at the fore of the chapel to examine what interior Warding had been done.

A thought had her turning back to Bishop: What about Franklin? Had he heard from him? Surely Blessing and Stevens would have welcomed the help outside. Yes, he was exhausted and had been taxed to illness by recent events, but it was odd for such a core Eterna Commission employee to miss the wedding of a woman whom she knew he considered a dear friend. Unease gnawed at her nerves until she displaced the feeling, as she could afford nothing but strength and vigilance here, with some room for happiness.

A hired florist had provided black tulle and varying white flowers drizzled with black paint. Lord Black was personally accomplishing the decor, making sure every placement had meaning behind its beauty. As Clara approached, he was adding a palm frond and bouquets to the end of each pew, creating a lovely line up the aisle toward the pair of large silver vases, exploding with the same arrangement, on the altar.

As he'd promised, Stevens supplied a case of Wards in a box on a rear pew. Clara picked them up and brought them to Lord Black, who was, like Mr. Stevens, in shirtsleeves, having draped his striped blue and white coat over a pew. "Will it disrupt you if I add Wards to these aisle decorations?"

"Not at all, it's the perfect addition," Black replied.

"With a bit of ritual around it?" she asked, producing a small few twists of sage from her drawstring bag of supplies.

Lord Black smiled. "As my soul knows you from ancient days, Clara, there would be nothing more fitting for us than performing rituals side by side. Well, if we were in a stone circle, perhaps—" He grinned and looked up at the graceful stone arcs of the chapel. "—but arches and crosses will do."

She chuckled softly, delighting in him, sure he was right. Her instincts regarding the Warding, perhaps why she'd taken to it so strongly, were as familiar as it was ancient.

Methodically Clara inserted the small glass vials into the tulle bows of the aisle bouquets, then lit each one. They flared bright and then went into a low smolder, small tendrils of smoke lifting up like incense. She set a match to the thin twists of sage as well, then held them before her in the air and moved them to draw a cross, a pentagram, a Star of David, and a crescent with the smoke. Gliding around the small chapel, almost dancing, she turned to honor the four cardinal directions and imagined that the beautiful Gothic building was alive and helping them in their task.

Spiritual matters were intimate, and as souls representing a wide spectrum would gather under these Gothic eaves this night, Clara wanted to respect a range of belief and identity as best she could. If the Society did not discriminate in its perversions, she would not discriminate in her protections.

The Trinity bells tolled again. All would soon be under way.

* * * * *

Spire, dressed in the nicest suit and frock coat he'd ever been in, courtesy of Lord Black, held open the plain, heavy, military-grade metal door of the three-storied British diplomatic safe house tucked into shadows of taller buildings on Whitehall Street.

Rose thanked him as she brushed past his arm, dressed in a lavender silk dress with fitted bodice that, while modest in its lace neckline and pearl-buttoned collar, had a few too many ruffled layers for her taste; as much a piece of finery as she was comfortable in. The British team, having boarded for New York unprepared, had given Black their measurements, and a wardrobe was there awaiting them in the safe house, details having been wired to his favorite tailor, who was only too happy to oblige one of his best customers. This delighted Miss Knight most, who was unabashedly eager for new gowns, but Spire and Rose would have preferred to wear their own clothes of muted colors and simpler fabrics, more sturdy and made for work.

They descended the stoop from the side of the brick building that seemed a basic warehouse, an incongruous look, as such nicely dressed persons seemed better suited to descend from a Vanderbilt mansion. Both of them were adjusting, shifting the tight lines of their finery around their middle and shoulders, making sure they'd clasped all the right panels and buttons. After a moment of this mutual fussing, Rose glanced at Spire and they shared a little laugh.

Once they were strolling northward on Broadway, the island's most arterial road, Spire spoke. "I shudder to think what we're in for tonight." When Rose raised an eyebrow, he clarified: "Please understand, the groom, Nathaniel Veil, is a sensitive subject with my father, who calls him a 'childe imitator' in all manner of the Gothic arts. From what I understand, Veil is the better performer. I'm sure my father was terrible to him, even though he was the boy's idol."

"Well, the young man does not suffer from a lack of devotees," Rose stated. "He has a society of fanatical followers, Her Majesty's Association of Melancholy Bastards."

At this, Spire genuinely laughed. "As much as I detest the Gothic, being raised in the tradition," Spire said, "I can't seem to escape it. It is the tale in which I must be told, it would seem my doom."

Rose chuckled. "That sounds a very Gothic thing to say. I hope it is not as dire as all that."

"Leave that to the biographers," Spire said with exaggerated weariness. Rose's chuckle became a laugh.

Spire held the gate for her as he had the door. She again brushed his arm, unintentionally but it was not to be mistaken. There was some part of her, clearly, that wished to be close to him and for that wish to be known. Neither made comment as they stepped under the church eaves.

"Mr. Spire, Miss Everhart." Clara Templeton approached them at the door with a warm greeting. The green and gold of her gown made her eyes of matching hues look positively supernatural in the glow of the bright gaslight at the door. "So good of you to come." She held out cream-satin-gloved hands in gentle supplication. "Might I put you right to work?"

"Of course," Rose replied.

"I need your keen eyes," Clara continued. "Before the space fills we need to make sure nothing within this space is tainted. You come from an Anglican tradition and this church, while Episcopalian, descends from that tradition. Before any of Nathaniel Veil's 'association' will enter, we must be sure nothing is out of place or disturbed. It was never fully examined by those of us trained in these matters after the initial unrest of the graves, I don't want to take any chances.

"Evelyn is to give the final appraisal, as she is Episcopalian and may recognize if something inside is 'off' in the way that only her denomination might notice," Clara explained. "I was raised in far less decorated Quaker spaces."

"But we know 'off' when we see it at this point," Spire muttered.

"Indeed," Clara said. "The clergy of Trinity maintains that the sanctuary within remained undisturbed during the shifting and exhumations of some of the graves, but as the Society's tradition was to overturn sacred practices of all kinds to glean the power of their inverse, I don't feel combing it with detective's eyes can be overdone."

"You'll never hear me argue that," Spire replied.

* * * * *

As Clara led her British partners into the dim, arched space, which was bathed in the last of the day's golden light from the deep amber and parchment-yellow stained-glass windows on the ground and clerestory level, she saw a dramatic, black-clad figure. The groom had arrived.

Dressed head to toe in black silk, his long black hair down around his shoulders, he was staring nervously at the altar. His black silk cape, fastened with a large silver wing clasp, cascaded down his back and rustled in the church's drafts as if it were alive.

"Hello, Mr. Veil," Clara said with a wide smile. The man turned, wide, dark eyes taking her in. "Clara Templeton. We met only briefly. I work with Lavinia." She proffered a handshake, an odd gesture when she was dressed so formally, but she wasn't one for hand kissing, especially when working.

Veil shook her hand eagerly.

"Ah, yes, her secretive work!" he exclaimed. "Makes you two all the more ripe for drama in my mind, can never have enough of that."

"I leave all the drama to you, Mr. Veil. These are my

associates, Mr. Spire and Miss Everhart." Here the two nodded, and Clara continued, "You'll see a few of us over the
course of the night."

"I never say no to a larger audience." He maintained his
sharp-toothed smile, which was damnably endearing. The
man positively oozed charisma, and Clara was, in that moment, so very glad he didn't have the gift of mesmerism, as
his association was devoted enough already. Any greater
powers and this man could be a Gothic menace.

Clara laughed. "It is a rite, not a show, my friend."

"All the world's a stage, my dear," he replied.

As if to prove the point, Miss Knight swept up behind
them, in an even more impossibly lavish dress than was her
usual style, a brocaded satin confection of emerald and royal
blue, a gilded fascinator cascading green feathers down the
side of her black hair. She greeted the groom with a hearty,
welcoming laugh, grabbing him by the shoulders and kissing
both cheeks.

"Nathaniel Veil," she crowed. "My beautiful Raven is all
grown up!"

"Marguerite!" he cried, throwing his arms around her.
"Why . . . how are you here? Please tell me the whole Cipher
troupe is with you!"

"Alas, just me; here on some . . . official business and
thankfully your timing is perfect. Mr. Blakely and Mrs. Wilson
remain in London on business of their own."

"And Reggie?"

"I, well . . ." At this, Miss Knight was caught off guard, but
she didn't seem able to lie to the young man. "We lost Reginald."

"No . . . how?!"

"An . . . accident on the wires, but let's not talk about that.
Do pay us all a visit when you're back in London. It's been
ages since we all performed together, oh, Gods those wild

years on the road!" The performers sighed. Knight continued, "Adira would be very glad to see you."

"Of course," Veil said. "Vin and I are honeymooning in London and Paris and we'll be sure to pay our respects."

Clara left Veil and Knight to chat further; good that Knight could keep him busy, and also psychically keep an ear out for disturbances.

Moving forward to join Spire and Rose as they examined the beautifully wrought altar of carved, gilded wood, the throne-like chairs for clergy decked in rich purple velvet, Clara compared the church to the spartan Quaker meeting houses of her youth. Here were splendid, external testaments of glory, whereas her ancestors focused on internal cathedrals and contemplative silences. To each their own, she thought, provided it was for the caring benefit of all.

"Nothing looks out of place to me thus far," Rose offered. Evelyn joined them in silent inspection, wearing a splendid black silk gown with a purple velvet wrap. She nodded in agreement that all looked well, and that was when they heard music from the street outside, which drew them to the front of the church.

Nathaniel Veil's association made quite a show of their arrival. In the manner of a funeral procession, they filed down Broadway, musicians at the lead playing a morose, downtempo dirge on French horns.

Clara, Evelyn, Spire, and Rose took up standing positions just inside the transept, keeping an eye on the space, both inside and out.

The moment the procession filed fully in, Trinity's organist took to the keys and stops from his choir loft nest amid the dark wooden panels. The silver pipes of the complex instrument sent tones ringing through the small church, making the sanctuary positively vibrate. The music was recognizable immediately; even the first notes had Clara holding back a laugh.

Bach. Toccata and Fugue in D Minor. Of course. Theatrical to the core.

As the music crested, Nathaniel Veil stepped out from the shadows and strode to the base of the altar, staring down the aisle with searing intensity and a stage presence as tall as the grand church's beams.

The dark, rolling music lifted into another fortissimo peak and the sanctuary doors were thrown open to reveal the bride in a gorgeous, royal purple gown. Her black veil was of a wide netting that allowed her face to be seen, a radical departure from the demure bride. This challenging, bold choice would not allow her audience to forget her intensity or that she was as compelling a presence as the man who waited for her at the altar.

In one hand she held a simple bouquet of deep burgundy roses. In the other she held a censer, its smoking ball exuding the richest, most exquisite frankincense Clara had ever inhaled.

That a woman would carry an implement of the cloth, meant for preparing a ritual space, was unheard of—that was the province of male clergy alone. The association murmured in titillated approval.

Lavinia had confided in Clara years ago that she had once wanted to become an Episcopal priest, as the American branch of the Anglican Church at least seemed able to conceive of women in leadership positions, and she held out hope for the future. Perhaps this moment of boldly sanctifying the space was Lavinia's way of living that dream; Clara knew this was an act of love and faith, with no intent of sacrilege.

Bishop stepped up to Lavinia's side, not taking her arm,

but simply walking next to her, a show of support to offset
the family that had abandoned her when she chose to marry
a lower-class actor.

Admittedly, Clara's breath was taken away by the sight of
her former guardian: Bishop's striking presence and distinguished features were displayed magnificently by the finest
of all-black dress. His gaze went right to her as if he felt her
stare, and his smile dazzled her. After they'd stared at one
another, captivated, for longer than was proper, Bishop returned his attention to escorting the bride.

As they processed up the aisle, Bach echoing through the
church, Lavinia swinging the censer expertly, Clara noticed
with excitement that the Wards at the center of the bouquets
glowed more brightly in response.

Lavinia reached the altar where Reverend Blessing, having
refreshed himself and donned a purple stole, glowed with se-
rene happiness, his bright smile wide against his brown skin.
Bishop presented Lavinia to Nathaniel and inclined his head
to the groom before retreating to the side of the altar.

Nathaniel stared at Lavinia with transported joy. He was
an actor, but this was no act. They were young, barely twenty,
but the supernatural trials they'd faced early in their courtship aged them and made them inseparable. Bonds made in
spiritual battle were like no other; Clara knew this fact too well.

The organ music died away to silence. After a moment,
Nathaniel once again broke with marital tradition and began
to recite, his voice clear and strong. It took Clara a moment
before she could place the grand words—and then she smiled
in true delight. Nathaniel was speaking stanzas written by
Edgar Allan Poe, though substituting his beloved's name for
those in the original text.

"And we loved with a love that was more than love, me
and Lavinia Leigh . . ."

Thankfully, he stopped before the poem's elaborate lines about Annabel's sepulcher. Clara felt there was only so much morbidity one should bring to a wedding.

Reverend Blessing now took over, with a simplified yet traditional liturgy. Toward the end of the vows, Clara spotted movement at the corners of her eyes. She blinked, assuming she was just tired, to no avail.

The shadows were distinctly denser toward the back of the chapel. Her stomach twisted as she wondered if they had missed something during their inspection. From her place toward the back of the sanctuary, she tried to catch Bishop's eye, but he was focused on the altar.

Looking cautiously around the space, Clara noted Evelyn's vigilance: The powerful medium was standing sentry at the front of the other side aisle. Miss Knight sat a few pews ahead with an erect posture; the expression on her face showed that her sensibilities were all alertness.

It seemed that despite their work in the graveyard and the church itself, Trinity was still a precarious, vulnerable spiritual space, the kind of space that Summoned shadows liked to take advantage of. A pushback against all their Warding.

Clara edged back toward the entrance foyer, where gas lamps had been turned low for the ceremony. Spire and Rose moved just a beat behind her; they had been watching her closely for the cues that only a Sensitive could give. Miss Knight looked back at Evelyn, then Clara, picking up on a concern. Clara shook her head and pointed to the couple, indicating she should keep focused on them.

Gesturing to Rose and Spire, Clara slipped under the entrance arch and toward the front door. A moment later they had slipped outside to walk around to the rear without intruding on the ceremony.

"I thought I saw something—inky shapes—around the

ambulatory," Clara said quietly as they circled the edifice. "It may be a trick of the eyes—"

"We cannot be too careful," Rose stated.

As they crossed the length of the church, a flickering caught the corner of Clara's eye and she turned to look. A little farther downtown, something was disrupting the intermittent electric lights between here and the Pearl Street dynamos. She had to turn away lest the unnatural blinking affect her epilepsy. Either Mosley was manipulating the grid or the Summoned were responding to their new puppet master.

The rear of the church had a less grand but still beautiful Gothic arched door. As they approached it, they heard a raucous bout of applause and cheers from inside. The ceremony was done, the couple wed. Everyone would be focusing on the receiving line at the front of the church, hopefully moving away from whatever lurked here.

Spire strode forward and opened the rear door; a coolness wafted out. This was troublesome; the space, lit with candles and filled with a hundred-some persons, should not have been cooler than this near-Halloween night. And yet.

The veil between the mortal and spirit worlds was thin these days indeed, and straining at the seams.

Clara pressed the beaded bodice line at her bosom and felt the combination of talisman and Ward she'd placed there like armor. Her own energetic reserves swelled.

As she made to step past Spire into the church, he stopped her with a hand on her arm, squinting into the shadows of the eaves.

There was a candlelit, hanging wrought-iron lantern at the rear steps, and Spire reached out toward the wall just beyond the pool of its light. Something of the stone he put his hand to seemed to be sitting with too much space between the other stones, removed of mortar and revealing a gap.

Carefully he slid out a brown box about the size of a brick, the same color as the rich brown sandstone of the church. With a grim expression, he drew Clara away from the building, then opened the box. Clara's hand went to her mouth at the sight of its contents: partially disarticulated fingers, the skin peeled back and bloody runes placed at the knuckles. A Society-styled offering if she'd ever seen one.

Over Clara's head the darkening sky went pitch black and the three companions realized it was one of the demonic shadows, perhaps drawn to the box. Spire reeled back and slammed the box shut and cast it away toward a headstone, where it fell half ajar.

"Mr. Spire, do you have a Ward?" Clara cried. At the sound of her voice, the lightless silhouette whirled toward her.

"Not on me," he replied nervously. "Isn't the church full of them? Isn't that enough?"

The pitch-black, lightless shadow took a swipe at her, stretching the vague form of a hand toward her breast. It seemed to strike a barrier, unable to come near, and Clara knew her personal Ward was keeping it at bay.

"I do," Rose said, placing herself between Spire and the form, which had begun to advance on him. She thrust one arm toward the vile essence, holding out a glass vial, and the inky abomination shifted back as if onto its haunches.

Clara ran to one of the disrupted grave areas nearby and plucked a Ward from within the small bouquet left there as protection. After rushing back, she handed it to Spire; as their hands touched, the strength of their energies made the Ward glow.

Bishop called Clara's name and rushed toward her out of the dark.

Something within her shifted like a pendulum. Time seemed to pause and Clara could see something rippling in the night air, spanning the space between her body and Bishop's, between Spire and Rose.

A compass. To Clara, it was unmistakable, and from the looks on the others' faces, she assumed they also saw the odd ripple of the air, like heat off a horizon line or the shimmering of a moonbeam across water.

Another movement in her peripheral vision had Clara turning to watch as one of her past selves peeled away from her body and floated a few paces away, as if it were a leaf detaching from a tree on a blustery day and hovering in the wind. Androgynous in dark hooded robes, something priestlike, the figure faced Clara, then craned their head as if listening, the hood falling back to reveal long, pale hair. They lifted long-fingered hands to both ears, gesturing that Clara be the one to listen now.

Wincing, Clara heard a sound that caused the same reflexive reaction as smelling decay. The discordant note in the air was a raw sound, a grinding, screeching sort of noise that echoed faintly off her inner ear, quite separate from the dramatic organ postlude that had begun in celebration of pronouncement; resonant tones emanating into the night.

"Do you hear that?" Clara asked. Rose and Spire shook their heads.

"There's an undercurrent," Bishop stated. "I can *feel* it, but I can't hear it. Like when you know there's a ghost present but cannot see it. You must be tuning to the sounds of disparate energies as Mosley suggested."

Clara glanced back at the life that had manifested itself. The figure had moved to where Spire had discarded the box, holding hands out over the runic abomination in an act of blessing in an ancient, cleansing rite her current self no longer remembered, and then the figure faded. But the grating whine remained.

"Come with me," Clara said, remembering the idea for an antidote to discordant currents, and the others rushed after her into the chapel.

There were shadows lurking behind the altar, waiting. It hadn't been a trick of her eye after all. Lightless, silhouetted forms dove at the quartet but were repelled by the boundaries of their new compass.

"Stay close," she instructed the others. "Between the Wards and our connection, the effects are keeping us shielded."

By this time all the guests had left and the organist was winding down the haunting, deep-noted postlude. Reverend Blessing stood alone in the center of the transept, his head cocked to the side.

"Reverend," Clara said, "there's something foul we had to discard out back that needs your tending. Bring friends, please," she commanded. He nodded and called to Evelyn, who was standing near the front, as Clara led her team up into the choir loft. The four of them tried to keep equidistant spacing even in single file, the wood creaking as they moved quickly.

The organist, sitting on a padded velvet organ bench, turned to them with a disapproving frown.

"Friends, you can't be up here—"

"I know, but it's an emergency, sir," Clara said.

"Please listen," Bishop said, bringing his power to bear. The musician's expression softened.

The Summoned were rising slowly, a line of tar-black, silhouetted head-like shapes floating in terrifying unison toward them. Rose and Spire shifted closer. The shadows wafted back. Clara forced her eyes away from their mesmerizing abyss, which would derail them if she looked any closer.

"What's this note?" Clara asked the organist, then hummed, trying to match the sound wafting in and out of her hearing.

"An F," the man replied, matching it on the organ by playing a key with his left hand. He pulled out a stop with his right hand and laid a foot on a pedal, amplifying the sound in the space; it was almost too much for Clara to have it so prominent in her psychic ear and then rattling in her bones as well.

Her vision swam. Seizure symptoms. She drew a deep breath. *Not now,* she commanded her body. "Say . . . there was a discordant note against it," Clara posited. At this, the organist pressed the next key up the scale, maintaining the F and adding the sharp. Clara grimaced at the unbearable jangle of sound and pressed one hand to her ear. "Could you cancel it out?"

"I could resolve it," the organist offered.

"*Resolve* it. Yes!" Clara exclaimed. "That is exactly what we need."

The organist released the sharp to play an A, creating a harmonious interval, made fuller by his adding a C.

"Perfect," she murmured. "Could you hold that chord a bit?"

"Of course."

He pulled out all the stops and doubled the sound into a full chord in a higher octave, sending a magnificent trumpet blast out from gusting pipes that positively shook from the glorious force. The demons wafted back as if suffering a direct blow.

As Clara watched the buffeted forms trying to re-form their grim line, the density of their opaqueness thinned.

"I renounce thee," she spat at them. Rose and Bishop echoed her. The last of their essence faded in snuffed wisps.

Wind gusted through the chapel, carrying the smell of smoke, signaling that Evelyn and the reverend had found and destroyed the foul box outside.

The looming seizure vanished and Clara's breathing was less labored, particularly for Rose putting a hand to her back, invigorating her lungs with their bond. Bishop also reached out to brush her cheek with the soft benediction of his fingertips, and when he did, her clenching muscles released to ease.

Clara steadied herself, clapped, kissed the organist on the cheek in a burst of effusive thanks, then darted down the choir loft steps, skirts flouncing.

Bishop grabbed her hand once she dropped her skirts to the floor, and she did not break her stride as she looked about for any other foe, squeezing his hand and pressing his palm against her Ward, their bodies clumsily colliding as they moved, rushing out the back to make sure Blessing and Evelyn didn't need more help with what had tainted the building.

Rose and Spire continued to follow, hesitant to break the compass.

"Banished," Clara assured Evelyn and the reverend, who were standing by the grim box that now lay charred before an old grave, the reverend's Bible open in hand. Both colleagues sighed in tired gratitude.

"Thank you, Mr. Spire," Clara said, turning and bowing her head toward him in a gesture of deepest respect. "You did not question us and you did not break our corners. I do not know if you could see what we saw—"

"Something in the light and air changed between the four of us," Spire said, looking thoughtful. "That was followed by a literal *pull* upon my body. If there is an element of action and reaction physical enough to believe in, then I will do what it bids. Though I amend my skepticism only on those points."

"I'll never ask for more," Clara assured him, swaying on her feet. Bishop took her in his arms.

"Are you in a countdown?" he asked.

"I was. I believe it has passed. Our collected efforts afforded me the necessary shielding and shelter."

"Thank you for keeping everyone safe," Evelyn said, touching Clara's cheek with a fond hand. "Your instincts remain unmatched."

"I'll not rest on any laurels, but I'm glad they served us tonight," Clara said. "But as for us, I'm . . . at the end of my usefulness. Let's go home. . . ." She looked up at Bishop, and his soft smile was the most beautiful welcome to her invitation.

"Do rest," Rose bid her gently. "For we've no idea what the moving-picture demonstration might bring."

"At least I keep learning," Clara said to Bishop hopefully. "I can indeed hear things, now, and Mosley was right about a tone of cancellation; resolving a chord. We've another weapon in our counter-arsenal, navigating the paths of these dark turns."

"I'll take that as a triumph of the night," Bishop stated. He glanced back at the altar. "Love triumphed tonight. . . ."

Clara could not help but notice their new compass was created between two couples with great care for one another. Perhaps love, though she'd never speak for Spire or Rose in that regard. In all the ways love had triumphed thus far, it still had been decidedly under attack. What the shadows or whoever wielded them likely couldn't understand was the attacks only strengthened their truths. While her love had never been stronger, and her spirit never so steeled, she had never been so sure that the attacks were about to worsen.

* * * * *

Celeste knelt on the floor of her feminine sanctuary, her boudoir, her favorite place to conduct rituals and divination, dressed in a thin shift hanging low.

Her arms were outstretched to Collect. She faced east, the

better to feel the heartbeat connection of her magic along the transatlantic cable, an essence that snaked into her body with a tingling hand that caressed her heart and pumped her blood with greater pressure. But this had lessened, nearly stopped since Moriel's death. She'd have to renew her booster boxes set along the cable grounding point on the American and English shores, as something had cut her co-opting line to the quick, likely the same forces that had been pushing back against Moriel's final displays of doomed might.

A map of Manhattan lay on her lap, with dried drops of blood marking the places of the most supernatural disruption, places where her operatives were actively involved.

The night was alive with activity, and she flexed her fingers to direct it more specifically. As if she were pressing against a wall with her palm, there was a pushing back downtown, along Broadway, a direct shove against her measures to open the corridors of the Summoned wider to let more in. Closing her eyes, she could feel the push and pull. Surely, again, the meddlesome Sensitives who had caused so much trouble for Moriel along the way.

There was a muffled sound from down the hall, a shuddering cry and then silence. Lord Tantagenet breathed his last; she could feel his spirit leave, eager to get out of his poisoned body. She rose and looked in the mirror, touching her face; her eyes flashed as she felt the life force that had drained from him being usurped into her ravenous, insatiable aura.

For a moment she was glad she did not see ghosts, for if she did she knew she'd be haunted forever—not by sentiment but by specters lingering in anger and betrayal. The funeral arrangements were already in place; the body would be taken in the morning.

Then she would be free to unleash an enemy directly upon his foe, and keep them both busy while she engaged her next target. She'd leave New York with another spectacle to preoccupy itself with while she boosted all its power into her hands for her body to wield. Hopefully the clash of old enemies would leave them all dead. Good riddance, as her path to Washington needed to be clear.

TWELVE

From a ceremony to a vaudevillian exhibit of unfolding new technologies. All the world was a stage indeed, every day a new trial. If there weren't a true evil underpinning her city, Clara could have delighted in the occupations of her life. But her world was clutched in a vise grip. Recent events had Shakespeare close to mind. . . .

We make trifles of terrors, ensconcing ourselves into seeming knowledge, when we should submit ourselves to an unknown fear.

As the line was sourced from *All's Well That Ends Well,* she hoped she could live into that title.

It was a glorious late autumnal day in the small, tree-lined confluence of Fifth Avenue and Broadway that created Madison Square Park—clearly a Halloween week if ever there was one. This was Clara's favorite time of year, even if the perilously thin veil between mortal and spirit world was hazardous to her health.

When she and Bishop reached the park, Evelyn Northe-Stewart, dressed in a saffron day dress of frothy layers, moved to Clara's side, touched a satin-gloved hand to the embroidered roses adorning Clara's long-sleeved bodice, and indicated the passersby around them.

"Let's have a listen in on the city's sanity," Evelyn said of the crowds. Clara nodded and the two took a silent stroll along a paved path around a copse of trees. Glancing up at Liberty's torch, Clara saw nothing green but the touch of patina on the seams of copper. Between her Warding and Stevens's chemistry, the partial statue remained free from perversion. They were, by each event, she hoped, closing doors the Summoned and their new mistress, the mysterious Celeste named in blood and confirmed by Rachel, would have preferred remain open.

Clara listened closely to conversations of milling passersby, to gauge just how much the Society had managed to tear holes in the fabric of New York's sense of safety, wondering how effective the supernatural terrorism of the downtown displays, the torch or Columbia's shambling corpses had been.

After enough time for empirical discernment, the two Sensitives returned to a waiting Bishop, tall and elegant in black top hat and tailcoat. Clara found herself blushing at the sight of the small white rose she had affixed to his lapel that morning, plucked from the bouquet he'd given her. Bishop noticed her blush and his piercing eyes of mercurial colors flashed. They had nearly fallen into a passionate kiss when she had bestowed the flower this morning, but the clock reminded them they would be late for the rendezvous and their ache was again prolonged.

"Well, my dear senator," Evelyn began, returning them to the moment, "I am heartened to discern that New York as a whole, sampling tidbits of conversations from all walks of life and background, is wary, but not on a precipice. It takes New Yorkers more than a few bouts of weirdness to be thrown. Clara, do you agree?"

Clara turned her face toward the breeze to cool her suddenly enflamed cheeks. "I do."

"Our teams best keep it that way," Bishop declared, and strode over to Spire and Franklin, Clara at his side.

"I'm so sorry for missing the ceremony," Franklin blurted. "I was ill. I've sent my regards to the happy couple, please don't think me rude."

Clara shook her head in absolution of any slight. The dear heart still looked so tired, drawn, with dark circles under glassy eyes. She almost told him to go right back home again, as he clearly still needed rest, but as a woman with a condition she was adamant about not being dismissed and she wouldn't visit low expectations on anyone, instead trusting him to tell her if he was beyond capacity.

Lord Black had excused himself from today's rounds to liaise with the British embassy about site-specific tree and flower planting around English holdings to act as additional Wards.

Clara reached out her hand to run gloved fingers over the elegant, palm-like leaves of a nearby green locust, which signified affection from beyond the grave. This made her smile wistfully, thinking of city elders watching over the metropolis by way of these trees. She would suggest the city plant more locusts, invoking the affection, and thus, protection, of spirits who loved this city as their own. Lord Black had encouraged her to consider every living thing as bearing a message. She was listening.

Bishop turned to the group and began. "We'll be in the audience for today's presentation. Fred and Effie are already backstage beside a friend, a rail operator. We, honestly, don't know what to expect today. I hope you are all carrying Wards."

"And perhaps a concealed pistol," Spire added. Patting his pockets.

At this, Franklin gestured. Spire reached into an interior pocket and smoothly deposited a revolver tucked beneath his palm onto Franklin's outstretched hand. Clara, knowing Spire wouldn't have thought to bring a Ward, plucked a corked vial from her reticule and took the liberty of placing it in Spire's front breast pocket, tucking it behind his rumpled linen pocket square. He grimaced a sort of thanks.

"*I* received gifts from my doting Blakely!" Knight said of her beard of a spouse, necessary in a world that would not accept her preferences. She opened a small wooden case decorated with floral marquetry and pearl inlay to reveal several small steel guns with carved wooden handles. At the top of the box marched a row of odd ammunition: arrow-like bullets and suctions filled with powders and chemical agents.

"The darling had it sent to the safe house. Filled with his inventions and compounds," she said proudly. "Don't worry, they've all been tested."

"Yes, some of them on me," Spire retorted bitterly.

Knight laughed gamesomely. "I'd not be near to one when it goes off. Good for cover, distraction and disorientation, not good to breathe in."

"I can assure you of that truth as well," Spire added. Rose held back a chuckle.

Arms surreptitiously distributed, the cluster of operatives began to stroll to the famous Park Theatre, which years ago had made its name and fortune downtown on Park Row. Now a grand affair nestled on Broadway between Twenty-first and Twenty-second Streets, all stately splendor, with flourished corners and Romanesque arches of the kind that matched the lavish shopping palaces and other theaters in this entertainment district, each attraction trying to keep up with the next in gilded glamor.

As to be expected in a vaudeville format, there were several acts before the signature piece. There was a distinct time-table for this matinee performance and showcase, however, as another act was to take over the stage that night: the highly anticipated American debut of famed actress Mrs. Langtry.

Bishop procured tickets and mesmerized the ushers so his

assembled company could come and go from their seats without censure or alarm. He chose strategic seats, back from the orchestra pit so the mezzanine above shadowed them, and house right, near the aisle, offering a perfect view of the stage and the grand staircases between levels.

The curtain closed over the stage was a lush red velvet bare of any design, great golden tassels catching the glow of the footlights trimmed low. A pianist on a raised dais in the orchestra pit was playing gamesome modern tunes and the occasional French art song as they took their wooden seats upholstered with a similar red velvet.

A top-hatted maestro of ceremonies in a red tailcoat stepped out onto the stage, and a gas-lamp spotlight shifted to him. He was heavily made up, and his black mustache was waxed to an impressive curl on either side.

Welcoming everyone to the theater, he promised the audience a string of superlative adjectives scripted to excite an audience, but something about him seemed too nervous for Clara to feel anything but the same nerves. Not in empathy, but dread. That wasn't stage fright. That man was generally frightened.

He didn't introduce himself and seemed eager to get back off the stage. He scurried off before scurrying back on again, the mezzanine spotlight operator doing a figure eight with the great glass that magnified the lantern behind it before the light landed again on the man's sweaty face.

He introduced the next "girls," offered a few more hyperbolic statements about their bewitching beauty, and was off again.

The curtain rose.

Clara and Bishop stared with skepticism at the dancers, this all seeming a bit scandalous for Evelyn, to their left, who stared at the scantily clad ladies with a mixture of horror and pity.

Above them, Rose and Spire were positioned in a clear mezzanine vantage point.

Miss Knight, on the other hand, sitting to Clara's right, was beaming. She leaned over to Clara once the song had ended and the audience was clapping and whistling for an encore.

"Times like this, I miss the old days of touring with the Ciphers," she said. "The thrill of a stage or a tent, there's really nothing else like it."

"I wouldn't know," Clara murmured.

"But you can guess. You can remember, I'm sure . . ." For a moment Miss Knight stared deeply, startlingly, into her, and Clara almost felt like there had been a direct touch to her head, but Miss Knight's hands never left her lap. "About two lives ago you were what, a singer, weren't you?"

Clara thought a moment and a piercing memory struck her. She saw this scene but in reverse, from onstage, staring out at powdered faces and feathered heads, the base of the wooden stage set with the most primitive of flame footlights, when women were first allowed in French theater. That particular, trailblazing life of drama and pain, snuffed out in a gale of bourbon and tuberculosis, had been overshadowed in her memories by the boldness of the next; the French sea captain. Even her own sense of her past lives minimized the presences of women. She didn't need to be an additional part of that oppression.

Snapping back to the moment, Clara stared at the beautiful woman, who did nothing but wink at her. Goodness, Knight was gifted indeed. Clara stared at the whole spectacle with a bit more understanding and respect.

Bishop, his forearm continually brushing her elbow, seemed to be entirely unaware of the performance, instead examining the attendees and glancing at Clara frequently, to make sure nothing was affecting her adversely. Knight looked between them and rolled her eyes in exaggerated bemusement, as if their pining, impassioned awkwardness had now become a travesty.

She glanced at a deliberately, ostentatiously prominent velvet-covered box above and to her right. Within, staring with a furrowed brow at the stage, Clara noticed a familiar face. She leaned over to Bishop.

"Rupert," she said, gesturing with an incline of her artfully coiffed head. "Look up. Isn't that Mr. Edison?"

He followed her gaze. "Why, yes it is."

Before they could muse further about Edison and his aims, a woman dressed head to toe in onyx beading over black satin that made her pale face look ghostly beneath a tulle mourning veil stepped out from the wings toward the foot-lights, a stack of folded papers in her hands.

She gestured into the wings and indicated a spot center stage. Turning to look out at the audience, she held a stare for a long, uncomfortable moment before leaving the stage again, clutching the papers in both black-gloved hands.

When Clara glanced at Rupert, his brow was furrowed in recognition; she knew that look when he pinpointed some-one gifted. She had some of his mesmerism, perhaps, but something else altogether. Clara suddenly had a bitter taste in her mouth, as if the woman had created an alchemical shift in the air.

It was a curious turn, as Clara could see no purpose in it, as if someone of import had merely wandered onstage, find-ing themselves suddenly in a play when they ought to have been holding a grieving court somewhere.

The same nervous man from the beginning of the show stepped out again.

"A thank-you to our anonymous benefactor for this per-formance," he said, bowing in the direction of the woman in black.

Clara turned to Bishop with a pointed look. "I'm not a betting woman but . . ."

"The mysterious Celeste, perhaps?" he murmured. Clara and Bishop looked up at Rose and Spire, and the policeman was already on his feet, seemingly ready to charge down and enter backstage to arraign and question her.

"Ladies and gentlemen," the man said. "Now for the moment you have all been awaiting. Monsieur Carre has brought his equipment from Paris to showcase something marvelous. Something that will change the world. As humans we are entranced by pictures, paintings, daguerreotypes, and now photographs. What if they moved? What if they quite truly came to life?"

There was a murmur from the crowd.

Clara and Bishop shared a familiar, wary look. They'd been to plenty of lavish stage performances put on by sham spiritualists who were talented magicians, but no mediums, taking advantage of the grieving and the lost. Tricks of light and sound through mirrors and curtains, levers rapping on tables, anything was possible and much of it was quite convincing, and many phantasmagorical images "moved" via tricks of light and perspective.

Part of their job in the Eterna Commission, as gifted, *true* spiritualists, was to quietly shut down impostors and redirect their efforts to cue up a good magic trick, not the faux dead. The famed magician Houdini was championing this same cause, but with more passionate—and public—effect. Clara and Bishop couldn't begrudge anyone trying to make a living, and some of these people actually had the beginnings of the gift. Eterna did not wish to ruin lives, whether those of the performers or audience.

But did this event promise spirit or magic?

This man didn't bear the hallmarks of a charlatan spiritualist, and to Clara's mind it shouldn't have been this man speaking about it at all. The enigmatic woman should have presented and introduced the keynote innovative attraction.

The gas lamps lighting the stage suddenly shifted and a curtain parted to reveal a wide white screen, darkness of the theatrical abyss on either side.

The screen at the center of the stage began to glow. A golden frame was lowered via another rail.

Something about the shift of light and the depth between screen and frame set Clara on edge and she couldn't place why.

An indistinct sound grew from the back of the stage, a loud whisper, a droning chant. To Clara's ear, it broadened to a grating whine. From the spotlight operator's mezzanine perch there came an image placed over that broad lantern.

It was the image of a man in lavish, royal robes.

Clara and Evelyn gasped in unison while the rest of the audience was silent. This man's projected image meant nothing to them. Several people—including Miss Knight and Franklin—turned at the women's audible reaction, wondering if they were seeing part of the trick the rest of the audience wasn't yet aware of.

Would it were that simple. Clara and her friends had reacted because they were staring at their enemy, a face they would never clear from their mind's eye.

Moriel.

The projection was a portrait of Moriel in kingly robes.

A portrait.

With a shuffling, metallic clank, the image changed. Moriel in the same robed costume but with arms raised, triumphant, eyes wild and crown slightly askew. Another tick and a younger Moriel in a suit coat loomed before them. Then another, reaching toward the audience. Then another.

The sequence of daguerreotypes repeated, faster and faster.

With their jerking, unrelated movements, the six images

looked like a horrific marionette, dancing and flailing. Clara turned to Rose in the mezzanine, and the war-weary friends shared a helpless look. Spire was gone.

* * * * *

There was nothing wrong to the outside eye, Rose thought, so the Bixbys could not be given the cue to stop the show. Nonetheless, something had to be done. The pictures of Moriel were undoubtedly a signal to whatever Master's Society operatives still existed in this city.

Rose thought to follow Spire out the exit, but then the tether to Clara made her stay; she had to keep an eye on her to help if a seizure was imminent. Needing to be on her level, she rose and made to descend the carpeted stair, and was stopped by a whole new, terrible movement.

In that tense moment, a figure stepped through the image, making it three-dimensional and bringing it to life. There was now a shadow with Moriel's face. . . .

It moved forward.

Rose clamped down on a scream, her tie to Clara allowing her to feel her soul sister doing the same. Before she could move or make a sound, a small flame whizzed out of the audience, toward the stage.

Knight must have used one of her various projectiles. The image and then the screen vanished in a flash of flame and heavy smoke. Many in the crowd screamed as people ran for the exits.

A great gust of unnatural wind swirled around the stage, kicking up embers. Parts of the curtain and baffles caught fire. Screams from the audience appeared to fan the flames. Another whizzing sound and a second arrow landed on the contraption that was still cycling the images, Knight's aim impressive, a smoke rising up from around the wide glass, the operator darting away with a curse.

"Where did Moriel go?" Rose gasped. "He could be anywhere." She made for the orchestra level as Effie Bixby, dressed in a simple black cotton dress, spiral curls all back in a bun, appeared from an upper-mezzanine side door, having used a stagecraft passage to get herself to the upper levels, and examined the lantern and the device that was hooked over it, damaged as it was from Knight's weaponry.

The woman of the hour was nowhere to be seen as smoke began to fill the auditorium. The ringmaster was gone; so, too, was Edison. But where was the form that had been summoned by this display? Where was Moriel's shadow?

Amid the harried rush to exit the theater, Fred emerged from backstage, carrying papers in his hand, rushing directly to Clara, Bishop, and Franklin, who stood to the side trying to account for their team. Knight joined them, her weaponry held tight in folded arms, a scowl on her lovely face.

"I found something," Fred said, holding the papers out. Bishop took them for safekeeping and put them in his interior breast pocket. "They look like letters but they must be clues. I saw the ringmaster go out the back," Fred offered.

"I'll follow," Franklin said, darting back in the direction Fred pointed, weaving through the skittish crowd.

"To the street," Bishop instructed. Rose folded in with them, gripping Clara's hand instinctively. Moriel was a shock, but it wasn't enough to have triggered a seizure, not yet at least. Rose's healing touch eased the problematic tension that led to an episode.

"I think Mr. Spire went after the lady," Fred told Clara as their company joined the panicked throng heading for the least congested exit. Fire in a theater was nothing to wait out. "When she exited I heard him accost her with a proclamation of police. There was a dark shadow, pursuing."

They exited on the Twenty-first Street side. The bells of fire pump trucks clanged along Broadway in response to the reports of a fire.

The famed Mrs. Langtry evidently wouldn't get her debut there tonight after all.

Out on the street, their assembled team looked around for Spire.

Effie was examining a part of the projection equipment she'd managed to pry loose, frustrated she hadn't gotten more before they were evacuated.

"Now, about those papers," Clara said to Fred.

"I found these set down backstage," he said. "I think they belonged to the woman in black." Fred cleared his throat and adjusted his cotton neck cloth in discomfort. "They appear to be love letters. Odd ones, but, who am I to judge? Though something tells me there's a pattern here I can't quite see."

"May I see them?" Rose asked. Fred passed them to her, his hands shaking.

"Patterns and ciphers are, if you recall, Miss Everhart's specialty," came a voice from behind them. They turned to see a flushed Spire, out of breath, join them. "She's better with them than I am catching a waifish suspect," he muttered.

Evelyn gestured that they get out of the congested street and move toward the park.

"What happened, Mr. Spire?" Clara asked as they walked.

"I followed the woman, thinking she might fit the bill via Miss Horowitz's suggestions: an anonymous benefactor of new industry. When she saw me approach, she set down the papers in her hands and darted out a rear stage exit. I made pursuit, and called after her. That's when I lost my way. A darkness fell all around me and I couldn't see a thing. I tripped on cobblestones and when I righted myself, she was down the street like a flying ghost, a Summoned shadow tearing off after her. Why it was following her when we are known targets, I couldn't tell you. Perhaps it was just following its mistress."

"But that was Moriel," Clara said.

"The shadow came through Moriel's picture, but we've no idea if that silhouette is Moriel, and how could we know?" Spire countered.

They came to the corner of the park and paused, Rose sifting through the pages.

"These are love letters indeed," Rose reported after inspection. "Between an 'M' and a 'C.'"

"'M' for 'Moriel,' perhaps, and 'C' for 'Celeste,' from the suicide note you found?" Clara posited.

"Surely," Evelyn replied. "Had Lord Denbury been with us, I'm sure he would have seen that her aura bore the telling hellfire color of the demons. Tonight I will see if the spirits can help me discern more, now that I have been in her presence."

"There *is* something else here," Rose began. "A pattern, but deeply buried. A cipher. Good eye, Mr. Bixby." Hearing this praise, Fred beamed. "May I take this to the safe house?" Rose asked generally, not sure who could give permission. "I need my books to speed the translation."

Spire, Bishop, and Clara looked at one another and shrugged.

"I'll escort you downtown," Clara offered.

"We've got to see to Gran again, she weathered her latest bout, thank God, but we'll be continuing to check along the docks as Apex is still likely doing damage and the more folks are warned the better," Effie said. "I'll enlist Franklin to help in this, too, once he's returned."

"I can peruse as many city records as might contain a Celeste, I know that's a needle in a haystack, but I'll do what I can," Fred offered. Bishop said his thanks to the siblings.

"I wish I could take everyone out to supper," Bishop explained, "but I must pin down the mayor, who has been avoiding me. Tonight he dines with a number of captains of industry that I managed to invite. I cannot miss this opportunity to speak to them all at once. I've arranged for Lord Black to come with me to help charm them."

Spire turned to Evelyn. "Miss Horowitz wrote to you about her concerns, yes?" Spire asked. "May I examine all your correspondence? Perhaps a clue will come to mind, something I haven't drawn a connection to just yet."

"By all means," Evelyn replied gladly. "Come with me and I'll open the study to you, where suitable amenities await. A glass of whiskey will take the edge off a failed chase," she offered, and Spire attempted a strained smile.

A few blocks away, the column of smoke from the theater was now black and ominous.

Once a carriage had been flagged for Clara and Rose and the two had climbed in, they were quiet at first during the trundling trip downtown, each looking out the parted curtains of the glass-paneled windows covered in a film of the city's innumerable particulate exhalations.

"How are you?" Rose asked. Clara turned to her.

"I am weary of one task after the next, desperate for it to crest to the same kind of battle like we all fought across Embankment. If nothing else I long to feel a sense of focus and accomplishment; this ebb and flow is unsustainable. But I am grateful for new talents, new emotions, and new possibilities . . ." Clara finished, a small smile playing at the corner of her mouth now whenever she thought of Bishop.

"I believe it is hard for us to express the true bent of our hearts, is it not?" Rose asked. Clara nodded. "We keep stalwart company."

"That we do. And despite the knowledge of mutual care, I simply don't know how to begin," she said quietly. "How to exchange something stable for something passionate."

"Nor do I. I would love for a day just to enjoy the company of a man I've come to so treasure, with no other requirement but delight," Rose stated. "To enjoy the bonds this work has created without the dreadful nature of it intruding."

Clara nodded. Their compass rose of dear souls was forged out of the deepest respects. She did not press Rose for a communal dinner; she could see her friend needing to work on the puzzle as if it were an opiate and she were addicted. It was something to seize upon and solve and that drive was tantamount. Clara understood.

She, too, needed meditative time. Her relationship to ley energy, and to time itself, was a lesson she needed to let settle in, digesting like an ancient meal across her many lives.

Taking warm leave of Rose, Clara bid her luck on deciphering, and arrived home. Harper had prepared simple food, soothing peppermint tea, and saw to it that modest fires were stoked. Glad for the quiet, Clara dined alone with more candlelight than was her custom, lit Wards sitting amid the tapers.

Her lives, the way with time, the sound of energies, were all becoming more and more under her control. She did not feel as helpless as she used to, when her seizures were at their worst. This gift was a new expansion and evolution.

Clara had never felt so powerful. Which meant, she thought with sinking surety, that something even more terrible would come to challenge her.

Ever more aware of energies sapping her, she had to take quiet moments when she could, and she undid her bodice, corset, and doubled skirts, her clothing fine enough to pass in high society but never so much as to require a lady's maid in such a capacity. In her chemise and petticoat, she put on a quilted and lace-decked robe and lay upon her boudoir fainting couch for a meditative rest.

After a time, something woke her. Upstairs there was odd movement. Scraping. Was someone intruding?

After darting to her small boudoir fireplace to grab the

poker, Clara opened her door a crack. Rupert's study lights were bright and he was half-dressed in shirtsleeves and waistcoat. She let the poker clatter to the floor, throwing open the door and stalking to his threshold.

"What are you doing?" she demanded. He turned to her at his desk and arched an eyebrow.

"Hello, my dear," he countered. It escaped neither of their attention that she was only in her nightdress and she hadn't bothered to button it up all the way.

"Where are you going?" she asked, gesturing to his open briefcase, lying on the desk, a scatter of papers tossed within.

"To Washington," he replied. "I've had quite a night. After a frustrating dinner with the mayor and industry, after which I went to Chief Patt directly to explain our latest concerns and clues, 'Celeste' and all, and being thoroughly dismissed, I was then tracked down and given this. From the president." He handed her a telegram that had been encrypted, bearing the Secret Service symbol. She recognized his own handwriting below as he decoded the typewritten message.

STRANGE SHADOWS IN CORNERS OF EXECUTIVE MANSION. PLEASE COME IMMEDIATELY. TELL NO ONE.

The seal of the president followed the text. Clara looked back at Bishop, wide-eyed.

"The reverend and I will go to the capital in response, on the pretense of the National Cathedral commission," Bishop continued. "His friend at the diocese can give us access to all sacred spaces in the District. From there we can assess the situation and what to do next."

"But . . . You're going without me?" Clara tried to process a burgeoning panic. "Leaving when I was sleeping? Do you give me no courtesies?"

"I was about to come and tell you—"

"I *should* go with you. It's unheard of, really. 'The heart of the matter,' you say; you praise my gifts and instincts, am I not an asset?"

"Clara," Bishop sighed. "Of course I want my greatest asset with me, but in a secondary wave. After I respond to the president directly. I think you'll be of more help here, tracking 'Celeste,' the city's changing energies and lines, and helping with what Rose finds. As women, you and she will have access if she's captured. I've already wired Chief Patt that he must advise you. Whether he'll listen or not may be our downfall," Bishop muttered.

"I think you're being too careful with me," Clara said, trying to stay calm. "Don't let the bent of our hearts now mean you treat me differently. You know I won't stand for that." She folded her arms.

Bishop sighed. "Clara, believe me when I tell you that I've every intention of bringing you along provided I can account for additional cover, clearances, and safety for the whole team. Washington is a different creature from New York, Clara. It lives in its own little world, one that changes people from the districts we represent, often into something monstrous and amoral. The president could be paranoid and I'll not drag everyone out there if that's the case."

She scowled. "We had very few safeties in England—"

"This is different—"

"I don't see that it is, Rupert. Don't treat me like I'm your ward again when we're *well* past that. I insist we move *well* past that," she stated, lowering her eyes at him, trying her damnedest to actually *say* what she needed.

He advanced upon her, a desperate light in his mesmeric gaze.

"I'm sorry. I want nothing to revert, everything to progress . . . All I've ever done has been for your safety and happiness," he said, his breath suddenly hot against her neck as he closed the distance between them. "For years I've been terrified the evil energies of the world would come for my bright treasure, burgeoning with gifts and powers, all the more a target." He grasped her by the arms, pressing against her, his forehead to hers, his breath ragged.

"Clara, you're such a magnet, you're such a light, if darkness came for you before I could—" His voice broke; his hands fluttered at her cheeks as if he wished to cup them. There was hardly space between their bodies anymore, and she was nearly against the wall.

Clara smiled. He seemed taken aback.

"What?" he said, wary of the shift in her expression.

"I realize it is hard to love something and be scared to lose it," she murmured. "But we can't live in fear." He stared at her, a bit wide-eyed. "Oh, don't be a coward," she exclaimed, pulled him to her by his unbuttoned waistcoat, and planted her lips directly on his.

It was a delicious, torturous, near-violent kiss, an instant explosion that spoke of years of their pent-up desires.

Clara's hands swept up to claw at his shoulders, rake his neck, and grab his thick mop of luminously silver hair. He returned the force of passion, snaking his arms behind her back to hold her tight, pressing her against the wall.

After countless moments he pulled away, both of them gasping for air, hearts pounding against one another. His hands remained a vise grip around her.

"Well *that's* about time . . ." Clara murmured.

"I'm sorry that I don't always know what's best to do," Bishop murmured after a long moment, running his nose along her temple, kissing her brow. "Worry ties me up in knots but my desire to see you as free and independent will always win, though not at cost to your safety if I can at all help it."

"You always help," Clara said, caressing his cheeks. "I will stay here for the next two days to follow up on our leads. But you, in turn, must promise that you and the reverend won't just charge in anywhere, the two of you, without reinforcements. Promise?"

"I do. Fair."

Clara stared at him, now that concerns were settled, neither of them ready to relinquish their grip upon the other. She smiled again. Another furious kiss.

"Now what . . . ?" she murmured in his ear.

"Now what, what?" he replied, drawing back.

"Are we . . ." She trailed off, allowing her expression and tone to become suggestive.

"Going to get married?" he stammered. "Of course we are, I'd never impugn your honor!"

Clara chuckled at his blustering insistence. "I didn't mean proposing this minute, Senator." She sighed and shook her head. He was so terrified of saying or doing the wrong thing when it came to her, his generally stoic and assured behavior turned flustered. It was both endearing and maddening.

He retreated an unsure step, his hands sliding down from behind her back, glancing over her hips, and then he clenched his fists at his sides. When he looked away, she noticed that his leather travel bag was lying out open on the floor beside his desk.

"You're taking the night train, aren't you," Clara said with disappointment.

"I was planning to, yes, per the request of 'immediately,' " Bishop said with evident discomfort, as if staying the night with her was as titillating as it was overwhelming.

"Very well then," Clara said. "Shall I pack your bag? You know I'm fond of our rituals."

He raked a hand through his mussed hair. "If you step into my room I . . . doubt I'd be able to control myself."

"Will you come kiss me good night before you walk out the door?" she countered.

Bishop cleared his throat and spoke carefully. "If I were to come to your bed to kiss you, my dearest, in matters of control, I am *sure* I would have none."

Clara saw that the dear man was visibly trembling, he loved, and wanted her, that much. She felt a bit faint realizing the magnitude.

"Gives us something to look forward to, then, I suppose?" she murmured, her cheeks flooding with heat as she dared to imagine spending an inseparable night together . . .

"Like nothing I've ever wanted," Bishop murmured. "But for now . . . Please leave me to it, you beautiful creature, lest you unravel me further . . ." He was staring at the descending line of her nightdress, which had come almost completely open in their passionate embrace.

If Clara had ever been trouble to him, she was glad it was now in this way, now when they were ready for such unwieldy passions, now when she could truly handle herself and hold her own.

"Be safe, my love," she demanded, moving to the threshold.

"I will, my love," he replied, relishing the word "love," his eyes still all fire.

She blew him a kiss and walked away.

The letters between Lord Beauregard Moriel and the woman, C—Lady C, according to the pages—were stuff and nonsense, Rose determined. Meaningless drivel about flowers and the weather, nothing of actual import, which made no sense. No one went to the trouble to write of such mundane goings-on, to offer such hackneyed phrases of affection, when planning to destroy a national government. By using demons.

Their true meaning would take time to decipher. Her codebooks might provide shortcuts, make things quicker, but it would still be a long night. Thankfully Lord Black had made sure that the small kitchen was fully stocked with stores of tea and simple foods so she could focus on the task at hand.

What was the purpose of these letters? And why had they been abandoned at the theater? Spire said she set them down before running out. If they were truly important to her, she'd have run with them. Rose was certain that her compatriots were meant to find them, and that was as unsettling a notion as any.

* * * * *

Evelyn Northe-Stewart had kept Rachel Horowitz's letters in a black lacquered box as ominous in looks as its contents. Ensconced in the den that had originally been the purview of her first husband, Peter, Harold Spire carefully reviewed each one, looking for ties between the woman they'd seen today,

that eerie, black-clad figure he'd chased, and the woman
Horowitz had warned them about. When Evelyn came to see
what progress he'd made, politely ignoring the cloud of cigar
smoke that floated through the room, he was pleased to share
his thoughts.

"This young woman, through contact with you, your
family, and the Society," Spire began, "began to wrestle with
the idea that the written word, the power of the name, was
the oldest magic of all. Now don't get me wrong, I do not
believe in magic, but there is something gratifying to me
about moving away from the idea of old crones standing
around pots stirring and cursing in meter."

Evelyn nodded in agreement. "Indeed, Mr. Spire. The
power of the name isn't like a thunderclap sent from a magic
wand, but it does focus energy, coalesces meaning and determination, for better or worse, and that in and of itself has
practical effects."

Spire looked at the material Miss Horowitz had gathered
as haphazard evidence, splayed before him across a gilded
writing desk. One note caught his eye, in careful, looping
script:

*Messages revealed as an invocation ritual were found written in
code at a slaughterhouse site. As an associate was attempting to
decipher, the spirits told me to burn the note immediately; that
devils would come through. I grabbed the note and put it into the
lantern, to the detective's chagrin, and the invocation was ruined
forever.*

Spire looked up, showing Evelyn the note that gave him
pause.

"What then about those letters from today?" he asked.
"The ones that Rose took?"

"An invocation ritual by which devils would come

through . . ." Evelyn murmured. She looked at him and her color paled. "A summoning spell."

When the words sank in, Spire felt ill.

Summoning spell.

Spire jumped up. "Rose is decoding the letters now . . ."

Evelyn followed him as he rushed out of the study. "Dear God . . ."

Rose would bring the devils right to her. Not that Spire believed in ghosts or demons, but Rose had been a target before. She was known to the perpetrators and he would take no chances. The Summoned he had seen with his own skeptical eyes, and as much as he'd tried to pretend it was just the power of suggestion, he *felt* their evil press upon his skin, his heart, his mind. He prayed—if there was a God, something else he was not sure of—that Rose would survive this night unharmed.

He ran out the door, his hostess calling after him.

"Gather everyone you can," he called back over his shoulder at her front door. "Our safe house may no longer be so. Regroup the team at the Eterna offices."

He was already down the block and up on a horse he untethered from a nearby post by the time Mrs. Northe-Stewart flung open her front door to follow. He'd return the animal once he was certain Rose was safe. It occurred to him that nothing else in the world mattered—had ever mattered—so much as this.

* * * * *

Rose was so focused on the letters she didn't notice the fog rising in the room. Working through the phrases, she'd slowly puzzled out the hidden messages in the texts. Long ago she'd learned not to read for meaning when decoding. Instead, she would record the deciphered symbols in order, avoiding drawing conclusions that might prompt an incorrect letter or number. Only when she read the entire phrase did the whole of the exercise fall into terrifying place.

"I summon you from the depths of time. I draw you from human misery and manifest you now. By blood you will take elemental form. Shadows, come to darken mortal skies."

Rose's throat constricted as the air grew thin. Coughing, she recalled that terrible moment back in London when dark shadows accosted her and she was knocked unconscious. This felt the same.

She stared at her writing, a dark spell working terrible magic. The paper rustled slightly in a wind that could not be present in her sealed room, yet was.

Between her unadorned wooden desk and the blank wall of the safe house, a dim speck hovering in midair expanded into a shimmering portal, through which she could see dark shadows darting along a gray corridor.

At the other end, barely glimpsed beyond the undefined shapes, was a spot of light. And in it, Clara.

Feeling desperate, Rose opened her mouth to ask for help . . . only then realizing that across these walks of life and death, her soul sister was also under attack.

CHAPTER

FOURTEEN

Clara lay back in her bed, taking passionate thoughts with her, eager for the time when she and Bishop could truly give over to one another. She could not sleep.

Ever since she'd said good-bye to Rose she felt something was off in the air, an odd ringing in her ears, and she hoped that was not a new epileptic symptom. Once she'd begun making connections to ley-line energy and discerning the difference of a co-opted industrial hum, she had to make sure she wasn't hearing things just by thinking of them, a psychosomatic paranormal response.

Mosley's words echoed in her mind; a great power was routing itself to her. And it wasn't electrical. The hum was, truly, undeniable, and as the strange man with that precarious relationship to the current predicted, the sound was rising. Surging. She shuddered to think what floated along the crest.

A beacon in reverse, the absence of light wanted her luminosity. Now that she could wield certain powers directly, shift time and energy with her lives and the lines, she was all the more visible to all parts of the spirit world, across the spectrum of intent.

Thinking of Rose, as she sat up suddenly, stock-still, unable to relax, she could feel her reaching out in the most basic of human impulses: a hand reaching for another hand.

Rose was nearby, Clara could feel her, but there was a cloud. Something of friction and interference.

Glancing worriedly at her writing desk, she noticed there were two spent Wards in small, decorative glass bottles upon her desk. They'd used so many and it was impossible to keep up with the demand. Could she relight them with any effect? Perhaps the material she'd worn like a poultice for the wedding . . . she'd placed it on her nightstand.

With a muttered curse she jumped up to remedy the vulnerability, grabbing the fabric and placing it under her robe, but with a sickening certainty she realized she was too late. At this point, the Summoned didn't need an invitation; they knew right where to find her.

The temperature dropped drastically as a shudder raced down her spine and her hair stood on end—but only on her right side. With one hand on a lit taper, moving to relight the cold Wards, she slowly turned her head, looking to her right.

A Summoned shadow lurked in the corner of her room. A cold black silhouette against the warm, cherry-paneled walls. Behind it, a vague rectangle began to shimmer, reminding her of the portal she'd seen in London, and the dark rectangles seen in the air when her lives had spread out before her. She was standing between worlds.

Staring into this seemingly endless, incorporate shaft, she understood with growing wonder that when facing death, it wasn't that your life flashed before your eyes; instead, it appeared as a series of frozen moments framed within. You crossed the threshold toward death and looked back on life. But she wasn't ready to die.

What would close the corridor? How could she hold to this world, this life?

Without Rose, without Bishop or Spire, could she be the whole of the compass? That was the only thing she had seen defeat this manifestation before. She had to be. No knight in shining armor was coming to rescue her.

For all that there was of import about the *team,* those precious dynamics as a part of a web of love-spun magic, at the end of the day, in the solitude of single consciousness, the human mind was alone. Even psychics were sole souls, for all their talk of interconnectivity.

Anything alone was an easier prey.

This is likely what the shadows had wanted all along: to separate them, to make them feel alone. Helpless. Then pick them off one by one.

The shadow in her room wafted closer, and the lightless silhouettes within the corridor took note of the movement.

Dimly down that corridor, Clara thought she saw Rose, also surrounded by shadows. A protective, sisterly rage bubbled up within her and what would have been the early countdown to a seizure was delayed by the emotional and energetic response.

Just as the transatlantic cable carried messages between continents, Clara's spiritual lines connected her to Rose and Rose to her. They were tied, no matter the distance. She murmured Rose's name and felt that sisterly press upon her palm, there when she called for it, just as she'd asked, desperate.

Clara watched as the echoes of her previous selves marched out around her, folding out from her in that peculiar accordion stretch of lives and time, each of them wafting just to the edge of that perilous portal but stopping, her ship captain self drifting to stare directly into the eyeless void that was the Summoned sentry.

"I renounce thee . . ." she exclaimed. This kept the shadow in the room and the others at the mouth of the corridor back, but the portal remained open.

Fumbling, trying to take advantage of the time her lives were buying her, she turned, in a slow, aching swivel, to her desk and grasped one of the cold Wards in a shaking hand. At her touch it smoked, reacting to her energy. She had to close that portal. If she did not, shadows would spill out all over her, then the city. She had to do *something*.

Trying to listen for the positive hum of Manhattan's natural ley line, she deemed it too faint against this dread press; even though it was easier to feel at the tip of the island, she could not seem to magnify it beyond the light note in her own ear.

On her desk was a small box containing treasures she pored over at least once a month: a small cross; a flower from her mother's grave, pressed in glass; an old letter from Mary Todd Lincoln, thanking twelve-year-old Clara for services rendered, bringing messages from her dead loved ones. Her psychic imprint was rich upon those small things.

She gathered up meaningful things, those symbols of life everlasting, and lifted the neatly trimmed gas lamp from the desktop, realizing only as she touched it that the base of the lamp was burning hot. The hiss of pain sucked through her teeth sounded like an amplified pit of vipers to her own ear, agony returning her to herself.

Her lives echoed her renunciation of the devils in a whisper through time.

Grounded by the compass field of her lives, jarred into focus by the pain of the burn, she used what strength she had in this suspended state—a netherworld that did not operate in the same laws of physics that governed everyday moments.

Again crying the exorcism liturgy of renouncement, thinking of Mr. Spire casting lit Wards at Moriel, she heaved everything at the portal. The Ward, the objects of meaning, and the lamp all passed through the foreground demon in a burst of multicolored light before hitting the flocked wallpaper and clattering to the floor.

Time, weight, and gravity returned to normal as the corner of her room burst into an immediate bonfire. Only now did she notice the tar-like pitch oozing from the portal threshold, fuel to the fire. Her lives slammed back into her with a pummeling blow and she flung open her door with a cry.

She ran into the hall. Harper was darting up the stairs toward her.

"Clara—"

"Fire! Get *out,* now," Clara shouted, rushing past the older woman, knowing she was racing not just the flames but now a seizure. Somewhere in the chaos one of the first symptoms must have started. She had only a few minutes.

Her legs were trembling even as she ran; tremors set her teeth clattering against her tongue. The taste of blood then blank warmth, taste gone—the first of her senses disappearing like a wire snipped from connection with one of Edison's dynamos.

Flinging open the front door of her home, Clara fled onto the street, feeling the cool night air penetrating her robe for an instant before the sensation vanished. There went touch. Smoke was acrid in her nose, near to choking her. Then the scent disappeared, though she kept coughing.

Extending what was left of her consciousness, she tried to feel Rose, to find Bishop; she couldn't tell what or who she connected to, but she found something—an infusion of strength that bought her enough time to reach the Eterna offices up the block. Giving a look back over her shoulder, she saw Harper standing out in front of the house, directing neighbors who had come to help, waiting for the fire brigade whose bells Clara could hear—for the moment.

Sight remained, along with a desperate desire to reach sanctuary—the office, where she could lie down and let the seizure happen in a safe, quiet place. . . . Sight allowed her to see people staring at a woman running down the street in her nightdress. Clara did not care.

When Bishop had guards installed in the Eterna offices, he'd required them to be there at all hours. Both were dozing as Clara crashed against the door to fumble with the knobs. The sound jarred them awake and they ran to help. When they opened the door she fell inward and to her knees.

Her vision was beginning to tunnel. Someone grabbed her from behind, lifting her. She had no capacity to scream.

Into her peripheral vision she saw Rose, thrust against her. Swimming into her other eye, her sight having trouble focusing, was Harold Spire, looking as pale as the ghosts he refused to believe in. He and the guards helped carry both lethargic bodies up to Clara's office.

Thank goodness intuition had told her not to set the trip wire when she last left the office, so their pass up the stairs went unimpeded.

Spire deposited them squarely in the middle of the room upon a fine Persian rug and sat close between, his eyes wide with anxious concern. Dimly she registered golden light behind Spire's head, coming in from the office window. The fire. It surely had grown.

"You're all right, my dear ladies," he murmured. "You'll be all right," he insisted. His were the last words—accented by fire bells—that she registered before hearing failed.

Sight remaining with her unto the end, Clara could see that Rose was neither dead nor bleeding, but fading. She lay back, reaching out to clasp Clara's hand as Spire placed his hands on both their shoulders protectively, part of their compass connecting. Something of this act allowed Clara to let the seizure come, now overdue but as safe as it could be.

While sensation was numbed, she could see her body go rigid as though she were turning to stone, her muscles prickling, burning, and clenching in shuddering spasms.

The spirit world was thick in her mind, the weight of purgatorial corridors heavy and close as if she were buried in

sand; the sixth sense always the last to go. The creeping tendrils of shadow were the last things Clara felt as she faded to
seizure black.

* * * * *

Clara woke up not in stages but in a rush, as if she had been
doused with water. Everything hurt. She was lying on a floor.
Where was she? A searing panic had her sitting up, the immediate wooziness had her lying back down.

She could smell smoke and see an orange glow outside.

Her memory came back in a wild rush and she began to
cry, turning away from the window. Her house was gone. All
her books, a few treasures from her family, everything she
possessed, gone. It wasn't fair, but then again, very little was,
especially for people in her line of work. At least she was
alive. *Be grateful,* she thought, trying to rally herself.

Rose was lying still and peaceful next to her. Asleep or
unconscious, Clara could not tell. Harold Spire was still on
the floor with them, having backed up to sit against the wall,
dozing.

The sickening feeling that something was off, not right,
had not left her mind or body. Generally a seizure resolved
the sense of dread. Here it was heightened. As she listened to
Rose breathing, Clara gauged the shadows of the room. The
hairs on her whole body rose in a slow, subtle wave.

A low, ominous bell rang downstairs.

In Lavinia's nook hung three bells. When Lavinia judged a
visitor, she'd ring to signal their intentions: friendly, neutral, or
dangerous. The dangerous bell—the deepest of the three—had
never been rung by Lavinia in all their years together. Now it
was clanging wildly.

Lavinia was not here.

Yet *something* was ringing danger.

Clara wanted to scream. Would the horrors give her no
peace? A moment's respite?

Rose began to rouse. Spire was up and alert thanks to the ghost-rung bell, bending over them both.

"Hello, ladies, welcome back," he murmured with relief, peering at them both before looking toward the stairs. "But why is that bloody bell clanging on?" He darted downstairs to see what all the racket was about.

"Rose," Clara mumbled, her tongue thick, her mind ahead of her body. She was in desperate need of water but it was a floor away. "Wake up. Rose, I'm not well, can you . . ."

The Englishwoman blinked up at Clara. "Where am I?"

"At the Eterna offices, but something's wrong. Maybe an intruder," she said quietly. Wouldn't she have heard an intruder? A living one, yes, but . . .

The remaining glow of the fire outside cast a frightening orange pall over the room, over their faces.

She tried again to lift Rose at least to a sitting position, one of her buttons catching the edge of the rug and tugging on it as she propped Rose up.

Her eye caught on something on the floorboard. A word stared up at her.

HELL

Carved into the floorboards . . . Clara lifted the carpet higher.

HELL IS HERE

She turned her head, bile suddenly churning with a violent lurch.

No. Not her offices.

"Rose," Clara gasped.

She could feel an unprecedented second seizure about to start.

Her offices were tainted.

"Rose, I need your help . . ." Clara cried.

"Yes, yes, Clara." Rose rubbed her head, her eyes, coughed. She put her hand out to steady herself and knocked over a vial on the floor. "What's wrong . . ."

Oh, God. The Wards. Spire had evidently taken spent Wards from Clara's office desk and set them around the perimeter of their incapacitated bodies, in an effort to keep protective watch, but in an already tainted space, it was an extra danger, a fouled space rendering the Wards moot.

They would become choked out. Dead just like Louis when he created the Wards in the first place, their lives snuffed out, taking the whole Eterna research team under in a violent suffocation.

Panic threatened to undo her utterly. She didn't know what to say or how to move; her jaw began to chatter.

"I may seize again, Rose. . . . This office, tainted . . ." She grabbed Rose's hand and put it down on the carved board to show her.

This snapped Rose into action, finally clearing the fog from her mind and vision.

Six silhouettes, Summoned shadows inky black, lightless and in vague human forms, the very picture of dread despair, peeled from the wallpaper as if they'd been waiting in hiding all along.

The bell rang again from downstairs, clanging an unbearable note, declarative of the danger they were now too late to avoid. Their death knell.

"Bloody hell!" Spire cried. "There's no one ringing that bell."

"Harold!" Rose screamed. Spire ran up the stairs to see the demons drifting closer and he cursed again. These shadows did not wait politely at the threshold as they had in her room, a space that was not the invitation that these carvings had become. Who had carved them was a mystery for another moment, if they lived long enough to solve it.

From around the shadows' airborne feet, issuing from their inhuman absence of life, their unnatural reversal, they exuded exhalations of death. . . . A distinct, sulfuric smoke rose and swirled in the room, behaving not as smoke would, but its own animate force, there to strangle and snuff.

Clara thought, dimly, that she was about to experience how Louis died, a thought through a glass. She tried to suppress her terror long enough to elongate time in this thickening air, trying to again cast out her many selves. But her body failed her. Having so recently seized, and on the verge of another seizure, she had nothing left.

"Clara . . ." Rose whispered, a soft cry. Then her throat constricted. A gasping cough. Rose managed to get to her knees as Spire hoisted Clara to hers.

The air grew closer; the mist of oppressive pall clouded up the entire office into a gray, opaque, sightless night, rooting their bodies and souls and stilling their breaths. The three of them stumbled as Spire was dragging them toward the threshold.

A shattering sound pierced the air, then a loud thud. Something hurled through the windows. The fog around them lessened, drained by a hole in the window. They took shaking breaths of lighter air.

Another sound of shattering glass, a pounding sound of something heavy, then sounds at the front door. More glass breaking.

Feet running upstairs. A voice.

"I renounce thee, I renounce thee," came a strong, youthful voice. Joe. Josiah. That trusted, wondrous boy, Clara thought with a flood of thankfulness. With one hand, he held a kerchief against his face to block the smoke and noxious odor. In his other hand, he held a silver dispenser.

Clara felt drops of water on her head, thrown about the room. Holy water. He had learned well from his idol Reverend Blessing. She could feel herself being picked up into Spire's arms.

"Help Rose, please," Spire pleaded, choking out the words.

"I've got her, come on," Josiah insisted, tying his kerchief around his mouth and nose as a mask. His young, strong hands pulled Rose toward the door.

"I renounce thee, I renounce thee," Josiah repeated over and over against the demons' approach. Blessing's trusted right hand was not far behind Josiah: Evelyn Northe-Stewart came charging up with Bible in one hand, nearly screaming texts before the smoke got to her and she gagged, a cross held out prominently in the other.

Clara's vision swam. Rose was coughing. As she was carried by a straining, choking Spire, Rose was walked out, Josiah helping her, while Evelyn took up the rear, facing the hovering, approaching shadows. Tucking the Bible to her chest the medium cupped a lace cuff of her sleeve at her nose, but still held out the cross with her other hand, struggling to speak the scriptures of protection and banishment as she edged away. Everyone coughed and gagged against the acrid, toxic air.

They all leaned heavily on the rail as they tried to inelegantly descend the flight to the front landing. Once they crossed the empty hall, the guards gone, perhaps helping with the fire, Josiah flung open the front door and the group tumbled toward the street, collapsing on a stoop a few addresses west.

"How did you know to help us, Josiah?" Spire asked before another coughing fit.

"When I first started working for the senator, he asked me to keep an eye on the house and offices as often as I could. So I make rounds whenever I can. Everyone was so focused on the burning house, even the Eterna guards. When I saw something wrong here, I thought to do what the firemen do; break windows to let smoke out. I didn't know it wasn't a natural smoke until inside when it smelled all strange and sulfur-like—"

"You brilliant child," Clara gasped. "Saved our lives."

"You called me family, remember, that's what we do," Josiah said with a grin. "Now breathe deep, get all that smoke out. I'm so sorry about this, and for your house, Miss Clara, it's too much," he said sadly.

The countdown to a second seizure was well under way. Terror perhaps had its uses in having staved it off thus far. But as an aftershock seizure like this had never happened, she was in entirely uncharted waters and didn't know if her body would again fail in sequence or all at once.

Clara clawed at Rose's forearm clumsily. "I may fade . . . Again . . ."

Rose clamped her hand on Clara, creating a renewed frisson of energy between them. "Stay with me," Rose demanded, her voice scratchy and broken from the acrid smoke.

"What now?" Josiah asked.

"What can I do?" asked Spire, coughing again, this time into a handkerchief, then grimacing at a black substance marring the fabric, a mixture of smoke and the acrid airborne poison made when Summoned entered tainted rooms. He wadded up the linen and tossed it onto the cobbles.

"Clara is about to have another seizure, we need to get her someplace safe," Rose explained.

"Nowhere is safe," Clara moaned.

"Come back to me," Evelyn demanded, and went ahead toward greater traffic to hail carriages as another figure rushed up to them in a tearing huff.

Clara's vision blurry, she shrank back, cowering behind

Josiah with a pathetic whimper. She didn't want to be attacked any more. . . . Rest . . . God, she needed *rest*. . . .

"It's Lord Black, Miss Clara, don't worry," Josiah said gently, pressing his hands on hers, steadying her. "And Miss Knight, too."

"My friends, thank God you're all right!" the nobleman exclaimed, breathlessly. "After dinner with the senator, I remained out, convincing a few magnates with British investments to take Warding to a more direct level. I raced downtown as soon as I was wired on the senator's trip. When the safe house door was found open, and the bells all clattering here, I feared the worst! What happened?"

Spire tried to answer but was still short of breath.

"Well, first there was a fire in Miss Clara's house," Josiah explained. "I saw that after it started. When I went looking for where she'd gone, I noticed smoke in her office so I broke the windows to get them out. The devil's smoke though, sir, is something terrible."

"What happened to Louis," Clara stammered. "Tainted. Something got to the offices."

"Both offices," Spire added, his voice raw. "Rose was attacked there, she decoded a summoning. We must stay together. Gather everyone in the team that remains, warn them all, no one should be alone. Go to Northe-Stewart."

"Of course," Black exclaimed, and ran to help Evelyn hail.

"Bishop. In Washington. Call for my Rupert," Clara begged, and began to wink out.

This time Clara's sight failed first. Only hearing and feeling remained in this unprecedented second wave. Her muscles began to twitch and lose control once she was aided into a carriage.

"Keep me from falling over," she mumbled, and dragged the tie of her robe out, placing it in her sore, raw mouth. The interior of the cab was padded enough. Knowing she was as safe as she could be, for the second time in one night, she let go as her internal clock ran out. She seized. Her body would feel beaten, but she was damned if she would not survive the night.

* * * * *

This time she woke more slowly, but memory still returned in a rush. Her body felt heavy and bruised everywhere. Everything hurt and her home was gone. Her safety was gone, her offices tainted. Every place she loved had been wrenched from her.

Where was she now? Dead? Trapped? Did she dare open her eyes? There was a noise down the hall, a familiar voice. A rush of relief flooded her as she remembered talk of Evelyn's house before she went under and heard her mentor's voice.

The terrifying events of the night paraded through her mind and she had to shift her thoughts lest the panic trigger another episode. Two seizures. That couldn't be a good sign. She tried to stave off fear that she was worsening, weakening.

Bishop. She longed for Bishop. The sight of his face, the feel of their impassioned kiss was a glorious alternative to the course of her thoughts.

She opened her eyes to a view of Tiffany glass and satin drapes, with daylight coming through them. Evelyn and Rose peered down at her, one on either side.

"Is everyone . . . safe?" Clara asked slowly, her voice thin and cracking. "The Summoned seemed to be making a sport of trying to kill one by one. . . . The rules of their coming and going are more fluid now, constant danger. Everyone needs to be accounted for," she insisted.

"Always looking after everyone else first," Rose said fondly. "We've asked everyone to check in."

"Rupert?"

Rose glanced at Evelyn.

"We haven't heard yet," Evelyn replied. "When Mr. Spire realized the danger Rose was in, I had my staff alert as many of our team as possible and headed downtown. Gathering you up, we brought you back and you've been asleep for nine hours. In the meantime, Miss Knight and I held a private séance here, trying to find out more from the spirit world about this possible Celeste."

"And?" Clara pressed.

"Nothing conclusive," Evelyn said angrily. "We were over-whelmed by the frenetic nature of the spirit world, it was so much *noisier* than usual."

"Rupert wired me about Washington and to keep watch on everyone." She turned to Clara and Rose, grieved. "I'm so sorry I wasn't there for you, I should have known—"

Rose put a hand on the woman's shoulder. "No. If the psychic realm was all turbulence then you wouldn't have been able to hear a distress call in the storm."

Evelyn helped Clara to a sitting position and pressed a glass of water to her lips. Clara drank desperately. Looking down, she noticed she'd been put into a fresh day dress with a shawl draped over her, a simple wool and thick lace frock with its ties, hooks, and cinches left open; her undergarments had been left on and alone.

"I put you in a fresh layer as I couldn't have you lying here in a bloodied, soot-stained robe, dear," Evelyn explained as Clara examined the dress with trembling fingers.

"Have you checked this house?" Clara asked Evelyn. "Nowhere is safe . . . the offices. Someone got to the offices." She heard her voice crack and closed her eyes, hot tears leaking out.

"I will inspect again, and when you can move, you can help me do so once more," Evelyn stated, patting Clara's hand. "We'll get through all of this, we have so far."

There was a knock at the guest room door. Evelyn looked to Clara, who nodded.

"Yes?"

Spire, Black, and Knight entered.

"We wanted to see you awake and well," Black said gently.

"Does anyone know . . . the extent of the damages to my home? I had to throw a lamp and the Wards to close a demon's corridor, I didn't know what else to do, I was alone in the room, Harper downstairs. *I* started the blaze, in a panic, because it's what stopped Moriel, and what if that shadow was him?" She felt tears itch her eyes. Evelyn placed a comforting hand on her shoulder. "Where did Harper go?"

"The damage to your home was extensive," Spire answered, moving toward Clara. "Fred and Josiah are seeing if anything is salvageable. Your housekeeper is staying with family."

"Well, I suppose that settles moving . . ." she said sadly, thinking how Bishop might take to the news. "Rupert will be so upset. . . ."

"The house is immaterial. You're Bishop's treasure, you're all he needs," Evelyn assured. "Now rest."

"No, I don't dare. Not after a seizure. Two, even. I need to stretch."

"Tea?" Rose asked.

"Yes, please. And I'm starving."

Clara helped herself up, waving Evelyn off. "If I don't move myself, it's like my body calcifies. I will rest, but when awake, I need to gently keep moving, lest the bruises really set in. Is . . . is someone missing?" She cocked her head to the side as if listening for something, the ineffable internal bells of her instinctual gifts ringing with a sudden urgency. "Where is Effie? I feel like Effie should be here. . . ."

"I don't know, dear," Evelyn replied. "She and Fred came

here when they heard what happened but stepped out. After that I haven't seen them."

Rose presented a porcelain teacup, and Evelyn fussed over pillows around Clara. Knight brought her a bowl of stew, which she began devouring immediately.

"Come down to the parlor when you're ready and you can tell us what happened," Evelyn said gently. "Take your time."

"We don't *have* time. I'm very worried," she stated, handing Rose her food as she stood, slowly adjusting the shawl over her shoulders and hooking the front panel of the dress to the side so that she wouldn't be hanging open exposed. Gesturing for her friends to follow with one hand, lifting skirts in the other, she called, "Let's talk this out and get to work."

She was bruised and battered, but if anything, this sequence of terror had strengthened her resolve to find ways to best the demons.

Once the assembled company was in the parlor, Evelyn dug in. "What happened?"

Clara explained the events as best she could, and even though the parlor was warm with a blazing fire, there remained a chill to the air and Clara shivered for what felt like the thousandth time. Spire put another log on the fire and rekindled the blaze.

"So that leaves us to wonder who tainted those offices," Spire stated. "Miss Kent, those guards, the Bixbys or Mr. Fordham, or even our dear senator."

"No!" Clara spat, horrified.

"But you have to think of all the possibilities. You have no choice," Spire said with a slight sharpness. "We cannot let sentiment cloud us, that's likely precisely what the enemy wants."

"Then I am glad you do not suspect me, Mr. Spire," Clara said, holding his gaze.

"It is far more likely that an enemy gained clearance to those offices," Spire replied. "Our poor, late Mr. Brinkman had no trouble doing so."

The ringing of the doorbell made both Rose and Clara start, nerves mutually frayed.

Sure enough, Effie was shown into Evelyn's parlor.

"There you are! I had a feeling I'd see you," Clara said with a warm smile that quickly faded when she saw her colleague's expression.

The lovely woman, dressed in a floral-patterned calico with ribbon and eyelet trim and matching bonnet, bore a look that was the jarring opposite of her dress. She looked pale and shaken, ashen against the soft peach and rose colors of her ensemble, a few brown spiral curls hanging distractedly from beneath the bonnet. Fresh dread overtook Clara, the day proving a further cavalcade of unfortunate events.

Spire studied Effie with intense scrutiny, reminding Clara that now none of her team were safe from suspicion. This did prompt Clara to look closely at Effie's eyes. Brown and tired, but not blackened. Effie didn't taint the offices, of that, Clara felt certain.

"Clara . . ." Effie came close, sitting next to her on the divan.

Evelyn poured the woman some tea and handed it to her directly. Clara knew from years with Evelyn that this was a part of the medium's process of assessment, seeing how a person would take to small but expected civilities. If there was hesitation, they were not themselves. Effie accepted the cup and saucer graciously, but the porcelain rattled a bit and she had to sit with it in her lap to still her own trembling limbs.

Evelyn shook her head, meaning she didn't suspect Effie either. But something else was wrong.

Effie took a deep breath. "I know you've been truly through

hell. So I'm sorry to make it worse. But . . . it can't wait. How *well* are you?" Effie countered.

"Well enough to do whatever needs to be done," Clara replied, "I'll take some palliative pills for the aches and bruises. Tell me, you look like you saw a ghost, and I should know."

"It's . . . Franklin. Something's wrong. I think you need to see his house. "I . . . If you're able to come and take a look, it's better explained by seeing it. I frankly don't know what it means, but if a clue is missed, it could be deadly."

"Very well," Clara murmured.

"I'd not trouble you, especially not in seizure recovery, if it weren't—"

"I know," Clara reassured, patting Effie's hand. "I'm glad you've come to me, you know I hate it when I'm coddled due to my condition."

"Still, please take extra care," Effie replied carefully. "What I've seen could easily be another trigger."

"She won't go alone," Spire stated firmly. "We are a team. None of us is allowed, from this point forward, to be split up. Police orders."

"There's something else," Effie said, producing a telegraph from her pocket.

Clara read the typed slip of paper on Western Union stationery.

BEAUTIFUL EFFIE, IF NY CAN SPARE YOU, NEW
ORLEANS NEEDS YOU. YOU AND FRED CAN
COMPLETE OUR COMPASS AS WE FIGHT FOR THE
SOUL OF THE CRESCENT . . . IT IS DIRE. SOON, IF
YOU CAN.

Nodding, Clara looked up with a steeled smile. "Of course," she murmured, squeezing Effie's hands in hers. "Go, with our blessing and love, both of you. There are enough of us here. I know London and New York have been hard on you. I hope New Orleans will be kinder."

"I think it will be . . . better," Effie murmured.

"Give those dear twins my best," Clara said, fighting back tears at the thought of Andre and Louis and all that had passed between them.

"I will," she promised, embracing Clara. "Stay sharp as ever. Let Bishop take care of you when you need it, and you him. We all need taking care of sometimes. Give that man my love and thank him for all he's done for my family."

"I shall. Let us know of anything New York can do to help."

Clara then turned to the assembled company, beginning with a rallying tone that to her own ear sounded entirely false and hollow. But perhaps in the acting of it she could be convinced. "Friends?"

Everyone gathered around her diligently. Knight and Lord Black came further into the room from the parlor entrance, Black in his usual bright whites and blues, Knight in an ornately embroidered Turkish ensemble fit for the theater, her expression all empathy for Clara's state.

"It would seem there's more grim work for the day," she announced. "No rest for the weary. Not everyone need accompany me, but while I'm not completely at my best, this new matter cannot wait until morning."

"Whatever you need, Miss Templeton," Spire offered. She could have sworn she had insisted he call her Clara, but at the moment, formality was its own comfort.

"We must examine Mr. Fordham's residence in Brooklyn, accessible by ferry from the Fulton landing. Once across the river, it's a short walk. We'd best go now."

"But before we do," Clara continued, "we must wish our Effie well. She and her brother have been called to New Orleans by Andre Dupris to be a spiritual compass in their efforts. The call has been urgent, and we are selfish if we keep them from noble tasks southward."

No one fought this, and everyone was quick to offer Effie embraces, well-wishes. Evelyn pressed money into her hands, and the young woman caught between worlds was further caught off guard by the outpouring of love and appreciation for her hard work.

Lord Black gave her the names of British embassy contacts in the city and Miss Knight moved forward to murmur something in her ear, to which the woman flushed. Whether it was clairvoyant prophecy or a flirtation, Clara would never know, and she was too much a lady to ask.

The valuable Eterna operative left their company with simply a quiet thanks, tears in her warm eyes, lingering last on Clara, offering a complicated gaze for a complicated life, and exited. Clara managed to hold back her own tears, for fear of what she'd find at Franklin's home was sobering and chilling a prospect enough to keep them at bay.

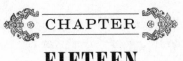

FIFTEEN

It was true that not everything had gone to plan during the moving-picture presentation and after, Celeste had to admit. However, she chose to count a few joys.

Waking the next morning, she was thrilled to wander a blessedly empty house in her robe. Lord Tantagenet's body had been taken away and done solemn ceremony with the day prior, all of his money in her account presently, and the freedom that society afforded a widow was hers.

Having been married she'd done her societal duty, having lost a husband she was afforded space and room, not expected to entertain suitors unless she wanted to, and no one would seize the money—as if only death could pry open men's permission for a woman to have her own. All remained still, of course, in his name, but as titles came with open doors, she did not mind the name, now freed from the tedious man who bore it.

As a hungry child who came from nothing, scrabbled and fought tooth and nail to have anything, respect most of all, she would do what she could to keep it.

Her workers had gone on ahead of her to prepare the next ritual site, and she would join them promptly. All would move forward. Once she tied up a loose end.

She hadn't expected to be chased by Moriel's shadow, the old king now given over purely to demonic force. It had been her hope that he'd pounce directly on the coterie of troublesome folks that had been the end of him and who stood in her way. Instead, the petty thing, he went after her. Again. She knew it was him. She knew his taste and the air was full of it: bitter, earthy smoke, blood and tar.

When he tore past the police officer chasing her out, bowling the man over in the process, she thought for a moment that the demon shade would gain on her, tear her into pulp as they did any servant deemed a betrayer. The shadow only stopped when she used the arcane Latin words she'd heard Moriel use against shadows before. Words he didn't know she'd listened in on in the early days of his prison sentence, words he never guessed he would be subject to. Listening women. More infernal that all those scribbling ones Hawthorne complained about.

The summoning code, those dear old letters, served their purpose. Having used them to bring the shadow forth into the theater was a closure of sorts. They'd been placed with deliberation, and they were picked up with the same consideration. Those government operatives couldn't help themselves; of course they'd try to crack the code. A trap too easy to lay for them. She felt the corridors of the darker realm widening, like a surging tide. Her foes had been overcome. How many died in an attack, she couldn't tell.

Having stretched out her hands over the map to Collect vitality last night at the witching hour, she had felt the push and pull between the forces she wielded and that which her foes were trying to wrangle.

She'd gotten their scent at the performance, a read on their potency. If she tried hard, she could feel them darting about now, proving not all of them succumbed. They were out of their depth but damn if they weren't full of pluck. She had to admire the enemy teams but surmised they were more lucky than truly gifted.

They managed to stumble onto the right ways to fight the

malevolent nature of Society magic by sheer instinct and happy coincidence, despite being constrained by cultural expectations of decorum.

That Celeste chose to champion the unnatural was not a judgment on the natural world, it was a matter of expediency. She could control the unnatural. She was in awe of the natural world, the organic flow of the Earth's cosmic energy. That these elder energies seemed to favor the fools who opposed her was an insult. So she gave herself more and more to the unnatural, a force that welcomed her gifts with open arms, and soon she would be entwined fully with the converse of all that was ley. Her body would become the dark line; the ultimate autonomy.

But she couldn't trust her loose ends. If she wasn't careful, she'd be unwitting prey twice. It was time to put the old king away for good.

Moriel was a liability and she couldn't risk another incident. So she would call him forth for the last time and secure his permanent fate. As a final outrage, the cage she'd had built for his essence was constructed from iron, a plain, pedestrian material he hated. The box was filled with salt and her own blood, and marked with every symbol of cherished faith, kept whole, all represented in small silver tokens.

She didn't need the letters to draw him forth now that she had the diadem a corrupted police officer had sent her from the site of burning Vieuxhelles, the night Moriel's castle lay in ruin.

She held it up, Lady Macbeth holding up the crown, and began what of the Summoned ritual she knew by heart.

Moriel came quickly at her call—too quickly, perhaps. Celeste was fairly certain he was not en route to do her bidding, but to do away with her. Rip her apart. She was prepared for that.

His Summoned shadow slid through the opening created

by Lady Tantagenet's incantations and her blood. Then, as if magnetized, the shadow drifted toward the blackened gold of the diadem in her hand, smeared with her blood. As so much of Moriel's magic was drenched in blood, hers slathered on the crown declared it as her own.

As the dark shadow dove, Celeste threw the talisman into the fireplace, into the hot iron box atop a glowing hardwood log. The shadow lunged after the diadem, coiling into the box, the lid slamming shut on it, salt spilling everywhere, the whole and unsoiled talismans of every faith Moriel had ever corrupted rattling as the box shook in protest.

What Moriel's essence couldn't have known was that the seal of his trap, hidden just under the lip of the container, was the small blade Moriel had run between her ribs when he'd grown too leery of her psychic and mesmeric powers, now the tool of her revenge.

The weapon used to kill her would be what held him prisoner. It had been doused in holy water and it was now a symbol of her superior power. It was now the barrier between his shadow and her soul.

Flinging out both her hands, she pulled on every rail track and electrical wire she'd ever fouled, the force of energy the same as any speeding train. A roaring sound crested in her ears; unbearable heat poured off her body as rivulets of sweat dripped off her brow.

The box melted slightly at the corners, the padlock edging into the metal, fusing. Dropping her arms, she stumbled forward, never yet having exerted that much of herself or the lines she was tying herself to. But the effect was thrilling and useful.

She lifted the glowing iron box out of the flames with a pair of fireplace tongs, setting it to cool on the tile of the fireplace.

Sitting in a brocade armchair, she stared at the box, feeling the heat wafting off it, and smiled. Leaning forward, she spoke to it as if it were the old friend it contained.

"It is always personal," she murmured to the box. "You *made* it personal, many times, and you never grew more powerful for your pettiness, Beau. I could use all your betrayals to my advantage. Did you really think I would die so quietly, put up no fight, not haunt you to the day one of us died and beyond?" She chuckled.

"I am ready to look beyond *attaining* power. Instead I will *become* it. Live beyond flesh's boundaries. If my sins were to finally catch up to me, I'll have gathered enough power to alchemically shift them, the avalanche will fall upon my shoulders, and I will be Atlas holding up a world of ill will, bloodshed, and avarice. I'll be strong enough to weather any reckoning, and even consume it, allow the sword of justice to be smelted inside me. I will remain standing and live."

Once the box had cooled enough to handle, she lashed it closed with a metal vise and padlock, tucking the container under her arm and walking casually out the door. A hired carriage awaited her, with her traveling case already lashed to the rear.

On the way to the train station, she asked the driver to circle Washington Square Park while she "ran an errand." When she'd last passed the park, a few days earlier, she'd noticed construction taking place at one corner. Now, dressed in a riding skirt, Celeste walked to an open corner.

"Excuse me, gentlemen," she said to the workmen who stared up at the black-clad woman with open mouths. "Allow me to pay some *respects*." At this last word, she lifted her veil, feeling heat surge in her body as she gave a psychic shove.

Mumbling, the men standing on street level turned away and the two on planks six feet below street level all dispersed, climbing up and shambling away like the reanimate. She took their place, climbing down a workman's ladder, holding the box under her arm and her layered black skirts in her hands.

Just under the street level lay an open chasm. Celeste moved bones to create a pit and left Moriel's spirit box within a pile of unnamed bones, hiding it within ignominy, abandoning him with the remains of the poor and the forgotten, the unnamed victims of plagues and injustices. The unfortunates. The common criminal. It was the greatest insult to someone who had prided himself as "the best" of men.

As she climbed back to the surface, she heard, echoing through the earth, a long, muffled, bellowing scream, the veritable definition of fear and defeat. Throwing back her head, unable to hold back joyful amusement, she loosed a howl of retribution that made the scar from Moriel's betrayal ache. It was worth the pain to hear that sound, to know she had bested him at last. She would hold his cry close as a lullaby for as long as her mortal coil clung to this earth.

But enough of that, Celeste chided herself, returning to her carriage. She had no time to indulge in the classic trope of the villain luxuriating in victory. She had a train to catch, and power to Collect along the rails, augmented as so many of them were with her befouling stamp. Her work was almost ready to be unveiled in Washington, her pinnacle nearly complete.

She would Collect her opposition, too, and fold them in with her, gaining their powers either when she broke them open or when the demons snuffed them out under her watch.

Franklin's family town house in Brooklyn Heights, a fine neighborhood that stared across the East River at the rising edifices of Manhattan with cool disdain, was a redbrick mansion in the Federal style, a simple, sturdy edifice that spoke of his family's long history in the city.

"Are we breaking in?" Spire asked, hanging back to address Clara, who was moving as fast as seizure-sore and uncooperative legs would allow as the cluster of operatives walked up the wide lane.

"No," she replied, drawing the fur-lined cloak Evelyn provided tighter over her aching arms. "The Eterna offices have spare keys for all our homes. Not one to mistake odd behavior or sound a false alarm, Effie procured the set from the office when Franklin was acting odd and handed them to me."

"Odd how?" Spire asked as they strode across the cobblestone under oval-globed streetlamps with tall flames, their somber faces alternately in glow and shadow, an eerie cycle.

"Distracted, gloomy, tired," Clara said. "I knew he was suffering from deeper melancholy than usual but I assumed that was because of the grimness of our work of late. I should have paid better attention."

"You were in England," Spire countered, "and returned to constant preoccupation."

"You are too kind, Mr. Spire. I doubt you'd afford yourself the same courtesy were our positions reversed."

"You're right, I wouldn't," Spire replied. "Still, I don't coddle, and I don't give women a handicap. I merely state the facts of your circumstances. We can't play counsel to everyone."

Clara smiled at him, her expression, she hoped, conveying her growing appreciation for this consummately sensible man. They stopped outside the town house.

"My senses perceive a sour taste," she said.

Evelyn Northe-Stewart agreed. "Yes, something is terribly off." Without asking, Evelyn plucked the key from Clara's hand, strode up to the door, and unlocked it, volunteering herself for the first psychic blow to protect the compromised Clara.

When the door opened in an unsettling creak to a dim hall beyond, Evelyn set her jaw. Clara felt it next; the wave of overwhelming despair that hit Sensitives like the stench of decay.

Spire was the first to step past Evelyn and into the house, pistol drawn, oblivious to the psychic miasma. Clara followed, pausing to turn the gas knob near the door and bring light to the interior of the house from the multiple, white, glass-globed sconces on the walls of the long front hall and along the stairs to the second and third floors. The rest of the group filed in behind them, then Evelyn closed the door and locked it.

"Franklin?" Clara called carefully. Nothing. "*Franklin*. It's Clara, I just want to talk with you, I'm worried about you, my friend. . . ."

Nothing.

"No one is here," Knight verified. "Nothing but sadness."

"It is most unlike Franklin to leave the place so cluttered," Clara stated as she stepped carefully through the entrance hall, noticing boots and hats strewn about in the hall. "He despises clutter—it causes him great unease. Tidying up makes him feel safer."

"Does he live here alone?" Spire asked.

"Unfortunately yes," Clara replied. "His parents are dead and his brother never returned from the Civil War. I've never thought it was a good idea for him to remain here, like an additional haunt, but he feels it is his duty."

The disorder of the entrance hall continued in the study and parlor that flanked it. In the parlor, books were tossed about haphazardly, lying on the furniture and the floor, looking as if they had been catapulted out of the study, where bookshelves stood empty.

Across the hall was his study, overrun by what appeared to be kindling, brush, and weeds, but which turned out on further examination to be bouquets tied with twine; bundles of herbs, flowers, ferns, and such.

Clara stepped into the study, her compatriots following.

"While the place is admittedly messy," Spire began carefully, "I see no signs of any particular scuffle or struggle."

"There wasn't one," Miss Knight stated, keeping to the threshold. "Death is here, but not murder." Evelyn, who was keeping close to Clara, flanking her with Rose on the other side, nodded, affirming the assessment with a grimace. Knight winced. "However . . . I sense some items of concern upstairs, Mr. Spire."

Spire wasted no time in brushing past Knight to ascend the stairs and she moved quickly to accompany him.

Lord Black examined all the dried plants around the study with meticulous care, touching, sniffing, and holding leaves up to the light.

Clara moved forward, to where Effie had instructed she pay close attention, Franklin's desk—a prized possession that Clara knew had been handed down within his family for generations. She looked down at the polished oak surface and her heart stopped.

A simple message was scratched across the wooden surface, probably created with the penknife lying nearby:

I'm sorry, Clara . . .

She sucked in a sharp breath, involuntarily uttering a thin, wretched cry.

Rose pressed a hand into the knot of corset laces at the small of her back, reminding her to breathe again and with regularity. Evelyn, hearing the sound, came near, looked at the message, and loosed a pained sigh.

"Sorry for what, Franklin?" Clara asked the text. "Sorry for *what*?!"

She felt herself sinking toward the desk chair. Rose grabbed her, brushing away a cluster of brown palm leaves from the seat before she could collapse on them.

Seeking an inner lighthouse of hope or ingenuity, Clara found she had no such lit tower within her by which to navigate her way out of horror; she was left with only tempestuous sea and jagged rocks. Even Rose in this moment, keeping hold of her hand, couldn't drag her away from the murky water, her heart a dark depth.

He was sorry for something he had done, would yet do. The scrawling scratch was the same on the desk as it had been on the floorboards of the office. It was him. He was tainted. He was sorry. Some part of him still knew that much. . . . Clara bit down on her lip hard to keep from crying. It would do no good.

"I'm trying to make sense of the plants," Black called, and this brought Clara to the active moment, desperate to seize on useful clues.

If Franklin had taken to the ideas of natural Warding, he had misinterpreted them. Strewn about the room were disheveled, dead bouquets that looked as if they had been dipped in browning fluids or made brittle by acids.

"What exactly turned the poor man, I wonder," Black mused, frowning at an unpleasant clump of nettles.

"He was such a good soul," Clara replied, feeling small and defeated.

"I don't know. Chemicals? Exposure to an operative? He's undertaken some missions privately, that must be when it happened."

"You must not blame yourself, dear," Evelyn said, seemingly all too aware of her precarious emotional state. "There is only so much any one of us can do to protect our teammates and friends."

Clara couldn't stop staring at her name, wishing she had Franklin's ability to touch an item or surface and dial back the clock. She would be able to see precisely where she had gone wrong, when Franklin had become lost.

Black returned to Clara's side.

"Each of these plants has had something sour done to it," he explained. "In some cases they've been dipped in resin or tar, or perhaps blood. In some cases they were blanched by something astringent. Damaging their natural chemistries and, I would imagine, inverting their properties as well."

"A Society specialty," Evelyn commented. "Overturning, inverting, perverting . . ." She closed her eyes and cocked her head to the side, listening. After a moment, she looked at Clara and shook her head. "The spirits don't even know what to say," she continued. "All they seem able to manage is . . . *protect.*"

"Tell them we're trying," Clara nearly growled.

Black moved to the desk to look at the carved message. Directly below the words lay one parched, floral branch. Running one shaking hand through his platinum hair, Black pointed at the branch, his words tinged with worry.

"That is a breed of lily," he said. "Many such flowers are, to use their Latin name, of the *Columbianum* species. Considering the sacred, life-giving meaning associated with many lilies, and the Latin root, I believe . . ."

"District of Columbia. He's going after Rupert," Clara cried. "We have to get to Washington. Now."

"Clara, your health—"

"If all of us go, together, I'll be fine," she said, her voice growing shrill as her words tumbled over each other. "If I seize along the way, at least we'll be en route. If no one wishes to accompany me, I'll go alone and take my chances." She burst into tears, her shoulders bowing in pain, body trembling from the aftershocks of the twin seizures of earlier.

Immediately Rose embraced her.

"I'm sorry," Clara sobbed. "I—"

"Don't apologize, Clara. You know we will do anything for Rupert," Evelyn said.

"I do understand," Rose assured quietly. "I would feel the same way."

Clara assumed Rose was thinking what might happen if Mr. Spire was in danger. Empathy was a vital asset in their team.

It was unlike Clara to be so revelatory of any emotion, and while she hated being seen like this, rubbed entirely raw, there should be no shame in admitting just how terrified she was at the possibility of losing what was most important to her. After Louis, she doubted she could survive another loss of such magnitude and keep her wits.

Black flanked Clara opposite Rose, asking quietly, "Clara dear, let us alert the senator. Did he not say he would await word from us?"

"Yes, I must wire him," Clara said quickly, pulling herself together, tamping down on the panic that bit at every nerve, patting her tear-stained face with her fingertips as she'd been too rushed at the house to procure a handkerchief.

"But . . . Edward . . . where can we wire *from?*" she asked the nobleman. "We are wholly breached."

"Train station," Spire offered from the landing, having heard at least part of their conversation. He descended at a clip, Knight gliding behind him in her elaborate costume.

"Perfect," Black replied. "I'll wire our Washington embassy to have refreshments, fresh linens, and changes for us. We should not stop for amenities but travel direct."

"Thank you, you are ever the gentleman and our foremost resource," Clara said, allowing both for Evelyn and Rose to hold a bit of her weight a moment as she shifted forward to walk again, her muscles having clenched in painful stiffness.

They'd done the same harried rush to get onto the steamboat across the Atlantic. Evil didn't wait for a prepared itinerary and well-packed trunks.

Here the fair-headed lord, his undaunted qualities never so valued as now, turned further into Clara's view, leaning forward and speaking near her ear: "Before we board, give me a few minutes at the florist, I'll be able to create a few bouquets suited for cleansing and Warding tasks, antithesis to these dead branches."

"Of course, thank you," Clara replied warmly. In these dark hours she could not help but thank God for such fellow travelers as these. "What did you find upstairs, Mr. Spire?" she asked as they all moved toward the front door.

"Troubling signs," he replied grimly. "Three small black boxes of the same provenance as that of the booster station, lying empty in the upstairs hallway. Blood trails in the washroom. Bottles of embalming fluids on the shelves."

Clara put a hand to her mouth and leaned on Rose as Spire continued, "It does appear that Mr. Fordham has participated in that ugly business of augmenting the mechanical lines."

Clara screwed her face up. "This isn't him, it's—"

"We know, Clara. He's been corrupted, clearly, by chemical or coercion," Rose assured. "And we'll find him alive, and we'll cure him."

The group wasted no time in darting to the Fulton Ferry's edge, but as there was not another scheduled departure for another half hour, Lord Black paid a small boat handsomely for their own private crossing in the immediate.

"Milord, your resources," Clara said in awe.

"Thank goodness you've a branch of my British bank in this city! I replenished myself on day one," he said with a smile. "Prepared for anything."

"Your generosity is such a balm," Clara continued. "I confess, spoiled as I am by my Rupert, I'm not always used to men of your station being so selfless."

Black shrugged and replied with good-natured earnestness. "I was put on this earth to be a loving, peaceful soul and to do less harm in the world than good. I believe our work is doing good, and thusly, by all of our work, so is my purpose magnified."

"The heavens are well pleased with you, milord," Evelyn murmured.

Once back across to Manhattan, they crammed inside the same wide carriage as had taken them down, Evelyn's driver a silent, patient man who was well paid and adored the lady of the house. At Grand Central, Evelyn took a turn, paying for everyone's tickets and securing a private compartment. Black and Clara sent their telegrams before His Lordship went in search of the plants he needed.

Lord Black bought at the very least one of every flower and fern variety within, to the young shopkeeper's great delight.

As their team boarded, Lord Black's arms were as full of flowers as if he were an altar to Demeter. In their compartment, furnished with divans, cushioned chairs, and a dining room set in the middle, he set them gently down on the lace-covered table and rummaged through the mass to extract a bouquet of small white flowers. Untying the bunch, he plucked at the blossoms and leaves, carefully disentangling them, working with a gentleness that spoke of solemn respect. As he separated them, he handed a white and green sprig to each of his compatriots.

"Lily of the valley," Black explained, "signifies 'a return of happiness' and that is most certainly what we need. It is also a relative of the soiled blooms we saw below the terrible declaration that drew us here. As the Society so loves inversion, so will we invert their dying rot with the powers of fresh, verdant, *living* tokens. Place this offering somewhere meaningful on your person, please. Let no bit of life go without celebration."

"Amen," Evelyn murmured.

"These can serve as makeshift Wards until we have a chance to make some," Black said. "Charge them up with the brightness of your wonderful souls, my friends."

Seemingly overcome by the wealth of flowers spread across the table, Miss Knight held her hands above the fragrant offering, as if praying over them or perhaps, drinking in their lush effect.

Spire accepted the sprig Lord Black offered him without argument. He knew when to pick his battles, and Clara could see the man considering that there was sense in all this. Every counterbalance they had made against the Society thus far had been granted some measure of success.

As the train screamed a whistle and jolted into motion, the travelers seated themselves on the compartment's wide, velvet-padded benches.

The hypnotic motion of the train urged Clara's body to calm. Her muscles began, finally, to unclench. She intended to distract herself during the journey by attempting to refine her newly honed awareness of the sounds of energies, learning to untie the knots of steel and Earth.

Sliding back the damask curtains of the train-car windows, she pressed her ear to the vibrating glass, trying to blunt the fangs of her terror. What if she found her beloved Bishop too late? It would be another lifetime—if they were granted such a chance again—before they could affirm what had become so precious between them.

Evelyn had seated herself beside Clara. At length the younger woman turned to her and whispered, "Can you feel him? I'm trying to sense him, but it's harder now, I don't trust my own sensitivities when it comes to him anymore . . ."

"Love gets in the way," Evelyn murmured. "Don't worry. I can feel him," she assured.

But Evelyn could feel ghosts, too. Clara knew she couldn't always make the distinction.

Rose sat very close to Mr. Spire. The other half of her compass magnetized to Bishop, always tied but never so much as now. They had to make it through this whole. Their team all had its pairs and alliances across so many lines. Their team was a network of compasses, all trying to point to a peaceful north. She tried to hear, to *feel* the sound, holding the vibration in her heart to strengthen her own channel, for she was the compass needle never so much as now.

Exhausted, Clara nodded off. She was roused as the train screeched to a sudden halt. They were at no station; instead they had come to a stop in the midst of a vast field of tall, swampy grass and nothingness under a bright, moonlit sky.

Spire stepped out of the compartment to investigate and soon returned carrying one of those horrid black boxes. There was a rotting finger inside.

"The conductor says we missed a switch and have to back up," he explained. "It won't take long. I walked with him and found this beside the switch point."

Lord Black approached Spire and set a few flower buds into the box.

"If you want to say any prayers, do it now," Spire said, drawing a box of matches from his pocket.

Clara, Evelyn, and Rose held hands and murmured prayers; Miss Knight chose to withdraw into a meditative state. Spire opened the window, holding the box out in the air. Black lit a match and handed it to Spire, who traced the flame around the top of the nasty device. Once it was burning brightly, he dropped it onto the rocks that formed the track bed.

The train whistle screamed. The car jolted into reverse for a few minutes before going forward again at a new angle.

Despite their worries and a few more delays along the tracks, the company managed some fitful sleep until the conductor cried "Washington" by morning.

Since each rail company had its own depot in Washington, the station was not as hectic as Grand Central, but the Pennsylvania Railroad operated a grand enough edifice of soaring archways and glass between riveted steel. Its well-dressed denizens moved with a slower, more deliberate pace than Clara was used to in New York.

"How tainted is this station?" Miss Knight asked Clara and Evelyn as they disembarked. She screwed up her lovely face, trying to ascertain the damage herself.

"We can't worry about that now, we'll have to come back to see to it," Clara said, smoothing her hair, tying the cloak about her neck, and striding through clouds of steam toward many doors and an impressive line of waiting carriages beyond.

They proceeded to Bishop's standard lodgings when in the capital, the luxuriant Willard Hotel, within view of Pennsylvania Avenue and the Executive Mansion. As they checked in, Clara asked about Senator Bishop.

The old clerk, looking at the name Clara signed and then up at her, grinned.

"Well I'll be, Clara Templeton. It's been years!" the man exclaimed. "Glad to see you back, my dear. No, I haven't seen the senator since he dropped his bags off."

"Do you know if he would have received my wire?" Clara asked.

The clerk glanced below the counter and pulled out a Western Union envelope marked *Bishop*. "No, I'm afraid he hasn't. But . . ." The clerk pulled out another envelope below. "Ah! It seems you've been anticipated." He handed over an envelope marked *For My Dear Clara Templeton Should She Arrive Searching For Me*.

Clara laughed, feeling tears itch her eyes. Tearing open the paper, she read:

My Beloved,

If instinct serves correctly, you'll come for me before I've wired you. Since I know there's no stopping you, find me at either the offices of the Episcopal Church, Representative Brown's office, the Executive Mansion itself, or the morning reception out front I plan to attend. Until soon, Bishop.

Clara gestured to her company to follow her out onto the wide Willard porch, a landing where dignitaries liked to smoke and drink, studying the Executive Mansion before them as if their scrutiny might change policy. For some of them, if they threw enough money into their cause, it might.

"That's the reception Bishop meant." Clara gestured ahead to milling, well-dressed folks on the lawn as the sun crested onto the reception. "Can we get in?"

Knight grinned and took Lord Black's arm. "Leave that to

us," she said, and strode off, Black skipping a step to keep up without being dragged.

Sure enough, Knight used charm and psychic persuasion, and Black's diplomatic papers didn't hurt. Spire didn't even have to show his badge, though Clara overheard him remark to Rose that security was too lax here and what was wrong with them, Garfield having been shot so recently.

Soon their company joined the lawn party and Clara had to keep herself from running through the crowd. Her hawk-like gaze found Bishop with preternatural speed; even in a sea of top hats and black coats, she could pick out his silhouette.

"Rupert!" she nearly screamed, rushing to him, not caring who saw or if she might cause intrigue or scandal. Throwing her arms around him, she let her tears flow.

"My dear! You must have gotten my note," he exclaimed. In the next instant he grabbed her by the arms and stepped back to take a good look at her. "What on earth has happened?" He gingerly touched her cheek; the gesture hurt, likely a bruise she hadn't bothered to notice. Clara leaned against him, and he welcomed her nearness; this alone helped ease her sore muscles.

"Your dear girl has been through hell and back, my friend," Evelyn said—she had been only a step behind Clara even during the younger woman's mad dash. "There were attacks and grim revelations yesterday. We're here to warn and protect you."

"What now?" Bishop asked, drawing Clara and Evelyn away from the crowd, many of whom had turned to watch them with a mixture of curiosity and disdain. Clara squinted back tears. Crying in a public space, in front of Bishop's colleagues, would not do.

"The house is gone," Clara choked, looking away in shame. "There was a fire. There was corridor of Summoned coming into my room," she added in a whisper. "I'm so sorry,

I had only a moment to think . . ." She looked down, tears inevitably falling on the grass. Bishop enfolded her in an embrace.

"Oh, my dear, my dear . . ." He kissed her on the crown of the braid she'd haphazardly set on the train. "It's all right, you're safe and that is all that matters." He held her tighter.

"That's exactly what I told her," Evelyn added. "Harper is fine, and there may be objects salvageable, we honestly haven't had time to check. It was one crisis after another, and now we are here."

"Franklin has been turned," Clara blurted from under his arm. "He tainted the offices. That's where I went for safety, after the fire, and then Rose and I almost died there, too," she murmured. Scenes from the horror flashed again in her mind and made her feel sick to her stomach. "Have you seen Franklin?"

"That's all so terrible, but no," Bishop said, shocked. "I'm so sorry . . . I should never have left you!" the senator exclaimed, lifting a covetous hand to cup her neck, gently turning her to kiss her forehead. "I'm so sorry . . ." His voice was suddenly small, terrified.

"All this would have likely happened whether you were there or no," Evelyn stated. "There is an escalation at work."

"Still . . ." Bishop trailed off ruefully. Clara recognized the self-censure.

"Let's not blame or regret," Clara said gently. "We're alive, thanks be to God."

"Yes," Bishop murmured, bestowing another kiss on her head. "Thanks be to God."

By this point the rest of the team had encircled them, once again attracting the attention of others. Bishop recovered himself, gently stepping back from Clara to address his company.

Rarely at a loss, Bishop loudly welcomed the company to

his "personal tour of the Executive grounds." This seemed to settle any lingering curiosity over their odd coterie. Bishop led them around to the rear of the famed edifice, where signs of construction were evident.

"I'm surprised you've not seen Mr. Fordham," Spire commented. "We assumed you were his target. Given when we assume he left New York, he would have reached you long since. If not you, then what?" Here Spire paused. "However, it is good to see you well, old chap," Spire added, as if he suddenly realized niceties sometimes were, actually, nice.

"And all of you," Bishop returned, keeping his hand on Clara's elbow, refusing to break contact. The simple tether eased so many of her bruises and sharp pains.

"What building is this?" Rose asked, gesturing before her to the large, stately building and evident construction around it.

"This, friends, is the Executive Mansion," Bishop explained. "Some will say the White House, or, if you're snide, the 'Presidential Palace.' Where our president lives while in office." Here, Bishop almost sounded nervous. Clara looked up at him, hearing the subtle shift in his voice. "The building is under present renovation."

"Perhaps new technologies?" Spire queried. His unspoken point was clear: The building was more vulnerable to corruption than usual.

"That's what we must determine," Bishop replied. "The president thought he saw *shadows* here. I haven't been admitted in to speak with him. I don't have full clearance to all government buildings and my mesmerism only goes so far."

"How long can you be seen giving us a 'tour'?" Spire asked.

"Long enough for an external search," Bishop replied. Everyone focused on their surroundings with an immediate, intense scrutiny.

Rose was already studying any disruption in the grounds where the landscape architects were arranging nature to their bidding. Spire was looking at the structure itself. Lord Black was noting every plant.

Evelyn and Miss Knight stood several yards apart from each other, eyes closed, inspecting psychically and asking for spirits to offer up information. Clara suddenly wished Mosley were present to listen for current misplaced or other issues only his ears could detect.

No, she reminded herself, not only his ears. She listened, too. Clara closed her eyes, listening. There was strange, grating whine. A dissonant note. A clear danger.

"I cannot detect any signs of disturbance on the ground level," Spire reported.

"There's nothing off outside. But *inside*," Evelyn stated, squinting at the foundations. Miss Knight nodded in agreement.

"There is a dissonant, raw, scratching note," Clara said to Bishop. "Lately, that has meant disaster," she said blankly. "Why are you nervous about President Arthur? What are you afraid to say? We must be entirely forthcoming with one another," she pressed.

Bishop sighed. "I've been unable to access him. I'm admittedly worried as one of his aides confessed to me he hasn't seen him all day. I don't believe him to be an unpredictable man. This could be a crisis, especially considering—"

"Garfield," Spire interrupted. "I was telling Rose I think all of your security in Washington is woefully lax. Forgive me for saying so."

"No, agreed," Bishop replied. "We may find the Secret Service becoming stronger still, when all is said and done. I admit, as the legislator responsible for the Eterna Commission, devised for the purposes of supporting the presidency, I feel more responsible for all of this than I can explain."

"As do I," Clara said, still keeping close to him, his vibrant presence like a fire she could warm her aching bones beside.

"Arthur is your vice president ascended to president, yes?" Spire asked. Bishop nodded. "Who becomes president if something happens to Arthur?"

Bishop swallowed. "There is no official line of succession after."

Spire frowned. If he planned to make a remark about the superiority of the English system he kept it to himself. "Well. Let's hope it doesn't come to that, then."

"This afternoon's event, inside, for government officials, is our best chance," Bishop explained. "Mr. Spire, if you and Black could accompany me to the door, Reverend Blessing knows some of the help so he has cover in the building's inner workings. I feel confident if I'm inside I can find Mr. Arthur and get to the bottom of this."

"And the rest of us?" Clara pressed, an edge to her voice.

He turned to her ruefully. "You and the ladies will have to sit this one out, my dear, I'm sorry, it's a gentlemen-only affair and my mesmerism mustn't be spread too thin."

Clara scowled, withdrawing from his side, folding her arms. "Unacceptable," she countered.

"My powers of suggestion, like your own sensitivities, have limits, Clara. I chafe at the division of the sexes here, exactly as you do, but I dare not be too interesting or attention-stealing, and you are both. We don't know what all will be asked of us today and beyond," Bishop said.

Clara gritted her teeth. She remembered that Louis declared her a psychically "loud" presence. She'd best not set off any further alarm bells right upon arrival.

"We'll be there to support you however you need, Senator," Spire stated.

Lord Black, sensing the extreme tension, changed the subject. "I have a suggestion for the landscapers—there are numerous plants and shrubs that might be more . . ." He chose his words to reflect practicality above magic and spiritual meaning. "*Hardy.* Better investments."

"Make a list if you would. I'll be sure it gets into the designers' hands and add enough mesmerism to enforce the plantings," Bishop promised. Black beamed. "And I will say that on an individual basis, the few senators I've harangued seem amenable to states adopting their own trees and flowers as Warding measures. I'll have to mesmerize the house again for maximum assurance. States' rights mean any measure would be a gradual adoption."

"I studied a map of the core of D.C. on the train here," Spire said. "If the rails are subject to the same . . . pollution as the electrical grid was in New York, you'd best have inspectors take to each of the railways' depots."

"Agreed," Bishop replied as they turned around the exterior of the west wing. "Representative Brown has been extremely helpful, and has been making sets of Wards for personal and building use. When I said I'd likely have company, he promised he'd send a set to the Willard, look for them and have them on hand."

"How much time do I have before the next reception?" Spire asked. "I'd like to let the police precinct here know about Mr. Fordham, and about Celeste, any of the details that might be similar to New York, have them ready to evacuate any problematic areas."

"You've three hours or so until I need you back here," Bishop replied. "But don't breathe a word about the Summoned, or any worry for the president."

"You think *I* would warn fellow police officers about demons?" Spire asked with an arched eyebrow.

"Right," Bishop said with a mordant chuckle.

"We'll need their help and I'd like them on my side from the start," Spire said. "Point me to the precinct."

"I suggest you speak with the sergeant of the Capitol Police inside the Capitol building itself, ask them if they've seen or noticed anything unusual," Bishop said, gesturing toward the white-domed building rising above the tree line a mile and a half away. "The building has been recently electrified. If they believe you and your badge, you could ask to see the generators, see if anything has been co-opted down below. Feel free to drop my name but I don't know if it will open any doors, as you can imagine they're hard to persuade."

"I'll do my best," Spire stated, off in the direction of the grand complex immediately. Rose seemed torn, looking at Clara, then after the retreating Spire.

"We can't let anyone go alone, right?" Clara said, gesturing after Spire. "Come back for afternoon tea at the Willard, please, when you're done," she added. Rose nodded and ran after him.

Spire paused, hearing her running footsteps, and smiled over his shoulder as he continued. When they reached the road, Spire helped Rose up into a waiting carriage stationed there for the express purpose of making visitor rounds to buildings of note.

That happiness of a perfect partnership, even when attending to harrowing duties, was moving to see.

Clara turned to Bishop and refused to hide the pain in her eyes. He couldn't take her with him for the most critical night of this next phase, and she hated the world that considered her less, a world that separated them, never so much as now.

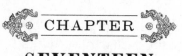

CHAPTER

SEVENTEEN

Washington was perhaps more divided by gender, race, and class than anywhere Clara had yet been. There were spaces women simply did not go. The goings-on of the rest of the day were for the gentlemen.

The ladies could have played tourist, seen art and other grand monuments, but none had the strength, the energy, or the inclination after the past week.

Clara, Evelyn, and Knight, situated in a large multiple-bedroom-and-bath suite, simply tended to themselves, which was admittedly a nice change, taking the time to clean, brush, and reset mussed hair, and to lounge in a scented bath, Clara adding a cup of Epsom salts to help her sore body. Humanizing things they'd let go in the past hectic days were attended to.

They changed into robes while their clothes were laundered. There were fresh, basic shirtwaists and skirts left for them thanks to Lord Black's consulate, and they gave their measurements to the Willard tailor for adjustments. Knight sent for an aquamarine silk evening gown instead, citing that her gifts were "simply useless in plain linen."

Clara took the liberty of sending Rose's garments on for her, as she was not yet returned from the Capitol and might not be for some time. Once Clara had changed into the crisp white shirtwaist with a lace collar and a cornflower blue skirt, she responded to a knock at the main door of the suite.

"Package for Miss Templeton," came a voice from the other side of the door. Clara opened it.

"That's me," she replied.

"From Representative Brown," the dark-haired maid in a starched uniform said, bobbing her head and holding out a box. Across the top was writ in Latin that Clara easily understood as:

For Protection.

In neat script below, the kindly man had added, *Welcome back to Washington, Miss Templeton.*

Wards.

"Thank you!" Clara exclaimed. As the door closed behind her, she swept into the parlor of the suite, where Evelyn and Knight sat with tea and District newspapers. Washington had not, it seemed, dealt with the outpouring of supernatural phenomena other cities had. Not yet.

"Bishop's dear friend Mr. Brown had local Wards sent over to us."

"Ah, good Mr. Brown!" Evelyn exclaimed. "Brown is one of Rupert's oldest, most trusted friends," she explained to Knight, who was braiding long black hair while staring in a mirror.

"He's the first associate Rupert sent a Ward recipe to, once we realized the worth of Louis's material," Clara continued. "Well before Rupert tried to mesmerize Congress to implement Warding, Brown was already creating these. I have to think it's why the District has fared better so far. Come on then, put one on your person," Clara bid, handing two to Evelyn and setting two on the vanity before Knight.

They were all in small bottles with cork stoppers. Clara poured the contents of two into a handkerchief and tucked it against her bosom to rest at the drawstring of her chemise; there the beat of her heart would charge that Ward as if she'd lit it. She placed others in her reticule and the other women did the same. Clara placed a few bottles on top of Rose's things so she wouldn't miss them either.

Eterna was, in its way, trying to do what it had been intended for. Protection at the highest levels of government, so the country would never be as rocked as it was when Lincoln was killed. That Garfield was taken down so relatively soon thereafter was a saddening, frustrating blow to the commission.

Clara so dearly wished they could have put these sorts of protections in place before the devastating effects of *another* assassination within their lifetime, the event having filled the whole team with a sense of forlorn failure. But the Wards, at least, were a push back against evil, even if it wasn't able to stop a bullet or reverse its damage.

Pressing the Ward against her heart, feeling the magical poultice heat up as if it were a living organism, she tried to reach out tendrils of her sensitivities, feeling for Bishop in the cacophonous realm of psychic navigation. If she could not be with him physically, she would try to hone her talents to be with him spiritually.

Knowing he was outside the Executive Mansion, or just having entered into it, she felt a pang of "what if" . . . and wasn't sure if the existential query was his or hers. She could feel a sort of boyhood wonder overtake him as he crossed the threshold of the "palace."

While they had never discussed it, Clara had often wondered if Bishop had ever considered running for president. But the obstacles were obvious.

A Quaker president? Not in her lifetime, she doubted. They were *too* sensible. Pacifist abolitionist suffragists . . . the bulk of the states and ever-usurping territories seemed to cherish warfare, seizure and inequality a bit too much for a man like Bishop, a stalwart Republican with progressive ideals, to ascend beyond his senatorial sphere.

That he'd remained in office for so much of his life was a

wonder. He happened to be very good at his job and very good at being the level, gamesome head in a room full of tempers at critical junctures. And, for what it was worth, he could not be bought or bribed. This was perhaps the most important factor in his being very good at his job. He *did* it, rather than parroting another platform, obstructing one, or bending on lobbyist marionette strings.

Lobbyist. That was what she'd be for the rest of the day, Clara thought bitterly; the origin of the word. Relegated to reception areas, hoping for a passing moment with a lawmaker deigning to rub elbows . . .

As the women descended for a late lunch, Clara passed through the Willard lobby, busy and brimming with the most expensive fabrics swishing about luxurious furnishings and innumerable crystals. Accents from around the country and indeed the world created a unique aural tapestry, sounds bouncing off marble and mahogany. Clara tried to lose herself in sounds to calm her nerves.

Down a lavish mirrored hall where chandeliers, potted palms, and hardwood paneling were reflected in endless iterations, the ladies of Eterna and Omega were ensconced in a private room with an adjoining parlor.

* * * * *

Spire escorted Rose back to the Willard, inquiring if the women had yet been seated for a meal. While Lord Black and Bishop were already inside the Mansion, Reverend Blessing was meeting with a member of the downstairs staff. Despite the importance of their investigation, it was embittering that Blessing's dark skin meant his freedom was as limited as the women's. Spire felt the same wave of anger he often felt at the closed doors between classes in England; so many iniquities dealt and opportunities missed at constant blockades.

A lobby concierge showed Spire the way to their team's private dining room.

"At least the sergeant took you seriously," Rose said of the encounter with the police.

"He seemed to be well-read, aware of the issues in other cities. That he knew what had happened in London surprised me," Spire stated.

"Washington may feel it needs to be aware of the outside world more than insular New York, which thinks it's the center of it. No offense to our New Yorkers," she said with a slight smile.

When Spire opened the dining room doors, his colleagues looked up at him hopefully, and he ached to see their capable, eager souls so constrained.

Spire lingered at the threshold while Rose came in and took a seat in a wingback chair.

Clara swept over to Spire and tucked two Washington Wards into his breast pocket.

"Here you are, my friend," Clara said, patting the pocket, trying to keep a measure of good cheer amid what was evident frustration. "Fresh local protection brought to you by New York Representative Ephraim Brown, one of Bishop's best friends and one of the only people he never has to mesmerize to do the right thing. He's been employing the Warding strategy here since we first started using it in the city."

"Thank you," Spire said. He looked around at the women before him, his usually neutral face unusually expressive with concern. "Are you sure you don't need someone to stand guard?" he asked.

The women—three clairvoyants and a code breaker par excellence—simply stared at him in silence. Rose folded her arms. Spire cleared his throat.

"Right then, I'll see you after the reception. We'll be sure to have a nice dinner, all of us. Take care." He strode off.

A moment later, he reappeared.

"Do not misunderstand me. I know all of you can take

care of yourselves and no offense was meant. I'm just . . ." Spire clenched his fists and stammered a bit. "Well . . . I've grown rather fond of you lot. And I don't like our splitting up. Bad things happen when we do. I'm not paranoid; at this point we've established empirical evidence."

Clara smiled warmly at him. "We'll manage, Mr. Spire, as none of us are alone, nor will any of us volunteer to be, but thank you."

He glanced furtively at Rose, who had unfolded her arms and was staring at him with a bit of pleased wonder at his unexpected display of emotion. Miss Knight breezed up to him and planted a kiss on his forehead.

"You *darling*, you," she cooed. His cheeks went scarlet and he moved to take his leave again.

"I'll be with the senator inside the Executive Mansion. Send word at the least inclination." Then he was gone, for good this time.

Evelyn loosed a chuckle when the mirrored door began to slowly close behind him and his flustered form caught a palm leaf to the face as he went out.

* * * * *

Spire met Bishop and Black on the Executive lawn at their appointed time; outside they could speak more freely.

"The sergeant at the Capitol was very helpful," Spire stated. "He said his men will look into anything odd around the electrical equipment, and will be on the lookout for Mr. Fordham, and what I could describe of the mysterious 'Celeste.' He was aware of the concerns in other cities, by which I am heartened."

Spire then conveyed the same objections to his fellows as he did in the Willard reception room.

"For the record, after what we've seen and done together, I don't like our team being divided in such a manner. Our strengths are varied and should be shared, and the pattern of late has been of dividing our team further and further."

"I agree, and we'll reunite as soon as we've swept this entire building and I've finally gotten an answer about where the damn president went," Bishop said.

Spire remained uneasy.

He'd begun to value the eccentricities of the team, though he'd never expected to. The Sensitives always managed to see the world in way he did not, a unique perspective that allowed him to build the strategy necessary in a war across a plane that he struggled to admit existed. Rose was his bridge between these worlds, and he was more grateful for her by the passing day; she understood her clairvoyant colleagues and Spire himself in equal measure.

Ascending the steps of the grand manse of the president, they checked in with a stern-looking footman in fine black dress who insisted only Bishop was on the list. Mesmerism employed, Bishop soon led the trio through the many stately rooms, Bishop explaining that there had been a recent change in decor thanks to the innovative Tiffany studios.

"Then how will we know if something is odd, out of place, or just 'art'?" Spire asked, grimacing at a mosaic installation he deemed rather gaudy. Black chuckled. "I'm being rather serious."

Black laughed further. "I know you are, my good man, and I don't know what to say. You're right. How would we know?"

"We'll have to hope small black boxes and disembodied parts are not part of the Tiffany vision," Bishop said mordantly.

They were ascending a carpeted stair that led to the west wing, Senator Bishop trying to explain to his British cohorts the particulars of their governmental system—one that to

Spire's mind seemed terribly inefficient—when Lord Black paused at a vase of calla lilies and frowned.

He swept back down to the wide stair landing, where a butler was directing the traffic of the distribution of hors d'oeuvres on the ground floor. Bishop followed a pace, Spire descending the stair enough to overhear.

"My good man," Black exclaimed to the butler. "I am very impressed with the new decor."

"It is very innovative indeed, glad you approve, sir," the butler replied with a smile. "Can I help you with anything?"

"I *love* the choice of flowers. Calla lilies, how stylish and modern. Are they always here or are these special for to-night?"

"For tonight's event, they were just brought in today."

"Thank you!" Black said, sweeping back to his associates.

"Why do the flowers matter?" Spire said. "I confess I don't share your particular expertise with or enthusiasm for plants."

"If the flowers were placed today, that's far too soon for a calla lily to be fading," Black said, inclining his head toward the middle blossom in the vase, which was yellowing and drooping.

"So it is," Bishop agreed.

"Is he still watching me?" Black asked. "I want to examine the pedestal but not if we're being watched."

"He is still looking in your direction. Somewhat dazzled, I'd say. I think you've an admirer," Bishop murmured, waiting for the staff to find the nobleman less fascinating.

"Damn. I wasn't trying for *that,*" Black muttered. "Just information."

"You're easy to like, milord," Bishop said. "Are you sure you're not a mesmerist?"

"No, he's just insufferably charming," Spire stated matter-of-factly. *"Insufferably."*

"My dears, you are too kind," Black said with a laugh.

"It's true," the policeman continued with a scowl. "I've tried to stay angry with you and I'm angry I can't stay angry with you."

Black laughed again, looking over his shoulder to see he still had the eye of the butler. "Well then, let's see if I can use that to further advantage. You take your opportunity as I do."

Moving away from Bishop and Spire, Black floated toward a server carrying a tray of food near the butler, making an excited sound.

As the staff watched Black, Spire took the moment to examine the console table. Bishop shifted the vase as Spire picked up the pedestal, lifted the lid, and made a face. Bishop leaned over to see a severed ear and Spire snapped the wooden box shut. They put the items back, turning to watch as Black engaged the butler further with some quiet words before returning with a porcelain plate with bits of meat and cheese on picks.

"Lost my appetite," Spire said as Black proffered the plate, gesturing to the pedestal.

"Ah. Evidence for the Capitol Police, I take it?" Black asked. Spire nodded.

"They need to sweep the place. I'd drop it in a fireplace, but the smell alone would end the soiree. I don't know if you want that kind of attention, Senator," Spire said.

"I'd like to handle this as quietly as we can," Bishop replied. "The country can't lose faith in Washington so close after an assassination. We can't be seen as too vulnerable."

Black gestured that they move into another room, pausing to bow his head briefly to the butler, who beamed a smile in return. "That's Mr. Taylor," Black explained of the butler. "When I asked if I could meet the president he said your commander in chief was found shuffling around one of the half-renovated halls in his dressing gown." Black leaned in.

"Raving about nightmares. They're not letting anyone see him. He's been taken to a private hospital."

Spire watched Bishop's eyes widen as Black flashed a smile. "If I've learned anything from my dear Francis, it's always ask the butler, he knows *everything*."

"I'm not sure he should casually tell British parliamentarians state secrets," Bishop said with a bit of bemused horror, which only widened Black's smile.

"See? Insufferable," Spire stated.

"Well at least he's . . . alive," Bishop said quietly. "But it does mean that token under the lily isn't the half of it. Arthur was never a man, from my knowing his New York politics, given to histrionics, which is why I took his telegram so seriously. It must have gotten worse."

"Mosley suggested that extensions like that box are connected to a source infinitely worse," Spire murmured. "My bet is that source lies below the main floor."

"If that is the case, we've placed our good Blessing in danger then," Bishop said as he instinctively moved away from several men who seemed about to corner him, but called over his shoulder with a wave of greeting.

"Haven't forgotten about your suggestion, Jim, the paperwork is on my desk, I'll have an answer for you this week," the senator called, then smiled and disappeared around the next corner, turning back toward the front entrance of the mansion. Spire kept up the pace as the senator continued urgently, "We shouldn't leave the reverend alone while Warding and sweeping, he'll be outmanned."

The trio breezed past a throng of men hovering around a dark wooden bar where drinks were being served in the front foyer. A round-faced man with an incandescent smile sought Bishop out and it was clear this was someone he didn't need to mesmerize away.

"Representative Brown, my dear friend, this is Lord Black

and Mr. Spire, helping us on our protective mission," he said quietly. "We need to find our friend on the lower levels. This building has been tainted by dark forces. How many Wards are here?"

The man's face flushed with shame. "Only a few on the outside. I haven't had luck gaining audience of late, and I don't have your gifts, my friend." He loosed a smile and spoke with furtive excitement. "But I do have a few in my pockets I plan to leave in strategic places."

"Wonderful," Bishop replied. "While we're belowstairs, if you might convince a few discreet, able-bodied officers to be on hand if we need them?"

Brown nodded and hurried off.

Spire peered closely at the wall near a copse of potted ferns, searching for a crack in the surface. Finding a hairline rectangle outline, he put his hand to the paneling, found the notch, and pulled; a door swung free. The help would need to come and go from every floor, and he knew from finer houses that such entrances and exits were to remain as hidden, out of the way, and close to invisible as the persons used to power a mansion. How the disregarded half lived.

Spire went on ahead down the first few steps to a darkened landing and turned back to see that Black had followed but Bishop faced a few legislators staring at their unconventional exit. Bishop held up a shooing sort of hand. Spire assumed some mesmerism was in play and continued descending once Bishop had joined them, letting the door close behind him.

Once their eyes adjusted to a dimmer light they descended a long and narrow set of stairs to discover a bustling underworld of activity where cooks and maids, butlers and footmen came and went along halls of arched, undecorated brick.

"Anyone seen Mr. Blessing?" Bishop asked gamesomely as their company tried to stay clear of hors d' oeuvres and drink trays coming and going, hoping not to sow concern or alarm. Polishing a silver plate, a ruddy-faced Irishman pointed down an unadorned hall dimly lit by a couple of plain gas sconces.

They turned a few narrow corners, Spire feeling as though they'd nearly gone in circles, before they found their colleague.

In the dim gaslight, the reverend was passing a dark hand along the whitewashed brick, as if seeking to draw information from it through touch. At the sound of footsteps in his tunnel, the reverend whirled to face the intruders; his look of fierce concentration softened into his characteristic ebullient smile at the sight of his friends.

"What have you found upstairs?" the reverend asked.

"An ear in a box," Spire stated matter-of-factly. "You?"

"Nothing tactile yet." Blessing shook his lightly graying head. "But my heart is exceedingly heavy and led me to this area as if I were dragged. Please understand." He paused, searching for words. "A place like this is fraught, for anyone who would have been killed or enslaved under the orders and decrees of this Masters house . . . haunted by injustices. I must try hard to separate my own emotional weight from the tenor of the air here. But we are here to do God's work, cleansing the horror of the works of men," the reverend concluded with a sigh.

Listening, Spire saw for the first time just how herculean the man's faith must be, for him to keep so hopeful and kind despite the breadth of injustice.

"I remain ever in awe and appreciation of you, and will keep fighting our good fight," Bishop said gently, placing a hand on his friend's shoulder.

As the group crowded into the narrow hall, Blessing took a step back to make room, passing a nondescript wooden door. Suddenly something shoved the clergyman away from the door, though no hand or body was visible. Thrust across the dim space, the reverend hit the bricks opposite with a thud, and Bishop was immediately at his side to right him.

Spire dipped his hand in his breast pocket and gripped his pistol.

"I don't know if that was a warning or a threat," Blessing said, shaking his arms. Spire felt a distinct chill pass through the moist air and over his warm face. "I can feel spirits, thick and agitated," the reverend continued. "There is something *dreadful* behind that door."

Spire drew his pistol, then stepped silently forward and pressed his ear to the door. For a moment, all he could hear was his colleagues' breathing, the symphony of activity back down the hall, and distant strains of hobnobbing above.

Then, as if it were right at his ear, he heard a shuddering, aching, wrenching gasp. Terrified to the core, he transformed fear to action, as was his wont. He took a step back to gauge the distance; after one hearty kick the latch gave and the door swung open.

All was darkness within; the dim gaslight of the corridor seemed not to penetrate beyond a pace or two.

Spire struck a match as Blessing handed him an oil lantern from a hook in the hall. Once he lit the wick within the metal cage, the space came into view; it was about the size of a small ship's cabin, its walls untreated brick as compared with the whitewashed hall outside.

It was filled with a pyramid built of palm-sized black boxes. Just like the ones Spire had seen on the bridge, in Franklin Fordham's town house, and just minutes ago upstairs.

At the sight of this cumulative formation, Spire was filled with revulsion and a hot wave of anger. How could anyone take the time to do something so awful? It was the constant bane of his life's work; he didn't want to twist his mind in such a manner as to understand evil, but he wondered what it would have taken for something constructive to prevail instead of the dark impulses he saw created and re-created through the course of his cases. A fresh desire to obliterate these monuments of horror seized him with a righteous fury.

Spire swung the lantern to and fro. There was no one inside. He stepped into the tiny space. In the hall, the smells of oil, of polish, and of food cooking had canceled out the miasma of decay. But in the room itself, that was almost overwhelming.

Lord Black joined Spire, circling the pyramid with one hand over his nose; the other was pressed to his fine beige frock coat lest the hem fall against any part of the pyramid.

A dark substance on the boxes glimmered in the lamplight. Spire leaned in and sniffed to get a better read. Dried blood. Apparently drizzled from top to bottom; the structure's base lay in a pool of pitch-black tar, whose oil kept some of the blood freshly wet.

Spire lifted the uppermost box. Two eyes—just eyes—stared back. Suspicions confirmed, he shut the box.

"There is nothing but unrest here," Blessing stated, "and it is at a precarious point. Any minute the spirits could set this all afire. With the tar . . ."

"It could easily consume the building," Spire declared. "We've not a moment to waste."

* * * * *

The meal was pleasant enough, but the ladies found small talk difficult and so most of it was spent in silence. Afterward they listlessly entered the adjacent private parlor, where they were soon offered an array of desserts, teas and cordials, wheeled in on a cart covered with a white cloth, by a maid who entered with her head bowed in what was either extreme shyness or deference to higher classes taken to an extreme.

Clara didn't feel well. Lunch didn't settle, but she didn't complain out loud. Perhaps mint tea would soothe her.

As the ladies took to the desserts and hot beverages, as much for the sake of having something to do as to assuage any lingering hunger, the maid stepped to close the room's pocket doors and locked them—with herself on the inside.

She lifted her platinum-haired head. When her gaze caught Clara's, Clara's already churning stomach plummeted. The intruder was beautiful, compelling, and familiar. Her deep-set, dark brown eyes, such a contrast from her pale hair, were not the eerily reflective blackened eyes of the possessed, but their umber abyss spoke of an exhausted and embittered old soul. Even a light mourning veil across a theater couldn't have masked an energy like this one. It was her.

Instantly, Clara heard the distant, quiet whine of the polluted energies, and she was certain they were all in distinct danger. The woman spoke softly.

"The poisons I added to your food will still your motor functions while we chart our next course, together." She procured a golden pocket watch and glanced at it. "We've a schedule to maintain."

The women stared at their captor in amazement and horror. Clara noted that Miss Knight's face was as impressed as it was offended. Evelyn's gaze was a bit blurry, an expression Clara knew indicated the medium was trying to reach out to the spirit world.

"We've seen you before," Rose stated. "The picture demonstration in the theater. What is your role in the Society?"

"I am its heir, I suppose," the woman murmured.

"The green fire of Liberty's torch?" Rose pressed.

"Kept you busy, didn't it? That, and Columbia. All while my minions were hard at work elsewhere." Her smile turned to ice. "This is no land of freedom. It's a land of *infinite* prisons and I wanted to express an . . . *artistic* protest to Liberty's lie."

"What is Moriel's plan?" Clara demanded. "Celeste, is it? Or do you have some abominable title?"

"Lady C, yes indeed, though I rather think of myself as Lady Macbeth to the world, urging it onward, born to kill while it fails at leading."

The woman smiled again, the expression a work of glamour, that of an old fae queen who invitingly led humans to ruin.

"I'd like, while in the presence of ladies for whom I have the utmost respect—"

"Poison and capture is hardly a mark of respect," Evelyn spat, trying to lift her arm.

"I've physically paused and detained you," Celeste countered. "There's a semantic difference."

"What do you want with us?" Rose asked. The toxin was slowing her speech. The numb, heavy weight down Clara's arm extended to leaden fingertips.

"I'll ask first for your willing participation, then I'll take it by force," the woman replied honestly. "The world does not respect you as anything but prize and property. You're too clever, the lot of you, not to be spared as the field is leveled, evils for evils."

"While women deserve equal footing," Evelyn said, "seizing any goal with the help of the Summoned will only drag you to hell."

"I'm interested in doing something quite different with the Summoned than Moriel did," Celeste countered.

"You're co-opting the rails, electrical and telegraph lines," Rose stated. "Poisoning them with your tainted boxes."

"Empowering them, rather," Lady C corrected.

"Those who work with the Summoned don't last long," Rose cautioned. "You'll be torn to bits. Or don't you know what happens when those who hold court with the demons fall out of favor?"

"No, I won't be torn to bits," the lady scoffed. "I pledged *no* loyalty to the Summoned, thus they have no leverage nor sway. I have no allegiance to anyone but myself. Evil—mind you that evil is conceptually subjective—will always adapt. It is a river that never runs dry, especially not in this country. All the bloodshed and dynastic horror of a colonial empire creates a perfect palette for channels of visceral, violent energy. You'll join this rising tide, one way or another."

"That's not what *we* were born for," Clara countered. She bit her tongue as she fought numbness to continue speaking. "Our minds and hearts were chosen for the fights of the angels, not devils."

"Yes, I suppose you think you're rather special," Celeste sneered. "All of you. *Gifted.* You stand out in a crowd." She narrowed her eyes at Clara and gestured around Clara's head: her aura. "You're very loud."

Clara set her jaw. "So I've been told."

"That's all right. Makes it easier for the demons to find you." She smiled again.

"So I've seen," Clara retorted. "Are you trying to intimidate or recruit us?"

"Can't I do both? Do you remember, each of you, when you first knew you were gifted? I began with small monstrosities in Chicago slaughterhouses. I saw what I could do, my gifts of persuasion and clairvoyance burgeoning in blood. Fed by the intersection of blood and steel blades. Moriel was the first kindred spirit I ever knew . . ."

Celeste's lovely face turned harrowingly angry. "But he, in his aristocratic blindness, discounted this country, and my superior power. He used the Industrial Revolution in his experiments, but hoped to do away with the very technologies that broadened his terrorism. There is no going back. One must embrace progress. One must use industry to rule. Moriel could not see that he underestimated the ingenuity of the American imagination, which can be turned to a beautiful, terrible purpose."

Clara wondered at this turn of events in Society legacy. If she wished women to be considered equal they must then consider each other capable of just as many terrible things as any human being. Beautiful and terrible.

"To what *end*?" Rose demanded.

"In constant momentum I gain the eternal," the Shakespearean villain replied. "In wielding all of mankind's energies into my body I will live limitless in a limited world. Men are *so* afraid of women's bodies. They deem us a mere collection of parts. Why not make them frightened of our holistic selves for a legitimate reason?" she asked.

"Proving women can be equally monstrous does our sex no favors," Clara retorted, fighting a wave of nausea.

"I'm not interested in favors. I'm interested in completion of a wondrous task. My slaves have been building pyramids!" she said excitedly. "I know you've been dismantling my boosters as you find them, but there are too many you've not found. Nothing can douse the bonfire that shall set the 'Presidential Palace' alight tonight.

"I've set up a pentagram. Moriel's perversion of the sacred, I will admit, does help the power I amass flow more quickly into me. And you, my dear ladies, are the arm of my star! You know, after all that mess in England, you should know better than to split up. When all together, you're quite a force. But alas . . ."

Staring hard at Clara, the woman continued, "Your Bishop, for all his powers, all his posturing about suffrage and women's rights, wouldn't take you to that precious house tonight because *society* says no. How bold. What a soldier for progress."

This cut Clara to the core. Surely he could have brought her and Rose along; using his power of mesmerism wouldn't have taxed him beyond the pale. Then their compass would have been present. Celeste seemed to see in Clara's expression that she had touched a nerve, and she smiled.

"You'll still defend him, even after this? After being *discarded* as second class?"

"We're not discarded—" Rose countered.

"Your *gentlemen* have left you here at my mercy. Leaving me the perfect offering." Celeste removed her apron, revealing a stunning black brocade dress beneath, and then whipped the white cloth away from the bottom of the cart. Sitting on the shelf below fine china teacups were black boxes, scraps of fabric, surgical tools, and a small pistol.

"From gifted bodies I require gifted tokens," she added, and licked thin lips.

Celeste rapped on the service door seamlessly folded into the wall. It opened and in walked Franklin Fordham in a soot-stained brown suit.

Clara's heart plummeted as he entered. His eyes were glassy, reddened, and full of pain. Her worst fears, what she'd tried to tell herself wasn't true, was. He'd turned, he'd tainted their offices, his home, and now . . .

"It's easy to mentally control someone so lacking in confidence and security," Celeste said, her voice sickly sweet. "To overtake them with your own agenda and make them act against their own interests, just by pulling the right strings of their deepest misery. Play upon a man's fear and he's yours for the taking. A few psychic tricks and mesmerism doesn't hurt."

Franklin took a step toward Clara, who couldn't move from the neck down. She lifted her head defiantly, her gaze drilling into her friend, willing his true spirit to fight to the surface of the water his soul was drowning in.

"Don't do this," she begged. "Remember the storm. Remember what I did for you in that life and in this one . . ."

"Shut up," Celeste hissed, and raised her arms, flexing her palms, and the environment in the pleasant room with all its fine furnishings reacted.

What had begun as a low hum in Clara's ear burst into a palpable vibration, as if all the energy from the electrical grids, telegraph wires, and railways was harnessed to her directly, pulled all along the New York rails. The white walls darkened, as if tar was bubbling forth—an overwhelming excretion of shadow. The Summoned would be upon them soon.

"Remember what we've been through," Clara demanded of Franklin before he pulled fabric from his pocket to wind around her mouth in a gag to silence her.

Clara closed her eyes and unfolded her many selves, allowing for time to stretch, for the power of her multiple lives to anchor the room.

First to step forward was the old ship captain, the one who had saved Franklin in a previous time. Long ago Clara had discovered that she and many of her close associates had gone through many lifetimes together, sometimes aware of their previous connections, sometimes not.

Something shifted in Franklin's expression as he stared at the captain; Clara saw a spark of recognition and detected a faint image superimposed over the man who stood before her. A gentleman dressed in eighteenth-century seafaring garb stared at Clara's potent former self.

Franklin swiveled his head from the captain to Clara, confused. It was like watching a man wake up from a nightmare, only to realize that the nightmare was still happening.

Clara couldn't tell if Celeste could see the layers of her lives or not, if she did, she refused to let further company daunt her.

Reaching under a warming tray on the cart, the woman withdrew a sharp golden dagger. Clara could see inverted symbols of many faiths and traditions etched into the hilt—

once again harnessing the perversion of the sacred. Celeste handed the blade to Franklin, who took it in a shaking grasp.

"You know what to do," Celeste said, the stretch of Clara's lives slowing her words as she touched Franklin's hand, moving it to point the blade at Clara's face.

Clara felt terror lurch over her in waves, the physical effect of which actually fought back against the lethargic toxin. She tried to force her lives, her energy, to be *more*.

However, this application of her lives had a cost, widening the spaces for spirits and dark forces alike. What Lady C was doing to the corridor between the worlds, Clara's extension only opened the door that much further.

The air shimmered and the now-familiar corridor appeared, where the Summoned waited. A few shadows slipped into the room, while others peeled away from the walls in a lightless line of silhouettes.

For now, the shadows were relegated to hang back from Clara and her Warded operatives, each of them having a Washington Ward on their person. One of the shadows floated toward Celeste, who shifted her head slightly, beholden to the same slow time as the rest of them. A low growl sounded from the back of her throat and the shadow backed away as if recognizing one of its own.

"Now," Celeste urged Franklin, gesturing to the dagger. Franklin balked, looking again at the sea captain, then back at Clara, wide-eyed.

"We've always lived to *help* each other, brother," the sea captain Clara once was said to the man Franklin used to be.

Franklin's gaze cleared, and awareness dawned to terror.

Behind them, the soul corridor that Clara had opened widened, enabling Clara to see the other end, where two familiar figures stood at the threshold of a dark room. Bishop and Spire. As if he could sense someone looking at him, Bishop turned to face her. Rose managed to touch a shaking finger to the back of Clara's hand to bolster their connection. Even Harold Spire turned his head, staring toward something he could not see.

"Damn it all, this is the final *piece,*" Celeste demanded, her voice in this altered state sounding far away. She seized the knife from Franklin and lunged at Clara, who screamed as she felt the blade dig into the side of her skull and begin to cleave . . .

* * * * *

The gentlemen stared at the pyramid of defilement.

"We need to alert the authorities to the nature of this offering," Blessing said, wiping sweat from his brow though the room was cold. Spire noticed that the reverend's dark brow was wet with perspiration. The idea of psychic exertion would have seemed absurd to Spire even a month ago, but time spent with persons of unique talents had kindled in him a growing awareness of the physical toll those talents could exact.

"This is an explosion awaiting a lit fuse," Blessing explained, "but emergency workers must understand this pyre will need to burn out to diffuse the power of this spiritual offal. If the spirits don't burn this denigration in offense, they'll never truly be free."

A vibration rippled through the room. Bishop clapped hands over his ears and moaned.

"What is it?" Spire asked.

"Do you hear that?" Bishop responded. "A terrible whine, a *scream* . . ."

"No . . . I don't . . ." the Englishman replied slowly, feeling a sudden sinking in the pit of his stomach. "However I . . . Do you feel something? Like something . . . *pulling* at you?"

He and Bishop both stared at the same invisible point on the wall of the dank chamber. As one, each said the name of his beloved.

"Go to them," Blessing urged. "Lord Black, Brown, and I will handle the authorities and the fire."

"I'll help the reverend with sacraments," Black said, nodding. "It's all right, none of us are alone and that's the important thing. Go to the heart of the matter!"

* * * * *

If there was a rising, grating whine in the air caused by polluted power and the growing presence of the Summoned, Clara did not hear it for the agony. All her lives screamed with her as the knife came away with her ear.

Blood rushed down the side of Clara's skull as the monstrous woman placed Clara's severed ear in one of the waiting black boxes.

When Franklin, seemingly returned to himself, moved to intercept as the woman next went for Rose's hand, Celeste cursed. Lifting the blade again, she drove it into Franklin's side, pushing him toward the open service door behind him. He collapsed beyond the threshold and slipped down a few of the steep steps.

Amid a renewed cry of grief, anger, and agony and the shudders of shock as the hot blood poured down her white shirtwaist, Clara closed her eyes and reached, no, *lashed* out to seize the eldest lines of life, perhaps the eldest throes of magic, ancient ley power, flowing in an unbroken river since the dawn of time, desperate for the help of such a primal force in her moment of most primal need.

In response a sudden frisson washed over her body and for a moment eased the pain, a flush of life leaching out the rest of the poisons, and her left hand flew to remove her gag as her right hand flew to the open wound, pressing in hopes of stanching the blood flow even against the burning pain and the sickening feeling of missing cartilage.

Marlowe the visitor had taught Clara to feel ley lines with her body, Mosley to hear them; both were in play in these cacophonous moments as Clara tried to focus only on the power itself, to live and breathe it, to embody it as Mosley did electricity and Celeste did the darkness.

With a ripping sound separate from the whine and hum of the battling lines, there she was: Marlowe, dressed in a simple riding habit. Wobbling on her feet a bit at her abrupt arrival, the woman steadied herself by clamping a vise grip on Clara's shoulder. Everything stopped save for Marlowe and Clara. They had paused time together, and every sensation was muted.

"Hello, Clara—*Heavens!*" the visitor exclaimed, staring at her bloody charge in horror. Marlowe looked at Celeste, frozen in a fierce scowl, knife in hand and eyes glowing coals of evil. "Well, well . . ." Marlowe murmured carefully. "We only have a moment, you and I, in this heartbeat we carved out of time. Let me help." Gently she pried Clara's hand away from her head as a whimper of pain escaped her lips.

Hissing at the gory sight of the wound, Marlowe reached into a pouch on her leather belt and withdrew a thick, padded patch marked with an unknown British Ministry seal and pressed it hard against her head, holding it there as a white-hot heat emanated from the center of the visitor's palm. Clara winced and groaned, clasping her hands together to keep from shaking, bloodying them both.

"Hush dear, just a lay of hands."

After a moment, Marlowe murmuring some private liturgy, the warm buzzing sensation she proffered took the edge off the agony and traded it for a throbbing pain instead. The visitor took the gag and used it as a bind around her head to keep the patch pressed to her ear.

"What will stop her?" Clara asked of the enemy before her.

"You, and the ley lines, all of you, have to be louder than all her wires and rails and the work she's done to make them sing devils' music," Marlowe replied, cocking her head to the side. "All of you can counter it. Just be louder. Be *more*." Marlowe hummed a note. "Hold to that . . ." Squinting at Celeste, Marlowe spoke with disdain. "Your soul is far older than hers; make her fear your age. Only a new soul would be so selfish as to do all this . . ."

And that was all the time they had, for Celeste lifted her arms wider and the air gusted around them suddenly, the Summoned rousing to their master and pressing in a step, bouncing off the boundaries of the women's Wards.

Marlowe was gone and the whine in the fouled air ground to a louder pitch. Celeste narrowed her eyes, staring at the bandage on Clara's head and how it could have gotten there. This moment of confusion was a distraction to Clara's advantage. Her heart swelled with purpose.

Behind them, in the corridor, Clara's gifts opened to connect the compass, she could no longer see their other half, Bishop and Spire. But a black pyramid was still visible as the dissonant chord vibrated through her bones.

If that pyramid was a vile magnifier, then Clara knew she must stand as the same to the vibrant, verdant ley energy, the counter to this woman's raw dissonance. Clara stood, letting her own bloodied hands rise to her sides. Rose's eyes went wide.

Evelyn, at her other side, was murmuring exorcism liturgy. It was helping to press the Summoned forms back against and into the walls.

The evil was all in parts, but those who fought it were whole. . . .

Miss Knight was the next to overcome the toxin fully and stood, withdrawing a hand from her skirt to produce one of her chemical pistols, pointing it at the enemy, who had backed behind the dessert cart, putting it between her and the women she had overtaken.

Evelyn, eyes blazing in fury, still murmuring renunciations in a growling hiss, rose to a crouch, seemingly prepared to charge. Celeste exchanged the dagger for the pistol from the cart, cocking it, ready to shoot, keeping it trained on Knight as she grabbed the box containing Clara's severed ear and backed out into the service stair Franklin's body had been so unceremoniously disposed into.

The sound of shouts on the other side of the locked parlor door, a key turning in the lock.

With the press of a lever the service door slid shut before Celeste's face, her eyes filled with fire to the last, and as Knight and Evelyn both rushed to pry back open the panel, there was a sound of heaving and dragging, the body being taken away. Rose was assessing Clara from top to bottom as the parlor doors were thrown open and Bishop and Spire rushed in, the power of the compass connection nearly lifting the four off the ground toward one another.

"Good God, Clara," Bishop choked, blanching at the sight of her, bloodied down one side.

Rushing to her, hands flurrying around her, he tried to discern where to help or heal. For just a moment Clara felt terrified that she would no longer be loved now that she was so damaged. But that petty thought vanished for the larger scope.

Behind them entered two Capitol Police officers, summoned at some point during the fray and concern, staring wide-eyed at all the blood in the room.

"The wretch has gone to ground," Evelyn declared, pointing to the service door. "Keep your compass together," she said to Bishop and Spire. "I'll come with you, gentlemen, as she is armed and has . . . unconventional tricks up her sleeve."

"No." Clara grabbed Evelyn's arm, her voice clear and calm, almost otherworldly to her own pained ear. "I'll need you. All of you, to help me."

"We'll find the woman," the officers assured.

"You'll need more than two of you," Knight cautioned. The officers paled, glancing at Clara and back at all the blood in the room, then ran out to ask for additional help.

Clara's head pounded in pain with every heartbeat, but, as one could lose a fair amount of blood before unconsciousness, the temporary fix the visitor had afforded her would hold for one battle, Clara surmised, choosing to remain clinical lest she panic. The amount of energy she was wielding crackled around her, and she was sure it was the only thing superseding a seizure. She had to act while this state held.

"I have the ley lines *with* me now," Clara said to Bishop.

"I see," he said, breathless with wonder. "Your eyes are glowing. You are the eldest magic *embodied;* tell me what I may do to magnify you," he begged.

The clarion song of the eldest forces was loud and sweet in her ear, especially in her injured one, a balm and salve to get her through.

There were screams from the outside lobby. Voices were heard shouting about devils and the work of evil, that Satan had taken the sky as his own . . .

Clara gestured onward. "We have to act while the tide is high. The enemy has created a storm and we have to fight from the center of it outward."

Spire seemed nearly as struck by her as Bishop was, bloody mess and all. She had assumed a heightened otherworldly command and none questioned it.

"Lead on," he bid.

EIGHTEEN

From the screams of the tourists and employees of the District, Clara could only assume the worst of the sky outside.

As she stepped out into the hall toward the front lobby, people took one look at her and screamed anew, running from her bloodied figure. She was flanked by Bishop on one side and Rose on the other, with Spire and Knight keeping pace.

"Do I look that much a fright?" Clara asked Rose, pausing before she stepped fully out into the lobby beyond.

"It's a wonder you're still standing," Rose said. "Whatever is happening, whatever you are wielding, it turned the tide."

"We all did," Clara countered. "Each one of us is doing our part, we are all fighting and all of it counts."

"I tried to root around in her mind for her next step," Knight said, shaking her arms as if fully clearing the poison. "She blocked me at every turn," she continued, tapping her temple in frustration, "but I did get a sense of taking something to a great height."

Evelyn had dashed to the coat check and returned with the cloak she'd procured for Clara after her seizures in New York, a deep green cloak with a hood. Seeing it again made Clara think of her ancient self that had appeared out in the Trinity lot to help her. Might all her souls be with her now, she pleaded.

"Here you go, my brave darling," Evelyn said, placing the

cloak over her with care, and squeezed gently. Clara smiled
warmly at the medium, who was clearly shaken to the core
by Clara's injury. "Let's not have you out in the field looking
so vulnerable," Evelyn said, blinking back tears. "I know
there's no stopping you but you must tell us when you flag."

"If I do, that wretch will win," Clara said simply. At this,
everyone straightened and stiffened, a simple call to arms. "I
saw you trying to communicate with the spirit world, Evelyn,
I hope they were useful."

"The spirits kept repeating *Washington,* which I thought
at first was a bit redundant and obvious," Evelyn said. "But
perhaps they mean—"

"The monument," Clara exclaimed. "It's an obelisk." She
turned to Knight. "At a great height. She'll use that to magnify her power!"

She rushed forward and her phalanx followed.

"That's one monument Brown made a *point* to Ward,"
Bishop stated. "As a Mason, he knows full well the ceremonial
and mystical power of an obelisk as a needle to the heavens.
I can only hope his efforts stem the dreadful tide."

Anyone in the way promptly dove out of it as their grim-
faced group descended the front stair, coats and skirts flaring
in the wind of crackling energy and surging powers, Clara's
cloak buffeted like wings of a swooping bird.

Outside, in any direction that there were people, they were
running to take shelter from the darkening sky, hands on
hats, parasols and walking sticks all akimbo, pleasant strolls
turned into harried displays of terror.

She looked up and swallowed hard.

There were black clouds in the sky, roiling, in intersecting
lines. A star, Celeste had said. The inky clouds formed in the
vague hazy shape of a stretched, thin, inverted pentagram,
one arm reaching directly up over the Willard, tethered now,
by her own sacrifice.

But of course it wasn't dark clouds that had taken up the sky but Summoned forms.

A celestial horror.

"And we're going into the center of the star . . ." Rose murmured, as if by stating just how mad it sounded they might make some other choice. Clara simply took her hand and they walked forward across the lawn with their company.

"She said she wanted to foul a pentagram," Clara said to Spire. "I assume boxes with parts are hidden below each of these points. My own included," she said, pointing to the shadows unfurling above the hotel and referencing her bandaged ear. At this, Spire stared at her in horror. "I saw, when psychically reaching out to you," Clara continued, "a pyramid below the mansion. I assume there's another offering below the Capitol building, a point at the monument, and the furthest wing?"

"Likely one of the main train stations," Spire replied.

"The police need to be alerted to each," Rose urged.

"I believe we may already have tapped the limited manpower of the Capitol Police just by calling upon them to help Blessing and Black with the Executive basement. Hopefully the sergeant I spoke with wired for reinforcements."

Bishop had to mesmerize two carriage drivers to take them near to the monument and even then, they refused to go out onto the Mall proper. The senator even had to calm the horses with his gift before they began, Clara helping by reaching out a hand to each forehead. The creatures must have felt the gentle but unmistakable hum within her as they settled, still stamping but no longer rearing.

In the mile it took, their compass four traveling together, Clara closed her eyes to feel precisely where Washington's ley line might be. It seemed to be ahead of her, right along the

Mall itself; no wonder the planners felt the need to secure green space there.

"Did Masons build the District to correspond with ley lines?" Clara asked.

"There is endless supposition about the nature of the layout," Bishop replied, "but, like everything else in Washington, it's a bit haphazard. Some say there's a pentacle that can be laid atop the grid, but as Brown has told me time and again, pentacles aren't Masonic, that isn't their symbol, so I don't understand what this woman thinks she's perverting, other than playing into satanic fears."

"The pentagram itself is a general sign of protection," Clara stated.

"She wants to make every area feel it has none," Rose replied. "This feeds the kind of power she's clearly addicted to."

Clara descended from the carriage carefully with Bishop's help; any hard jostling was agony on her ear, despite the warming hum of the lines she tried to keep stoking within her. The group stepped out onto the gravel path, and the carriages were off again with a start and shrill whinnies.

They were left to the Washington Monument section of the green; from what they could see from here to the Capitol, the area appeared cleared of anyone but them.

Clara stepped onto the grass, giving herself clearance of a good number of yards away from the base, looking up at the unfinished top of the monument, the needle pointing to heaven not yet complete, open to the elements in jagged stone.

A line of Summoned forms floated above the monument's uneven mouth as if a sequence of pitch-black flags were unfurled from a pole. The silhouettes did not touch down as close to the monument as they had seemed to over the Willard, or even over the Capitol, where the Summoned seemed to cluster around the top of the white dome as if ready to pounce.

She credited the distance to the Warding done on the monument. Lady C wouldn't necessarily know to look for them, as she'd have demanded they revoke the ones on their person when she attacked them if she knew to disarm them.

"Now what?" Spire asked, grimacing up at the roiling sky, the pitch of the figures swarming. That the man remained undaunted was a credit to his heart and soul. "Shall I search the monument?"

"Please stay within sight," Clara replied, gesturing to Bishop and Rose as the compass points near her, knowing she had to let the policeman do something useful, as he couldn't be one to help with the magnification of psychic transmission. He nodded and moved away from them to inspect the base of the obelisk for foul tokens.

Clara lowered herself to her knees. Her company folded in around her in an instinctive, protective circle.

She placed her palms flush down on the earth, never minding the roaring pain that a bent head caused her ear, murmuring simple prayers taught in Quaker youth, focusing on the pleas for peace that her congregation had championed during the Civil War years.

"Let me magnify your power, as much as you will let me," Clara murmured to the ley line below her hands, humming the note Marlowe had put into her ear.

The line hummed back. Sang. Nearly shouted a tone, as if screaming a hallelujah. In that moment, she felt almost like she'd discovered a soul that had been lost, imprisoned, and given up for dead. The line seemed to be so eager to be recognized. To be given a voice again in a world that had seemed to have moved on without it. All the exterior noise, dread, pain, and confusion was wiped away; there was only a blissful *I am here.*

The androgynous self of Clara's past lives, likely of druidic clergy, peeled away from Clara, without her even having to make the extension. The form wafted before her like a ghost, but in full colors. That body did as she did, bent to the ground and placed hands flush upon the grass and laughed a joyous laugh.

"It is good to hear you, too, old friend . . ." the old soul murmured to the earth.

Clara beamed, suddenly unaware of anything but this joy, and even if no one could sense or see what she was seeing, all seemed very aware that she was in the midst of a transcendent state.

From this place, she hummed the song of the lines, and her compatriots picked it up. So even did the wind around them. The air around their circle was distinctly brighter than the air outside of it.

Out of the corner of her eye there came a speeding, inky cloud rolling toward them, a misty, wispy black ball that smacked against the base of the obelisk and vanished in a large explosion of smoke. Spire, who had been examining the exterior base of the pedestal, rocked back as if he was shoved by unseen hands.

The countermeasure, the fouled lines, sang back, a grating response to what Clara had woken from the ground. It was almost as if the cloud approaching the obelisk was a renewed jolt of the dark power and there was an aftershock of the impact. Clara stood and wobbled on her feet, steadied by the strength of her compass.

"There is bound to be pushing and shoving out here, a war of the currents indeed," Clara said. "We must stand our ground. Feel the ley harmony, the resolved note, within you," Clara said to those inclined, and unfolded her selves, the act of doing so easier every time.

Her lives took up the note in turn, and she shuddered a

convulsion of refreshed energy from the sacred line, rolling off her not in seizure waves but in what felt like a burst of angel song. Her compatriots focused on the note, too, humming lightly, ignoring the dread press of the Summoned as they floated lower and lower, as if seeking to blanket the earth in dread.

Distantly, across the Mall and beyond the tree line, a bell tolled. Off from their note, but resonant into the air. It kept ringing. It didn't seem possible, but to Clara's augmented ear, it grew louder.

Then, some streets away, in another direction, behind them, another tolled. Others took up the ringing. And with each new bell, Clara chose not to hear cacophony but willed the echo to tune to a resolved note. She pushed against the air, physically lifting her hands up. The pitch rose just slightly from reverberate off-tune to amplifying the resolved note of the ley song.

"Do you hear that?" Clara murmured. Glancing at Evelyn, she saw that the woman was crying, saying thank you and wiping her eyes.

Evelyn caught Clara's gaze and she quietly explained, as if not wanting to disturb the reverberate bells. "I asked every ghost that could possibly hear me, I begged them to help us. . . ."

"And they are . . ." Clara murmured. "This is working, my dears, keep this up. . . ."

As the bells crested, rung by phantom hands, holding and vibrating the ley note so well it almost drowned out the fouled whine, a figure approached them from the shaded lane beyond at a trot, wiping perspiration off his close-shorn graying hair and from his face with a handkerchief.

Reverend Blessing was on his way to them, his vestments smeared with soot and tar, Lord Black at a dash behind him, glancing up at the sky with a grimace, trying to get closer to the reverend as if to be next to him meant protection.

"Yea, though I walk through the valley of the shadow of death," Blessing intoned approaching his fellows, arms wide as if welcoming congregants into a chapel.

"I will fear no evil; for Thou art with me," Evelyn replied.

"How fares the mansion?" Bishop asked.

Blessing gestured at the distance behind him. "See the line of smoke? A private bonfire in the back garden, carefully monitored. I will bless the ashes when I return. Brown is overseeing it now."

Clara squinted past the smoke and tried to see if the Executive Mansion arm of the Summoned star was mitigated. It appeared to be so, but they needed to keep pushing until the sky was clear. The shadows were like an infection, and they had to be eliminated, along with their puppeteer.

Two Capitol officers galloped up on horseback, dismounting at the tree line and making straight for the obelisk. Spire stepped up to greet them. "Did you see the woman? She was heading right here," said one of them, exasperated.

"We have not seen her," Spire countered. "I've personally been inspecting the site. She may have entered ahead of us."

The men opened the door to the interior, gesturing to Spire. "Well, come on then, you're a man of the law, let's stop this monster."

Spire looked uncomfortable, glancing at Clara and Rose. "I can't."

"Beg your pardon?" the other officer asked, hand on his pistol.

"Go ahead, Mr. Spire," Clara said watching the proceedings as she examined the brightening sky. "Our bond will hold provided you stay open to us, and listen if we call."

He bowed his head and followed the officers into the structure.

There was a loud, explosive pop from the Capitol building, and all the electrical lights that had been turned on as the sky had become so preternaturally dark now exploded. From the distance near the monument, Clara couldn't see much but a flash of light. Several Summoned forms in the cluster over the Capitol dome wafted away as if cut from a lifeline, washing down a stream to vanish.

"That has to be a good sign," Lord Black declared. He took in the sight of Clara, the blood on her sleeve, and his eyes widened.

"I'll be all right," Clara murmured to him. "But help me magnify the ley lines, you understand them, too." The noble-man nodded, and rummaged in his pocket, pulling out small flower buds.

"Gathered these along the way. Here. For healing," he in-sisted, tucking a small white bud into the bloodstained lace of her collar.

From far above them there was the sound of a scuffle, a roar and a scream. Clara and her compatriots cried out as a head was seen hanging over the top of the open obelisk. Then came a garish horror. A gush of scarlet blood splattered down the white stone and kept running in thin rivulets toward the base. The Summoned forms wafted closer, freshly encouraged by the ghastly sight.

"Harold!" Rose cried. There was a sharp tattoo, gunshots. A high-pitched scream of fury from above. The Summoned that had thinned fleshed out their ranks once more.

Clara returned to her knees. Her lives knelt with her. She couldn't get too distracted, even for the sake of Mr. Spire; the best thing she could do to help him was to keep extending the line.

"Tell the ghosts to keep up their aid," Clara begged Evelyn, who was staring up above in horror. Even if a swarm of ghosts threatened to shift Clara toward a seizure, she knew if there wasn't another push, they'd lose any ground they'd gained.

Blessing began circling their group reciting the exorcism liturgy, Evelyn falling in as his second, renouncing the dark forces above.

Rose ran to the base of the obelisk and called for Spire once more. There was a growl in response, echoing down the stone. Knight followed, raising her chemical pistol at the open door.

Clara fought for the note again; the bells had grown faint, only one nearby carillon still keeping unconventional mass with them.

Rose screamed as a roiling cloud of black mist tumbled out from the door of the obelisk, snarling and fighting forms, scrabbling limbs visible in a tangle within.

Clara dug her nails into the grass and pulled, as if she were reaching into the earth and dragging up an actual rope.

"Come fight with me, old friend, louder, harder, I *desperately* need you, here in the valley of the shadow of death," she murmured to the ley force. It answered.

She stood, and the surge of the energy up her body nearly lifted her off the ground. The glorious hum blasted again through every fiber of her being and she strode directly toward that hazy, frenetic knot that had tumbled out of the monument.

Bishop raced after her, and as Clara approached, holding her hands out as if they were weapons, the mist fell away. Summoned forms floated up as if blown back from the power, revealing the fight within: Celeste clawed and raged in Spire's faltering hold.

Behind them, the second of the two guards stumbled out, wide-eyed, and ran away from the site, screaming of devilry as he fled.

Blessing kept up with his liturgy. Clara looked up. The sky was nearly clear, not entirely, they were close . . . Returning her attention to the fight, stepping closer toward them, Clara

was horrified to see blood dripping from Spire's fingertips
from an unseen wound.

But their compass was reunited and the surge between the
partners forced the Summoned, who were still near enough
to swipe at Spire, clawing at his face and gagging him with
their toxic essence, to be dissolved into mist and evaporate
in the instant.

Knight fired at Celeste and in an explosion of acrid smoke
the two were flung apart. Rose and Bishop rushed forward to
catch Spire before he struck his head on the ground. Rose
tended to Spire immediately while Bishop turned his focus
back to Clara and Celeste.

The villain, snarling, dress ripped, hair wild and grayed as
if she'd aged a decade in a mere hour, regained her footing
and like an animal, made to lunge at Knight, but there was a
sudden arc of light that came down like the lash of a lightning bolt.

The blast flung Celeste to the side like a rag doll, after
which she lay crumpled on the grass, looking withered, the
hem of her dress singed and smoking.

Mosley, small and mousy in a too-large suit—Clara had
never seen him in one that fit—came into view from around
the side of the obelisk.

"*That* is on behalf of every electrical grid you've ruined,"
Mosley declared matter-of-factly to the crumpled form
before he sheepishly looked at Clara. "Keep watch, that
wouldn't have been enough to kill her. I assumed you'd want
to question her."

"Yes, thank you, Mr. Mosley," Bishop said in halting surprise.

Knight moved to the enemy, nudging the limp body onto
its side, and bent to bind her wrists tightly together with a
wide ribbon from her own dress.

"I fixed the Capitol," Mosley added. "They'll need new fixtures but the abomination from the sub-basement is clear."

"Thank you," it was Clara's turn to offer. So that was what the electrical explosion was about.

Their unpredictable ally looked up at the garish swath of crimson marring the monument and grimaced, and then he noticed Clara's bloodstained blouse and gown, her cloak having folded back over her shoulder, her battle wounds revealed. As he was watching her, she noticed that a line of dried blood extended from one of his nostrils, a rivulet of which had dripped onto his brown coat. Every act, every gift, it had a cost; a physical toll.

"Is he all right?" Mosley asked, pointing at Spire. Rose had ripped his shirt and waistcoat open to determine the source of the wound. She folded the torn hem of her petticoat to make a compress.

"A bullet hole in his side that seems to have gone clean through," Rose stated, and Clara could hear her trying to control her panic as she whipped off the loose silk bow at her throat to bind his torso, pulling hard on the fabric. "But the battle and the shock has knocked him unconscious."

Mosley came close, bent down over Spire, and held an open palm out a few inches over his heart. He then poked him with his index finger, hard in the chest, and there was a little *zap*. Spire's body shook reflexively, stirring in Rose's hold.

"Thank you," Rose murmured to Mosley, her voice catching.

Spire opened his eyes to see Rose looking down at him. He smiled. Mosley turned away, excusing himself from their tenderness, moving to examine the obelisk.

"Hello there," Spire said jovially. "Did we survive?"

"Yes." Rose exclaimed, the relief clear in her voice.

"We really shouldn't split up," Spire murmured, and Rose

helped him sit up on the grass. "Oh, that does hurt. Shots were fired."

"Yes, one through you," Rose murmured.

He glanced up at everyone before looking down at his makeshift dressing. "I say, women should always have on multiple layers of finery, else all of us would have bled to death in one attack or another."

Rose laughed. Clara did, too, until it hurt and she groaned, her hand rising to her wound as if she could pull away the pain.

"I should also say that there are foul offerings inside the base of the structure," Spire added. "Might want to tend to those."

Blessing gestured to Evelyn and they set to work cleansing and sanctifying the boxes from within the memorial structure.

"There's that fallen officer, too," Spire continued. "Dreadful stuff. Have we cleared the skies, though, Templeton?" he asked with a wan smile.

"Nearly, sir," she replied. "All the better thanks to your bravery."

"Oh, you set the tone for that today," he countered.

"How *are* you faring, Clara?" Bishop asked gently, taking her hand. "With all of this, I expected you might be staving off a seizure."

"Surprisingly, the force of the ley current seems to have stalled one. I am better than I should be, by all accounts."

"I'd like to get you to a doctor immediately," he replied, gesturing toward the bandage on the side of her head now caked with blood.

"Ah. Yes. It does hurt something fierce, and I expect I'm going to have a hard time looking in a mirror," she murmured, suddenly ashamed.

"My beautiful treasure," Bishop murmured, moving to her

and caressing her bruised cheek, lifting her bloodied hand and kissing it. "Nothing could make me see anything different."

"Thank you," she murmured, blinking back tears.

Mosley was wandering around, looking up at the sky and the few remaining Summoned that still floated there.

"Shall we finish this?" he asked Clara. "Between your line and mine, I think we can cancel out the damage she's done. Man-made and natural light don't *have* to be currents at odds," he added quietly.

Clara realized he felt about electricity the way she felt about the ley line, proprietary and protective about something that was often misunderstood.

Clara blinked at him a moment. "Of course," she stammered.

"All right, then." Mosley closed his eyes, holding out his hand before him. There was a buzzing in the air, a whine rising before it settled out to a vibrating hum at a high pitch. Hair rose on his head, and sparks flew up from his palm as if he held tiny fireworks.

Bishop drew Clara a few paces away from the rising voltage for safety's sake.

Clara knelt again, feeling for the lines as she did, against the ground, and the ley hum rose in her ears and shifted in pitch off the buzz nearby, as if either was a tuning fork for the other. The notes made a chord.

Some bells in the distance picked up on and tolled the tones, the effect of their work still having preternatural reach.

Looking up, they watched as the Summoned dissipated. Only a few hung over where the train stations clustered in the distance.

"That'll be easy enough to clean up," Mosley stated, gesturing toward what remained. "Are you going back to New York?"

"I assume, once . . . affairs are taken care of."

"Then I shall see you there," he said, and walked away without another word.

Bishop and Clara watched him go for a moment. He didn't look back, his fingertips fluttering at his side as if he were playing an instrument on the air.

Clara looked up at Bishop, standing over her; she was thinking of what was left undone. "Oh, God . . . Franklin's body," she murmured as the sequence of loss came back to her in a rush. "He woke up from her spell and she killed him. . . . He'll be in the basement of the Willard, she killed him and I couldn't stop it. . . ." Tears spilled down her face, the pressure of flushed cheeks making her whole head throb; the full breadth of the past days was too much to consider.

Bishop helped her up. As she rose, a wave of dizziness accosted her and she stumbled in Bishop's hold, but he held her steady.

Blessing, having returned from a rite over the boxes, stepped toward Clara, speaking quietly. "I'll take care of Franklin and see that he is returned to lay in the family plot, I'll pray over him with my colleagues. I'll stay in Washington another day to help them be sure of their own Warding and loose ends."

"Thank you," Bishop and Clara chorused.

"The pain is getting harder and harder to ignore," she murmured.

Blessing reached in a breast pocket for a small tin. He held out something for Clara. She opened her hand and he deposited two white pills into it.

"For the pain. I always carry some with me, for the agonies prayer can't immediately heal." He smiled. From another pocket he procured a small clear bottle and held it out.

"You're bidding me take aspirin with holy water?" she asked incredulously.

"I think God understands practicality, dear, and I happen to think He thinks you've suffered enough."

She took a small sip and tried to appreciate it as a taste of something priceless as she swallowed the pills. Blessing moved to Rose and Spire, who had been discussing matters quietly, and offered the same succor to Spire, who downed the rest of the bottle eagerly, not realizing it was sacred. This almost made Clara laugh again; her desire to weep, shout, scream, rage, rejoice, and laugh all held equal court.

Two more Capitol officers on horseback arrived, this time one Spire recognized and he struggled to get to his feet. "Sergeant!" he called.

"Mr. Spire. A fresh hell around every corner," the man murmured, staring up at the dreadful scarlet marring.

The men discussed what happened and the protocol of the prisoner, still lying unconscious on the grass, Knight keeping a vengeful watch, Spire drawing Bishop over to inquire about jurisdictions.

Clara lay back on the grass, tried to ignore the throb of her head, the strange sensation of missing a part of one's body that was there and gone in such a split second. She tried to find peace in the ley energy again, but perhaps it, too, was tired; its hum was faint, or perhaps it was coursing onward to others who called upon it, too.

Soon she was lifted up into Bishop's arms.

"Shall I help you walk or carry you home?" he asked.

"I can walk, let's not make any *more* of a scene," Clara chuckled. "But Rupert, we've no home to return to," she exclaimed, one painful reality hitting her after another.

"Yes we do. You are my home."

As he gingerly set her down, she nuzzled against him. "Yes," she murmured, "you are my port in the storm." She leaned in, kissing the hollow of his throat as she shivered in delight. "Being parted from you now causes a physical pain it never did before. If I lost you, I'd never find peace. Not now, not in any lifetime . . ."

He pressed his forehead to hers. "There was a time when I accepted a guardian's role with the gravest responsibility. But now . . ." He kissed her brow. "Do you know what I've done every year on the anniversary of your father's death?" he asked quietly.

"No . . ." Clara said warily, taken completely by surprise by what she assumed was a change of topic.

"I've asked him, since you were of age, if he would grant me your hand. The most recent anniversary fell—"

"While we were in England," Clara interjected.

"Yes. While I'm hardly the medium that Evelyn or you are, I will say that after years of silence, he replied."

Fresh tears wet Clara's cheeks. "And?" she asked breathlessly.

"He assented. Clara Templeton," Bishop said softly. "I was inelegant when I spoke of marriage before. I beg your forgiveness and ask you now. Will you?"

"Yes . . ." she breathed. "A compact made lifetimes ago, finally manifest in this one." Their ensuing kiss created a subtle haze of smoke curling up from their clothing.

Alarmed at first, they drew back, but kissed again when they realized the wisps were a protection; they'd lit their own Wards with adoration.

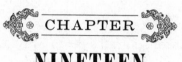

NINETEEN

The Pennsylvania Railroad station was all grand arches and beams, plumes of steam and shafts of light, as Eterna and Omega gathered for their return to New York. Rose paused to drink in the sight, not knowing when she'd see it next, if ever. The District seemed stately and quiet in comparison to the raucous bustle of New York, holding the methodical pace of bureaucracy.

Bishop and Mrs. Northe-Stewart had procured a private car and guided Clara toward it. Having been cleaned up, her wounds properly dressed by a doctor at the hotel, Clara had shifted dark blond locks to sweep down over the bandage. She kept the green cloak she'd worn during the battle drawn tight around her shoulders.

Lord Black went to a florist's stall, delighting the matronly woman running it by paying her to haul her entire stock into the designated car.

From across the platform, where he had been in ongoing conversation with Sergeant Walczek about their captive, Harold Spire moved toward Rose as if she were his only mission. His wound caused him to move more slowly than he would have normally, but something about his gaze stilled her breath. When he came near, he kept a decorous distance but Rose could feel him wanting to step closer. She wished he would.

"All set?" Rose asked.

"She's still unconscious thanks to Mosley, Knight has refused to let her out of sight, and our medium is now holding
court with the deputies and telling their fortunes for money.
They're all in her thrall."

Rose laughed.

Spire chuckled before growing serious.

"You know that I don't . . . I can't believe in half of what
has transpired over the last many months."

"Yes," Rose replied without judgment.

"But I felt something, when I was in the mansion
basement—a pull. The same thing that dragged me with
you, Bishop, and Clara at Trinity. I've never encountered
precognition, but I assume it would feel like that. It was . . .
disconcerting."

"I empathize. When the inexplicable began to open mysterious petals to me, I felt the same way."

"I knew that you were in danger though you were
nowhere near me," Spire said softly. "It was visceral and
terrifying."

"I'm sorry," Rose said.

Spire shook his head, took a step closer, and continued, "If
the paranormal serves no other purpose than to bind me to
you . . . then it is not altogether unwelcome."

Overcome, Rose grabbed his hand impulsively and
brought it to her lips. This made him smile and reach to touch
her cheek.

Their sweet moment was cut short by a great sound like a
cresting whine that seemed to come from everywhere around
them. The tiny hairs all over Rose's body stood straight up.
From far below came a pain-filled shriek, followed by a per-
vasive buzzing sound.

Spire and Rose hurried to where Clara stood leaning on
Bishop. Evelyn hovered close, looking angelic in a cream silk

day dress with golden embroidery, her gray-golden hair pinned up beneath a beige felt hat decked with golden ribbon. No one would have guessed that mere hours ago, the woman was standing over severed body parts giving sacraments and last rites.

"I think Mosley's just neutralized the last source," Clara said.

As if cued, the man in question strode into view through a cloud of steam, a dramatic entrance as fine as any theatrical effect.

"The abomination in this station's basement is neutralized," he said, hurrying right to Clara and speaking quickly. "I should also tell you I already dealt with the unholy mess that I found under Edison's plant back in Manhattan, six sub-basements belowground. The torn human bodies, the wiring, it's all so . . ." Mosley trailed off, tucking a shaking hand into his coat pocket and retrieving a singed handkerchief with which he wiped moisture off his brow, dabbing at the remains of a fresh nosebleed.

"Too much to bear, I know," Bishop said gently. "We cannot thank you enough for your help and your bravery, Mr. Mosley."

"We are yet again in your debt," Clara added.

"If you take that woman back to New York with you, you know what will happen," Mosley said, gesturing toward the police holding area.

"She'll try to amass power along the rails and attempt to overcome us?" Clara replied.

"You'll have to counter it," Mosley stated.

"If you come back on the same train, you'll feel it," Clara said. "Between the two of us, we could make a great difference. The way you wield electricity seems similar to the way I can now wield ley energy."

"I believe so. Look at us and these strange . . . conditions of ours," the man murmured with a sad chuckle. Rose watched as he stared at Clara, yearning for a connection.

"Mr. Mosley," the senator began warmly, "should you remain in New York, would you accept a position as an inspector of the grid? This whole war of the currents is problematic. We'd never reveal your abilities but you would be an invaluable asset."

Studying Bishop for a moment, Mosley spoke with disconcerting honesty. "I have much to atone for. Sins untold. I shall pay penance by serving in this capacity. Yes. Thank you. I agree."

The men shook on it, Bishop wincing as a shock passed between them. Mosley blushed and apologized. Bishop chuckled. He handed the man a train ticket. Mosley bobbed his head at Clara and moved to walk away, smiling at her as if he'd just discovered there might be family in the world after all, sudden tears in those Tesla coil eyes.

The train whistle screamed. It was time to go.

"I'll check in with Harold. I'll make sure you don't have to see her," Rose murmured to Clara, moving on ahead.

It had been agreed that "Lady C" would be returned to New York for trial. Spire and Knight arranged to keep watch on their incapacitated charge, with Rose moving between cars to keep the rest of the company apprised.

When the guards brought her out, Rose gasped. She appeared at least two decades older than when she had attacked them. Not only did she crave the powers she wielded, but they kept her young and beautiful. A refreshed chill slid down her spine. The queen could never get word of this, as it was evidence of gains in immortality . . . the whole reason their departments had been founded in the first place.

She glanced at Spire, and his wide eyes confirmed that he, too, was shocked.

"Not a word of it," he murmured, proving that his thoughts went exactly where hers had gone.

Spire opened the compartment and gestured that the guards who had kept her in holding should take their quarry into the train car. They hesitated. Sighing, he flashed his badge. "I have been granted authority of this charge by Sergeant Walczek."

"Who do you work for, Scotland Yard?" the officer asked.

"Something like that," Spire replied. "Her Majesty's government, and on behalf of the honorable Senator Bishop and the great state of New York."

"Mind telling me what these two have to do with it?" he said, gesturing to Rose and Knight.

"They are my operatives," Spire said indignantly.

The officer looked at the women in surprise and shook his head. "England," he muttered, and the prisoner was taken into the car.

"America," Knight countered with equal disdain as she climbed inside.

The company and their quarry took seats on the benches within. Lady C was beginning to rouse. Knight had supplied another length of cloth to gag her, lest she try silver-tongued charms or incantations to demons.

Spire set the woman roughly on her feet and shoved her to an open bench inside the compartment. Knight maneuvered to face her, leaning forward suddenly as Celeste opened her eyes with a cry.

"Bradley Volpe, Edmund Cornyn, Mitchell Bannen," Knight ground out through clenched teeth. "There!"

Withdrawing an embroidered silk handkerchief from her sleeve, she dabbed at her upper lip and then her temples, taking measured breaths. After a few minutes, Spire and Rose watching her, she straightened and spoke matter-of-factly.

"Her primary accomplices, at the Edison plant and be-yond," she explained. "I've been trying to extract them from her mind for an hour."

"You're certain," Spire said questioningly. Knight offered a somewhat deadly glare and he raised his hands in a ges-ture of surrender. "That is an *incredibly* useful skill," he murmured.

"I can't always manage it," Knight admitted. "It's why I don't volunteer the ability. I never know if I will succeed and I don't offer false hope unless I'm being paid to do exactly that. However, she's been digging into my head since she cor-nered us, and that helped create the channel."

Lady C narrowed her eyes.

"We met Volpe at the Edison plant and planned to arrest him," Spire said. "Thank you for the rest, Miss Knight."

"You know," Rose began, "I doubt a simple holding cell is sufficient for this creature. She has mesmerism, en-chantments, clairvoyance, and Lord knows what else in her arsenal."

"I can sense what she fears," Knight declared. "So I know how we can Ward the cell to mute her gifts. Do you want to know something else that's rather wonderful about this psy-chic wrestling we've been doing?" Knight continued.

"Do tell," Spire replied with a grim smile.

"Near or far, I can always keep track of her. I'll always know where she is. I'll always be able to sniff her out, and now I have leverage to push back."

"Useful indeed," Spire said eagerly.

"This, too, will help," Knight said, reaching around to the back of her neck to unclasp a thin golden chain that had been hidden below the seemingly endless ruffles of blue silk. A small, golden, heart-shaped locket dangled from the long chain, which Knight leaned forward to place around the lady's neck. At this intrusion the woman growled at Knight, who countered with a similar sound.

Rose was suddenly very glad Knight was on their side. She could be terrifying if pressed.

"That locket was a gift from my childhood best friend, the first girl I ever loved. I knew I could never have her, she was promised to a baronet and married off too young, but I've always remembered that stolen kiss I took from her one stormy night just before her wedding. And I've never loved another as I love her.

"Now *you* will wear my misery and regret. I'm done carrying them around—but I'll always know where they are."

Knight leaned forward, taking a shaking breath, her voice tremulous as she continued. "I could have so easily become like you . . . full of hate and desperate vanity, misunderstood and without recourse, feeling more kinship with demons than humans in this prison of a world that thinks so little of us. I understand you, Celeste," Knight murmured. "And I thank you. For reminding me why I did not choose your path."

Lady C leaned forward with another growl, and Knight was physically shoved back by her powers.

With a cry, Knight lowered her head and hissed. In a countering blow, Lady C flew back against the metal wall so hard that she again slumped into unconsciousness.

Spire gaped at her.

"I'll be in the powder room," Knight declared, then rose and swept off in a whirl of silk.

Watching her go, Rose felt newfound awe for her friend. Her theatricality was a weapon, and those who thought her a fraud did so at their peril; when Knight was serious, she was deadly so.

Glancing back at the rumpled form across the car, Rose dreaded what terrible things would be said of "womankind" on public record, depending on how the trial would proceed. But one thing at a time, one life at a time.

Rose pondered the scope of what they'd seen and done these past harrowing months, from public displays and parades of wild sacrilege in the streets and parks of New York and London to a celestial fight over the skies of Washington to this more intimate turn, where a lone set of paranormally augmented people fought for an upper hand while modernity barreled along on swift rails to unknown futures.

* * * * *

The rest of the team settled into their private car.

"I can sense that woman," Clara said quietly to Bishop. "Would you please help shield me?"

He nodded, breathing in and lifting psychic shields. It felt as if dressing screens made of light were erected all around her. She thanked him with a careful embrace as he helped her to a sofa and made sure that water and coffee were at her fingertips on a small table beside her.

Lord Black arranged flowers, kissing each bouquet and quietly thanking the blooms for their service. He surrounded Clara with them as if she were a living monument. At her feet he set two small pots of ivy, denoting fealty and unwavering strength. Verdant powers aside, the compartment smelled heavenly.

Evelyn sat on a velvet-lined fainting couch with an open notebook of paper, writing letters to clairvoyant colleagues across the continent, sharing her experiences in hopes the information would help them better help cities, townships, and native nations.

"Don't let my quietude during this journey worry you, friends," Clara said to her companions. "But I must go inward in order to Ward out."

"I love you, Clara," Bishop said boldly. At that, not even

the wound at her head hurt; she was too full of contentment, staring into his warm, glimmering eyes.

"I love you, Rupert. And I always have," she replied before closing her eyes and folding her hands over the bouquet Lord Black set in her lap: a collection of multiflora roses, hazel, and reeds that together meant "Heavens be with you, grace and peace."

Even the blooms trembled with life force, and Clara suddenly understood why Black kissed and thanked them. When attuned, everything had a vibration, and everything was in a harmonic conversation, it just took a keen ear and a deft touch.

She turned inwardly to her lives, asking their help, their senses to layer on top of hers, for everything she had known and lived through and to come to a vibrant fruition. The ley line felt thankfully not far off from the rails. She would not have to pull at a great distance.

Once the train took a slight jog along another set of rails, Clara could feel that these had been tainted; there was the grating note in the distance. If she were to open her eyes, she might see floating silhouette demons floating over the darkening countryside like plumes of toxic smoke. But she did not. Instead, she let the warmth from the ley line subsume her.

The harmony of the ley lines sound reverberated, like an organ note deep within Clara. She mused upon, relished, and savored that note, letting it be the echo emanating from her heartbeat, breath, and every thought.

If the grating note of co-opted rails grew loud, Clara put out a hand and drew her fingers together, isolating a string or snuffing a candle. At times there was a crackling hiss, and she knew that was the assistance of Mosley, neutralizing the black boxes set along the course, snapping out the spiritual interference with an electrical blast from the other side of the train.

Clara felt time bend like a young green branch in a warm spring wind. Deep within this sightless dance of sound and sensation, she felt as though she floated, winged and weightless in a great night sky. Any number of esoteric sects might be ecstatic at the prospect of such a transcendental state.

It wasn't until the conductor shouted "New York!" that she had any sense of time or place. The whole journey had been taken in one meditative leap. She opened her eyes and saw the arches and girded trestles of Grand Central Depot beyond, stirring to the sensation of Bishop's lips upon her temple.

"Brilliantly done, my dear, you lit up the whole line."

"I just let nature sing," she replied.

"If only we all would," he murmured.

* * * * *

It was an unspoken agreement that everyone would stay at Mrs. Northe-Stewart's home that night and gather themselves. Clara and Bishop had no safe residence, and soon the English contingent would return home; New York could not keep them indefinitely.

After a lavish meal, Northe-Stewart having clearly wired ahead to her staff to prepare something fit for royalty, the ladies retired to the parlor and the men to the den. Knight was exhausted; her mental battle with the villain had given her a fever. Evelyn was tending her on both a physical and psychic level.

This left the soul sisters to themselves.

Rose approached a reclining Clara with tears in her eyes.

"I don't want to leave you. But I can't stay," Rose said.

Clara allowed her own tears to fall, grasping her hand. "We were born an ocean apart for a reason. We're forever bonded, but we've different shores to guard."

"Are our battles over?" Rose asked hopefully. "What do you sense?"

"The specific threat of the Society, I believe, is now neutralized. And we have strategies to keep its fangs from growing again. But aside from the paranormal, there are terrible, normal, human failings ahead of us all."

Clara took a deep breath and spoke heavily.

"There will be a war, in the next century. We'll be older then, but still sooner than we'd hope. Miss Knight, Evelyn, and even I now sense it." She shook her head. "But here and now, my dear, your task is to make sure that this wretched door we've closed is as sealed and as solid as the best bit of masonry ever assembled."

"Yes. Of course," Rose promised.

"Meetings twice a year," Clara demanded. "At *least*. Besides, I've got to come to your wedding."

"My what?! I'm ..." Rose trailed off, her cheeks heating with a blush. "We're not ..."

Clara tapped her temple. "You will be. Sorry, I don't want to spoil the surprise, but if you two don't marry, then two of my favorite people, not to mention two of the best-suited people I've seen if ever there were, would miss the best companionship two humans could offer. You and I are soul sisters. You and he are soul mates."

Rose bit her lip, trying to restrain a gleeful grin. He was such a good man, and incalculably dear to her.

"You don't need to hide happiness from me, dear," Clara murmured, leaning in. "We need it. Let it shine. It helps the magic. It boosts the Wards we must keep lit. I always thought the idea that love was 'magic' was just stuff and nonsense, but, in a way, the romantic poets had a point."

"And you?" Rose asked. "When shall I attend the wedding of a magnificent senator and his most precious treasure?"

"We'll get around to it, I'm sure. Likely before the new

house. We're thinking of relocating to Greenwich Village rather than returning to Pearl . . ." She shuddered, and Rose understood that it would be a while before she felt entirely settled. Once a bastion was overtaken, nowhere felt safe for a while.

"We have to keep the compass held fast across the ocean. It will keep the ley lines clear. Are you up to that, the kind of energy that requires?" Clara asked.

"Absolutely."

"If you ever aren't, just tell me, we'll come up with a solution, a surrogate, those who can take over for us when our bodies eventually fail and we'll return as new family once more. Although to be perfectly honest I am very ready for an extended holiday. I could use a few centuries off after this body's day is done," Clara said with a weary laugh.

"I don't blame you. When I see all your lives expand, it's exhausting even to look at."

"I hope I've a period of relative peace and quiet ahead of me. The same for you."

"We'll see. Depends on what the queen demands of Har—Mr. Spire and me."

Clara snorted. "You can call him Harold around me, Rose. Don't hide familiarity any more than you should hide that smile of yours. Why is it working women are so pressured to be so stoic all the time? That isn't fair."

"Add it to the list of double standards, my dear," Rose laughed.

"Let's get some rest," Clara said. "And dream of a hopeful future."

* * * * *

Arriving back in England, Rose took in the port at Southampton with an overwhelming sense of relief. The familiarity of English sky and water, the drama of cliffs and seascapes; she now began to understand Clara's sense of tether, of the lines, and of the gravity of being. She was the other side of the great bridge. The hand at the end of the telegraph wire interpreting the taps on the machine that carried spirit messages from an ocean away.

She considered whether or not the sense of closure was realistic or a trapping she was putting on for comfort, a blanket against a draft. No. The closure stood, even upon careful examination. Even as she took to the London-bound rails with Spire, Black, and Knight, the ponderous silences between them were comfortable, not laden with the weight of countless worries left unaddressed.

Rose was sure none were naive enough to think that there would never be a flare of supernatural pique, but hopefully London's secretive spectral patrol, the elusive one Lord Black was always on about, would take care of it and they'd never really know.

The Omega department had opened her eyes to how much eluded the traditional senses' capacity to comprehend. There was vastly more beyond the slightly parted veil through which she now saw, but she had no desire to explore further.

There would always be work to do to ensure that Omega did not become something it dare not try to be and to ensure that certain questions, while asked, would remain bereft of answers that would only prove to unravel the world.

The returning team was met at King's Cross station by the recent widow Mrs. Wilson, dressed in a black dress and head scarf, and Mr. Blakely in his favorite aquamarine coat, heartily glad to see their fellows returned safely home. Rose now understood what soldiers must feel for their comrades when relieved from front lines.

Their reunion was full of long embraces, words of comfort and necessity on pressing matters before the team separated to attend to manners and expectations, with assurances they'd return to Lord Black's house for a sumptuous dinner that night.

* * * * *

Lingering a moment before traveling to the Black estate, Rose and Spire stood on Westminster Bridge under the shadow of the great clock tower and stared out over the bustling Thames. Neither of them being the sort that insisted upon hats, their bare heads were buffeted by a distinct breeze. Rose didn't bother to try to pin back loose brown locks that blew against her cheeks.

Spire seemed very intent on the river traffic, glancing alternately between the ships and the clock tower.

A movement up the bridge, crossing from the south to the north bank, caught Rose's eye. A group of six distinct individuals, men and women from different classes by the look of their attire, strode up the bridge toward Parliament, on a mission. A large raven flew above them as if a part of their coterie.

If Rose wasn't mistaken, the air before them shimmered, strangely, the look the air took on if there were ghosts present. . . .

This must be that group that Lord Black was always on about, London's hidden ghost patrol. . . . There was a particular woman at the fore who caught Rose's eye. The raven squawked loudly, as if confirming she was right in noticing them.

At her side strode a striking man all in black, but it was the woman who held Rose's attention. She was severe and compelling, with brown hair in a tight bun and steel-bright eyes fiercely set before her, gloved hands wafting the air as if shooing something unwanted toward the river.

The woman must have sensed her, for she snapped her head in Rose's direction. Perhaps there was a gaze of mutual understanding or recognition; Rose couldn't be sure. Something passed between them and the woman put a finger to her lips, bidding Rose keep her secret. There was no way Rose could do anything but. She knew then that she and her team weren't the only ones guarding London.

Spire saw none of this; he was fixated on a small schooner that didn't seem to be taking its proper time downstream and instead drifted too close to Parliament's base, and he narrowed his gaze as if the craft were suspect, glancing up at the clock in turn before the craft picked up its drift and disappeared below their bridge, and Spire relaxed.

They were silent for some time before Spire, his words precise and carefully curated, volunteered:

"I truly wish to return to the Metropolitan force. While our . . . *adventures* here have hopefully subdued, there will always be crimes that need a careful eye to solve them."

Rose took a moment to consider him. He stared up at the beautifully wrought clock as if the tower might provide him a certain benediction. Behind its bold face surrounded by gilding and grandeur, Big Ben began tolling the afternoon hour of three. Perhaps the London icon did just that: bless him.

"What do you think, Rose?" Spire asked.

"Are you asking my permission, Harold?" she replied gently. When he turned to stare deeply into her eyes, he stilled her breath. The breadth of his steadfast, earnest nature was so evident in the rich brown pools of his eyes. The tried, true joy of her heart. She smiled. "You needn't ask permission, but I am pleased you ask my thoughts. The city needs a man like you, as long as you can bear it. Simply so long as I might assist you?"

"Are you asking permission? You needn't," he countered. Then he smiled, continuing. "You'll be the front. The ostensible leader of Omega. You will see to its maintenance and presence. And yes." He took a step closer to her, took her face gently in his hands. "I want your assistance. In . . . *everything* in my life."

If it were possible, he would have looked deeper into her eyes, into her spirit, but those doors were already wide open for him. Spire bent his head to kiss Rose ever so softly, the pressure of his lips the most gentle, delicate dance, a reverence so opposite his forceful nature.

After a long moment they drew back, arms around one another's waists, turning again to the river, standing in silent appreciation of the space between two independent souls, a river they had laid a bridge across, now a partnership over that unfathomable abyss.

Their world stood, and remained, Warded.

EPILOGUE

The Bishops had only just returned to New York from their Parisian honeymoon. Evelyn and Blessing had spiritually cleansed the Eterna offices while they were away, new boards had been laid, and every trace of sacrilege had been removed before anyone else set foot inside.

As Clara and Rupert attended to correspondences in the Eterna offices side by side, Lavinia rang the "neutral" bell at her front desk, indicating that a visitor to the Eterna offices had arrived and her read on the caller indicated that middle tone.

"Proceed," Clara called down the stairs, offering Bishop a quizzical look, wondering who had sought them out. Perhaps a well-wisher regarding their recent union. She smoothed a lock of hair down over the scars remaining where her ear had been, an unfortunate new self-conscious habit.

Bishop, at the top of the morning, to Clara's delight, had managed to move his smaller desk, one he had rarely used across the large third-floor open office, over to sit next to her massive rosewood desk, twice the size of his and covered in papers and trinkets. For a woman who loved control in so many aspects of her life, she allowed her desk to be the one area of abandon. She felt it suited the nature of their work. But when receiving company she did feel a little self-conscious, so she rose and stood behind Bishop at his spotless desk, placing a hand on his shoulder.

In walked a man of average height, black hair and mustache trimmed close and corralled by a pomade, dressed in a fine black frock coat, beige waistcoat with white neckwear, black trousers, and shined black shoes—a look that bespoke a man of business. His arched brow was offset by a sharp nose, and dark eyes that were watery in a way that made them look impossibly glassy. Bishop stood upon his entrance, Clara at his side. The man strode forward.

"Senator, my name is Felix Saxton," the man said, shaking Bishop's hand. "I'm filling the vacancy in my Brooklyn congressional district, Williamsburg, but I've been active in local politics all my life."

"Rupert Bishop, pleasure to meet you, Congressman Saxton. This is my wife, Clara." Bishop gestured toward her. He was also careful to add, lest there be any question, "She is my colleague, partner, and fellow director of this program."

At this, Clara felt her whole being fill with light. He would never put her second, and he would not let marital convention change that status even if society insisted she step behind.

She thanked the heavens and all her lives, which had led up to this, to him. The men of this life, the few there had been, had done nothing but respect her, and that would be perhaps this life's greatest victory, as not all women were even half so lucky. She remembered to bob her head in the manner of a slight curtsey upon the introduction.

"What brings you here?" Clara asked with a smile. "Are you one of the very rare legislators who know of our existence?"

"I am. I was recently appointed to the Secret Services committee and I'm trying to follow up with any and all ventures under its . . . wide net."

It was clear to Clara that Eterna was either suspect to him, curious, surprising, or all three.

"Please do sit," Bishop said. Clara could tell from the tone of his voice that he was as wary as she. "Shall I ring for some tea or coffee?"

"Either would be lovely," Saxton replied. Bishop rang for Lavinia to offer amenities.

"I'll be straightforward with you, Senator, Mrs. Bishop. We're New Yorkers, let's not play games. I'm not sure I agree with the continuation of this commission as it was explained to me."

Bishop blinked and replied evenly, with no hint of worry or defensiveness. "Well, how has it been explained to you?" Clara knew this was hardly the first time he'd been questioned about the commission, even by the few who had ever known about it.

The man's colorless lips thinned. "It wasn't. Explained. I happen to prefer transparency in government."

"As do I," Bishop replied, "when it comes to matters of direct democracy. When it comes to public safety, that changes the equation. Aren't you a bit, beg your pardon, and your local political experience notwithstanding, *green* to have been appointed to a committee straightaway?"

Saxton shrugged and smiled. His watery eyes glittered but he was not in tears nor did he spill one when expressive. "I suppose I am a man to fill vacancies wherever they appear."

There was an edge to this man that Clara simply did not like. It was no wonder that Lavinia rang him as a "neutral" presence on the bells. There was nothing outright hostile, but there was a sense that this conversation could go either way. Politicians wouldn't get violent, not directly, but policies could, and laws and restrictions could become all too cutting.

"I have a . . . proposal for you." The man leaned forward. "Say you were to add another mission to your docket of immortality."

"We've veered away from the immortality search," Bishop replied. "Not only was it not fruitful, it was dangerous.

Eterna led us instead to providential protections. To pick up any other thread would be unwise."

"So what, then, does the Eterna Commission *do*? We can't have a government office that does nothing."

"We haven't done nothing," Clara snapped. She could feel Bishop's energy take her by the arm and squeeze as if he'd actually physically done so, encouraging her to keep calm.

"If you followed any of the goings-on these past many months, you'll realize that there are a great deal of paranormal knots that we tied up. We are here to make sure they stay tied, not frayed, not slipped into loose ends once more," Bishop stated evenly.

"So you're not interested in my proposal of an additional branch to your services?" Saxton pressed.

"What did you have in mind?" Bishop countered warily.

"Time, Senator. Look into *time.*"

Clara and Bishop looked at one another. Bishop remained expressionless. Clara tried to but wasn't sure she avoided a scowl. Everything within her, all her lives, any part of her body, mind, and soul that was attuned and resonant with her generally impeccable instincts screamed *no.*

"No," Clara said calmly. "As we said, it became clear chasing immortality was chasing death. Chasing time? Similarly imprudent. Unnatural. It would become the undoing of this department and the nation."

"And you're certain of this how?" he asked. He took on that tone some men take when they don't think women ought to speak their mind let alone speak for policy.

Clara smiled icily as she replied. "Were you aware when you stepped across that threshold, Congressman, we deal in the fantastical? The unknowable. I happen to *know.* By means one might call paranormal."

"Then my request, more, my *suggestion,* shouldn't surprise or meet with objection," Saxton replied.

"When one confronts the most basic laws that govern humanity, death being one and time being another, one should know that the law stands and is more powerful than human intervention or experimentation," Bishop stated. "Sorry to disappoint you, sir. I couldn't in good conscience either work on or support such a venture. Not after what we've been through."

"And what, exactly, has that been?"

"Exactly what that has been remains classified," Clara replied. "But unsettling things happening of late that you may have read about in the papers? That."

"Any resolution? Arrests?"

"Yes. And yes," Bishop replied. "Also classified."

After what happened to Moriel and the queen not executing him, Clara wasn't about to intimate that Lady C still lived, lest anyone find her as fascinating or as much of a lure as Victoria had found Moriel. After a private trial, Celeste had been moved upstate to a small ladies' asylum and kept in solitary confinement.

"Good," the man said, rising to his feet. "Well. I shall have to find some other obscure department behind closed doors to satisfy the most compelling issue of future centuries."

"As a fellow legislator, I would advise against that, Congressman," Bishop said quietly.

"I will take that under advisement, Senator, truly. I do respect you a great deal, have followed your career my whole life. You've done a lot of good for New York." The man seemed sincere enough in this. He turned to Clara. "Mrs. Bishop, take care of him."

"Of my jobs, that one is my favorite," Clara assured.

He strode toward the door. "If you change your mind . . ."

"We won't," Bishop and Clara replied in unison.

The man waved at them with a partial smile. "Still, you'll know where to find me. See you in Washington, Senator."

His tread sounded down the stairs and after a quiet courtesy to Lavinia and the guards, the front door was closed behind him.

Clara and Bishop turned to one another, taking hands and folding into a long embrace.

When they returned home, they found that a bouquet had been delivered from Lord Black. Around its copper vase hung a beautiful silver compass, with its back inscribed:

To My American Family

There were four flowers in the arrangement. Left to right, they were: flowering almond branches, heliotrope blossoms, a cedar branch, and oak-leaved geraniums. Signifying hope, faith, strength, and true friendship.

At the center of the lush bouquet was a freshly bottled Ward from London, strengthening the bonds of their protective lines. They would devote their lives to tending those lines and making sure that all, from every background and circumstance, would be covered in that care.

"And *that* is our denouement," Bishop stated, nodding at the bouquet.

* * * * *

After a lengthy discussion between its two founders in the pleasant parlor of their new Greenwich Village town house on Waverly, the Eterna Commission, as it had been known, closed its doors that day.

It would be target, suspect, and vagary no more.

What their team, and Omega, would take from it would be their own.

The Bishops agreed that they should, along with devoted friends and colleagues, remain open, available, and amenable to paranormal investigation should it arise or be brought to their attention. Not to mention keep a wary eye on anyone who did manage to set up an office looking into the great mystery of time itself, as everything about that proposition and encounter had filled Clara with great unease.

Clara had spent the better part of her life chasing elusive ideas and grasping at phantoms. It was time for some unmitigated peace.

She took Bishop's hand. They stared out at the sooty, steamy, ever-climbing skyline.

For a moment she thought to call upon all her past lives, to ask them what to do to be sure this life was lived to the best of its balance and mission.

Instead, she let the idea of her future self begin to set its course. No matter the century, the world would always need beings like her to listen to the old songs, the power of ancient lines, and adjust dissonant notes toward beautiful harmony.

AUTHOR'S NOTE

In this particular Eterna adventure, please forgive me for taking a few more liberties with historical time lines for the sake of iconic imagery than I usually do.

Firstly, the actual time line for the arm of Lady Liberty. While it was indeed showcased in Madison Square Park, it was not dedicated until 1886. At the late 1882 time of this novel, Liberty was being constructed full scale in Paris before being shipped to New York in 1884. The 214 crates sat unopened for more than a year, as the struggle to raise funds was very real; only after the *New York World* publisher Joseph Pulitzer—a Hungarian immigrant—promised to print the name of every donor in his paper, even if the gift was only a penny, was the necessary money raised.

Secondly, Edison's involvement with and envisioning of the Kinetoscope was not until 1888. He did, however, have an incredible penchant for stealing other people's ideas and taking credit, as well as snapping up patents with ravenous zeal.

Thirdly, while Thomas Edison's Pearl Street dynamos and the Lower Manhattan grid were very real, and there were indeed booster stations for Edison's plant all around Manhattan, there was never one exactly *inside* the bridge. There was an additional plant below the Brooklyn Bridge on the Brooklyn side.

* * * * *

A special thank-you to my editor, Melissa Ann Singer, for allowing me this wild journey of "boundlessly creative gaslamp fantasy"; thanks to Thom Truelove for extensive research help, to critique partner C. Wormwood for keen discussion, to my agent Paul Stevens for keeping such a good eye on me, and to you, dear reader, for journeying with me. Happy Haunting!

Please join us for *Miss Violet and the Great War*.